William John B. W. V. Vernon

Readings on the Purgatorio

chiefly based on the Commentary of Benvenuto da Imola - Vol. 2

William John B. W. V. Vernon

Readings on the Purgatorio
chiefly based on the Commentary of Benvenuto da Imola - Vol. 2

ISBN/EAN: 9783337886578

Printed in Europe, USA, Canada, Australia, Japan

Cover: Foto ©Andreas Hilbeck / pixelio.de

More available books at **www.hansebooks.com**

READINGS

ON THE

PURGATORIO OF DANTE

CHIEFLY BASED ON

THE COMMENTARY OF BENVENUTO

DA IMOLA

BY THE

HON^{BLE.} WILLIAM WARREN VERNON M.A.

With an Introduction

BY THE

VERY REV. THE DEAN OF ST. PAUL'S

IN TWO VOLUMES

VOL II

London

MACMILLAN AND CO.

AND NEW YORK

1889

DRYDEN PRESS:
J. DAVY AND SONS, 137, LONG ACRE, LONDON.

ERRATA.

THE PURGATORIO.

VOL. II.

CANTO XVIII.

THE FOURTH CORNICE.
SPIRITUAL SLOTH (ACCIDIA).

S in the last Canto Dante demonstrated how all sins have their origin in some kind of "love," in the present one he describes the purgation of *Accidia* or Spiritual Sloth, which comes from remissness in love for the Only True Good.

Benvenuto divides the Canto into Five Divisions.

In the First Division, from v. 1 to v. 39, Dante defines Love.

In the Second Division, from v. 40 to v. 75, he puts forward a doubt which is the consequence of this definition.

In the Third Division, from v. 76 to v. 105, he speaks of the punishment and purgation of the slothful in general.

In the Fourth Division, from v. 106 to v. 129, he introduces the shade of the Abbot of St. Zeno at Verona.

In the Fifth Division, from v. 130 to v. 145, he shows how the sin of sloth is to be rooted out.

Division I. The mental questionings of the Poet have been partly quieted, partly roused. What is that Love, the right or wrong direction of which is the cause, on the one hand, of all holiness; on the other, of all evil? Virgil accordingly once more appears as an expounder of St. Thomas Aquinas :—

> Posto avea fine al suo ragionamento
> L' alto Dottore, ed attento guardava
> Nella mia vista, s' io parea contento :

The lofty teacher had brought his reasoning to a close ; and was looking attentively into my face, to see if I appeared satisfied.

Then Dante relates that he had still certain doubts.

> Ed io, cui nuova sete ancor frugava,
> Di fuor taceva, e dentro dicea :—" Forse   5
> Lo troppo dimandar ch' io fo gli grava."—

And I, whom a new thirst was yet goading on, did not utter any words, but kept saying to myself: " Perhaps this excessive questioning of mine may be an annoyance to him."—

He leaves it to be inferred, that he had reasoned within himself whether enough had been said in the matter of " Love," and he came to the conclusion that there had not. He adds that Virgil restored his confidence by saying to him, in words which he does not quote, that he need not be afraid of telling of the doubts that he felt.

> Ma quel padre verace, che s' accorse
> Del timido voler che non s' apriva,
> Parlando, di parlare ardire mi porse.

But that true Father (Virgil) who comprehended my

timid wish that kept itself concealed, by speaking, gave me hardihood to speak.*

He must have spoken words like those of Beatrice that we just read (in note). Dante, with renewed confidence, proceeds to unburden himself of his doubts, but before doing so, he breaks out into an exclamation of affection and gratitude to Virgil. Benvenuto says that he does him honour by a cumulative process. First he speaks of him as *alto Dottore*, then *padre verace*, and now calls him *Maestro*.

> Ond' io :—" Maestro, il mio veder s' avviva   10
>   Sì nel tuo lume, ch' io discerno chiaro†
>   Quanto la tua ragion ‡ porti o descriva : §

* Virgil had read his thoughts, as we found him doing, in Canto XV, 127 :—
> " Se tu avessi cento larve
>   Sopra la faccia, non mi sarìeno chiuse
>   Le tue cogitazion', quantunque parve."

In *Par.* Canto XVII, 7, during Dante's interview with his great grandfather Cacciaguida, Beatrice observing in Dante's face a wish to ask further questions, and his hesitation to do so, says in words equivalent to " Come, out with it,"
> Per che mia Donna :—" manda fuor la vampa
>   Del tuo disio," —mi disse,—" sì ch' ella esca
>   Segnata bene della interna stampa ;
> Non perchè nostra conoscenza cresca
>   Per tuo parlare, ma perchè t' aúsi
>   A dir la sete, sì che l' uom ti mesca."—

† Benvenuto interprets *discerno chiaro*, I see now without the shadow of a doubt.

‡ *La tua ragion*, by natural and moral science.

§ This is very like his affectionate outburst to Cacciaguida in *Par.* XVI, 16-21.
> Io cominciai :—" Voi siete il padre mio ;
>   Voi mi date a parlar tutta baldezza,
>   Voi mi levate sì, ch' io son più ch' io."

Whereupon I: "Master, my sight is so vivified in thy light, that I clearly discern all that thy reason imports or describes.

Dante explains to Virgil that he had been telling him what Love did, and in what it was the cause either of good or of evil, but he says: Thou hast not yet told me to begin with what Love is! Define it for me! Thou hast told me the conclusions without having even stated the terms of thy proposition.

> Però ti prego, dolce padre caro,
>   Che mi dimostri amore, a cui riduci
>   Ogni buono operare e il suo contraro."—   15

Therefore, I beg of thee, dear gentle Father, to define for me the Love, which thou makest responsible for every good action, and its contrary."

Virgil answers Dante's petition, but first points out to him the difficulty of the subject.

> —" Drizza (disse) vêr me le acute luci
>   Dello intelletto ; e fieti manifesto
>   L' error de' ciechi che si fanno duci.

"Fix on me," said he, "the penetrating eyes of intellect, and then will be clear to thee the error of the blind, who style themselves leaders.

The error of the blind leaders of the blind is that of the Epicurean philosophers, who contended that, as a man's desires naturally turned to good, every such desire must, by that fact alone, be worthy of praise, and ought therefore to be gratified. Benvenuto puts it that such teachers, in saying that all love is praiseworthy, are guilty of a fallacy.

In the lines that follow here we are reminded of the beautiful figure in the last Canto but one (XVI, 86).

> L' animo, ch' è creato ad amar presto,
>> Ad ogni cosa è mobile che piace,   20
>> Tosto che dal piacere in atto è desto.

The soul, which is created disposed to love, is easily moved towards everything that pleases it, so soon as it is, by pleasure, awakened to action.

Benvenuto reminds us that we read in the last Canto that neither Creator nor created thing was ever without some kind of love, and that therefore the soul is naturally inclined towards everything that, at first sight, seems pleasing to it, as soon as it is awakened, and set in motion from the delectation born within it. For Benvenuto reads *piacer innato*, instead of *piacere in atto* ; just as when you see a beautiful woman, her form enters through the windows of your eyes into the chamber of your mind, and moves it to love her, although she is absent and the mind will never behold her.

> Vostra apprensiva da esser verace*
>> Tragge intenzione, e dentro a voi la spiega,
>> Sì che l' animo ad essa volger face.

Virgil explains this by saying :

Your power of apprehension draws the image† from a thing that really exists, and spreads it out within you so that it makes the mind turn to it (that image).

There is nothing in the intellect which was not in the senses, and which afterwards entered into the intellect by seeing or hearing.

---

* *da esser verace.* Pascal says, " Les appréhensions des sens sont toujours vraies."

† The scholastic philosophers called images, or likenesses of things, by the names " species " or " intentions."

> E se, rivolto, invêr di lei si piega,   25
>   Quel piegare è amor ;* quello è natura,
>   Che per piacer di nuovo in voi si lega.†

And if it does turn back towards such image and bends itself to it, that inclination is love,‡ it is nature, which by pleasure is united to you by a new tie.

---

* *È amor:* Biagioli says that the following words of the *Convito* (tr. III, ch. 2), admirably explain this passage :—" Amore, veramente pigliando e sottilmente considerando, non è altro, che unimento spirituale dell' anima e della cosa amata ; nel quale unimento di propria sua natura l' anima corre tosto o tardi, secondochè è libera o impedita........ E perocchè il suo essere dipende da Dio, e per quello si conserva ; naturalmente disia e vuole a Dio essere unita per lo suo essere fortificare. E perocchè nelle bontadi della natura umana la ragione si mostra della divina, viene che naturalmente l' anima umana con quelle per via spirituale si unisce tanto più tosto e più forte, quanto quelle più appaiono perfette ; lo quale apparimento è fatto secondochè la conoscenza dell' anima è chiara o impedita. E questo unire è quello che noi dicemo amore."

Therefore, Biagioli adds, as it is natural to the soul to desire to unite itself to God, as a support to its existence, so, by like motive, is it natural for it to unite itself to the goodnesses of nature, which is a radiance of the chief good.

† *Si lega*, is binding itself anew within you ; or, is striking a fresh root.

‡ The faculty of apprehending, perceiving, and comprehending, is set in motion by the reality of external things round us, and this develops in us the wish to show it worthy of love.

" Apprehension or conception consists in the power which the mind has of forming an image of attributes. Images so formed are first intentions (εἶδη, *species intelligibiles*) as when we regard the individual Socrates as man, white, &c. Second intentions are obtained by abstracting the relations of first intentions to one another, as humanity, whiteness, &c. First intentions are predicable, second not."—Mansel (*Artis Logicæ Rudimenta.*)

" Therefore," says Benvenuto, " Love is shown to be the inclination of the soul towards a thing agreeable to itself offered to it by the external senses."

And now Virgil, having given the definition of Love shows by a comparison its power and efficacy.

> Poi come il fuoco muovesi in altura,
>> Per la sua forma, ch' è nata a salire
>> Là dove più in sua materia dura ;   30
> Così l' animo preso entra in disire,
>> Ch' è moto spiritale ; e mai non posa
>> Fin che la cosa amata il fa gioire.

Afterwards as the fire moves on high, by virtue of its form which is made for rising to where it dwells more in its element ; * so the captive soul enters into a longing which is a motion of the spirit, and never rests until the thing it loves causes it joy.

Virgil, having shown what love is and how it is born in men, exposes the error of the blind teachers, of whom he had previously spoken.

> Or ti puote apparer quant' è nascosa
>> La veritade alla gente ch' avvera   35
>> Ciascuno amore in sè laudabil cosa ;

Now canst thou see how much the truth is hid from those people who maintain that each love is in itself a praiseworthy thing.

---

* That is to say the sphere of the moon which the ancients thought was the sphere of fire :

"Tutta la sfera varcano del fuoco."—(*Ariosto*).

The ancients did not know that the air, by its specific gravity, drives fire upwards, and thought it was made to rise naturally. Dante says, in the *Convito* (tr. III, 3), "Onde è da sapere che ciascuna cosa . . . . ha il suo speciale amore. E però il fuoco ascende alla circonferenza di sopra, lungo il cielo della luna, e però sempre quello."

Tasso has : " Come va fuoco al ciel per sua natura."

And he points out to Dante what is the cause of
the error of those who consider the substance of love
must be good, whereas nothing is really loveable but
what is good ; for they did not consider that anything
may appear good, which, in itself, is evil, but yet is
loved because it appears good.

> Però che forse appar la sua matera
> Sempre esser buona ; ma non ciascun segno
> È buono, ancor che buona sia la cera."—

Because its matter perchance may always appear to
be good ; but it is not every signet that is good, although
the (impression on the) wax may be admirable."

And thus love, however good in itself, may become
evil, if it takes its impress from an unlawful object ;
if it turns itself to anything that is wrong.

Division II.   Benvenuto tells us that we shall find
this Division much more difficult than the first, and in
it Dante puts forth a question which arises from
Virgil's answer, to clear up this doubt : If love comes
to you from without, that is, from the attractiveness of
the thing offered, in what can the mind be deserving
either of blame or praise, when the cause is from
without ?

In the following dialogue we have a type of the
scholastic disputation between master and scholar of a
mediæval university, such as Dante may himself have
taken part in.*

---

* Compare *Par.* XXIV, XXV, and XXVI, wherein Dante
relates his successive examinations, by St. Peter on Faith, St.
James on Hope, and St. John on Love.

—" Le tue parole, e il mio seguace ingegno "— 40
    Risposi lui,—" m' hanno amor discoverto ;
    Ma ciò m' ha fatto di dubbiar più pregno :

" Thy words," I answered him, " and the attention
my mind gave to them, have discovered love to me,
but that has left me more pregnant with doubt.

All operations, therefore, whether good or bad, proceed from love, and love is generated from some
pleasing object, which is presented to us from without,
to which pleasing quality the soul feels irresistibly
drawn ; therefore it would seem to me neither to
deserve merit nor censure. But if the mind has
received from its Maker the attribute of being born
to take pleasure in external objects presented to it,
and through such disposition loves ; if it loves badly
it is not its fault, and if it loves well it is not its
merit.

    Chè se amore è di fuori a noi offerto,
        E l' anima non va con altro piede,
        Se dritta o torta va, non è suo merto."— 45

For if love be offered us from without, and the soul
goes not with other foot, then it can neither be praised
if it goes right, nor blamed if crooked.

As representing human wisdom, Virgil offers but a
partial solution of the problem of free will. The full
explanation must come from Beatrice, as Theology,
the Scientia Scientiarum.

    Ed egli a me :—" Quanto ragion qui vede
        Dir ti poss' io ; da indi in là t' aspetta
        Pure a Beatrice ; ch' è opra di fede.

And he to me : " As far as reason sees here, I
can tell thee ; beyond that look only to Beatrice, for
it is a work of faith.

Virgil now begins to solve Dante's problem, but first assumes a general principle to be necessary for his purpose. And the better to understand this very stiff passage (says Benvenuto), you must first know that the vegetative and sensitive soul is evolved out of the power of substance, and is born with it and dies with it, as we see in plants and in animals ; but the rational soul is not evolved out of the power of substance, nor does it come into life with a body, but is infused into it by God, and given instead of a form. Now here Dante wishes to say that each rational soul has a certain power innate in itself, which cannot be recognised unless it is brought into outward action ; therefore, if natural science sees that the soul has a delight in what is good, it judges it to be good, and if it sees the contrary, it judges the contrary.

> Ogni forma sustanzïal,* che setta
> È da materia, ed è con lei unita,   50

---

* On v. 49, Dean Plumptre says :—

"The soul is, in scholastic terminology, the 'substantial form,' *i.e.*, the essence, of man's nature. Without it the man is not. As such, it has its own specific virtue, *i.e.*, its own ideas, tendencies and capacities. These are known in their effects, as the nature of the plant is known by its leaves and flowers and fruits, as the instinct of the bee is seen in its making honey ; but what is the source either of the primal conceptions or the primal desires, whether innate, inspired, or determined by stellar influences or a law of heredity, Dante will not say. The first desires, even if directed to counterfeits of good, are simply neutral, deserving neither praise nor blame ; but with them there is innate in the soul (here Dante is not doubtful, for with him it was a primary fact of consciousness) a power that judges, warns, advises,—what we know as conscience. This stands as warder at the gate through which desire passes into act, brings with it the sense of merit or demerit, is the foundation of human

Specifica virtude* ha in sè colletta,
La qual senza operar non è sentita,
Nè si dimostra ma' che† per effetto,
Come per verdi fronde in pianta vita.

Every substantial form that is separate from matter, and which is united with it (that is, the body), has a specific power collected in itself, which cannot be recognised or known until it is brought into operation, nor is it made manifest except by effects, as life is in plants by green leaves.

We do not think of primal motive powers, and it is only by their being brought into operation that we can perceive them, or when we put into action the special power given to us—and so by them we have no special merit, or demerit.

Però là onde vegna lo intelletto   55
Delle prime notizie, uomo non sape,
Nè de' primi appetibili l' affetto,
Che sono in voi, sì come studio in ape
Di far lo mele ; e questa prima voglia
Merto di lode o di biasmo non cape.   60

---

liberty, and therefore of all systems of ethics which are worthy of the name, chiefly that of 'il maestro di color che sanno.' *Inf.* IV, 131.   Hence, if we allow that every desire in men may be traced to a law of cause and effect, and admit so far the postulates of Determinism, there is yet a 'noble virtue' in man, which theology, embodied in Beatrice, recognises as keeping man from being bound hand and foot in the iron chain of necessity." Compare *Par.* V, 19.

Forma substanziale was, in the schools, the name for that form, which, united to primal matter, common to all bodies, forms the different species of them.

* *Virtù speciale* is, according to Dante in the Convito, the natural appetite of the soul.

† *Ma che* = magis quam = more than.

Therefore, man does not know whence comes the understanding of the primal conceptions, nor the bent of the first appetites, which are in you, just as there is in the bee the instinct to make honey; and this primal desire is not capable in itself of praise or censure.

> Or, perchè a questa ogni altra si raccoglia,
>   Innata v' è la virtù che consiglia,
>   E dell' assenso de' tener la soglia.

Now, in order that every other will* may cluster round this first will (may come into harmony with it), there is innate in you a power that you receive from nature, which counsels, and this power ought to guard the threshold of assent.†

There are several explanations of this terzina. I have in my translation followed Benvenuto, whose interpretation is practically the same as that of Witte and Philalethes.

> Quest' è 'l principio là onde si piglia
>   Cagion di meritare in voi, secondo   65
>   Che buoni e rei amori accoglie e viglia.

This is the principle whence emanate the grounds of your deserts, according as it receives or winnows out good and bad loves.

Benvenuto considers *principio* to be Free Will, which is the intrinsic principle of volition. He translates *viglia*, "receives and expels," and says it is a word used by rustics, when they are purging corn in

---

* And this, according to Benvenuto, is Free Will; or, as in verse 68, innate liberty.

† Lamennais translates: "Or afin qu'à elle viennent s'unir toutes les autres, innée en vous est la vertu qui conseille, et qui doit garder le seuil du consentement."

a threshing floor, and drive out all that is superfluous to good grain.

Virgil states that Aristotle and Plato, and others of the wisest of men, have been the inventors of moral doctrine by means of which men may go through life with prudence.

> Color che ragionando andaro al fondo,
> S' accorser d' esta innata libertate,
> Però moralità* lasciaro al mondo.

They who penetrated to the inmost depths of reasoning, took note of that innate freedom and therefore they left morality to the world.

> Onde pognam che di necessitate   70
> Surga ogni amor che dentro a voi s' accende ;
> Di ritenerlo è in voi la potestate.

Allowing, then, that every love which is kindled in you arises of necessity, there is still implanted in you a power to control it.

On this passage Benvenuto says: " Now mark here, reader, that if this reasoning be well considered, it ought to convince everyone. For what medical man would agree that it is no use curing a sick person ? But that *would* be true, if everything happened by necessity. What astrologer would be willing for his art to be condemned, when he maintains that one can avert coming misfortunes, if they be foretold by his lore ? What judge would not be indignant, were he told that he punishes evildoers unjustly ? What merchant would not say that negligence is very prejudicial to trade ? What wise man does not prove

---

* By *moralità* understand moral philosophy, which would have been of no avail without the principle of freedom of the will. Benvenuto says they left it to the world, by putting a check on liberty to prevent its declining to evil.

that much wisdom (*multa concilia*) is necessary for the world? What husbandman does not know that agriculture is profitable for fertilising crops? But all men try to make excuse, throwing the responsibility for all their vices and sins upon Heaven, upon destiny, upon fortune, saying like the philosopher, Cleantes:

"Volentem fata ducunt, nolentem trahunt."

And now, in conclusion, Virgil refers Dante to theology, and says briefly that he himself by his human knowledge or science cannot rise to any more elevated interpretation of the question, for he can only judge of cause by effect; but Beatrice understands that the noble virtue, the most excellent that there is in man, is Free Will, for by it we deserve either eternal life, or everlasting punishment.

> La nobile virtù Beatrice intende
> Per lo libero arbitrio ; e però guarda
> Che l' abbi a mente, se a parla ten prende."—   75

The noble faculty, Beatrice understands by Free Will; and therefore look that thou bear it in mind, should she take in hand to speak to thee of it."

Benvenuto says: Beatrice spoke of it to Dante in *Par.* V, 19: "Lo maggior don che Dio, &c." And again *Par.* I, 109, where he says that the order God has given to nature causes in us the first impulses.

———

Division III. In this Third Division of the Canto Dante describes the penance of the slothful, but he first gives a very exact description of the position of the moon.

> La Luna, quasi a mezza notte tarda,
> Facea la stelle a noi parer più rade,
> Fatta com' un secchione che tutto arda.

The moon, as it were towards midnight late, shaped like a pitcher all afire, was making the stars appear to us more rare.

I follow Benvenuto in the reading *secchione* "pitcher-shaped," which I must prefer to *scheggione*, a log all in a blaze.*

On this particular passage, Dr. Moore (*Time References*, p. 101) says "The majority of Commentators have assumed (as it appears to me quite needlessly), that this must refer to the actual hour of Moon-rise, which would certainly be, according to the principle we have been advocating, about 10 P.M., or perhaps 10.30., since the Moon is already well up, and producing a sensible effect in quenching the lesser stars.† Philalethes says the Moon rose *Etwa um* 10 *Uhr*, also *schon ziemlich gegen Mitternacht*. . . . I do not think it at all certain that Dante intends to speak of the hour of Moon-rise at all. . . . The effect here indicated of the quenching of the lesser stars by the light of the gibbous or pitcher-shaped moon (*secchione*) as it is graphically described, would be much more striking if it were some little time above the horizon than if it were just rising. I think it probable the whole passage is only a poetical and slightly elaborate way of saying the hour was

---

* Benvenuto explains *secchione* as half round and red, like fire, in a lighthouse, which burns all night to direct mariners into port; *scheggione* is like a pine torch burning naturally and emitting fire.

† Lubin thinks that it is natural to suppose that (when referring to the moon) Dante should have followed the Calendar of the Church ; and, in other words, all his allusions are to be connectedly and consistently explained as referring to the calendar moon and not the real moon.

approaching midnight, described, as usual, by some
striking visible aspect of the fact. It is not half so
elaborate or artificial a way of describing a simple
fact or phenomenon as many other passages that
might be cited. It was surely quite a natural (poetical)
description of such an hour (it being allowed that the
Moon was up, as a fact) to translate : ' And now the
moon, as it were, towards midnight late, shaped like a
pitcher all afire, was making the stars appear to us
more rare.' "

> E correa contra il ciel* per quelle strade
> > Che il sole infiamma allor, che quel da Roma   80
> > Tra i Sardi e i Corsi il vede quando cade ;

And it (the moon) was moving in the contrary direction to the heavens through those paths which the
sun sets aflame, when the man at Rome sees it going
down at a point between Sardinia and Corsica.

---

* Dr. Moore (*Time References*, p. 104): " The words which
follow in v. 79 describe evidently the backing of the moon
through the signs from west to east (as in *Par.* IX, 85, contra
'l sole, and again, in *Par.* VI, 2, the removal by Constantine of
the seat of Empire from Rome to Constantinople is described as
contro il corso del ciel.)

"This causes the daily retardation to which we have so often
referred ; and more particularly he says she was in that path of
the Zodiac which is illuminated by the sun, when the people of
Rome see him setting between Sardinia and Corsica. This is
stated by Mr. Butler, no doubt correctly, to be towards the end
of November, when the Sun sets west by south. If so, the Sun
would then be in Sagittarius, and that is precisely where the
Moon's Right Ascension would bring her on this night, as is
pointed out by Della Valle. Dante's indication of the Sun's
position here, as seen from Rome, is curious. These islands
being invisible from Rome, the Sun can only be said to be seen
setting between them, from a knowledge of their position on the

> E quell' ombra gentil, per cui si noma
>   Pietola più che villa Mantovana,
>   Del mio carcar deposto avea la soma :

And that noble shade (of Virgil), from whom the little village of Pietola (his birthplace) is better known to fame even than the city of Mantua, had laid aside the burden of my lading.

> Perch' io, che la ragione aperta e piana   85
>   Sovra le mie questioni avea ricolta,
>   Stava com' uom che sonnolento vana.

Whereupon I, who had received a manifest and plain answer to my questions, stood like a man who wanders through drowsiness.

The drowsiness reminds us of Canto IX, 11 ; and XXVII, 92, and may be connected with the sin of *accidia* from which the pilgrim is now to be purified ; perhaps with the weariness of the natural man after the tension of the brain occupied with profound mysteries.

Benvenuto says that Dante, after the fashion of the slothful, fatigued with but slight labour, was giving himself up to sleep—but before he could do so, he was

---

map, compared with the observed direction of the Sun. (Compare statement of moon setting beneath Seville in *Inf.* XX, 126). In this sense only can it be true that (as some of the old commentators say) Dante observed this himself when at Rome ; and in this sense it is very likely indeed to have been true, since he was actually at Rome at the moment of the disastrous entry of Charles of Valois into Florence on November 1st, 1301, and for some time afterwards, *i.e.*, at the very time of year here described."

Benvenuto thinks this happened in the middle of October about midnight, and when the sun was in Scorpio.

suddenly roused by a band of penitents, who to purge themselves of sloth, were running so rapidly, that they had already gone completely round the cornice, and were coming up behind the Poets.

> Ma questa sonnolenza mi fu tolta
> Subitamente da gente che, dopo
> Le nostre spalle, a noi era già vôlta.   90

But this drowsiness was suddenly taken from me by persons, who had already come round upon us behind our backs.

These are the slothful whose penalty is unceasing activity and display of energy in running, talking, meditating and whatever else is contrary to their mortal natures.

Benvenuto says the slothful man sins in a threefold way. (*a*) In his heart: by not thinking of God, his own and his neighbour's salvation, and not sorrowing for his sins. (*b*) With his lips: by not praising God, and praying to him, not instructing his neighbour by exhortation, reproof, and such like. (*c*) In his actions: by not giving alms, not going to church, and so on.

> E quale Ismeno già vide ed Asopo,
> Lungo di sè di notte furia e calca,
> Pur che i Teban di Bacco avesser uopo ;
> Tale per quel giron suo passo falca,*
> Per quel ch' io vidi di color, venendo,   95
> Cui buon volere e giusto amor cavalca.

---

* The word *falcare*, in French *faucher*, here translated "curve," is a term of equitation, describing the motion of the outer fore-leg of a horse in going round a circle. It is the sweep of the mower's scythe.

And as of old (*già*) Ismenus and Asopus saw the rush and throng at night along their banks, provided that the Thebans were in need of Bacchus, so these along that cornice curve their steps running round and round it, as much as I could see of those advancing, who by good will and righteous love are ridden.*

> Tosto fûr sovra noi ; perchè correndo,
>> Si movea tutta quella turba magna ;
>> E duo dinanzi gridavan piangendo :
> *Maria corse con fretta alla montagna ;* †   100
>> E : *Cesare, per soggiogare Ilerda,*
>> *Punse Marsilia, e poi corse in Ispagna.*
> —" Ratto, ratto ! che 'l tempo non si perda
>> Per poco amor,"—gridavan gli altri appresso ;
>> —" Chè studio di ben far grazia rinverda."— 105

Soon they were upon us, for the whole of that great band came up running ; and two in front cried out, weeping: " Mary in haste went to the mountain." And " Cæsar, to subdue Ilerda, stung Marseilles, and then hastened into Spain." " Haste, haste ! so as not to waste time through lack of love !" cried out all those that came after ; " that zeal of doing right may cause grace to bud again."

---

* Ismenus and Asopus were rivers of Bœotia, on whose banks the Thebans ran at night with lighted torches to invoke the aid of Bacchus—to give them rain for their vineyards—which is what Dante means by "*Purchè avesser uopo.*" The comparison comes from Statius (*Theb.* IX, 434).

Benvenuto draws a moral from this simile. He says if the Thebans were in the habit of arising at night to chant the praises of the heathen Bacchus, who was the god of wine and triumph, how much the more ought not Christians to arise and hasten to sing the praises of the One True God.

† vv. 100-105. The examples here given are, as usual, drawn both from sacred and profane history. As before, the first

Division IV. Dante now introduces one of the
shades of the slothful, but before doing so he tells us
that Virgil asks the spirits to point out the opening of
the stairway to the next Cornice.

> —"O gente, in cui fervore acuto adesso
> > Ricompie forse negligenza e indugio,
> > Da voi per tiepidezza in ben far messo,
> > Questi che vive (e certo io non vi bugio)
> > > Vuole andar su, pur che il sol ne riluca ;   110
> > > Però ne dite ond' è presso il pertugio."—

"O ye in whom the present fervid zeal perchance
redeems neglect and procrastination shown by you in
lukewarmness to do good, this man who lives (Dante),
and indeed I am telling you the real truth, wishes to
go up as soon as ever the sun shines forth again upon
us ; therefore pray tell us where the passage is near."

> Parole furon queste del mio duca :
> > Ed un di quegli spirti disse :—" Vieni
> > Diretro a noi, e troverai la buca.

---

reference is to an incident in the life of the Blessed Virgin.
St. Luke, I, 39 : "And Mary arose in those days, and went into
the hill country with haste."

These facts about Cæsar are related by Lucan *(Pharsalia)*
in books III and IV. Cæsar, who was on his way to subdue
Ilerda, now Lerida in Spain, besieged Marseilles, leaving there
a part of his army under Brutus to complete the work.

Benvenuto says : No example could be more appropriate, for
no man alive was ever a greater enemy to sloth than Julius
Cæsar—not only for his wonderful endurance, but also for the
incredible rapidity of his marches.

Dean Plumptre thinks that, in v. 105, Dante seems to teach
the scholastic doctrine of "Grace of Congruity ;" *i.e.* that the
efforts of men to do good are effective in making them meet to
receive grace for doing it. The doctrine is condemned by the
Church of England in Article XIII, which teaches to recognise
God's grace even in those efforts.

These words were spoken by my guide, and one of those spirits said : " Come close after us, and thou wilt find the opening."

The answer had come from the Veronese Abbot of Zeno, and we may note, Benvenuto tells us, that his whole demeanour shows how actively he is purifying himself from sloth. He was running fast, without his long robe, he did not delay his rapid course to answer, he did not involve his speech with a tedious exordium, but answered briefly, sharply, and to the point. He then goes on to excuse himself to Dante for not stopping, lest the latter should think his haste ill bred.*

---

* Benvenuto wishes us to take note that Dante has depicted this refusal of the Abbot to stop and talk, with an express purpose ; for he remarks how often one sees people, when engaged in honest useful business, stop on their way to gossip so that they may please men, and engage in delightful conversation. That hard working man, Cato the Censor, remarked that an account must be rendered to God for all our hours of ease, not only of our actions during that time, but even of our words ; and in another place he wrote this graceful idea : Human life resembles a sword, or piece of iron; if a sword be but little used, it is consumed by rust ; but if continuously used day by day it becomes more bright and shining.

The beautiful lines of Miss Proctor apply well to *Accidia* :

> One by one thy duties wait thee,
>   Let thy whole strength go to each,
> Let no future dreams elate thee,
>   Learn thou first what these can teach.
> *   *   *   *   *
> Every hour that fleets so slowly
>   Has its task to do or bear ;
> Luminous the crown, and holy,
>   When each gem is set with care.

Noi siam di voglia a muoverci sì pieni,   115
   Che ristar non potem ; però perdona,
   Se villania nostra giustizia tieni.

We are so full of desire to keep ourselves in movement, that we cannot rest.   Pray excuse us then, if
thou shouldst hold as want of courtesy that which
is our (obligation to satisfy divine) justice.

After his few words of apology for his haste the
spirit continues :*

---

  * Benvenuto says : For the better understanding of this text,
one must know that this spirit says that he lived in the time of
the Emperor Frederick I Barbarossa, of Suabia, who reigned
37 years.   Frederick was at first a friend of the Church, but
later on had a quarrel with Pope Alexander III, who excommunicated him.   About that time he had many wars in Italy
with the Lombard allies of the Pope.   He conquered them all
—destroyed Spoleto and Tortona, *Lodia transmutavit ;* he
built Crema, and Cremona was given up to him ; he assaulted
and took Milan in 1163, pulled down its walls, burnt, ploughed
it up, and sowed the site with salt.   He slaughtered the Romans
horribly.   Alexander, fearing his power, took refuge at Venice,
where he was received with great reverence.   By his favour the
Milanese rebuilt their city in 1168.

  The leader of the Venetian fleet in a naval action, took
prisoner Henry, the Emperor's son, and brought him to Venice.
Frederick Barbarossa, seeing his fortune was deserting him,
and that Pope Alexander was being strengthened by the support
of Louis VII, King of France, Henry II of England, and
William, the excellent King of Sicily, and the allied Venetians
and Lombards, asked for peace and pardon by ambassadors,
and came to Venice and fell on his knees before the Pope.
Pope Alexander placed his foot on the Emperor's neck, saying :
" Thou shalt go upon the serpent and basilisk, and tread the
lion and dragon under thy feet."   The Emperor said, " I kneel
to Peter ; not to you."   And the Pope answered, " I am the
Vicar of Peter."   Frederick went afterwards to the Holy Land
on a crusade in 1190, and was drowned in the Salef in Armenia.

> Io fui Abate in San Zeno a Verona,
>> Sotto lo imperio del buon Barbarossa,
>> Di cui dolente ancor Melan ragiona. 120

I was Abbot of San Zeno at Verona, when the good Barbarossa was Emperor, of whom Milan still speaks with sorrow.

This was a former Abbot of San Zeno, of a life blameless except for sloth, which he is purifying in this Cornice. Benvenuto says: He calls Frederick good, because he was brave, virtuous, energetic, a most successful general, and of a very handsome person, and called Barbarossa from the colour of his beard. During the sack of Milan 82,000 men were scattered abroad, and the ruins remained deserted for five years.

> E tale ha già l' un piè dentro la fossa,
>> Che tosto piangèrà quel monistero,
>> E tristo fia d' averne avuto possa ;
> Perchè suo figlio, mal del corpo intero,
>> E della mente peggio, e che mal nacque, 125
>> Ha posto in luogo di suo pastor vero."—

[Before translating these lines, it is well to mention that the speaker, formerly Abbot of San Zeno, had ruled it admirably.   He now complains of the present Abbot Giuseppe, a son of Alberto della Scala, who being deformed, and of less honourable origin than his half brothers Bartolomeo, Alboino and the famous Can Grande, ought to have been disqualified from so great a distinction as Abbot of San Zeno.   His character moreover ought to have been an insuperable bar to his appointment, but his father Alberto, in his old age, forced him upon the unwilling inmates of the monastery.   So the Abbot in Purgatory proceeds :]

And there is one (Alberto della Scala), already

with a foot in the grave, who soon will weep for that Monastery, and will lament that he ever held the mastery over it,* because he has placed his son (Giuseppe), a man of deformity, of a worse mind, and baseborn, in the room of its true pastor."†

Dante concludes his narration of the interview, by saying—

> Io non so s' ei più disse, o s' ei si tacque,
>> Tant' era già di là da noi trascorso ;
>> Ma questo intesi, e ritener mi piacque.

I know not whether he said more, or whether he was silent, for he had already run so far beyond us ; but I did hear that much, and was glad to retain it in my memory.

Benvenuto thinks Dante means that he noted this one circumstance, that he must remember to severely censure the violators of sacred things.

———

* Dante is here reproving the lay lords who have unjustly taken possession of the goods of the Church.

† Benvenuto tells us : Zeno was the eighth Bishop of Verona, in A.D. 165, during the papacy of Dionysius. He was a man of deep sanctity, learning, and eloquence. Three churches are named after San Zeno at Verona : one on the hill, another by the Adige, which is only a small oratory or chapel, and I think it is this San Zeno of which St. Gregory writes in the Dialogues that on one occasion the Adige had inundated Verona, but did not enter the windows of the Church of San Zeno. The third Church is about a javelin cast from the river, and there is no fairer Church that I have seen in all Verona. And it is of this Church in particular that Dante is speaking here, because it has monks, and also the spirit speaking Abbot, Albert, was Abbot there.

Division V.   This is the last Division, in which Dante teaches how sloth is to be avoided, by showing its unfortunate effects.

The examples are followed by warnings.   The Israelites who came out of Egypt (compare Canto II, 46) perished through their coward sloth, and did not enter on the inheritance of Canaan (*Numb.* XIV, *Deut.* I, 26-36, *Heb.* III, 13-19).   Many of the companions of Æneas chose to remain in Sicily with Acestes (*Æneid,* V, 746-761), and so forfeited their share in the inheritance of Italy.   They chose safety rather than glory, and that was the evidence of the sin of *accidia.*   Benvenuto begs us to admire how gracefully Dante makes Virgil introduce two spirits who are both showing their detestation of sloth.

> E quei, che m' era ad ogni uopo soccorso,   130
> Disse :—" Volgiti in qua, vedine due
> Venire, dando all' accidia di morso."—

And he, who was always at hand to assist me in need, said, " Turn round, and look at those two spirits coming up behind you, uttering reproaches against sloth.

Benvenuto thinks Dante shows great skill in representing the two first spirits singing the praises of the energetic, such as the Virgin Mary and Julius Cæsar, while the two now arriving, walk, on the other hand, singing the bad examples offered by the slothful.

Dante next describes the song of the new arrivals, and tells us how they first sang of the disastrous effects of sloth on the children of Israel.

> Diretro a tutti dicean : *Prima fue*
> *Morta la gente, a cui il mar s' aperse,*
> *Che vedesse Giordan le rede sue;*   135

Coming behind all the others they shouted: " That nation to whom the sea opened its waters were all dead before that the Jordan saw their heirs." [It will be remembered that Joshua and Caleb were the only Israelites who witnessed both these miracles.]

> E : *Quella che l' affanno non sofferse,*
>   *Fino alla fine col figliuol d' Anchise,*
>   *Sè stessa a vita sanza gloria offerse.*

And: "That folk that would not endure fatigue unto the end with the son of Anchises offered itself up to a life without glory."*

The glory would have been to share in founding the great Roman Empire. Benvenuto says that Dante now brings to a conclusion what he has to say about sloth, and with it this noble Canto, by preparing for what has to be described in the Canto that follows, which contains his account of a wonderful dream.

> Poi quando fûr da noi tanto divise
>   Quell' ombre, che veder più non potèrsi,   140
>   Nuovo pensier dentro da me si mise,
> Del qual più altri nacquero e diversi ;
>   E tanto d' uno in altro vaneggiai,
>   Che gli occhi per vaghezza ricopersi,
> E il pensamento in sogno trasmutai.   145

Then when those spirits had passed so far away

---

* Benvenuto says that this episode relates an effect of disgraceful sloth among the Trojans who followed Æneas, and when in Sicily he was celebrating funeral games by the tomb of his father Anchises, certain persons, both old men, young men and women, wearied out by their long voyage and hard toils, burnt Æneas's ships, so that they might not have to leave Sicily and confront new dangers. Æneas constituted them as a colony, and left the whole unwarlike crowd in contempt.

from us, that we could no longer see them, a new thought arose within me, from which in turn were born other thoughts many and varying ; and so from one to the other I rambled on, I closed my eyes, and transformed my thoughts into a dream.

It is noticeable that in this circle alone there is no request for the intercessory prayers of others. Is there an implied retribution in the omission ? Were they, who had been so negligent and apathetic on earth, now to undergo their fate unaided by the sympathy of others ?

END OF CANTO XVIII.

CANTO XIX.

___

The Fifth Cornice.
Avarice.

As in the last Canto Dante treated of the sin of sloth, so he follows on in this Nineteenth Canto to speak of avarice, which is atoned for in the Fifth Cornice of Purgatory.

Benvenuto divides it into four parts.

In the First Division, from v. 1 to v. 33, Dante tells of his dream.

In the Second Division, from v. 34 to v. 69, he describes his entrance into the Fifth Cornice, and the appearance of an angel who points out the way to him, and purifies him from the sin of Sloth.

In the Third Division, from v. 70 to v. 126, he speaks of the penance of the avaricious in the person of the spirit of Pope Adrian V.

In the Fourth Division, from v. 127 to v. 145, he clears up a doubt respecting the above named spirit, namely, whether temporal dignity ends with life.

Division I. Dante relates his dream, and premises his account by telling us that it was the hour before dawn ; by that implying that it was a dream that was to be fulfilled as he had already shown us in Canto IX, 13, and *Inf.* XXVI, 7.*

___

* Dr. Moore (*Time References*, p. 105) says: " In this passage

> Nell' ora che non può il calor diurno
> Intiepidar piu il freddo della luna,
> Vinto da Terra, e talor da Saturno ;

At the hour, when the heat of the day, vanquished by the earth, and sometimes by Saturn, can no longer warm the cold caused by the moon ;

> Quando i geomanti* lor maggior fortuna†
> Veggiono in oriente, innanzi all' alba,   5
> Surger per via che poco le sta bruna ;

When the geomancers see, before dawn, their Fortuna Major rise in the east, by a path which will not long remain dim ;

---

we have the hour before dawn on Tuesday, April 12th, described by two indications (or, as Benvenuto says : *dupliciter* = doubly.) 1. It was the coldest hour of the twenty-four. 2. The later stars of Aquarius and the foremost ones of Pisces were on the horizon. This, perhaps, we may be allowed to take for granted is the meaning of the *maggior fortuna* of the wizards, *v.* 4. It was a peculiar arrangement of dots, corresponding to one that can be formed out of certain stars on the confines of these two constellations. These were now in the east before the dawn."

* Compare Chaucer, *Troilus and Cressida*, III, 1415.

> "And whan the cock, commune astrologer,
> Gan on his brest to beate and after crowe,
> And Lucifer, the daies messenger,
> Gan to rise and out his beames throwe,
> And estward rose, to him that could it know
> Fortuna Major."

Benvenuto says, that *geomantia* is called *astrologia minor*, and it is said to be a common refuge for astrologers, and ought never to be entirely despised, as it has some of its principles in astrology. But he adds : "They may say what they will, I do not believe at all in geomancy, any more than I believe in astrology."

† Benvenuto says that geomancers use many figures made of

And now Dante, having stated what time it was, proceeds to relate a wonderful vision.   And Benvenuto says that by the dream he wishes to foreshadow the subject he is going to treat of, for, as he has already discussed the first four deadly sins, which are sins of the mind, viz., pride, envy, anger, and sloth, so now, being about to discuss the three remaining, viz., avarice, gluttony, and self-indulgence, which are of the body and are sins that are ever seeking pleasures, he pictures them to be represented by the Siren.   The vision seems in part a reproduction of *Prov.* VII, 10-12 ; the distorted eyes, the bent form, the crippled hands, the extreme pallor corresponding to the physiognomic signs of those evil passions.

Benvenuto supports this view, as it is a mistake to suppose that the Siren represented avarice alone.

> Mi venne in sogno una femmina balba,*
> > Negli occhi guercia, e sovra i piè distorta,
> > Con le man monche, e di colore scialba.

There appeared to me in a dream a stammering

---

dots, but one especially, which they call *Fortuna Major*, which was taken from six stars happening to be seen in an exactly identical position to the six dots, as in the annexed figure:

$$* \quad *$$
$$* \quad *$$
$$*$$
$$*$$

These stars rise in the East, and are said to be at the end of the Constellation Aquarius and at the beginning of Pisces. He says the Indians and Saracens used to go to the sea-shore at sunrise, and mark their dots, either odd or even, on the sand.

* Benvenuto says that *the stammering tongue* means avarice, which never speaks openly and clearly but deceitfully ; it means

woman, with squinting eyes, and distorted feet, with her hands cut off, and of a pallid hue.

In the person of this woman, who is presently described as a Siren, Dante sees the three deadly sins of avarice, gluttony, and luxury.

> Io la mirava ; e come il sol conforta   10
> > Le fredde membra che la notte aggrava,
> > Così lo sguardo mio le facea scorta
> La lingua, e poscia tutta la drizzava
> > In poco d' ora, e lo smarrito volto, ·
> > Come amor vuol, così lo colorava.   15

I looked at her ; and, as the sun revives the chilled limbs which night benumbs, so my gaze restored .liberty to her tongue, and then caused her whole body to become straight in a short space of time, and brought into her pallid cheeks that warm colour which pleases a lover.

And now Dante describes the soft seductive strains that issued from the mouth of her who had assumed beauty which was a mockery and deceit.

> Poi ch' ella avea il parlar così disciolto,
> > Cominciava a cantar sì, che con pena
> > Da lei avrei mio intento rivolto.

After that she had thus unloosed her speech, she

---

gluttony because drunkenness makes a man speak thick, and luxury because it makes him a liar and a flatterer. *The squinting eye* denotes avarice, because the miser is blind from the craving of acquisitiveness and of hoarding ; it denotes both gluttony and luxury, because over indulgence destroys the eyes both bodily and mentally. *It is lame* because in those three sins man never walks in the right paths. *It is maimed* because the miser never uses his hands to give, and the gluttonous and luxurious never work, but are idle and slothful. All three, the miser, the glutton, and the voluptuary, have pallid faces.

began singing so sweetly, that it would have been hard indeed for me to have turned my attention from her.

> —" Io son (cantava), io son la dolce Sirena,
>   Che i marinari in mezzo il mar dismago ;   20
>   Tanto son di piacere a sentir piena.

" I am," she sang, " I am the sweet Siren who bewilders the sailors amid the ocean, so full am I of pleasantness to hear.

Benvenuto explains that the sirens were marine monsters who used to bewitch mariners by their sweet song, lull them to sleep, drown them and then spoil their ships ; so here Dante appropriately comes with pleasure to the· Siren, who not only ensnares the incautious, but even the most wary.   In proof of which she says :

> Io volsi Ulisse del suo cammin vago
>   Al canto mio ; e qual meco si ausa,
>   Rado sen parte, sì tutto l' appago."*—

I drew Ulysses from his wandering path to my song, and whoever accustoms himself to me rarely departs from me, so abundantly do I satisfy him."

---

* Pope unconsciously reproduced Dante when he wrote, in his *Essay on Man*, II, 219 :

> Vice is a monster of so frightful mien
> As, to be hated, needs but to be seen ;
> Yet seen too oft, familiar with her face,
> We first endure, then pity, then embrace.

Benvenuto notices Dante's mistake in making out Ulysses as having been fascinated by the Siren, for he remarks (erroneously) that in the *Odyssey* Homer tells us that Ulysses avoided the Sirens and filled his ears with wax so as not to hear their song. He thinks Dante must have meant Circe, who detained Ulysses for one year, or Calypso, who kept him a prisoner for several years.

Dante then introduces a lady in his dream, typifying
Wisdom, who puts to shame the false one, the type
of pleasure.

> Ancor non era sua bocca richiusa,   25
>> Quando una donna apparve santa e presta
>> Lunghesso me, per far colei confusa.

Her mouth was hardly closed again, when swiftly
there appeared at my side a saintly Lady to put that
one to confusion.

Benvenuto points out that whereas Dante had called
the Siren *femmina*, a female, he styles this one *donna*,
a far more honourable term.   Benvenuto's words are :
" *Bene vocat istam dominam, ubi illam vocaverat famu-
lam, quia ratio debet dominari, et passio famulari.*"

Scartazzini says that the commentators have differed
very considerably as to what this lady symbolises, and
that he does not agree with those who think she is
the symbol of wisdom, or of Lucia (symbol of truth),
or of the Church, but he thinks with the older commentators that she represents reason, or temperance,
or philosophy, or intellectual virtue.

Whoever she is supposed to be, we now read that
she addresses Virgil in a tone of indignant remon-
strance for allowing Dante, their joint pupil, to gaze
on the deceitful pleasures of the world.

> —" O Virgilio, Virgilio, chi è questa ? "—
>> Fieramente diceva ; ed ei venia
>> Con gli occhi fitti pure in quella onesta.   30
> L' altra prendeva, e dinanzi l' apria
>> Fendendo i drappi, e mostravami il ventre ;
>> Quel mi svegliò col puzzo che n' uscia.

"O Virgil, Virgil, who is this ? " said she, sternly ;
and he advanced with his eyes fixed upon that honour-

able one only. She* seized the other one, laid her
bare in front, rending her drapery, and showed me her
belly; this woke me with the stench that came from it.

Benvenuto praises the words of the Poet with much
enthusiasm ; and asks if the filth of the miser does
not befoul everything beautiful and honourable with
its misery, just like the harpies befouled the feast.
How great the filth of the glutton. Into what mire
does not the drunkard fall from his drunkenness. And
of the filth of sensuality Benvenuto prefers not to
speak.

————

Division II. Dante now tells us of his entrance
into the Fifth Cornice and his purgation by the Angel.

Virgil roused him, and on waking he found it was
broad daylight.

> Io volsi gli occhi, e il buon Virgilio :—"Almen tre   35
>   Voci t' ho messe (dicea), surgi e vieni ;
>   Troviam la porta per la qual tu entre."—

I turned my eyes, and the good Virgil said : " I have
called thee at least three times ; arise, and come. Let
us find the opening through which thou mayest enter."

> Su mi levai. E tutti eran già pieni
>   Dell' alto dì i giron del sacro monte,
>   Ed andavam col sol nuovo alle reni.

I rose, and already were all the cornices of the holy
mountain beaming with the light of broad day ; and

————

* *L' altra prendeva.* Scartazzini says that the holy lady
seized the stammering one, and he says that is the view of the
commentators, the Ottimo, Benvenuto, Buti, Danielli, Venturi,
Biagioli, Witte, Ozanam, and others ; but some think that it
was Virgil who took the Siren: among these are Landino,
Vellutello, Cesari, Brunone Bianchi, and Philalethes.

we were walking towards the west with the newly risen sun right at our backs.*

It is now full daylight of the morning of Easter Tuesday, 1300, Dante's third day in Purgatory.

> Seguendo lui, portava la mia fronte 40
> Come colui che l' ha di pensier carca,
> Che fa di sè un mezzo arco di ponte ;

As I followed him I carried my head as one who has it full of thought, and makes himself look like half the arch of a bridge.

In two lives of Dante we find that this was his habit, Boccaccio (Vita di Dante) says : *Andò alquanto curvetto* ; and Filippo Villani (*Vita Dantis*) says : "*Is dum annis maturuisset, curvatis aliquantulum renibus incedebat, incessu tamen gravi, mansuetudoque aspectu.*"

He was thinking about his wonderful dream.

> Quando io udi' : *Venite, qui si varca,*
> Parlare in modo soave e benigno,
> Qual non si sente in questa mortal marca.† 45

---

* Dr. Moore (*Time References*, p. 106). "In lines 37-9 it was now full daylight, with the sun on their backs, so that they were still journeying towards the west, when they enter the Fifth Cornice, where Avarice and Prodigality are punished. Observe here also the admirable fitness with which Dante times his progress so that the time spent in the Cornice where Accidia, or Spiritual Sloth, is punished is exactly coincident with the hours of the night—'the night in which no man can work.' He enters it as darkness comes on (as we read in XVII, 70-80) and leaves it next morning, as soon as he awakes with the *nuovo sol* (XIX, 38), being mildly chided by Virgil for the length of his slumbers (XIX, 34). I might, perhaps, mention here that it will be found that in each of the other Cornici he spends from three to five hours."

† *Marca*, march, is used in the same sense as it is in *Marca Trevigiana*, the region or district of Treviso. The word is found in the Gothic *Marca*, a border country (see Skeat's *Ety-*

When I heard : "Come, one can pass here," uttered in so sweet and gentle a tone as one never hears in this region of mortals.

> Con l' ale aperte che parean di cigno,
>   Volseci in su colui che sì parlonne,
>   Tra i duo pareti del duro macigno.

With outspread wings, as those of a swan, did he who thus spoke to us make us turn upwards through walls on either side of hard rock.

Benvenuto says *macigno* is that kind of stone from which are cut *macinæ*, mill-stones.

Another P is now erased from Dante's brow by the Angel.

> Mosse le penne poi e ventilonne,
>   *Qui lugent* affermando esser beati,   50
>   Ch' avran di consolar l' anime donne.

He moved his pinions, and then fanned us, (with the words) "Blessed are they that mourn," affirming that they that mourn on earth will in heaven have their souls as ladies of consolation.

In the last line I follow Benvenuto ; not one other translator or commentator that I have looked , at, except Fraticelli, seems to give the true meaning. We are supposed to understand that the angel had, with one stroke of his wings, effaced from Dante's forehead the fourth P, so that there are still three remaining.

Virgil now asks Dante what is the matter with him.

> —" Che hai, che pure invêr la terra guati ? "—
>   La guida mia incominciò a dirmi,
>   Poco ambedue dall' Angel sormontati.

---

mological Dictionary of the English Language), and also in the Icelandic *Mark*, border-land. Vigfusson (*Icelandic Dictionary*) says it is a word common to all Teutonic languages, and the original sense is outline, border.

" What ails thee that thou gazest only on the earth?"
My guide began to say to me, when we had both ascended a little above the Angel.*

> Ed io :—" Con tanta suspizion fa irmi 55
> Novella visïon che a sè mi piega,
> Sì ch' io non posso dal pensar partirmi."—

And I : " A sight so new, and which draws my mind
to ponder over it so much, that I cannot dissever it
from my thought."

Virgil briefly explains :

> —" Vedesti (disse) quella antica strega,
> Che sola sovra noi omai si piagne ;
> Vedesti come l' uom da lei si slega. 6o

" Hast thou seen, (said he), that ancient sorceress,
whose wicked work has to be wept for only in the
three cornices above us ?† Hast thou seen how man
is delivered from her ?

Virgil admonishes Dante respecting this vision, that
a man shall let each of his members do its own office,
that he shall, with his feet, walk upon the earth, and,
with his eyes, look up to heaven.

> Bastiti, e batti a terra le calcagne,
> Gli occhi rivolgi al logoro, che gira
> Lo Rege eterno con le ruote magne."—

Let that suffice, and strike the earth with thy heels
(*i.e.*, quicken thy steps), and turn thine eyes upward to

---

* *Sormontati.* This passage can be translated in two ways,
and commentators interpret it, either, " When we had ascended
a little above the point where the Angel stood " ; or, " Being,
where we both stood, surmounted by the Angel," that is, the
angel being still a little above the point we had reached.

† Benvenuto gives this interpretation, but with the choice of
another, viz., ' who is weeping alone because we have departed
from her, and she was not able to turn us out of our way.'

the lure, which the Eternal King whirls with vast revolutions."*

Virgil noticed Dante's eyes bent upon the ground. The Almighty is compared to a falconer; meaning that man must use this world's goods, such as wealth, food and luxuries, only so far as are necessary to sustain life, and treat them as things to be trodden under foot, as little and vile, but let his mental contemplation be towards heaven, eternal and immortal. And then Dante shows, by a noble comparison, how eagerly he proceeded to follow Virgil's advice.

> Quale il falcon, che prima a' piè si mira,
>   Indi si volge al grido, e si protende   65
>   Per lo disio del pasto che là il tira:

Like as the hawk, which first looks down towards its feet, then turns him to the call and darts forward, through strong desire for food which draws him there.

Benvenuto notices how appropriate is this comparison. . As the hawk, which is by its nature light, flies in a spirited manner on high by a number of great wheels, so did our Poet fly by the wings of his mind wheeling round and round the cornices of the high mountain. And as the falcon first looks down at its feet, so was Dante doing now; and as the falcon, raising its head, stretches itself forward to fly for its food, so now Dante, raising his head, stretches himself forward with the hopes of heaven, at the call of Virgil,

---

* Comp. Ovid's *Metamorph.* 1, Dryden's Trans.:

> Thus, while the mute creation downward bend
> Their sight, and to their earthly mother tend
> Man looks aloft ; and with erected eyes
> Beholds his own hereditary skies.

who, like a noble falconer, was leading him in search
of his quarry.* And he concludes the Second Divisicn
by telling us how he ascended.

> Tal mi fec' io ; e tal, quanto si fende
> La roccia per dar via a chi va suso,
> N' andai infino ove il cerchiar si prende.

And so did I act, and I went on as far as the rock
cleaves to give a passage to him who would mount up .
to where one begins again to circle.

Benvenuto says that the stairways always mounted
straight up, and all the cornices were circular throughout the Purgatorio.

Division III. In the person of a modern spirit, the
penance and purgation of the avaricious are described.
Benvenuto says that Dante purges the avaricious in
the most perfect manner. He represents them all
lying on the ground with their faces to the earth and
their backs turned towards heaven, and with their
hands and feet tied, and weeping and lamenting.
What Dante represents is explained a little further
on. One must imagine that he who wishes to
purge himself from the sin of avarice has to recollect
and mourn over the life that he has wasted on earth.
For if the slothful man abstains from doing good
through laziness, the avaricious man does all manner
of evil from wickedness ; he turns his back on heaven
and worships the world ; he keeps his hands and feet

---

* This is another of Dante's favourite illustrations from the
sport of falconry. See also *Inf.* XVII, 127 ; *Inf.* XXII, 130,
and *Par.* XIX, 34.

bound, for he gives to no one, nor goes to any one's
assistance, and is the most miserable of men.   He is
just like some animals who will sacrifice, of their own
accord, some part of their body to save their lives—
the fox, for instance, has been known to bite off, with
its teeth, its own foot when caught in a trap—as Pliny
tells us.   So does the avaricious man expose his soul
to manifest death, for the sake of acquiring or pro-
tecting a small modicum of money.

> Com' io nel quinto giro fui dischiuso,   70
>   Vidi gente per esso che piangea,
>   Giacendo a terra tutta volta in giuso.

As soon as I came forth into the fifth circle (from
the stairway wherein I had been, as it were, shut up),
I saw persons upon it that lay upon the ground weeping, with their faces turned downwards.

> *Adhæsit pavimento anima mea,**
>   Senti' dir lor con sì alti sospiri,
>   Che la parola appena s' intendea.   75

---

* Dean Plumptre observes : " As in *Inf.* VII, 25-66, the misers
and prodigals are grouped together as exhibiting different aspects
of the same evil, on earth their looks, like those of Milton's
Mammon (*Par. Lost*, I, 681) have been ever " downward bent,"
and their penance is to lie prostrate on the earth, uttering the
words of *Psalm* CXIX, 25.   These words form part of the service
of Prime in the Roman Breviary, and it was at this hour that
Dante hears them in Purgatory. . . . We may also call to
mind the concluding words of the verse which begins :

"My soul cleaveth unto the dust : quicken Thou me according to Thy word."

Dean Plumptre also notices the courteousness of the address
to the spirits in v. 76 : " Such should be the tone of every soul
seeking its own purification towards others who are under a like
discipline for like sins."

I heard them say: "My soul cleaveth unto the dust" (*Psalm* CXIX, 25), with such deep sighs that one could hardly distinguish the words.

Virgil then addresses the spirits ;

> —"O eletti di Dio, gli cui soffriri
> E giustizia e speranza fan men duri,
> Drizzate noi verso gli alti saliri."—

"O ye elect of God for salvation, whose sufferings are rendered less hard by justice and hope, direct us towards the high ascents." This means : Show us the way to the next stairway that we may ascend to the cornices above.

And now one of the spirits answers, being evidently in doubt whether Virgil and Dante have gone through their course of penance, or whether they have come into Purgatory by the special grace of God :

> —"Se voi venite dal giacer securi,
> E volete trovar la via più tosto,   80
> Le vostre destre sien sempre di furi."—

"If you come, being exempted from lying prostrate, and wish to find the path soonest, see that your right hands are always outward."

> Così pregò il Poeta, e sì risposto,
> Poco dinanzi a noi ne fu ; per ch' io
> Nel parlare avvisai l' altro nascosto;

Thus did Virgil make his request, and thus did answer come from a little beyond us, and therefore by the speech I was able to make out where that other (spirit) was concealed.

To really appreciate the next *terzina* one must have lived in Italy, and know Italian ways of sign-language. Dante heard the voice, turned his head to Virgil, gazed at him straight in the eyes, turned his head again towards the recumbent spirit, and then again looked Virgil full in the face, the triple gesture signifying: " That is the person who spoke, can I go and speak to him ? " Virgil probably answered with a graceful wave of the hand, meaning, " Do so."

E volsi gli occhi allora al signor mio :   85
   Ond' egli m' assentì con lieto cenno
   Ciò che chiedea la vista del disio.

And I turned my eyes then to my Master, on which he, with a pleasant gesture, signified consent to what his sight of my wish expressed.

Poi ch' io potei di me fare a mio senno,
   Trassimi sovra quella creatura,
   Le cui parole pria notar mi fenno,   90
Dicendo :—" Spirto, in cui pianger matura
   Quel senza il quale a Dio tornar non puossi,
   Sosta un poco per me tua maggior cura.

So soon as I was enabled to do according to my will, I moved on until I was leaning over that being whose words had first made me notice him, saying : " Spirit whose weeping is bringing to perfection that, without which one cannot turn to God, lay aside for awhile thy greater care, for my sake.

Dante asks the spirit three questions :

Chi fosti, e perchè vôlti avete i dossi
   Al su, mi di', e se vuoi ch' io t' impetri   95
   Cosa di là ond' io vivendo mossi."—

Tell me who thou wast, and why you have your backs uppermost, and if there is anything that thou wishest to be asked for in prayer by me on thy behalf over there whence I came alive ?"

Benvenuto points out that by this last verse Dante shows in which of the two ways he is *sicuro dal giacer*, viz., because he is alive. The commentator points out how different the whole scene is from Dante's interview with the wicked Pope Niccola degli Orsini in `Inf.` XIX.

The spirit now tells Dante that he will answer the two questions in turn.

> Ed egli a me :—" Perchè i nostri diretri
> Rivolga il cielo a sè, saprai : ma prima
> *Scias quod ego fui successor Petri.*

And he to me : " Thou wilt learn why heaven wishes our backs turned towards it ; but first know that I was a successor of Peter.

This reminds one of the scene in *Inf.* XIX. Dante having been carried by Virgil to the place where Pope Nicholas Orsini is being punished, has to stoop down to the ground to converse with him.*

The speaker is Ottobuoni Fieschi, who was elected Pope as Adrian V, July 12, 1276. He died at Viterbo on the 3rd of August the same year. Sestri and

---

* See v. 49 of *Inf.* XIX.
> Io stava come il frate che confessa
> Lo perfido assassin, &c.

So, too, here has he to stoop to converse with this Pope. In *Inf.* XIX, Nicholas tells him (v. 69):
> Sappi ch' io fui vestito del gran manto.

At the end of his conversation with Pope Nicholas, Dante breaks forth into a reproach against the avarice of the Pastors of the Church. At the end of his interview with this Pope, also doing penance for avarice, he humbly bends the knee to do homage to his high dignity. And even in *Inf.* XIX, v. 100, while using words that were somewhat forcible, he says :
> E se non fosse ch' ancor lo mi vieta,
> La riverenza delle somme chiavi
> Che tu tenesti nella vita lieta,
> Io userei parole ancor più gravi, &c.

Chiavari are two towns of the Eastern Riviera, which
were subject to Genoa. The river is the Lavagna,
whence the Fieschi family took their title. Adrian
died before his admission to the priesthood, and was
therefore neither consecrated nor crowned as Pope.
He had been sent by Innocent IV in 1268 as a legate
to reconcile Henry III, King of England, and his
barons, and to reform abuses in the church. Adrian
was, Benvenuto tells us, a nephew of Innocent IV,
and when his friends and relations came to congratu-
late him on his election, he is reported to have said :
" It was better for you to have a live Cardinal than a
dead Pope." He only sat on the throne of St. Peter
one month and eight days. Benvenuto gives the date
as 1273. Pope Adrian's speech is one of the fine
passages in the Purgatorio :

> Intra Siestri e Chiaveri si adima   100
>   Una fiumana bella, e del suo nome
>   Lo titol del mio sangue fa sua cima.

Between Sestri and Chiavari a beautiful river flows
down, and from its name, the Lavagna, the title of my
race takes its origin.

> Un mese e poco più provai io come
>   Pesa il gran manto a chi dal fango il guarda ;
>   Che piuma sembran tutte l' altre some.*   105

For one month and a little more I experienced how
weighs the grand cope on him who keeps it from the
mire, so that all other burdens seem but feathers.

---

* Compare *Purg.* XVI, 127, 129 :

> La Chiesa di Roma
> Per confondere in sè duo reggimenti,
> Cade nel fango, e sè brutta e la soma.

> La mia conversione, omè ! fu tarda ;
>> Ma, come fatto fui Roman Pastore,
>> Così scopersi la vita bugiarda.

My conversion, alas! was delayed : but when I became Pope of Rome then I discovered how false was life.

> Vidi che lì non si quetava il core,
>> Nè più salir poteasi in quella vita ;   110
>> Per che di questa in me s' accese amore.

I saw that the heart had no rest there, nor in that life was any further advancement possible, wherefore the desire of this (eternal life) was kindled in me.*

> Fino a quel punto misera e partita
>> Da Dio anima fui, del tutto avara :
>> Or, come vedi, qui ne son punita.

Up to that time I was a wretched soul, and severed from God, the prey of avarice ; now, as thou seest, here I am punished for it.

Benvenuto says that Adrian speaks true, for the followers of avarice are cut off from communion with God ; nor, indeed, is the avaricious man satisfied by the gratification of his desires, as happened once to a kinsman of this same Adrian.   For the head of the Fieschi, who was the richest of all churchmen,

---

* Benvenuto considers this is very good reasoning, for what sovereign has such dignity and power as the Pope ?   Others have to rule over mortal affairs ; but he over spiritual matters. Others get their pre-eminence from man ; but he from the eternal wisdom of God.   Others have power over earthly matters ; he has the freedom of eternal ones, and indeed, as they say, he is the ruler over both living and the dead.   Therefore there neither is, nor can be anything greater in the whole Christian world, although now-a-days it does not seem to be · greatly esteemed.

obtained from the Emperor Rudolph to be Vicar
of the Empire, and the expense utterly ruined
him.

The avaricious man seeks immoderately what is not
his own, and tenaciously holds what is his own—as
did Adrian.

In the early days of the Christian Church the
dignity of the Papacy was not one at all to be coveted,
as nearly all the early Pontiffs were dragged off to
execution and martyrdom ; but now the dignity is
sought after with such ambition, that fraud, bribes,
and promises have a large share in influencing the
election.   That is the probable explanation of Adrian
saying, in vv. 103-4, that now-a-days the office
is not greatly esteemed ; it is coveted and intrigued
for by churchmen ; and laymen, in consequence, hold
the office in less respect from the election not being
merely the result, as it used formerly to be, of the
free choice of holy-minded men, who had prayed to
God to direct their selection without any thought of
personal ambition for themselves.

And then Adrian answers Dante's other question as
to why he and other spirits are lying in that posture.

> Quel ch' avarizia fa, qui si dichiara   115
>   In purgazion dell' anime converse,
>   E nulla pena il monte ha più amara.

The effects of avarice are here displayed in the
purgation of converted souls ; and the mountain contains more bitter punishment than this.

> Sì come l' occhio nostro non s' aderse
>   In alto, fisso alle cose terrene,
>   Così giustizia qui a terra il merse.   120

As our eyes were not uplifted on high, but fixed on

earthly things, so justice here has sunk them to the
ground.

> Come avarizia spense a ciascun bene
>> Lo nostro amore, onde operar perdèsi,
>> Così giustizia qui stretti ne tiene
> Ne' piedi e nelle mani legati e presi ;
>> E quanto fia piacer del giusto Sire,   125
>> Tanto staremo immobili e distesi."—

Even as avarice extinguished in us the love of all
good, which caused all our work to be in vain, so
justice now confines us here in restraint, fast bound
and fettered by the hands and feet; and, for so long
as the righteous Lord wills it, so long shall we remain
stretched and motionless."

Division IV. In this concluding division of the
Canto, Dante solves a point which was always a
doubtful one to him, viz. : whether temporal dignity
ceases with temporal death. He pictures himself as
having knelt down with the intention of doing homage
to the Pope's high office :

> Io m' era inginocchiato, e volea dire ;
>> Ma com' io cominciai, ed ei s' accorse,
>> Solo ascoltando, del mio riverire,
> —" Qual cagion (disse), in giù così ti torse ? "—   130
>> Ed io a lui :—" Per vostra dignitate,
>> Mia coscïenza dritto mi rimorse."

I had knelt down and was about to speak ; but, as
·I began, he perceived my act of reverence solely by
hearing. "What cause," said he, "has bent thee
downward there ?" And I to him : "By reason of

your rank my conscience gave me compunction* (or my conscience stimulated me to kneel)."

We now have Adrian's answer, proving that after death no demonstrations of respect are due or even decorous.

—" Drizza le gambe, levati su, frate,"—
    Rispose: "non errar, conservo sono
    Teco e con gli altri ad una potestate.   135

"Straighten thy legs, rise up, my brother," said he in answer, " Err not; I am a fellow-servant with thee and others to one Power.†

---

* Benvenuto wishes us to take note that to no living person among Christians is any greater reverence paid, than to the Pope, even though he may be the vilest and most vicious of men, and many think this is almost a miracle. Dante himself touched elegantly on this once at Verona, when, supping with some distinguished persons, someone asked out of curiosity: "Why is it, most learned Dante, that a sailor who has suffered shipwreck ever goes to sea again: that a woman who has once borne a child ever wishes to conceive again: and that such thousands of poor do not swallow up the few rich?" To which the very prudent Dante, fearing to furnish error to the least intelligent guests, evading the question, replied: "Add a fourth question, Why do all the kings and princes of the earth reverently kiss the foot of the son of a barber and washerwoman when he is made Pope?"

† Benvenuto says: "These words are taken out of the XVIIIth chapter of the *Apocalypse* (XIXth in A. V.), where, when St. John had cast himself at the feet of the angel, it was said to him: 'See thou do it not: I am thy fellow-servant and of thy brethren who have the testimony of Jesus: worship God.' And notice how Adrian brings forward an excellent example from a most excellent book of Holy Scripture; for if it be lawful to make a comparison of such a nature, Dante, a man of a highly speculative nature, can be compared to St. John, who was of a most contemplative nature, each of whom, although in

Adrian had learnt the lesson of *Acts* X, 26—*Rev.* XIX, 10—XXII, 9.

Another token of humility is that instead of using the usual formula of a Pope, who addresses others as "my son," he speaks to Dante as a brother. And Adrian confirms his words by adding testimony from Holy Scripture.

> Se mai quel santo evangelico suono,
> Che dice *Neque nubent* intendesti,
> Ben puoi veder perch' io così ragiono.

If thou hast ever heard those words from the Holy Gospel, "Nor are given in marriage,"* thou canst well perceive why I speak as I do.

> Vattene omai ; non vo' che più t' arresti,
> Chè la tua stanza mio pianger disagia,   140
> Col qual maturo ciò che tu dicesti.

Now go thy way, I will not have thee linger more : because thy stay here inconveniences my weeping, with which I bring to perfection that which thou hast said.

And then Adrian answers the third question that Dante had asked him, as to whether he could make any prayers for him on earth.

---

different manners, while in rapt ecstacy of the mind, saw wonderful and various imageries. As then St. John had knelt at the feet of the angel, so did Dante kneel at the feet of the great High Priest ; and as the angel did not accept this honour, calling himself the fellow-servant of St. John, and of all them that had the testimony of Jesus, so did Pope Adrian now, calling himself the fellow-servant of Dante, and all other Christian men."

* " For in the resurrection they neither marry, nor are given in marriage, but are as the angels of God in heaven."—*St. Matt.* XXII, 30. Dante uses these words in an allegorical sense.

Nepote ho io di là ch' ha nome Alagia,
   Buona da sè, pur che la nostre casa
   Non faccia lei per esemplo malvagia
E questa sola di là m' è rimasa."—   145

On earth I have a granddaughter named Alagia, good in herself, unless, indeed, our house does not corrupt her by its evil example, and she alone remains to me yonder."*

The Pope is the spiritual bridegroom of the Church. Compare *Purg.* XXII, 20-22 :

     e quella faccia
Di là da lui, più che l' altre trapunta
Ebbe la santa chiesa in le sue braccia :

But in the other world there is no marriage, and there no longer exist there those prerogatives of the spiritual union contracted between the Pope and the Church. Therefore Adrian was not any more to be revered as the Head of the Church.

 * Madonna Alagia was the wife of Marcello Malespini, that friend of Dante, with whom, during his wanderings, he took refuge in the Lunigiana in 1307.—See *Purg.* VIII, 115-139.

END OF CANTO XIX.

CANTO XX.

THE FIFTH CORNICE.
AVARICE (*continued*).

As in the preceding Canto Dante defined the general penance and purgation of the avaricious, he now teaches us to avoid that common evil of the human race in two ways. First, by considering the good effects of liberality and voluntary poverty, and secondly, by considering the evil effects of avarice and cupidity.

This Canto is divided by Benvenuto into four parts.

In the First Division, from v. 1 to v. 33, Dante expresses his hatred of avarice and commends liberality.

In the Second Division, from v. 34 to v. 96, he introduces the spirit of a noble, himself avaricious, and the head of a long line of avaricious persons.

In the Third Division, from v. 97 to v. 123, the spirit runs through the hideous sins of many avaricious men with marked brevity.

In the Fourth Division, from v. 124 to v. 151, Dante describes a wonderful phenomenon that took place, viz.: the shaking of the mountain of Purgatory and a simultaneous outburst of all the spirits into a song of *Gloria in Excelsis Deo*.

Division I. The first division of the Canto opens with a short continuation of the closing scene of the last Canto, in which Dante tells us that, although he was obliged to yield to the will of Adrian that he should pass on his way, yet he did so unsatisfied, as there were many things he would have liked to have asked him, but could not.

> Contra miglior voler, voler mal pugna ;
>   Onde contra il piacer mio, per piacerli,
>   Trassi dell' acqua non sazia la spugna.

The will (of man, however good) strives ill against a will that is better.* Therefore, although it was not what best pleased me, to please him (Adrian), I withdrew from the water my sponge (*i. e.* my desire for information) not filled.

> Mossimi; e il duca mio si mosse per li
>   Luoghi spediti, per lungo la roccia,   5
>   Come si va per muro† stretto ai merli ;
> Chè la gente che fonde a goccia a goccia
>   Per gli occhi il mal che tutto il mondo occúpa,
>   Dall' altra parte in fuor troppo s' approccia.

I moved onwards, and my guide went along the spaces left vacant underneath the cliff; as happens when one walks along the top of the wall close up to the battlements, because those people (the spirits), who with tears pour drop by drop from their eyes the ill which occupies the world (*i. e.* avarice or cupidity), approached too near to the other side (*i.e.,* were lying so close to the edge of the precipice, that we were obliged to pass between them and the cliff).

Benvenuto quotes Euripides as affirming that avarice carries its own punishment with it, costing a vast amount

---

* Dante desired further information. Adrian wished to return to his penance, which was a holier and better desire, and Dante's will could ill strive against it.

† By *muro* is meant the wall of a city, on the top of which, in the middle ages, a footway ran, so that one walked close up to the battlements.

of toil and of tears ; and so unhappy is the covetous
man, that, whatever he fails to get hold of he esteems
a great calamity.

Dante now inveighs against avarice.

> Maledetta sie tu, antica lupa,*   10
> Che più che tutte l' altre bestie hai preda,
> Per la tua fâme senza fine cupa !

Accursed be thou, old she-wolf, that gettest more
prey than all the other beasts on account of thy insatiable greed of unfathomable depth.

He implores Heaven for aid against so ferocious a
wild beast.

> O ciel, nel cui girar par che si creda
> Le condizion' di quaggiù trasmutarsi,
> Quando verrà per cui questa disceda ?   15

O Heaven, in whose revolving courses some appear
to think the conditions of the earth are correspond-
ingly changed, when will He come, before whom she
(the wolf, avarice) will retreat ?

Benvenuto takes this mysterious personage to be

---

* *Antica lupa:* Scartazzini says that this passage is most
important, nay, even decisive for the true understanding of the
fundamental idea of the Divina Commedia. For if the *lupa* of
which Dante speaks here is the same that he spoke of in *Inf.* I,
and if the wolf that he curses here is Avarice, it follows of
necessity that the wolf in *Inf.* I can only be a symbol of avarice.
And if there the wolf is the symbol of a vice, it also follows of
necessity that the other two wild beasts, the *lonza* and the
leone, must each also symbolize a vice, and not some political
power. There can be no doubt that the wolf here cursed by
Dante is the identical one that opposed him at the commencement of his journey. In this passage the wolf is styled *antica ;*
in *Inf.* I, 111, it is the *prima invidia*, which at the beginning of
the world Satan called forth from Hell, and therefore it is as
ancient as the world. In *Inf.* I, 51, the wolf *fé già viver grame
molte genti ;* the poet curses the one here because *ha preda più*

the Veltro, the greyhound, mentioned before in *Inf.* I,
99-101.

Now Dante, having uttered his curse against avarice,
sings the praises of voluntary poverty and liberality.

> Noi andavam co' passi lenti e scarsi,
>> Ed io attento all' ombre ch' io sentia
>> Pietosamente piangere e lagnarsi :
> E per ventura udi' : *Dolce Maria,*
>> Dinanzi a noi chiamar così nel pianto,   20
>> Come fa donna che in partorir sia ;

With slow and scarce steps we picked our way, I
listening to the spirits whom I heard lamenting and
bewailing piteously; and by chance I heard "O
gentle Mary" cried out in front of us, as a woman
does in the hour of delivery.

It was the spirit of Hugh Capet* who had uttered
this exclamation, as we shall see further on.

---

che tutte l' altre bestie, and because it makes the penitents in
this cornice *viver grane* who are *molte genti.* In both passages
is its ravenous hunger mentioned. Finally, Dante concludes his
malediction of the wolf by exclaiming: *Quando verrà per cui
questa disceda?* And what other motive can he have had for
thus expressing his impatience, but that Virgil had prophesied
to him (*Inf.* I, 101), *che il veltro verrà, che la farà morir di
doglia?* Dante makes use of the same word, *verrà,* for both.
Therefore the two wolves are one and the same. The wolf in
this cornice is cursed by Dante for being the cause of the torments of the avaricious, and therefore the wolf is Avarice, and
consequently the wolf in *Inf.* I is also certainly a figure of
Avarice.

* The spirit that speaks is not that of King Hugh Capet, but
that of his father, Hugh Capet, Duke of France and Count of
Paris, better known as Hugh the Great. Pasquier, in his *Recherches de la France,* describes him as both valiant and
prudent, and says that although he was never king, yet was he
a maker and unmaker of kings. He died in 956. His name

E seguitar: *povera fosti tanto,*
    Quanto veder si può per quell' ospizio,
    Ove sponesti il tuo portato santo.

And following: How poor thou wast can well be seen by that humble cot (at Bethlehem) in which thou didst deposit thy sacred charge.   .

And for fear, says Benvenuto, that anyone might
• say: Ah! but it is not everyone who could endure · the inconveniences of poverty like the Virgin Mary, he brings forward another example of sober poverty in a virtuous heathen, Fabricius Caius Luscivius, whose whole life was a protest against greed of gain. When he was censor he had banished P. Cornelius Rufinus for his luxury and prodigality. He refused the gifts offered him by the Samnites, and the bribes of Pyrrhus, and died so poor that he had to be buried at the public expense, and the Romans were obliged to give a dowry to his daughters. Virgil, in *Æneid* VI, 844, calls him " powerful in poverty." Dante extols him in the *Convito.*

Seguentemente intesi: *O buon Fabbrizio,*   25
    Con povertà volesti anzi virtute,
    Che gran ricchezza posseder con vizio.

Thereafter I heard: O good Fabricius, thou didst prefer virtue with poverty to the possession of great wealth with vice.

Queste parole m' eran sì piaciute,
    Ch' io mi trassi oltre per aver contezza
    Di quello spirto, onde parean venute.   30

---

is said to have been more accurately Huon Chapet, some say, because when at school he was always pulling off other little boys' caps. Ducange, *Gloss.* under *Capetus*, repeats this story from an old chronicle, but ascribes the name, with more probability, to the hood or cowl which Hugh was in the habit of wearing.

These words were so pleasing to me that I walked a little further on, to get knowledge of that spirit from whom they seemed to come.

The allusions to the Virgin Mary and Fabricius seemed so appropriate, that Dante had reason to hope that he might enter into a profitable conversation with him, which might not be so abruptly broken off as the last one had been. He felt inclined to talk, and he seems to have been fortunate in meeting with a kindred spirit in Hugh Capet who at once proceeded to tell him a story of the noble liberality of St. Nicholas, Bishop of Myra in Lycia.*

> Esso parlava ancor della larghezza
>   Che fece Niccolao alle pulcelle,
>   Per condurre ad onor lor giovinezza.

He furthermore began to speak to me of the liberality that Nicholas used to the three damsels to conduct their young life to honour.

---

* Benvenuto tells us: Here the Poet brings forward an example of noble generosity in a few short clear words; how the holy Nicholas, having lost his parents, wished to spend his money on the poor. There was a nobleman with three grown-up daughters, who was reduced to such extreme poverty that he had determined to send them out to beg for the support of the family. One night St. Nicholas, passing the house, took a bag of gold from under his cloak and threw it in at the window, the eldest girl was thus dowered and, as all three were beautiful girls, was at once married; St. Nicholas repeated this a second and a third time, with short intervals between, and thus secured for all three daughters honourable marriages. Not long after the marriage of the youngest girl the father ascertained who was their benefactor, and kissed his hands and feet, but Nicholas made him promise to tell no man.

Division II.   Hugh Capet talks to Dante at length
about the avarice of the Kings of France, his descendants.

> —" O anima, che tanto ben favelle,
>   Dimmi chi fosti (dissi) e perchè sola   35
>   Tu queste degne lode rinnovelle ?
> Non fia senza mercè la tua parola,
>   S' io ritorno a compiér lo cammin corto
>   Di quella vita, che al termine vola."—

" O soul," said I, " who speakest such good words,
tell me who thou wast, and why thou art the only one
who seemest to care to renew these well deserved
praises (that is to bring back to one's recollection these
beautiful instances from sacred and profane history of
voluntary poverty and open-handed liberality) ; and
if thou dost tell me what I want, thy words shall not
be without a requital, if I return to finish the short
journey of that life which is speeding on to its end."

The requital being, that he would convey to any of
his surviving descendants a message that prayer might
be offered up for his early deliverance from Purgatory,
or, that Dante might *confortare la sua memoria,* (Inf.
XIII) speak a good word for his reputation.

Hugh Capet answers, and declines Dante's proffered
good offices :

> Ed egli :—" Io ti dirò, non per conforto   40
>   Ch' io attenda di là, ma perchè tanta
>   Grazia in te luce prima che sie morto.

And he : " I will tell thee, not for any ease that I can
expect from the world yonder (from my descendants),
but because so large a measure of divine grace shines
forth in thee before thou art dead.

Benvenuto says that it is either that he wishes to
say that he has no more care for the empty fame of

the world, or because his descendants are too much given up to avarice to think much about him.

Hugh continues :

> Io fui radice della mala pianta,*
> Che la terra cristiana tutta aduggia,
> Sì che buon frutto rado se ne schianta.   45

I was the root of that malignant tree (the Capets) which casts its evil shadow over the whole Christian world, so that good fruit is seldom gathered from it.

"And yet," says Benvenuto, "there were some illustrious kings of that line, such as St. Louis, and Charles of Anjou, his brother, and this family down to the present time (Benvenuto wrote about 1375) is most powerful *in our west*, where there are such men as the King of France, Charles V. the Wise, 1364-80 ; the King of Navarre (probably Charles the Bad) ; the King of Hungary, Louis the Great, 1370; the Queen of Apulia (probably daughter of the Emperor Charles IV)."

Hugh proves what he said by alluding to the reigning prince, Philip the Fair.

> Ma, se Doagio, Guanto, Lilla e Bruggia
> Potesser, tosto ne saria vendetta ;
> Ed io la cheggio a Lui che tutto giuggia.

But if Douai, Ghent, Lille and Bruges had the power, they would soon take vengeance (on Philip), and I invoke it from Him who judges all things.†

This passage shows the hatred which Dante felt for the Kings of France.

> Chiamato fui di là Ugo Ciapetta :
> > Di me son nati i Filippi e i Luigi,   50
> > Per cui novellamente è Francia retta.
> Figliuol fui d' un beccajo di Parigi.

I was called Hugh Capet there (on earth): from me the Philips and the Louises sprang, by whom in recent times France has been ruled.* I was the son of a butcher of Paris.

---

ever preferred the subtle negotiation, the slow and wily encroachment ; till his enemies were, if not in his power, at least at great disadvantage, he did not venture on the usurpation or invasion. In the slow systematic pursuit of his object, he was utterly without scruple, without remorse. He was not so much cruel as altogether obtuse to human suffering, if necessary to the prosecution of his schemes ; not so much rapacious, as finding money indispensable to his aggrandizement, seeking money by means of which he hardly seemed to discern the injustice or the folly. Never was man or monarch so intensely selfish as Philip the Fair : his own power was his ultimate scope ; he extended so enormously the royal prerogative, the influence of France, because he was King of France. His rapacity, which persecuted the Templars, his vindictiveness, which warred on Boniface after death as through life, was this selfishness in other forms." Milman's *Latin Christianity*, XI, ch. 8. He was defeated at the battle of Courtrai, 1302, known in history as the battle of the Spurs of Gold, from the great number found on the field after the battle. This is the vengeance imprecated on him by Dante, and, as Benvenuto says, had already taken place when Dante wrote these lines.

* For two centuries and a half, that is, from 1060 to 1316, there was either a Louis or a Philip on the throne of France. The succession was as follows :

> Philip I. L'Amoureux,   1059.
> Louis VI. the Fat,   1108.
> Louis VII. the Young,   1137.

Benvenuto tells us that France is a small province
in Gaul which has several subject provinces such as
Provence, Burgundy, Normandy, Piccardy, Aquitaine,
Vascony (*sic.*), &c.　He says Dante was a most curious
investigator of things worth remembering, and while
studying at Paris, he found out the real facts, and
treats all that is said to the contrary, as said for the
sake of covering Hugh Capet's low birth.　Villani
says the father was a great and rich burgher of Paris,
of a race of butchers or dealers in cattle.　Hugh
Capet is now considered to have descended from a
noble line of Counts of Paris and Dukes of France.
Possibly the legend arose out of the fact that his
father, or he himself, had been described as a butcher
on account of the severity of his punishments.　The
French commentators vigorously deny the truth of
this statement of Dante.*

Philip II. Augustus,	1180.
Louis VIII. the Lion,	1223.
Louis IX. the Saint,	1226.
Philip III. the Bold,	1270.
Philip IV. the Fair,	1285.
Louis X.,	1314.

* Pasquier (*Recherches de la* France Liv. VI. ch. 1), thinking it
is King Hugh Capet that speaks, protests: "Et au surplus combien
Dante Poëte Italien fut ignorant, quand au livre par luy intitulé
le Purgatoire, il dit que nostre Hugues Capet avoit esté fils d'un
Boucher . . . . Et depuis Agrippa Alleman en son livre
de la Vanité des sciences, chap. de la Noblesse, sur ceste
première ignorance declame impudemment contre la genealogie
de nostre Capet.　Si Dante estima Hugues le Grand, du quel
Capet estoit fils, avoir esté un boucher, il estoit mal habile
homme.　Que s'il usa de ce mot par metaphore, ainsi que je le
veux croire, ceux qui se sont attachez à l'escorce de ceste parole
sont encore de plus grands lourdauts."

I think we may, with confidence, take it for granted
that the consensus of the best modern historical critics
treat the story as a fable, and that Hugh the Great was
really descended from illustrious ancestors.

> Quando li regi antichi venner meno
> Tutti, fuor ch' un, renduto in panni bigi,

When the ancient kings (the Carlovingians) had all
passed away, save one who had taken the grey frock.

The *Ottimo* thinks this unnamed king was Rudolph,
who became a monk and afterwards Archbishop of
Rheims. Benvenuto gives no name, but says "only a
monk in poor coarse garments." Francesco da Buti
states the same. Daniello thinks it was "some Franciscan, perhaps St. Louis"! forgetting that St. Louis did
not see the light for some two centuries afterwards—
nor did the Order of St. Francis exist then. Some say
Charles of Lorraine. Biagioli decides that it must be
either Charles the Simple, who died a prisoner in the
Castle of Péronne in 922 ; or Louis d'Outre-Mer, who
was carried to England by Hugh the Great in 936.
The Man in Cloth of Grey, says Longfellow, remains
as great a mystery as the Man in the Iron Mask.

> Trovámi stretto nelle mani il freno   55
>   Del governo del regno, e tanta possa
>   Di nuovo acquisto, e sì d' amici pieno,
> Ch' alla corona vedova promossa
>   La testa di mio figlio fu, dal quale
> .   Cominciàr di costor le sacrate ossa.   60

I found fast in my hands the reins of government
of the kingdom, and so great power of new ac-
quisitions, and such an array of friends, that the
head of my son was promoted to the widowed (*i.e.*

vacant) crown : from whom the consecrated bones
(*i.e.* the anointed line of the Capets), took their
descent.

Hugh Capet, son of the speaker Hugh le Grand,
was crowned King at Rheims in 987. The above
terzina makes it perfectly clear that it is Hugh the
Great who speaks. Benvenuto tries to make out that
the son who was crowned was Robert.

Now Hugh goes on to tell Dante the evil deeds
wrought by his descendants through avarice.* Benvenuto says that up to that time the descendants of
Hugh had been somewhat avaricious, but not to such
an extent as to usurp unjustly what belonged to
another.

> . Mentre che la gran dote Provenzale
>   Al sangue mio non tolse la vergogna,
>   Poco valea, ma pur non facea male.

Until the great appanage of Provence deprived my
posterity of shame, their power was small, but still it
did no harm.

---

* Hugh begins by speaking of their first avaricious annexation.
He tells us, says Benvenuto, that Louis IX. (St. Louis) and
Charles of Anjou, his brother, who was afterwards King of
Sicily, married the two daughters of Raymond Berenger of
Toulouse, and under the pretext of claiming their dowries, they
usurped the province of Narbonne, of which, Provence fell to the
share of Charles of Anjou. Raymond Berenger had two other
daughters, married to our Henry III of England and his brother
Prince Richard.

Louis IX married Margaret the eldest daughter, and Charles
d'Anjou married Beatrice, a younger daughter. In the increased
wealth and power, which they brought to the Royal house of
France, Dante saw the source of all the miseries of Italy, and
the failure of the Empire, which was to him the ideal polity.

Observe in the two next terzine the thrice-repeated ironical *per ammenda* (for compensation); to atone for the preceding fault, they committed a succession of others always worse and worse.

> Lì cominciò con forza e con menzogna
>   La sua rapina ; e poscia, per ammenda,   65
>   Pontì e Normandia prese, e Guascogna.
> Carlo venne in Italia, e per ammenda,
>   Vittima fe' di Curradino ; e poi
>   Ripinse al ciel Tommaso, per ammenda.

Then it began by violence and fraud its plundering; and afterwards to make amends took Ponthieu, Normandy and Gascony. Charles came to Italy, and to make amends made a victim of Conradin ; and then again to make amends sent Thomas back to Heaven.*

---

* Three Charleses are mentioned in this Canto : 1. Charles d'Anjou, brother of St. Louis, who had Conradin beheaded, and possibly poisoned Thomas Aquinas. 2. Charles de Valois, brother of Philippe le Bel, who used the *lancia con la qual giostrò Giuda*. 3. Charles II of Naples and Apulia, son of Charles d'Anjou. He was taken prisoner in a naval action off Naples, in 1284, by Ruggieri di Lauria, Admiral of Pedro of Arragon. He was imprisoned four years, and was not restored to his throne till 1288, three years after his father Charles of Anjou had died. It was he who accepted a large bribe to give his daughter in marriage to Azzo d' Este.

Normandy had been taken from King John in 1202, Gascony, Guienne and Ponthieu had been formally ceded by Edward I to Philip the Fair, 1295, with a secret understanding, afterwards repudiated, that it was to be formal only. Guienne was recovered 1298. Conradin, son of the Emperor Conrad IV, when only 16, was beheaded in the square of Naples by order of Charles of Anjou in 1268. He was captured after his defeat at Tagliacozzo and imprisoned in the Castel dell' Uovo at Naples. A graphic

Benvenuto says that all Charles's best friends and counsellors repudiated the act.   Did not this Charles receive unpunished Guy de Montfort, who had slain a kinsman of the King of England, even "in the bosom of God?" (in sanctuary).   Did he not condemn to perpetual imprisonment Henry, brother of the King of Spain, his own kinsman, for some sum of money that he would not pay to him?   He adds that a just Judge inflicted heavy adversity on Charles before his death, for just when he seemed at the zenith of his success in arms, he saw the rebellion in Sicily and the captivity of his son, whom his victorious adversary Pedro of Aragon might well have slain, to revenge Conradin, had he chosen to so abuse his victory, 1284. And Charles died of grief, while his son was still in prison.   And now we pass on to another Charles, only too well known in Florence in the time of Dante.

---

account of his end may be read in Milman, *Lat. Christ.* XI, 3.

Dean Plumptre says that the story of St. Thomas Aquinas having been poisoned by order of Charles of Anjou, 1274, has fallen into such discredit, that it is not even mentioned in the current biographies of the great Dominican Doctor.   In Dante's time, however, it was currently believed throughout Italy, and is mentioned by Villani, and by all the early commentators. Thomas had lived some years at Naples, and had been much respected by the King, at all events outwardly.   On his departure to attend Gregory X at a Council at Lyons, the King asked him what he should report of him.   "I shall tell the truth," was the answer.   This alarmed Charles, and he commissioned a physician to follow and poison him at the Cistercian Monastery of Fossa Nuova, near Terracina, when he was 47 years old.

> Tempo vegg' io, non molto dopo ancoi,   70
>   Che tragge un altro Carlo fuor di Francia,
>   Per far conoscer meglio e sè e i suoi.

I see a time, not long after this, which brings another Charles forth from France, to make him and his race still better known.

This is Charles de Valois, surnamed " Sans Terre,'' brother of Philip the Fair, who was summoned into Italy to settle the disorders of Florence by Boniface VIII, as pacificator, and was guilty of many acts of treachery.   Dante's opposition to his intervention led to his own banishment and that of the other Bianchi.

> Senz' arme n' esce solo, e con la lancia
>   Con la qual giostrò Giuda ; e quella ponta
>   Sì che a Fiorenza fa scoppiar la pancia.   75

He comes forth without other arms than the lance that Judas tilted with ; and with that thrusts in such fashion as to rend the paunch of Florence.

Let us paraphrase this : He comes without any exhibition of open strength, but only with the weapon of Judas, that is, treachery bought by corruption ; for as Judas betrayed our Lord to the Chief Priests for money, so is Charles de Valois bribed by Boniface VIII to carry out his policy at Florence ; and with such malignant dexterity does he use these weapons of deceit, that he tears out from overgrown Florence its very vitals, in the persons of its chiefest citizens, and among them Dante himself.

> Quindi non terra, ma peccato ed onta
>   Guadagnerà, per sè tanto più grave,
>   Quanto più lieve simil danno conta.

And from that (treachery) he will gain for himself no territory, but reproach and shame, so much the

more grievous to himself, as the more light such
damage counts in his eyes.

An old writer says of him—" Carlo venne in Toscana per pace, e lasciovvi gran guerra; passò in Sicilia
per guerra, e riportonne ignominiosa pace."

We now turn to the third Charles, the son of Charles
of Anjou, II of Naples and Apulia.

> L' altro, che già uscì preso di navé,
>   Veggio vender sua figlia, e pateggiarne,   80
>   Come fanno i corsar' dell' altre schiave.

The other, who but lately went forth from his ship
a prisoner, I see selling his own daughter, haggling
for the price to be paid, just as corsairs do with
other female slaves.

We must remember that at that time the whole
coast of Italy was subject to the depredations of
Saracen corsairs, who used to seize maidens and sell
them for slaves in the East. Benvenuto tells us,
that in 1284, while Charles d'Anjou had gone into
Provence, to collect troops to revenge the massacre of
the French at the Sicilian Vespers, he had particularly
charged his son Charles, who is mentioned in these
lines (79-81) not on any account to be drawn into
any action by sea or by land during his absence.
Ruggeri d' Oria, a most distinguished naval com-
mander of Pedro, King of Aragon, knowing this,
came with a great fleet to Naples, and even entered
the port, shooting missiles into the city, and luring
Charles the younger to come out. Ruggieri well
knew that Charles d'Anjou was already off Pisa with
a great fleet on his way back from Provence.

Charles the younger fell into the trap, and embarked

with all his chief officers and engaged d'Oria. Like the King of Syria, in battle with Ahab, said to his chief captains, "Fight neither with great nor small, but only with the King of Israel," so did d'Oria order his captains that their chief duty was to capture young Charles, and only to attack that galley which bore the royal standard. The result satisfied his expectations. The youth was captured with nine long ships, and all his great officers of state, who were utterly useless in a naval action. He was taken to Messina. Two hundred of his nobles were slain with the sword to requite the death of Conradin, but young Charles was reserved with a few of his companions, and Benvenuto says he would certainly have been slain, had not Queen Constance (wife of King Pedro, and daughter of Manfred, who alludes to her, Canto III, 115), ordered his life to be spared. The following day his father, Charles of Anjou, touched at Gaeta, and hearing the disastrous news, broke out into a great explosion of wrath against his son and said : " I wish he had died, rather than disobey my distinct orders." After four years' imprisonment, during which Charles the Elder had died, the younger Charles made peace with Pedro, and was restored to his kingdom in 1288. It was then he gave his beautiful daughter Beatrice in marriage to Azzo, Marquis of Este, either for 30,000 or 100,000 florins, according to two different authorities, Azzo being much older than Beatrice, and of evil reputation.

Then Hugh continues :

> O avarizia, che puoi tu più farne,
>> Poi ch' hai il sangue mio a te sì tratto,
>> Che non si cura della propria carne ?

N N 2

O avarice, what canst thou do more with us, since thou hast so drawn my race to thyself, that it loves not its own flesh.

But now Hugh comes to speak of what he evidently thinks a crime which leaves all the above mentioned ones in the shade.

> Perchè men paia il mal futuro e il fatto,*   85
>   Veggio† in Alagna entrar lo fiordaliso,
>   E nel Vicario suo Cristo esser catto.

In order that evil, both past and future, may appear less, (I will tell thee that) I see the fleur-de-lys enter into Anagni (the home of Pope Boniface VIII in 1303), and Christ Himself taken captive in the person of his vicar.

> Veggiolo un' altra volta esser deriso ;
>   Veggio rinnovellar l' aceto e il fele,
>   E tra vivi ladroni esser anciso.   90

---

   * This line is very obscure, and the explanation of Jacopo della Lana seems much the most clear. He says that Dante wishes to feign that Hugh was prophesying to him what was going to happen, though as a matter of fact it had already taken place, and he says to Dante : "In order that the horror of what is going to happen may seem to you somewhat less, when it does take place, I will foretell it to you."

   † *Veggio.* Dante means, ' I see with the eyes of a Catholic.' He is alluding to the indignities to which Pope Boniface VIII was subjected at Alagna (now Anagni) by Nogaret and Sciarra Colonna by order of Philip the Fair in 1303, and from the mortification of which he died shortly afterwards at Rome. The event is related by Milman (*Lat. Christ.* Book XI, ch. 9). Although Dante entertained feelings of bitter hostility towards Boniface, he viewed with the utmost abhorrence his treatment by the emissaries of Philip. No personal enmity could make him forget that, as Pope, he was the vicar of Christ. See

I see Him mocked a second time: I see renewed the vinegar and gall; and Him again slain between living thieves (*i.e.* Sciarra and Colonna).

> Veggio il nuovo Pilato sì crudele,
>> Che ciò nol sazia, ma, senza decreto,
>> Porta nel tempio le cupide vele.

I see the new Pilate (*i.e.* King Philip the Fair, by whose orders these outrages were perpetrated), so relentless, that even this does not sate him, but without decree he sets his covetous sails towards the Temple.*

Hugh concludes by calling God's vengeance upon such infamy.

> O Signor mio, quando sarò io lieto
>> A veder la vendetta che, nascosa,   95
>> Fa dolce l' ira tua nel tuo segreto ?

Oh! my Lord, when shall I be made joyful by seeing the vengeance, which, concealed in Thy secret, makes Thine anger sweet ?

Benvenuto points out that this means that when a

Inf. XIX, 100.

> " E se non fosse che ancor lo mi vieta
>> La riverenza delle somme chiavi
>> Che tu tenesti nella vita lieta,
>> Io userei parole ancor più gravi."

* In 1314 Philip suppressed the Order of the Templars on a number of trumped-up charges. He seized on their Preceptories, their property and their persons, and after putting them to the most inhuman tortures obtained from Pope Clement V a reluctant assent to these illegal proceedings. Dante especially censures in these lines the absence of a fair trial, and the real motive of Philip's zeal against the Templars, which was his covetousness of their possessions.

man who has suffered an injury knows that speedy vengeance will fall on the offender, he secretly rejoices in his heart—and he says the same thing will happen here with the anger of God, which in brief space will fall on Philip and his descendants.

———

Division III. Several flagrant instances are now given of avarice as exhibited in persons, both of sacred and profane history, and Hugh the Great answers the second of the questions which Dante had put to him* as to why he alone of all the spirits in the Cornice seemed to care to renew these well deserved praises. That, we may remember, was the recalling to notice certain instances of voluntary poverty and great liberality.

> Ciò ch' io dicea di quella unica sposa
>   Dello Spirito Santo, e che ti fece
>   Verso me volger per alcuna chiosa,
> Tanto è disposto a tutte nostre prece,   100
>   Quanto il dì dura ; ma' quand' e' s' annotta,
>   Contrario suon prendemo in quella vece.

What I was saying of that one only Spouse of the Holy Ghost (the Blessed Virgin), and which occasioned thee to turn to me for some commentary, that invocation has been ordained for all our orisons only for so long as the day lasts, but when night comes, then we sing a contrary strain.

In the daylight they sing of virtuous persons con-

———

* See v. 35   " Perchè sola
                Tu queste degne lode rinnovelle ? "

spicuous for their voluntary poverty, and liberality, but at night only of those who were friends of avarice and cupidity. Liberality makes men shine, Avarice makes them obscure.

Hugh next runs rapidly over several examples of the hateful sins of avaricious and covetous persons. First he mentions Pygmalion, the brother of Dido who, through blind greed of gold, murdered her husband, Sichæus, King of Tyre, and drove his sister an exile to Carthage.

> Noi ripetiam Pigmalione allotta,*
>   Cui traditore e ladro e patricida
>   Fece la voglia sua, dell' oro ghiotta ;   105

We commemorate Pygmalion then, whom his insatiable desire for gold made a traitor, a thief, and a parricide.

He was a *traitor*, because when bound to Sichæus by an oath of faith, he killed him unawares while sacrificing at the altar of Hercules, in whose temple he was priest. A *thief*, because he took his brother-in-law's gold ; and a *parricide*, because Sichæus was not only his brother-in-law, but also his kinsman. Parricide, Benvenuto tells us, is commonly used as a term for the murderer of any kinsman.

The next example of avarice is that of Midas, King of Lydia, who tied the famous Gordian knot, and who was supposed to have obtained from Bacchus the faculty that everything he touched should become gold.

> E la miseria dell' avaro Mida,
>   Che seguì alla sua domanda ingorda,
>   Per la qual sempre convien che si rida.

---

* *Allotta* for *Allora*.   At that time, that is *quando s' annotta*, when it is night.

And the distress of the miser, Midas, that followed his covetous request, at which one always needs must laugh.*

Benvenuto says he feels sure Dante must have been laughing when he wrote this. He next turns to Sacred History.

> Del folle Acám ciascun poi si ricorda,
> Come furò le spoglie, sì che l' ira   110
> Di Josuè qui par ch' ancor lo morda.

And then again each of us remembers the story of the foolish Achan, how he stole the plunder, so that the wrath of Joshua seems still to chastise him.†

> Indi accusiam col marito Safira :
> Lodiamo i calci ch' ebbe Elïodoro ;‡
> Ed in infamia tutto il monte gira
> Polinestòr § ch' ancise Polidoro.   115

---

* " Pan tuned the pipe, and with his rural song
  Pleased the low taste of all the vulgar throng ;
  Such songs a vulgar judgment mostly please :
  Midas was there, and Midas judged with these."
              —Ovid, *Met.* XI.

† Achan said : " When I saw among the spoils a goodly Babylonish garment, and two hundred shekels of silver, and a wedge of gold of fifty shekels weight, then I coveted them, and took them ; and behold, they are hid in the earth in the midst of my tent, and the silver under it."—*Joshua* VII, 21.

‡ This refers to the miraculous horse that appeared in the Temple of Jerusalem, when Heliodorus, the treasurer of King Seleucus, went there to remove the treasure. We read of it in II *Maccabees*, III, 25 : " For there appeared unto them an horse with a terrible rider upon him, and adorned with a very fair covering, and he ran fiercely, and smote at Heliodorus with his forefeet, and it seemed that he that sat upon the horse had complete harness of gold." This subject is one of the chief ornaments of Raphael's Stanze in the Vatican.

§ Polydorus, the youngest son of Priam, King of Troy, being

Ultimamente ci si grida : *Crasso*,*
Dicci, che il sai, di che sapore è l' oro ?

Then we accuse Sapphira with her husband : we
laud the kicks that Heliodorus received ; and (the
name of) Polymnestor, who murdered Polydorus, goes
round the mount in infamy. And last we hear shouted
out : "Crassus, tell us, for thou knowest, of what
taste is gold ?"

Hugh finishes by explaining that the reason Dante
only heard him singing the praises of the non-
covetous and virtuous persons was, that they vary the

---

too young to take part in the defence of Troy, was placed under
the care of his father's friend, Polymnestor, King of Thrace.
The latter murdered him for the sake of the treasure which he
had brought with him.

See Virgil, *Æneid* III, 49.   Conington's Translation.

" This Polydore awhile by stealth
With store of delegated wealth
Unhappy Priam in despair
Sent to the Thracian monarch's care
When first Troy felt her prowess fail,
Encompassed by the leaguering pale.
There when our star its light withdraws,
False to divine and human laws,
The traitor joins the conqueror's cause,
Lays impious hands on Polydore,
And grasps by force the golden store,
Fell lust of gold ! abhorred, accurst !
What will not men to slake such thirst ? "

* Crassus, who, with Cæsar and Pompey, was one of the
three Triumvirs of Rome, was defeated and killed by the
Parthians, B.C. 59.   On account of the reputation of Crassus for
avarice and cupidity, their king is said to have cast his head
into a vessel full of molten gold, with the words :

"Aurum sitisti, aurum bibe."
" Thou didst thirst for gold, drink gold."

modulation of their strains, and he happened to be the
only one in that place at that time who was singing
aloud.

> Talor parla l' un alto, e l' altro basso,
>   Secondo l' affezion ch' ad ir* ci sprona,
>   Ora a maggiore, ed ora a minor passo ;   120
> Però al ben che il dì ci si ragiona,
>   Dianzi non er' io sol ; ma qui da presso
>   Non alzava la voce altra persona."—

Sometimes we speak, one loud, the other low,
according to the impulse that urges our steps, at one
time at a greater, at another at a lesser pace ; all the
same, as regards the good (examples) which are cited
by us during the day, I was not alone (as thou didst
imagine) in uttering them, but it so happened that no
other person was uplifting his voice just near here."

———

Division IV. In the Division on which we now
enter, Dante describes the occurrence of a wonderful
phenomenon, viz. the shaking of the entire mountain,
and an outburst, from the spirits, in all quarters, of
Gloria in Excelsis.

> Noi eravam partiti già da esso,
>   E brigavam di soverchiar la strada   125
>   Tanto, quanto al poter n' era permesso ;
> Quand' io senti', come cosa che cada,
>   Tremar lo monte : onde mi prese un gelo,
>   Qual prender suol colui che a morte vada.

---

* Most editions read *che a dir*, but Fanfani (*Studi ed Osserv.*
p. 11) observes that whoever adopts so strained a metaphor
must have thought Dante was asleep ! In the Codices the
readings are *che adir, cheadir,* or *chadir*, which ought, from the
sense, to be divided as *che ad ir*, or *ch' ad ir*.

We had already departed from him* and were
endeavouring to overcome the way as much as was
permitted to our power, when I felt the mountain
trembling like a thing that falls,† at which a chill
seized me, as that which seizes a man who is about
to die.

> Certo non si scotea sì forte Delo,   130
>   Pria che Latona in lei facesse il nido,
>   A partorir li due occhi del cielo.

Certainly Delos did not quake so violently before
that Latona made her nest there to give birth to the
twin-eyes of Heaven (Apollo and Diana, the Sun and
the Moon).

The Island of Delos, in the Archipelago or Ægean
Sea, was thrown up by an earthquake by order of
Jupiter in order to receive Latona, one of his wives,
when she gave birth to Apollo and Diana.   Other
accounts say it was left floating about after the separation of land and sea, and Jupiter made it stand
still.   Herodotus and Thucydides both mention its
constant earthquakes.   Benvenuto says that the comparison is very apt, for, as Delos sent forth two shining
lights, the sun and moon to Heaven, so now was the
Mountain of Purgatory sending forth Dante and
Statius, two eminent poets.   Benvenuto does not
mention Virgil, who did not go to Heaven.

Dante now describes a loud cry that followed the

---

* Benvenuto says that, if Hugh Capet was a miser or covetous
as regards money in his life, he certainly cannot be accused of
want of liberality in his words, judging from this long speech.

† We shall hear in the next Canto (XXI, 70) that this earthquake was occasioned by Statius having completed his term in
Purgatory.

earthquake.   It was the jubilant shout of the spirits
in Purgatory at the liberation of Statius.

> Poi cominciò da tutte parti un grido
>> Tal che il maestro invêr di me si feo,
>> Dicendo :—"non dubbiar, mentr' io ti guido."— 135

Then there arose on every side a cry so great, that
my Master drew nearer to me and said : " Doubt
nothing while I am guiding thee."

> *Gloria in excelsis*, tutti, *Deo*
>> Dicean, per quel ch' io da' vicin compresi,
>> Onde intender lo grido si poteo.

Gloria in Excelsis Deo was the cry of them all, by
what I could make out from those near, wherefore
their cry was more easily distinguishable.

Benvenuto thinks Dante deserves much commenda-
tion on account of this beautiful idea.   For, as the
Angel Host sang with joy the hymn *Gloria in Excelsis
Deo* on the evening of the Nativity of the Redeemer of
the World, so now the spirits in Purgatory do so when
a soul is set free to go to heaven.

> Noi stavamo immobili e sospesi,
>> Come i pastor' che prima udîr quel canto,   140
>> Fin che il tremar cessò, ed ei compièsi.

We remained unmoved, and in rapt attention, as
were the shepherds who first heard that song, until
the trembling ceased, and it (the hymn) had come to a
conclusion.

Virgil calls poets shepherds in his *Bucolics*, whence
Benvenuto discovers an appropriateness in the shepherds' hymn.

> Poi ripigliammo nostro cammin santo :
>> Guardando l' ombre che giacean per terra,
>> Tornate già in su l' usato pianto.

We then resumed again our holy path, watching the

shades that lay on the ground, already returned to their customary wailing.

Some read *tornate giù* alluding to the posture of the spirits. And then Dante adds that this wonderful phenomenon had excited his intense curiosity to know the cause of it.

> Nulla ignoranza mai con tanta guerra   145
>   Mi fe' desideroso di sapere,
>   Se la memoria mia in ciò non erra,
> Quanta parémi allor pensando avere :

If my memory about this is not at fault, no matter, of which I was ignorant, ever gave me so great a desire of knowing it (and the desire was striven against with all my might), as I seemed to have about this matter then when I thought it over.

>   Nè per la fretta dimandarn' er' oso,
>   Nè per me lì potea cosa vedere.   150
> Così m' andava timido e pensoso.

Nor did I dare to ask, on account of our haste, nor of myself could I perceive anything there, so I walked on timorous and thoughtful.

Benvenuto adds, by way of a corollary, " And there really was not time for talking any more in this XXth Canto, which contains in itself so many noble histories, fictions and opinions."

END OF CANTO XX.

ᵥ\

CANTO XXI.

The Fifth Cornice (*continued*).
Appearance of Statius.

BENVENUTO remarks that, whereas in the preceding
Canto Dante taught his readers in many ways (*multi-
pliciter*) how to avoid the sin of avarice, so in this one
he treats of prodigality, which is chastised with the same
punishment and in the same cornice as avarice.

Benvenuto divides the Canto into four parts.

In the First Division, from v. 1 to v. 33, a spirit
is introduced, who has just completed his purgation of
the vice of prodigality, to whom Virgil explains the
respective conditions of himself and Dante.

In the Second Division, from v. 34 to v. 75, the
spirit, in compliance with Virgil's request, tells the
poets the reason of the quaking of the mountain, and
of the universal chant mentioned in the preceding
Canto.

In the Third Division, from v. 76 to v. 102, the
spirit declares himself to be the poet Statius.

In the Fourth Division, from v. 103 to v. 136,
Dante reveals to Statius who Virgil was.

Division I.   Dante opens the Canto by describing
the intense desire that he had for more knowledge.
His first words are spoken in confirmation and
reiteration of the last few lines of the preceding Canto,
in which he ill-concealed his disappointment at not

have placed Statius, who was not a Christian, in
Purgatory, and do not see the reason for it ; but I
declare, to begin with, that Dante might imagine, from
many signs that Statius was a Christian. For if Virgil,
who lived before Christ, had some foreknowledge of
Him, from the songs of the sibyl, as Augustine
testifies, how much more might not Statius have had,
who saw the Christians ever increasing, although he
had seen them nearly exterminated by cruel and
unheard of persecutions, even before the time that
Titus dealt, as he did with the Jews ; and besides this,
he had seen so many miracles performed by the
martyrs whom Domitian, the brother of Titus, so
cruelly persecuted, when the Christian name was
continually waxing. . . . Statius was most high-
minded and moral in his writings ; but as to whether
or no he was a Christian I do not attach much importance, for Dante has probably with much ingenuity
pretended that he was, because many subjects have to
be treated by him, as we see in the XXVth Canto
and in other passages, which could only be treated by
a Christian. But our Poet rather introduces him here,
because it is known that he lived in the greatest
poverty and want ; which one would not think would
happen to a man of such distinction in the city
(Naples) in which he taught rhetoric, unless he had
fallen into the fault of great extravagance."

> Ed ecco, sì come ne scrive Luca,*
> Che Cristo apparve a' duo, ch' erano in via,
> Già surto fuor de la sepulcral buca,

---

* See *St. Luke* XXIV, 13 : "And, behold, two of them went
that same day to a village called Emmaus, which was from
Jerusalem about three-score furlongs. And they talked together

Ci apparve un' ombra, e dietro a noi venia   10
  Dappiè guardando la turba che giace ;
  Nè ci addemmo* di lei, sì parlò pria,
Dicendo :—" Frati miei, Dio vi dea pace."—
  Noi ci volgemmo subito, e Virgilio
  Rende' gli il cenno ch' a ciò si conface.   15

And lo ! in the same way that St. Luke tells us
(*lit.* writes to us) that Christ, lately risen from the
sepulchral cave, appeared unto the two that were in
the way, so did a shade appear unto us ; and came
behind us, looking down on the recumbent throng ;
nor were we aware of him, so (the shade) was the
first to speak, saying : " My brothers, may God give
you peace." We turned round suddenly, and Virgil
rendered him the countersign that corresponds.

Benvenuto interprets this last line as only meaning
that Virgil courteously returned the greeting of Statius,
but Longfellow says that among the monks of the
Middle Ages there were certain salutations, which had
their customary replies or countersigns. Thus one
would say : " Peace be with thee," and the answer
would be : " And with thy spirit ! " Or, " Praised
be the Lord ! " and the answer, " World without
end ! "

Virgil then goes on to reply to the words, "May
God give you peace ! " for he perceived that Statius
was under an erroneous impression that both he and

---

of all these things which had happened. And it came to pass,
that while they communed together and reasoned, Jesus himself
drew near, and went with them."

* *Nè ci addemmo.* Blanc (*Vocabulario Dantesco*) refers to
this word, which Dante on y uses in this one place. It comes
from *addarsi*, " di origine incerta, accorgersi, avvedersi."

Dante were bound for Paradise after completing their purgation, and so in his answer he shows Statius that he (Virgil) is not destined to enjoy that peace which he had augured them.

> Poi cominciò :—" Nel beato concilio
> Ti ponga in pace la verace corte,
> Che me rilega nell' eterno esilio."—

He then began : " May the tribunal of truth, which relegates me into eternal exile, establish thee in peace within the blessed council."

" See," says Benvenuto, "how Virgil enlists the good-will of Statius by wishing for him what he (Virgil) can never hope to obtain himself."

Statius is greatly astonished at this intelligence.

> — " Come ! (diss' egli, e parte* andavam forte),
> Se voi siete ombre che Dio su non degni,   20
> Chi v' ha per la sua scala tanto scôrte ?"—†

" How!" (said he, and meanwhile we stepped quickly onwards), " if ye are shades whom God does not deign to admit above, who has escorted you so far up His staircase ? "

Virgil replies.

---

* *Parte andavam forte,* is the reading of all the best commentators. Some read "e perchè andate forte?" But Benvenuto expressly points out that *parte,* as used here, is not a noun, but an adverb and has the sense meanwhile (*interim*). " Interim ibamus velociter, nec tardabamus illis loquentibus, ita quod parte non denotat portionem, nec est nomen, imo adverbium, et tantum valet quantum in isto medio, et est vulgare florentinum (is used in the popular speech at Florence)."

† *Scorte* is the past participle of the verb *scorgere,* to be an escort to anyone, and it is in the feminine plural to agree with *ombre,* understood.

E il dottor mio :—" Se tu riguardi i segni
Che questi porta e che l' angel profila,
Ben vedrai che coi buon convien ch' ei regni.*

And my teacher: "If thou wilt look at the signs
that this one (Dante) bears, and which the angel
traces (on the brow of every shade that enters Purgatory), thou mayest well perceive that he must (in due
course) reign among the good.

Virgil then goes on to answer a doubt unspoken, but
none the less felt, in the mind of Statius ; such as this :
" I (Statius) understand from what thou tellest me
how it happens that Dante is here, but what hast
thou to do here, who art not alive ? "

So Virgil says :

Ma perchè lei che dì e notte fila,   25
Non gli avea tratta ancora la conocchia,
Che Cloto imponet a ciascuno e compila,
L' anima sua, ch' è tua e mia sirocchia,
Venendo su, non potea venir sola ;
Però che al nostro modo non adocchia.   30

But because she who spins day and night (Lachesis)
had not yet for him (Dante) wound off the full yarn
which Clotho puts on (the distaff) for each, and packs

---

* Scartazzini observes that as Dante has been admitted by
the angel warder to the seven cornices, he will, as a natural
consequence, be admitted to pass on into the Kingdom of the
Blessed in Paradise.

† *Compila.* Lombardi tells us that two operations take place
in putting the wool on the distaff : the first is to lay on a great
mass of it twisting the distaff round till it gets attached, this
operation Dante calls *imporre* ; the second is to run the palm of
the hand over the wool to unite and compress it, this he calls
compilare, which Mr. Butler very aptly translates " packs
together."

together, his soul, which is sister to thine and mine, could not come alone in its upward ascent, for the reason that it does not behold in our manner.

The meaning of this is that, as Dante had not exhausted the full span of life and was yet alive, his soul joined to the body could not see after the fashion of spirits.

> Ond' io fui tratto fuor dell' ampia gola*
> D' inferno, par mostrargli, e mostrerolli
> Oltre, quanto il potrà menar mia scuola.†

On this account was I drawn forth from the wide throat of Hell to guide him, and I will direct him further still, so far as my teaching (*lit.* school) has power to conduct him.

The meaning of this is, that Virgil will guide Dante as far as mere human science can be efficacious ; after that he must expect Beatrice, type of Divine science, to lead him on.

Division II. In this division we have an explanation by Statius of the causes of the earthquake and

---

* *ampia gola.* Scartazzini says that by the throat of hell is meant Limbo, because it was situated at the beginning of Hell, and it was wide, because Hell, according to Dante, was funnel-shaped, and the circles diminished in size as one went lower down. Limbo being the uppermost, was the widest.

† *mia scuola.* Compare *Purg.* XVIII, 46 :

> —" Quanto ragion qui vede
> Dir ti poss' io ; da indi in là t' aspetta
> Pure a Beatrice ; ch' è opra di fede.

the *Gloria in Excelsis* of which we read in the last
Canto.   Virgil asks him:

> Ma dinne, se tu sai, perchè tai crolli
> > Diè dianzi il monte, e perchè tutti ad una   35
> > Parver gridare infino ai suoi piè molli ?"—

But tell us, if thou knowest, why the mountain gave
such shakes just now, and wherefore, down to its
watery base, all seemed with one voice to send forth
a shout."

Benvenuto says that *piè molli* are the roots of the
mountain where the rushes grow in the soft mud.*

Dante exclaims that the mere fact of Virgil asking
this question quieted his mind, as he could now form
a hope of knowing what he wanted.

> Sì mi diè dimandando per la cruna†
> > Del mio disio, che pur con la speranza
> > Si fece la mia sete men digiuna.

In asking this question, he (Virgil) so hit the very
eye of my desire, that with the hope alone my thirst
became less violent.

Statius replies that the earthquake cannot be as-

---

* See *Canto* I, 100, where Cato informs the poets that no other
plant than the humble reed could stand the shocks of the surf:

> Questa isoletta intorno ad imo ad imo,
> > Laggiù colà dove la batte l' onda,
> > Porta de' giunchi sovra il molle limo.
> Null' altra pianta che facesse fronda,
> > O indurasse, vi puote aver vita,
> > Però che alle percosse non seconda.

† *Cruna* is properly the eye of a needle.   Blanc (*Vocabolario
Dantesco*), interprets this passage : "toccò propriamente ciò
ch' io desiderava."   Others read : "cuna del mio disio"; *cuna*
being a cradle, and Benvenuto, who adopts this reading, speaks
of it as the desire of a child in the cradle for its food.   *Cruna*
seems much the more intelligible reading.

cribed to any natural causes, but only to the Will of
God.

> Quei cominciò :—" Cosa non è che sanza   .   40
>   Ordine senta la religĭone*
>   Della montagna, o che sia fuor d' usanza.

He began : " There is nothing which the usage
of the mountain observes without its due order, nor
which is unwonted.

This is one of the many passages in the *Divina
Comedia* that has caused much dispute among the
commentators.   Benvenuto says that *religio* is the
same thing towards God as *reverentia* towards parents
or elder persons.   He interprets : " Nothing here in
Purgatory happens by chance, but yet what does
happen does not occur from natural causes, as is the
course in the world."

Others translate: " This earthquake is a thing
which does not, without divine ordinance, observe
the rule of the mountain, nor is it unusual."

Statius adds :

> Libero è qui da ogni alterazione ;
>   Di quel che il ciel da sè in sè ricevet
>   Esserci puote, e non d' altro, cagione   45

---

* Compare *Par.* XI, 93, where the word *religione* is used to
signify the monastic order (of St. Francis) :

>   " e da lui ebbe
> Primo sigillo a sua religione."

† Before reading the translation it will be well to consult
Scartazzini's explanation of this difficult passage.   He says :
" Let us interpret it by the context.   Virgil has asked Statius
the reason of the earthquake and of the universal song that had
occurred shortly before.   Statius commences his answer by
telling the two wayfarers that what they heard was neither
extraordinary nor contrary to the regulations of the mountain.

Perchè non pioggia, non grando, non neve,
    Non rugiada, non brina più su cade,
    Che la scaletta dei tre gradi breve.

This place is free from every permutation : in what
Heaven receives into itself from itself may be found

---

v. 40-42. He goes on to say that the mountain of Purgatory
from its entrance-gate up to its summit is free from all those
alterations to which the earth inhabited by man is subject, and
that therefore the cause of the marvels that occur upon it (the
mountain), cannot be from other than what Heaven receives
into itself from itself, v. 43-45. This terzina already contains
in nuce the answer to Virgil's question. But Statius develops
two conceptions that are expressed in it more fully. First he
explains to him why the mountain is free from every permutation, 46-57 ; next the cause of the wonderful phenomena that
take place upon it, 58-60. After having explained when such a
cause generally occurs, 61-66 ; and why it had just occurred
then, 67-69 ; he draws the conclusion that for that very reason
the two wayfarers heard the earthquake and the chant. Verses
43-45 are therefore, so to speak, *the theme* of all that Statius
goes on to explain in the lines that follow. And as verses 46-57
unfold the idea of verse 42, so do verses 58-69 unfold the idea of
verses 43-44. Now, if the mountain quakes when a soul rises to
ascend to Heaven, the cause of this quaking is that Heaven
receives that soul into itself (*il cielo riceve* essa anima *in sè*).
But the soul originally issued from the hand of that God whose
throne is in Heaven, and therefore when it ascends to Heaven
it returns to God : ("siccome a quello porto, ond' ella si partio
quando venne a entrare nell' mare di questa vita."—*Conv.* IV, 28).
When, therefore, a soul ascends to Heaven, that Heaven does
not receive a being strange to itself, but one that takes its origin
in Heaven ; *riceve dunque in sè quel che è da sè.* Statius means
then that nothing of what happens up there can be caused by
anything which Heaven may receive from elsewhere (as is the
case lower down, where the sky receives the vapours that rise from
earth and cause its permutations), but only from what it receives
into itself from itself, as in fact is the case with that soul which
returns to the Heaven from which it originally issued."

the reason why neither rain, nor hail, nor snow, nor dew, nor hoar-frost fall higher up than the short staircase of the three steps (*i.e.* at the entrance-gate of Purgatory).

According to Lubin it must be understood that the atmosphere is supposed barely to reach the three steps at the Gate of Purgatory, and above the uppermost one there are no rains, winds, earthquakes, &c. Therefore in that elevated region, as Statius says, there can only be those influences that Heaven undergoes (*il Cielo in sè riceve*), caused and produced by the heavens (*prodotto da sè, cioè dai cieli*).

We afterwards see Dante in the Terrestrial Paradise (*Purg.* XXVIII, 85-120), wondering, after this explanation from Statius, that there should be a light wind in the thick forest. Dante remarks to Matelda that the phenomenon appears to be at variance with the principles that Statius had laid down. Matelda confirms the doctrine of Statius, and makes it clear to Dante that the uniform current, which he then feels, comes (according to the Ptolemaic system) from the revolution of the air, caused by that of the Primum Mobile, which communicates its motion to all the other spheres.

I am surprised to see that all the translators pass over the difficulty of this passage. Pollock, Longfellow, Plumptre, Lamennais, simply translate "from itself to itself," whereas the commentators write pages about it.

> Nuvole spesse non paion, nè rade,
> Nè corruscar, nè figlia di Taumante,*   50
> Che di là cangia sovente contrade.

---

* *figlia di Taumante.* According to heathen mythology, Iris was the daughter of the Centaur Thaumas, and of Electra. Her sisters were the Harpies. She was the goddess of the rain-

Neither dense nor rarified clouds appear, nor flashes of lightning, nor the daughter of Thaumas (the rainbow), who yonder (on earth) often changes place.

Statius now touches upon the natural causes of winds and earthquakes, for wind (says Benvenuto) is a dry and impalpable vapour raised by the sun ; and an earthquake takes place when the wind enters into the bowels of the earth, and being imprisoned (*incarceratus*) cannot come forth: therefore it causes a violent disturbance in the earth and makes it tremble.

> Secco vapor non surge più avante
>> Che al sommo dei tre gradi ch' io parlai,
>> Ov' ha il vicario di Pietro le piante.

No dry vapour ascends any higher than the summit of the three steps I mentioned, on which the (Angel) vicar of St. Peter, sets his feet.*

> Trema forse più giù poco od assai ;
>> Ma, per vento che in terra si nasconda,   55
>> Non so come, quassù non tremò mai :

It may perchance tremble more or less lower down (*i.e.* below the top step at the Gate of Purgatory) ; but, by reason of wind that is hidden in the earth, how I know not, it never quaked up here.

Statius finally assigns the real spiritual and moral cause of the recent earthquake.

> Tremaci quando alcuna anima monda
>> Sentesi, sì che surga, o che si mova
>> Per salır su ; e tal grido seconda.   60

---

bow, the joiner or conciliator, the messenger of heaven, restoring peace in nature.

* Aristotle (*Metaph.* II) says that from humid vapours are derived rain, snow, hail, dew, and hoarfrost; from dry vapour, if it be light, is produced wind ; but if it be strong then the earthquake.

It trembles in this place (*ci*, *i.e.* above the three steps) whenever any soul feels itself so purified that it rises, or that moves to ascend ; and this cry accompanies it.

As soon as every one of the spirits within the gate of Purgatory proper has completed its purgation, and if its penance was on the ground rises up from it, or, if not lying down, sets itself in motion to ascend up to Heaven, immediately the mountain quakes down to its lowest base, and all the spirits upon it break out simultaneously into a song of *Gloria in Excelsis.*

But in case Virgil should ask : " In what manner, or by what token canst thou become aware of the fact that a spirit has completed its term of purgation ?" Statius anticipates the question by saying :

> Della mondizia il sol voler fa prova,
> Che, tutta libera a mutar convento,
> L' alma sorprende, e di voler le giova.

The sole volition (Free Will) gives proof of its purification, which, while wholly free to change its abode (*lit.* convent), suddenly lays hold on the soul ; and the soul rejoices at having such a will.

Some read *ed il voler le giova*, which would be translated : " and that will turns to its advantage."

Benvenuto remarks that Statius keeps on anticipating possible questions or objections of Virgil ; and now he seems to say : But thou wilt ask if the soul does not always desire to escape from punishment ? and Statius answers that, however desirous the soul is to ascend forthwith to Heaven, yet God instils into it the will to continue in penance, so as to satisfy Divine justice.

Prima vuol ben ; ma non lascia il talento*
    Che divina giustizia contra voglia,   65
    Come fu al peccar, pone al tormento.

At first (before it is purified) it has indeed the wish (to ascend to Heaven), but that inclination (*talento*) does not allow it, which (inclination to be purified) Divine Justice imposes as a chastisement in opposition to the wish (to ascend) just as, (in life, there was in it the desire to ascend) contrary to the inclination to sin.†

And now Statius cites his own case as an example in

---

* *Talento.* The modern meaning of "talent" is comparatively recent. By Dante it is nearly always used to express an impulse or desire. Compare *Inf.* V, 38 :

    "I peccator carnali,
    Che la ragion sommettono al talento."

And *Inf.* X, 55 :

    "D' intorno mi guardò, come talento
      Avesse di veder s' altri era meco."

† The following passage from St. Thomas Aquinas (*Summ. Theol.* p. III, *Suppl. Append.* qu. II, art. 2) elucidates better than any commentary what is Dante's idea of there being an absolute and conditional will : "Aliquid dicitur voluntarium dupliciter. Uno modo voluntate absoluta ; et sic nulla pœna est voluntaria, quia ex hoc est ratio pœnæ quod voluntati contrariatur. Alio modo dicitur aliquid voluntarium voluntate conditionata ; sicut ustio est voluntaria propter sanitatem consequendam. Et sic aliqua pœna potest esse voluntaria dupliciter. Uno modo quia per pœnam aliquod bonum acquirimus ; et sic ipsa voluntas assumit pœnam aliquam, ut patet in satisfactione : vel etiam quia ille libenter eam accipit, et non vellet eam non esse, sicut accidit in martyrio. Alio modo quia quamvis per pœnam nullum bonum nobis accrescat, tamen sine pœna ad bonum pervenire non possumus, sicut patet de morte naturali ; et tunc voluntas non assumit pœnam, et vellet ab ea

confirmation of what he has said, and tells Virgil that
the earthquake and the chant were on account of him.

> Ed io che son giaciuto a questa doglia
>> Cinquecento anni e più,* pur mo'† sentii
>> Libera volontà di miglior soglia.‡
> Però sentisti il tremoto, e li pii   70
>> Spiriti per lo monte render lode
>> A quel Signor, che tosto su gl' invii."—

And I, who for five hundred years and more have

---

liberari : sed eam supportat, et quantum ad hoc voluntaria
dicitur."

Jacopo della Lana says of this passage : " The will ever
desires the ultimate and perfect end, but the justice of God wills
to be fully and entirely satisfied, that, as the sinner had the will
to sin and sinned, so he may have the impulse to stay, and may
stay for his subjugation and purgation ; so that *lo talento* is the
will *secundum quid.*"

* Statius had been undergoing penance in the cornice of the
avaricious, but for prodigality, not for avarice, as we shall read
in the next Canto, where we shall also find (XXII, 92) that
before passing his 500 years in the cornice of avarice, he had
had to pass 400 in the cornice of sloth, 900 years in all.

Statius died 96 A.D. Dante supposes his vision to take place
in 1300. Counting 500 years in the cornice of avarice, 400 years
in the cornice of sloth, 96 the year A.D. that Statius died, gives
996, which, deducted from 1300, leaves 304 years unaccounted
for, and these he may be supposed to have passed in the Anti-
purgatorio.

† *pur mo'*. Compare *Inf.* X, 21 :
> E tu m' hai non pur mo a ciù disposto.
And *Inf.* XXVII, 20 :
> E che parlavi mo lombardo.

‡ *soglia* is the name given to the different degrees or spheres
of heaven, as *Cornice* is for those of Purgatory, and *Girone* or
Cerchio for those in hell. Compare *Par.* III, 82 :
> Sì che, come noi sem di soglia in soglia
>> Per questo regno, a tutto il regno piace.

lain in this pain, but now have felt in me the free
will for a better sphere. On that account thou didst
feel the earthquake, and hear the devout spirits all
over the mount render praise to that Lord, Who will
(I trust) soon send them up (to Heaven)."

Dante's unceasing desire to know the causes of these
phenomena is completely satisfied by these words
of Statius.

> Così ne disse ; e però ch' ei si gode
>   Tanto del ber quant' è grande la sete,
>   Non saprei dir quant' ei mi fece prode.   75

Thus he spoke to us ; and, seeing that one's delight
in drinking is in proportion to how great is one's thirst,
I could hardly describe how much good he did me.

Benvenuto says : "And here note that a drink is
agreeable, not so much from the quality of the wine, as
from the disposition of the drinker ; as for example,
when Xerxes, the mighty Persian king, had been ig-
nominiously defeated, and was timidly flying, he saw,
by the side of the way, some muddy dirty water, and
immediately stooped down and began to drink greedily;
on his soldiers expostulating with him for doing so, he
said he had never in his life drunk better, for he had
never, till then, known what thirst was."

Division III. In this Division Virgil asks Statius
who he was in life ; but, before doing so, he tells him
that his explanation had cleared away all difficulty of
understanding the matters in doubt.

E il savio duca :—" Omai veggio la rete
  Che qui vi piglia, e come si scalappia,*
  Per che ci trema, e di che congaudete.
Ora chi fosti piacciati ch' io sappia,
  ˙ E, perchè tanti secoli giaciuto   80
  Qui sei, nelle parole tue mi cappia."—†

And my wise leader: "Now I perceive the net
that encloses you here, and how one may escape (*lit.*
get disentangled) from it ; why it (the mountain) here
trembles, and whereof you all rejoice together.   Now
may it please thee that I should know who thou wast,
and I pray thee to let it also be contained in thy words
to me, why thou hast lain here for so many ages."

Statius begins by answering Virgil's first question
as to who he was, and he does so in precisely the same
fashion as Virgil in the first Canto of the *Inferno* had
replied to a similar question from Dante.   Virgil
answered Dante "*Nacqui sub Julio,*" and only ten
lines lower down is the name of Virgil mentioned.
Here the same order is followed.   Statius first says
that he lived in the reign of Titus, and he discloses
his name just ten lines after.

—" Nel tempo che il buon Tito‡ con l' aiuto
  Del sommo Rege vendicò le fora,
  Ond' uscì il sangue per Giuda venduto,

---

* *Scalappiare* is from the "s" privative, and the German, and
has the sense "to unloose, disentangle oneself from a *calappio*, a
trap, a snare."

† *Cappia.*   Scartazzini says that nearly all the commentators
are agreed that this word is derived from the verb *càpere*, to
contain, and distinctly not with the meaning of *capire* to understand.

‡ *Il buon Tito.*   The siege of Jerusalem under the Emperor
Titus, surnamed "The Delight of Mankind," took place in the
year 70 A.D.   Statius was born at Naples in the reign of

Col nome che più dura e più onora   85
    Era io di là (rispose quello spirto)
    Famoso assai, ma non con fede ancora.

"In the days when the good Titus," answered that
spirit, "with the aid of the Supreme King, took vengeance for the wounds, from which gushed the blood
sold by Judas, was I in the world yonder, famous
enough for that name which most endures and most
honours, but not as yet with faith (of Christianity).*

Statius continues:

Tanto fu dolce mio vocale spirto,
    Che, Tolosano,† a sè mi trasse Roma,
    Dove mertai le tempie ornar di mirto.   90

Claudius, and had already become famous as a poet before that
of Titus.   His works are the *Silvæ*, or miscellaneous poems;
the *Thebaid*, an epic in twelve books; and the *Achilleid*, of
which he speaks in verse 92 as being unfinished at the time of
his death.   He also wrote a tragedy, *Agave*, which is lost.

Juvenal says (*Satire* VII, Dryden's translation):

  "All Rome is pleased when Statius will rehearse,

    And longing crowds expect the promised verse;
    His lofty numbers with so great a gust
    They hear, and swallow with such eager lust:
    But while the common suffrage crowned his cause,
    And broke the benches with their loud applause,
    His Muse had starved, had not a piece unread,
    And by a player bought, supplied her bread."

* Dante seems to have ranked Statius as a poet next to
Virgil.   The epics of Statius were extremely popular in the
middle ages.

† *Tolosano.* Dante has evidently confused Statius the poet,
who was born at Naples, with Statius the rhetorician, of Toulouse, Statius himself speaks of Naples as his birthplace, but he
does so in the *Sylvæ*, one of his books which was not discovered
until after Dante's death.

So sweet was my genius in song, that, although
I was a native of Toulouse, Rome drew me to herself,
and there I was thought deserving to have my brows
decked with myrtle.

He now tells his name.

> Stazio la gente ancor di là mi noma:
>   Cantai di Tebe, e poi del grande Achille,
>   Ma caddi in via con la seconda soma.

Yonder (in the world) people still call me Statius:
I sang of Thebes, and then of the great Achilles; but
I fell on the way with the second load.

This means that he died before he had completed the
Achilleid, the second of his works.   Benvenuto relates
that Statius, seeing the great disagreement that existed
between the two brothers Titus and Domitian, took as
his subject for their instruction the history of the two
brothers Eteocles and Polynices (the rival kings of
Thebes).

Benvenuto sees two interpretations in the six lines
that follow, according to the first of which Statius, unaware of who is standing by him, would show that
Virgil was the model from whom he became a poet:
or secondly, that he became a Christian from reading
Virgil's poems.   We will adopt the former, which is
preferred by Benvenuto, as we have no evidence whatever that either Virgil or Statius had any pretence to
be Christians.

> Al mio ardor fur seme le faville,
>   Che mi scaldâr, della divina fiamma,   95
>   Onde sono allumati più di mille;
> Dell' Eneida dico, la qual mamma
>   Fummi, e fummi nutrice poetando:
>   Senz' essa non fermai peso di dramma.

The sparks of the divine flame from which more than a thousand (poets of the Latin race) have been illumined, were the seed which kindled me to my fire ; I speak of the Æneid, which was to me a mother and a nurse in poesy : without it I did not balance the weight of a drachm.*

Benvenuto says that Statius tried to imitate Virgil in the Thebaid, not only in the number of books, twelve, as in the Æneid, but also in everything (*in omnibus*), so that he was not undeservedly called Virgil's monkey (*simia Virgilii*).

He concludes by showing the immensity of his love for Virgil.

> E, per esser vivuto di là, quando   100
>   Visse Virgilio, assentirei un sole†
>   Più che non deggio al mio uscir di bando."—

And, to have lived yonder, when Virgil lived, I

---

* At the conclusion of the *Thebaid* (811-817) Statius shows in what honour he held the Æneid.   Addressing his own poem, he says :

> " O mihi bissextos multum vigilata per annos
>   Thebai ! jam certe præsens tibi fama benignum
>   Stravit iter, cœpitque novam monstrare futuris.
>   Jam te magnanimus dicatur noscere Cæsar,
>   Itala jam studio discit, memoratque juventus.
>   Vive, precor : nec tu divinam Æneida tenta,
>   Sed longe sequere, et vestigia semper adora."

† *un sole.*   The word is similarly used to express a year in *Inf.* VI, 64-68.

> " Dopo lunga tenzone
>   Verranno al sangue, e la parte selvaggia
>   Caccerà l' altra con molta offensione.
>   Poi appresso convien che questa caggia
>   Infra tre soli. . . ."

would consent to do penance for a year (*lit.* a sun)
more than I need do before my going forth from
bondage."*

Division IV. In this concluding Division of the
Canto, Dantes describes how Virgil made himself
known to Statius, who was quite unaware that the
subject of his encomium was standing by his side.
Virgil, by a rapid contraction of his eyes (*col viso*),
imposes silence on Dante, who cannot all the same
restrain himself from giving a smile, for which Statius
in his turn, is quick to ask the reason. The whole
scene is thoroughly Italian, and would not occupy
more than five seconds.

> Volser Virgilio a me queste parole
> Con viso che, tacendo, disse : *Taci.*
> Ma non può tutto la virtù che vuole ;　　105
> Chè riso e pianto son tanto seguaci
> Alla passion da che ciascun si spicca,
> Che men seguon voler nei più veraci.

These words (of Statius) made Virgil turn round
(to me) with a visage that, though speechless, said :
" Be silent !" but our will cannot always perform
all that it desires ; for laughter and weeping follow
so promptly the passion from which each takes

---

* Scartazzini points out how well Francis Bacon illustrates
this passage (*De dignitate et augmentis Scientiæ*, I, VII, c. 1) :

" Legimus, nonnullos ex Electis et Sanctis viris optasse se
potius erasos e libro Vitæ, quam ut salus ad fratres suos non
perveniret, ecstasi quadam charitatis et impotenti desiderio
boni communis incitatos."

its origin, that in the most truthful men they least obey the will.

It is only the most sincere and ingenuous people who are unable to disguise their emotions. If they feel a desire to laugh, the laugh shows itself on their countenance, and the same with weeping.   It is only the deceitful man who feigns a smile while rage is in his heart.   It is only the hypocrite who can simulate grief for some misfortune at which he really secretly rejoices.

Dante now shows exactly how this difficulty of concealing his thoughts happened to him, for though he uttered not a word, he spoke by his expression, and Statius detected his thought.

> Io pur sorrisi come l' uom ch' ammicca ;*
> Perchè l' ombra si tacque, e riguardommi   110
> Negli occhi, ove il sembiante più si ficca.†

Notwithstanding, I smiled, like one who gives a wink ; on which the spirit stopped speaking, and looked me in the eyes, wherein the expression is best marked (*lit.* fixed).

---

* *ammicca.*   Blanc (*Vocabulario Dantesco*) derives the word from the Latin *micare*, to make a sign with the eyes.   Others derive it from the Latin *nictare, adnictare.*   Tommaséo (*Dizionario dei Sinonimi*) says : "*Ammiccare*, sebbene riguardi segnatamente l' occhio, comprende un po' l' atto di tutta la faccia . . . Si *accenna* e con gli occhi e col capo e con le mani.   Si può accennare senza ammiccare, ma non vice versa."

† In *Convito*, tr. III, c. 8, Dante lays down that the eyes are the window of the soul, in which all the passions can be observed, and says it has even happened to some to put out their own eyes in order that their shame from within should not be seen without (perchè la vergogna d' entro non paresse di fuori).

Statius makes his petition.

> E :—" Se* tanto lavoro in bene assommi,"—†
> Disse,—" perchè la tua faccia testeso‡
> Un lampeggiar di riso dimostrommi ?"—

And : " As," said he (I pray that) " thou mayest bring to a happy conclusion so great a work (as thy journey), so do I pray thee to tell me, why just now did thy face reveal to me a flash of merriment ?"

Dante is fairly perplexed.

> Or son io d' una parte e d' altra preso ;   115
> L' una mi fa tacer, l' altra scongiura
> Ch' io dica : ond' io sospiro e son inteso
> Dal mio maestro, e :—" Non aver paura,"—
> Mi disse,—" di parlar ; ma parla, e digli
> Quel ch' ei dimanda con cotanta cura."—   120

Now am I caught both on one side and the other ; the one (Virgil) makes me silent, and the other (Statius) entreats me to speak : on which I heave a sigh, and am understood by my Master, and said he to me: "Fear not to speak, but say on, and tell him that which he asks with so much anxiety."

Francesco da Buti says that Virgil had stopped Dante speaking before, so as not to interrupt what Statius was saying : but when he saw Statius look perplexed, he thought it would be kinder to tell him what it was, about which they were making signs.

---

* *Se* is a deprecative particle.

† *assommi*: from *assomare*, from the Latin *summa*, to bring to an end, terminate, finish.

‡ *testeso* : an ancient form of *testè*, which means "now ;" and also "just now," "lately."

Ond' io :—" Forse che tu ti maravigli,
    Antico* spirto, del rider ch' io fei ;
    Ma più d' ammirazion vo' che ti pigli.†

On which I : " Perchance thou marvellest, spirit of
days gone by, at the smile I gave ; but I will that even
greater wonderment seize upon thee.

Questi che guida in alto gli occhi miei,
    È quel Virgilio dal qual tu togliesti   125
    Forza a cantar degli uomini e de' Dei.

This one, who is guiding my eyes up on high, is that
Virgil from whom thou didst gain strength to sing of
men and of Gods.‡

Scartazzini points out that *in alto* means as far as
the summit of the mountain, beyond which Virgil,
representing Reason, would have no power to go, and
not as Benvenuto interprets it, as meaning to Heaven.

He now adds :

Se cagione altra al mio rider credesti,
    Lasciala per non vera esser, e credi
    Quelle parole che di lui dicesti."—

---

* *Antico spirto.* Benvenuto remarks that Statius may well be
called ancient, since he wrote poems more than a thousand years
before the scene here described is supposed to occur.

† *più d' ammirazion vo' che ti pigli.* This almost reminds one
of Mark Anthony, who first shows the mob Cæsar's mantle
stabbed all over, and then, suddenly plucking it aside, shows
them the body.

" Kind souls, what weep you, when you but behold
    Our Cæsar's vesture wounded ! Look you here,
    Here is himself, marred, as you see, by traitors."
        —Shakespeare (*Julius Cæsar*), Act III, Sc. II.

‡ In the Thebaid, Statius introduces both Gods and men as
performing feats of arms, and therein imitated Virgil, who in his
turn had imitated Homer.

And if thou didst believe in any other cause for my smiling, abandon it as not true, and believe those words that thou didst speak of him ?"

Statius is dumbfoundered, and, with the utmost reverence, bends down to do obeisance to Virgil.

> Già si chinava ad abbracciar li piedi   130
>   Al mio dottor ; ma e' gli disse :—" Frate,
>   Non far, chè tu se' ombra, ed ombra vedi."—

Already was he stooping to embrace my Teacher's feet : but he (Virgil) said to him : " Brother, do not so, for thou art a shade, and a shade thou seest !"

Statius makes a courteous excuse for having forgotten their want of substance, and says that it arose from his intense delight at seeing so unexpectedly before him the spirit of one for whom he felt such deep reverence.

> Ed ei surgendo :—" Or puoi la quantitate
>   Comprender dell' amor che a te mi scalda,
>   Quando dismento nostra vanitate,   135
> Trattando l' ombre come cosa salda."—

And he (Statius) rising : " Now canst thou comprehend the sum of the love which burns in me towards thee, when I am able to forget our emptiness, treating shades as substantial things."

END OF CANTO XXI.

CANTO XXII.

—

Ascent to the Sixth Cornice.
Statius (*continued*).
The Gluttonous.

At the beginning of the last Canto, Benvenuto stated that in it would be treated the purgation of prodigality, but it is an error on his part, for the subject is not mentioned at all until the present Canto. Here again, in his opening words, Benvenuto continues his error, saying : " As in the preceding chapter, our poet treated of the vice of prodigality in the person of Statius, so now in this chapter XXII, he concludes the subject of prodigality in the same spirit, and enters upon the subject of gluttony, which is punished in the sixth circle."

Benvenuto divides the Canto into four parts.

In the First Division, from v. 1 to v. 54, Dante tells how he found that his purgation from Avarice had already taken place, and how he learns that it was for prodigality and not for avarice that Statius had to suffer.

In the Second Division, from v. 55 to v. 93, Statius informs Virgil, in answer to a question, that it was from Virgil's writings that he had learnt the Christian faith.

In the Third Division, from v. 94 to v. 114, Statius asks Virgil what has become of certain illustrious writers of antiquity.

In the Fourth Division, from v. 115 to v. 154, the poets reach the sixth cornice, and the purgation of the sin of gluttony is described.

Division I. It would seem that between the conclusion of the last, and the commencement of the present Canto, Dante had passed before the Angel of the Fifth Cornice, who had erased another P from his brow, so that two only now remain upon it, the P of Gluttony, and the P of Luxury, which will be erased in the Sixth and Seventh Cornices above.

The three poets, Dante, Virgil, and Statius, appear to have already entered upon the stairway leading up to the Sixth Cornice, and Dante tells us that they have left the Angel behind them at the foot of the steps.

> Già era l' Angel dietro a noi rimaso,
> L' Angel che n' avea vôlti al sesto giro,
> Avendomi dal viso un colpo raso.

The angel was by this time left behind us, the angel who had made us turn to the sixth circle, and who had (before doing so) erased from my brow one mark (*lit.* stroke of the sword of the Angel Warder).

Benvenuto remarks that, although nothing has been said about the Angel, he is here introduced by an artificial abbreviation. With the erasure had come the appropriate Beatitude.

> E *quei ch' hanno a giustizia lor disiro,*
> Detto n' avea,* *Beati,* e le sue voci ·   5

---

* *N' avea.* Scartazzini says that this is one of the passages that have been terribly tortured, first, by the amanuenses, and then by the commentators. The variations in the reading are many, but the most common alternative reading is *n' avean,*

Con *sitiunt*,* senz' altro, ciò forniro.

And he (the Angel) had said to us, " Blessed are they that have their craving for righteousness;" and his words completed the sentence (*ciò forniro*) with *sitiunt* (they who thirst), not adding more.

Scartazzini says that these last words imply that as there are seven Angels, into whose mouths Dante wishes to put a Beatitude, he finds himself obliged to

---

which would imply that it was not the Angel, but the spirits of the fifth cornice, who pronounced the words, " Beati quei ch' hanno a giuztizia lor disiro." But such an interpretation would simply destroy the beautiful symmetry of the poem. While everywhere else it is the angel guarding the exit who, when dismissing the purified souls, chants the appropriate Beatitude according to the reading *n' avean*, the angel in this cornice would be made to act differently, and to allow the travellers to depart unnoticed by him. Dr. Moore, in his recent valuable work (*Textual Criticism of the Divina Commedia, Cambridge University Press*, 1889) says at page 405 : "the right reading *n' avea* (unless I am mistaken) is not found in any of the earlier Commentators, yet it has considerable support among the MSS., being found in about half those examined . . . . on fuller and wider consideration, both of context and parallel passages, *avea* will, I think, prove to be decidedly more appropriate."

* *sitiunt.* The same process of reasoning can guide one in preferring this reading to *sitio*, which occurs in by far the greater number of MSS. Everywhere else the angel guarding the stairway chants one of the Beatitudes, *Purg.* XII, 110 ; XV, 38 ; XVII, 68 ; XIX, 50 ; XXIV, 151 ; XXVII, 8 ; and the analogy requires that in the case of the Fifth Cornice also he should dismiss the poets with a Beatitude. The words in this passage are taken from *St. Matt.* V, 6, and are "Beati qui esuriunt et *sitiunt* justitiam," not *sitio*. Therefore *sitiunt* must be the right reading. It is adopted by Scartazzini, Fraticelli, Lubin, Pollock, Moore, and Butler.

leave out from this text the words, " Blessed are they that hunger," *" Beati qui esuriunt,"* which comes in very appropriately in the next Cornice, where gluttony is chastised.

Dante, having been disburdened of five out of the seven mortal sins, of which the emblems, the seven P's, had been traced on his brow, tells us how relieved he feels.

> Ed io, più lieve* che per l' altre foci,
>> M' andava, sì che senza alcun labore†
>> Seguiva in su gli spiriti veloci.

And I was walking on, lighter than when passing through the other entrances, so much so, that I could follow those two quickly moving spirits (Virgil and Statius) without any distress.

Benvenuto tells us that Virgil now addresses Statius in a few noble words, and, to win his good graces, prefaces his remarks with a noteworthy opinion about honourable love.

> Quando Virgilio cominciò :—"Amore   10
>> Acceso da virtù, sempre altro accese,
>> Pur che la fiamma sua paresse fuore.

---

* Compare *Purg.* IV, 88, where Virgil, in answer to Dante's inquiries as to the ascent, replies :

> " Questa montagna è tale,
> Che sempre al cominciar di sotto è grave,
> E quanto uom più va su, e men fa male."

and *Purg.* XII, 112, where Dante compares the cornices of Purgatory to those of the circles of Hell.

> " Ahi ! quanto son diverse quelle foci
>> Dalle infernali ; chè quivi per canti
>> S' entra, e laggiù per lamenti feroci."

† *labore.* A primitive word from the Latin, used instead of *lavoro,* and has the signification of fatigue. Dante makes use of it in the Convito.

When Virgil began: "Love, kindled by virtue, always causes another to burn (*i.e.* is reciprocated), if only its flame appear outwardly.

Francesco da Buti says: "Purchè sappia l' amato esser amato incontanente ama." " Provided that the person loved is aware of being loved, immediately he loves?"

And Benvenuto: "From this we see that we often love a virtuous man, even though we have never seen or known him, just as I, Benvenuto, love Dante."

Virgil states this proposition in order to show that on hearing of the writings of Statius, in which admiration for himself is expressed, he too had felt a sympathetic touch of love for Statius.

After laying down this opinion on the reciprocity of love, Virgil proceeds to tell Statius that, though only knowing him by hearsay from Juvenal, whom he had met in Limbo, he had loved him for many centuries.

> Onde, dall' ora che tra noi discese
> Nel limbo dello inferno Giovenale,
> Che la tua affezion mi fe' palese, 15
> Mia benvoglienza inverso te fu quale
> Più strinse mai di non vista persona,
> Sì ch' or mi parran corte queste scale.

Wherefore, from the hour that Juvenal, who made me acquainted with thy affection for me, descended into the Limbo of Hell, my good will towards thee has been as great as ever bound me to an unseen person, so that now these stairs will appear short to me.*

---

* Virgil does not appear to mean that he had hitherto found the ascent toilsome, but only wishes to express his regret that he will not be able to go beyond the summit of the staircase of the

Benvenuto says that, having addressed the above graceful words to Statius as an exordium, Virgil asks him how it is possible that he can have been guilty of the sin of avarice.

> Ma dimmi (e come amico mi perdona
>   Se troppa sicurtà m' allarga il freno,   20
>   E come amico omai meco ragiona)
> Come poteo trovar dentro al tuo seno
>   Luogo avarizia, tra cotanto senno*
>   Di quanto per tua cura fosti pieno? "—

But tell me (and forgive me as a friend if too much freedom loosens the rein of my speech, and henceforth converse with me as a friend) how could avarice find a place within thy breast, amid wisdom so great as thou wast filled with by thy care?"†

Statius cannot help smiling at this misapprehension on the part of Virgil, just as Dante had previously laughed at that of Statius.

> Queste parole Stazio muover fenno   25
>   Un poco a riso pria ; poscia rispose :
> —" Ogni tuo dir d' amor m' è caro cenno.

These words made Statius somewhat inclined to laugh at first; then he answered : " Every speech of thine is to me a dear token of love.

---

cornice above, and will have so short a time to pass in the company of Statius.

* *tra cotanto senno.* The same words occur in *Inf.* IV, 102 :
    " Sì ch' io fui sesto tra cotanto senno."

† Scartazzini thinks that Virgil's mistake was very natural. The poets had heard from Adrian V that in the fifth cornice was punished the sin of avarice, *Purg.* XIX, 115. Moreover, Statius, in *Purg.* XXI, 67, has told them that he had lain in that cornice for five centuries. Nothing had been said about prodigality being punished there, and Virgil consequently took it for granted that avarice had been one of the sins of Statius.

Statius says this because Virgil had asked him for pardon, if he used too much freedom in speaking about his supposed sin of avarice.

Benvenuto observes that, after this preliminary remark, Statius commences his speech, and does so in a manner which one cannot sufficiently admire, both from its artistic merit, worthy of so great an orator, and also as being quite after Virgil's manner. He introduces, as the basis on which he forms his speech, a noteworthy expression of opinion.

> Veramente più volte appajon cose,
>   Che dànno a dubitar falsa matéra,
>   Per le vere ragion che son nascose.   30

In truth, oftentimes appear things which afford false material for doubt, because of the real causes which are hidden.

Benvenuto says it often happens that things which are perfectly true are not believed, from ignorance of causes. It seems incredible that, under a clear sky and on a tranquil sea, a ship should suddenly go to the bottom and not be seen again, if you do not know that a hidden rock was the cause ; or, the statement in the last Canto, that Titus attacked Jerusalem to avenge the death of Christ, which Benvenuto says is false, as Titus made war against the Jews on his own account.

Statius next deals with Virgil's misapprehension.

> La tua dimanda tuo creder m' avvera
>   Esser, ch' io fossi avaro in l' altra vita,
>   Forse per quella cerchio dov' io era.

Thy question convinces me that it is thy belief, that I was avaricious in the other life, possibly on account of (seeing me in) that cornice where I was.

And he immediately shows where the mistake lies.

> Or sappi che avarizia fu partita
> Troppo da me, e questa dismisura   35
> Migliaia di lunari* hanno punita.

Now learn that avarice was too far removed from me ; and this disproportion thousands of moons have chastised.

Francesco da Buti remarks that, instead of hoarding the things he ought to give away or reserve, he gave away both the things he ought to have given away, and also the things he ought to have reserved.

Statius now goes on to relate that it was a passage in Virgil's writings that had wrought an amendment in him.†

> E se non fosse ch' io drizzai mia cura,
> Quand' io intesi là dove tu esclame,
> Crucciato quasi all' umana natura :
> *Per che non reggi tu, o sacra fame*   40
> *Dell' oro, l' appetito dei mortali ?*
> Voltando sentirei le giostre grame.

And had it not been that I turned my solicitude aright, when I understood the passage (*là*) where thou, almost indignant against human nature, ex-

---

* Statius had spent altogether 14,448 months in Purgatory. He died A.D. 96 which, deducted from A.D. 1300, leaves 1204 years, of which, as we noticed before, he had spent 500 in the cornice of avarice ; 400 in the cornice of sloth ; 304 in the Anti-purgatorio. Total, 1,204 years = 14,448 months.

† There is a graceful courtesy in Statius quoting a passage from Virgil's own writings, and telling him the influence it had upon his life. It reminds one of Casella the musician, mentioned in the second Canto, who, when asked by Dante to comfort his soul with song, after the bodily and mental prostration he felt from his passage through Hell, commenced singing one of Dante's own sonnets set to music of his own.

claimest : " Through what (crooked channels) dost not thou, accursed hunger of gold, drive the appetite of mortals ? " I should now be experiencing the dismal jousts, rolling (the weight among the misers and prodigals in Hell.* See *Inf.* VII, 25-26.)

---

* Some read *perchè* and translate : Why dost thou not regulate and confine within due bounds the appetite of mortals ? Others, limit *a che* ; translating : To what pitch dost thou not drive. Some take *sacra* in a good sense, as though the words meant Why dost not thou, O holy hunger of gold, restrain the desire of mortals :

Scartazzini says that it is clear, before everything else, that Dante intends here either to translate or to imitate the well-known verses of Virgil (*Æn.* III, 56) :

> " Quid non mortalia pectora cogis,
>   Auri sacra fames ? "

This is evidently the opinion too of Benvenuto, who translates it :

> " O execrabilis cupiditas auri."

Scartazzini says that, of four different ways of interpreting the passage, he prefers the last : " Per che distorte vie, per che malvagità, non conduci e guidi tu, o esecranda fame dell' oro, l' appetito degli uomini ? " (Through what crooked ways, and through what wickedness, dost thou not conduct, &c.) He also cites a number of commentators who say that rightly to understand how Virgil's severe censure of the hunger of gold serves to condemn prodigality (for both the miser and the prodigal have the sinful love of money), the following passage from Aristotle (*Ethics*, book IV, ch. 1, R. W. Browne's translation) may be quoted : " But the majority of prodigals, as has been stated, also receive from improper sources, and are in this respect illiberal [in the Italian version ἀνελεύθεροι is translated, " guilty of the sin of avarice."] Now they become fond of receiving because they wish to spend, and are not able do it easily, for their means soon fail them ; they are therefore compelled to get supplies from some other quarter, and, at the same time, owing to their not caring for the honourable, they receive

Statius, having quoted the words of Virgil, tells him how reflection on those weighty lines influenced his life, for he then began to understand that both misers and prodigals have a sinful thirst for gold, though with the intent of using it in opposite ways; and that they often seek it by sinful fraud, or violence.

> Allor m' accorsi che troppo aprir l' ali*
> Potean le mani a spendere, e pentémi
> Così di quel come degli altri mali.   45

Then did I perceive that the hands could spread their wings too widely in spending; and I repented me both of this as of other sins.

Statius next condemns prodigality in men, who

---

without scruple from any person they can; for they are anxious to give, and the how or the whence they get the money matters not to them."

Biagioli has the following note: "*Sacra*, esecrabile. *Fame*, per desiderio smoderato. It is used by Petrarch: *Quella perch' io ho di morir tal fame.* Every one can see that this is the Virgilian *Quid non mortalia pectora cogis, Auri sacra fames?* When I read for the first time this *perchè*, written thus as one entire word, I confess that I did not succeed in understanding the construction of it, although the sentiment of it can be so clearly seen. . . . I returned to my house and commenced the analysis, separating the preposition *per* from the adjective *che*, knowing that, in whatever aspect it presents itself, *che* is nothing but an adjective, and therefore connected with a noun either expressed or understood, and I quickly found that I could fill the void, by writing *per che* (per quali) *scelleraggini non reggi, &c.* (through what crimes dost thou not conduct, &c.) and in this way the construction becomes quite simple."

* In *Purg.* X, 25, Dante gives wings to the eyes, as here to the hands:

> " E quanto l' occhio mio potea trar d' ale
> Or dal sinistro ed or dal destro fianco, &c."

seem to be ignorant of how great a sin it is, and of
such had been Statius himself.

> Quanti risurgeran coi crini scemi,*
> Per ignoranza,† che di questo pecca
> Toglie il pentér vivendo, e negli estremi !

How many shall rise again with shorn hair, for
ignorance which bars repentance for this sin, both
in life, and at the extreme hour.

Benvenuto has a fanciful interpretation for *estremi,*
"the extremes," for such are avarice and prodigality.
He supposes that Statius now anticipates the possibility

---

* *Crini scemi.* Compare *Inf.* VII, 46, where Virgil in
describing to Dante the punishment in hell of the avaricious
and the prodigal, says of the former :

> " Questi fur cherci che non han coperchio
> Piloso al capo, e papi e cardinali,
> In cui usa avarizia il suo soperchio."

And at verse 55 :

> " In eterno veranno agli due cozzi.
> Questi risurgeranno del sepulcro
> Col pugno chiuso, e questi co' crin mozzi."

† Scartazzini explains that there are two kinds of ignorance :
the one sinful, and the other not. That ignorance is sinful which
could be overcome by exercising and perfecting reason.
See St. Thomas Aquinas (*Summ. Theol.* P. I, 2ᵃᵉ, qu. LXXVI,
art. 2) : " Quicumque negligit habere vel facere id quod tenetur
habere vel facere, peccat peccato omissionis. Unde propter
negligentiam ignorantia eorum quæ aliquis scire tenetur est
peccatum ; non autem imputatur homini ad negligentiam si
nesciat ea quæ scire non potest. Unde horum ignorantia
invincibilis dicitur, quia studio superari non potest. Et propter
hoc talis ignorantia, cum non sit voluntaria, eo quod non est in
potestate nostra eam repellere, non est peccatum. Ex quo patet
quod nulla ignorantia invincibilis est peccatum ; ignorantia
autem vincibilis est peccatum si sit eorum quæ aliquis scire
tenetur, non autem si sit eorum quæ quis scire non tenetur."

of Virgil asking him : " Why then didst thou remain so long doing penance among the misers ? " and makes him answer that the two sins of avarice and prodigality, opposed to each other, are rightly punished in the same cornice.

> E sappi che la colpa che rimbecca*
> > Per dritta opposizione alcun peccato,   50
> > Con esso insieme qui suo verde secca.

And know that the fault which offers itself in direct opposition to any sin, here (in the fifth cornice they have just left) together with it dries up its green.†

The first of the two faults undergoes the same purgation, and is punished in the same place in Purgatory, as the fault which is the direct opposite to it. Benvenuto says of *la colpa che rimbecca* " idest, adversatur et occurrit a becco a becco," and of *qui secca suo verde,* " id est luit pœnam æqualem."

" And mark here, reader," adds Benvenuto, " that our poet rightly assigns the same penalty to both those sins, for although avarice is always the most detested of the two, yet in real truth prodigality is a damnable pest, and hostile to the public weal. For the prodigal, who spends more than nature requires, and more than fortune supplies, soon replaces plenty

---

* *rimbecca.* Blanc (*Vocbulario Dantesco*) says that *rimbeccare* is a word of uncertain origin, and that Dante uses it in the sense of being directly opposed to anything. It properly signifies to strike the ball backwards and forwards from one player to another. The word is used in Corsica as the title of a kind of song to incite the backward when unwilling to carry on a vendetta.

† Compare *Ezekiel* XX, 47 : " Thus saith the Lord God ; Behold, I will kindle a fire in thee, and it shall devour every green tree in thee, and every dry tree."

with emptiness, sweet with bitter, light with darkness, praise with derision, much with nothing. The prodigal soon renders himself contemptible in the eyes of those, by whom, but shortly before, he was held in respect . . . O how many worthy and great men has this sin cast down into rage and despair!"

And Statius concludes :

> Però, s' io son tra quella gente stato
> Che piange l' avarizia, per purgarmi,
> Per lo contrario suo m' è incontrato.*"—

Wherefore, if I have been for my purgation among that folk, that bewail their avarice, it has happened to me by reason of its contrary," (*i.e.* the sin for which I have had to suffer was prodigality, the contrary of avarice.)

————

Division II. In the Second and principal Division of the Canto, Statius relates to Virgil the cause of his conversion to the Christian faith, of which Virgil had expressed some doubt, thinking rather that in his books Statius seemed to speak like a heathen.

Virgil begins :

> —" Or quando tu cantasti le crude armi   55
>   Della doppia tristizia di Jocasta,
>   (Disse il Cantor de' bucolici carmi)
> Per quello che Cliò teco lì tasta,
>   Non par che ti facesse ancor fedele
>   La fè, senza la qual ben far non basta.   60

————

* *m' è incontrato* is here used as an impersonal verb, with the sense: " it has happened to me." Scartazzini observes that the prodigality of Statius is a mere poetic fiction of Dante, as whatever is recorded of Statius in history would show him not to be possessed of sufficient means to be very extravagant.

"Now when thou (in the Thebaid) didst sing of the cruel war of (Eteocles and Polynices) the twofold sorrow of Jocasta" (their mother), said the Singer of the Bucolic Poems, "from the matters about which with thee in that poem (*li*) Clio touches, it would not seem to me that the (Christian) faith had as yet made thee a believer, without which good works do not suffice." *

Virgil means to say : I do not find in the Thebaid any evidence whatever that thou hadst acquired the Christian faith. And he further asks:

> Se così è, qual sole o quai candele
> Ti stenebraron sì, che tu drizzasti
> Poscia diretro al Pescator† le vele?"—

---

* Statius begins the Thebaid with an invocation to Clio, the Muse of History, whose office it was to record the heroic actions of brave men. See *Thebaid* I, 55 :

> "What first, O Clio, shall adorn thy page,
> The expiring prophet, or Ætolian's rage?
> Say, wilt thou sing how, grim with dismal blood,
> Hippomedon repelled the rushing flood,
> Lament the Arcadian youth's untimely fate,
> Or Jove, opposed by Capaneus, relate?"

Eteocles and Polynices, sons of Œdipus and Jocasta, having succeeded their father as Kings of Thebes, had agreed to rule in alternate years, and that the non-reigning brother should pass the year in voluntary exile. Eteocles reigned first, but, when at the end of the year, Polynices came to claim the sceptre, Eteocles refused to give it up, and thence arose the celebrated war of the Seven Kings against Thebes so magnificently described by Æschylus.

† *Pescator.* According to Dean Plumptre the image had become familiar through the Sigillum Pescatoris used by the Roman Pontiffs, on which there was a representation of Christ

If it is so, what sun (*i.e.*, light from heaven), or what candles (*i.e.*, light from earth), so took thee out of the darkness, that after the time I speak of (*poscia*) thou turnedst thy sails into the wake of the Fisherman (St. Peter)."

Statius replies.

> Ed egli a lui :—"Tu prima m' inviasti
> Verso Parnaso a ber nelle sue grotte,   65
> E poi, appresso Dio, m' alluminasti.

And he to him : " Thou first didst lead me towards Parnassus to drink (from Helicon) in its grottoes, and then didst illumine me on the road to God.

> Facesti come quei che va di notte,*
> Che porta il lume dietro, e sè non giova,
> Ma dopo sè fa le persone dotte,
> Quando dicesti : *Secol si rinnuova;*   70
> *Torna giustizia, e primo tempo umano,*
> *E progenie discende dal ciel nuova.*

Thou didst, like him who walks at night, who bears

---

fishing with a line, and St. Peter with a net. The first mention of this seal occurs in a letter of Clement IV in 1265, the year of Dante's birth.

* *quei che va di notte.* An allusion to the attendant who at night walks in front of his master, carrying a lantern behind him, so that, while giving light, he himself remains in the dark. A passage nearly identical is found in a sonnet of Messer Polo da Reggio in Lombardy who flourished about 1230 :

> " Sì come quel che porta la lumiera
> La notte quando passa per la via,
> Alluma assai più gente della spera,
> Che sè medesmo che l' ha in balia."

According to Dante, Virgil walking in the darkness of ignorance, but bearing the light of wisdom, gave to Statius, who came after him, the knowledge of the true faith.

a light behind him, and profits not himself, but makes wise (*i.e.*, gives knowledge of their way to) the persons behind him, when thou saidst : " The ages are beginning anew ; Justice is returning, and man's primeval time; and a new progeny descends from heaven ?"*

Scartazzini, drawing his information chiefly from Comparetti (*Virgilio nel medio evo*, Livorno, 1871, vol. I, p. 128, &c.) says that this prophecy of the Cumæan Sibyll is applied by Virgil, who was a courtier, to the birth of the son of Asinius Pollio, but that Dante sees in the words an announcement of the birth of the Redeemer. Nor was Dante the first so to understand it. The presentiment that breathes through the whole Eclogue of a speedy renewal of the world, in an age of happiness, justice, love, and peace, and the way that such expectation is linked on to the birth of an infant, were things too seductive for Christians to read, and not to connect them with the birth of Christ, and the renewal of the world in the new and gentle doctrines which He offered to it. In fact the Christian interpretation of the Fourth Eclogue is seen to have been exceedingly in vogue among the Christian writers of the Fourth Century. The fullest interpretation of it in this sense is to be found in an allocution delivered (according to Eusebius, *Vita Const.* IV, 32), by the Emperor Constantine before an ecclesiastical assembly. The Emperor, examining that composition

---

* The passage referred to is from *Ecl.* IV, 5 :
    " Magnus ab integro sæculorum nascitur ordo
      Jam redit et virgo, redeunt Saturnia regna ;
      Jam nova progenies cælo demittitur alto ;"
and it will be seen that Dante translates it almost literally.

of Virgil in its various parts, sees in it the prediction
of the Advent of Christ, shown forth very circum-
stantially ; the virgin that returns is Mary ; the new
progeny sent down from Heaven is Jesus ; the serpent
that shall be no more is the ancient tempter of our
fathers ; the *amomum* that will be born everywhere
is the Christian race, cleansed from sin ; and he goes
on interpreting after this wise other details in the
Eclogue.   He maintains that Virgil wrote with the
clear intention of predicting the birth of Christ, but
that he expressed himself in veiled language, mixing
up with the words even the names of heathen divini-
ties, so as not too openly to shock the beliefs of that
time, and not to draw upon himself the displeasure
of the spiritual authorities.   Lactantius also, who lived
in the same century as Constantine, interprets this
Eclogue in the Christian sense, referring it however
not to the first, but to the second coming of Christ.
(Lactantius, *Div. institut. lib.* VII, *ch.* 24.) . St. Augustine, while admitting the existence among the heathen
of prophets who foretold the coming of Christ, also
cites the Fourth Eclogue, and curiously enough takes
up verses 13 and 14, which he refers to the remission
of sins through the merits of the Saviour.   (August.
Epist. 137 *ad Volus.* ch. 12. *Epist.* 258, ch. 5.   *De Civ.
Dei, lib.* X, ch. 27).   In vain did St. Jerome inveigh
against such ideas, ridiculing those who could believe
that Virgil could be a Christian without a Christ.
(Hieron. *Epist.* 53, *ad Paulin,* ch. 7).   Christian theologians continued to interpret the famous Eclogue in
their own way, and even those who did not believe
that Virgil had himself understood his own words in
the sense which they attributed to them, still main-

tained, that though personally unconscious of the fact, he offered a testimony and an argument for the true faith.   The pretended irresistibility of that argument also gave rise to ecclesiastical legends of conversions due to the verses of the Fourth Eclogue, as that of Statius, and that of the three heathens Secundianus, Marcellianus, and Verianus, who being suddenly enlightened by Virgil's lines, from being persecutors of Christians became martyrs for Christ. Pope Innocent III quotes the lines in confirmation of the Christian faith in a Christmas sermon (*Serm.* II, *in fest. Nativ. Dom.*), and they were understood in the Christian sense during the middle ages and afterwards. We may conclude then that Dante is here following the exegesis of a tradition generally accepted in his time, that made Virgil a prophet of Christ.

Benvenuto, without going so far as to deny that the lines refer to the birth of Jesus Christ, is far more inclined to think that they allude to that of Augustus Cæsar.   Statius continues,

> Per te poeta fui, per te cristiano.
> Ma, perchè veggi me' ciò ch' io disegno,
> A colorare* stenderò la mano.   75

Through thee was I poet, through thee a Christian. But that thou mayest discern what I outline, I will put forth my hand, to fill in the colours.

That is to say, I will now explain in detail what I merely hinted at before.   This Statius proceeds to do.

---

* Blanc (*Vocabulario Dantesco*) says that *colorare* is here used in the figurative sense, and thus signifies : " to explain anything in detail."

> Già era il mondo tutto quanto pregno
> Della vera credenza, seminata
> Per li messaggi dell' eterno regno;
> E la parola tua sopra toccata
> Sì consonava ai nuovi predicanti,   80
> Ond' io a visitarli presi usata.*

Already was the whole world teeming with the
true faith, sown abroad by the (Apostles) messengers
of the Eternal Kingdom ; and thy words which I
touched upon above, harmonized with (the teaching
of) the new preachers, whereupon I took the custom
of visiting them.

He then relates his sympathy for the Christians
under their persecutions.

> Vennermi poi parendo tanto santi,
> Che, quando Domizian li perseguette,
> Senza mio lagrimar non fur lor pianti.

Afterwards they got to appear so holy to me, that,
when Domitian persecuted them, their lamentations
were not unaccompanied by my tears.

But he did more than merely pity them.

> E mentre che di là per me si stette,   85
> Io gli sovvenni, e lor dritti costumi
> Fêr dispregiare a me tutte altre sette.

And while I remained yonder (in the world), I gave
them assistance, and their upright fashions made me
despise all other sects.

And then he shows how he became a Christian.

> E pria ch' io conducessi i Greci ai fiumi†
> Di Tebe poetando, ebb' io battesmo ;

---

* *usata* for *usanza*. Scartazzini says that the past participles
were anciently used as nouns ; *il destinato* for *il destino; la
disposta* for *la disposizione; il cogitato* for *la cogitazione*.

† There are twelve books in the Thebaid. In the ninth book
Statius describes how the Greeks, under Adrastus, their king,

> Ma per paura chiuso cristian fúmi, 90
> Lungamente mostrando paganesmo ;
> E questa tepidezza il quarto cerchio
> Cerchiar mi fe' più ch' al quarto centesmo.

And before that, in my poem on Thebes, I had taken the Greeks as far as the rivers (Ismenus and Asopus), I had received baptism ; but from fear I remained a concealed Christian, for a long while professing Paganism : and this lukewarmness made me encircle the fourth cornice (where spiritual sloth is punished) for more than four centuries.

Division III. In the Third Division Statius asks Virgil what has become of certain of the Latin writers whom he had most honoured. Virgil in reply, gives him the information, and also tells him about many other Greek and Latin writers.

Statius begins :

> Tu dunque, che levato hai il coperchio
> Che m' ascondeva quanto bene io dico 95
> Mentre che del salire avém soverchio,
> Dimmi dov' è Terenzio nostro antico,*

---

came to the assistance of Polynices, and how they reached the Ismenus and Asopus, rivers of the Thebais. Statius then is made to say that he was baptized before he had completed his poem, and his lukewarmness would be shown by there being no profession of his faith, or praise of the Christian religion, in the three last books.

* The readings vary between "*Terenzio nostro antico*" and "*nostro amico.*" I prefer the reading "*antico,*" for "*nostro*" distinctly implies friendship.

See Dr. Moore's *Textual Criticism,* pages 410-414, on this passage.

Cecilio,* Plauto e Varro,† se lo sai,
Dimmi se son dannati, ed in qual vico."—

Thou then, who didst lift for me the veil which was
hiding that good which I now proclaim (*i. e.* the
knowledge of the Christian faith), while in our ascent
we have time to spare, pray tell me, where is our old

---

* Statius Cæcilius was a dramatic author, and died B.C.
168.

† Scartazzini says that, in the history of Roman literature,
two poets of this name are recorded. The most renowned was
Marcus Terentius Varro Reatinus, born at Reate, B.C. 116. He
filled various public offices with great credit. During the civil
wars he at first followed Pompey, but promptly abandoned him
to go to Rome with Julius Cæsar, who intended employing him
to collect the public library which he wished to form at Rome.
After Cæsar's death he was included in the proscription of the
Triumvirs, but concealed himself until he was taken under the
protection of Augustus. He passed the remainder of his life in
studies and died at the age of 89, B.C. 27. He was the friend of
Cicero, who (*Brut.* XV, 60) styled him *Diligentissimus investigator antiquitatis.* Seneca (*Consol. ad Helv.* ch. 8) calls him
"the most learned of the Romans," Quintilian X, 1, 95, "*Vir
Romanorum eruditissimus.*" Lactantius (*Institu.* I, ch. 6) styles
him the most learned man among the Latins and Greeks. Far
less distinguished was the other Varro, Publius Terentius Varro
Atacinus, born at Atace in Gallia Narbonensis, B.C. 82. There
has been much controversy as to which of the two Dante is
speaking here.

Witte was the first to suggest that the reading ought to be
Vario, and that the person spoken of is Lucius Varius, a dramatic poet, friend of both Virgil and Horace. But Scartazzini
concludes a long and very close argument by saying that, as
both Varros were poets, either can well be mentioned by Dante
with the others he names in this passage. And when one remembers that all the old MSS. and all the old editions read
Varro or *Varo,* not *Vario,* and that M. Terentius Varro, as
being much the more renowned, would have been so much the

friend Terence.   Tell me where are Cecilius, Plautus
and Varro, if thou knowest ; tell me if they are
damned, and in what circle (*lit.* street)."

Virgil answers :

> — " Costoro, e Persio, ed io, ed altri assai,"—   100
>   Rispose il duca mio,—"siam con quel Greco
>   Che le Muse lattâr più ch' altro mai,
>   Nel primo cinghio del carcere cieco.*
>   Spesse fiate ragioniam del monte,
>   Che sempre ha le nutrici nostre seco.   105

" They," my leader replied, " and Persius, and I,
and many others, are with that Greek (Homer), whom
the Muses suckled more than they ever did another,
in the first zone of the dark prison (*i. e.* Limbo, the
first circle of Hell).   Often do we converse about
that mountain (Parnassus), which always has on it
our nurses (*i.e.* the Muses).

Benvenuto says that Virgil, having named Homer
as the prince of Greek poets, under whose care are
all poets, now proceeds to mention certain other
Greek poets.

---

better known to Dante than Varius, one must come to the
resolution of rejecting the ingenious conjecture, and admit with
the many that Dante intended to speak of ·Varro, though it is
not impossible that he may have made the two Varros into one
person.

   * *carcere cieco.* Compare *Inf.* X, 58-9, where Cavalcante
Cavalcanti uses the same expression, when asking Dante for
news about his son Guido, Dante's great friend :
>   —" Se per questo cieco
>   Carcere vai per altezza d' ingegno,
>   Mio figlio ov' è ?   E perchè non è teco ?"—
   Compare also I *St. Peter* III, 19 : "by which also he went
and preached unto the spirits in prison."

Euripide v' è nosco, ed Antifonte,*
  Simonide,† Agatone,‡ ed altri piùe
  Greci, che già di lauro ornâr la fronte.

Euripides is there among us, and Antiphon, Simonides, Agathon and many other Greeks, who in days
gone by (*già*) decked their brows with laurel.

Benvenuto says of *ed altri piùe Greci*, that Dante
means Greek poets not less famous, such as Pindar

---

* Antiphon, also a tragic poet, lived first at Athens and afterwards at Syracuse at the court of the tyrant Dionysius, who had
him put to death for being too frank in his speech (see Arist.
Rhet. II, 76). Aristotle praises him as a poet, and Plutarch
speaks particularly of him as one of the best tragic writers.
The reading *Antifone* is adopted by all the best codices, and
the first four editions, and many of the best commentators, including Benvenuto, Buti, Lana, Pietro, Dante, Witte, &c. ; but
others read *Anacreone*, the lyric poet. Scartazzini points out
the improbability of Dante, a grave, serious poet, making
mention of one who was all softness and effeminacy, and placing
him among the greatest representatives of the drama, and the
epic and lyric poets. Especially does this argument gain force
when one notices that Dante neither mentions Catullus nor
Propertius, nor Tibullus, nor Ovid, with whose names he would
be far more familiar than with that of Anacreon. Moreover, it
would not be in the least probable, that amanuenses would
change the well-known name of Anacreon into the much less
known name of Antiphon, but an amanuensis, who had never
heard of Antiphon, might quite well be supposed to yield to the
temptation of altering the word into Anacreon.

† Simonides was a distinguished Greek lyric poet, born B.C.
559. He was brought to Athens by Hipparchus. He beat
Æschylus in a competition for a prize offered by the Athenians
for the best elegy upon the warriors who fell at Marathon. He
also wrote celebrated compositions upon Thermopylæ, Arte-
misium, Salamis and Platea. He died at Syracuse B.C. 469.

‡ Agathon was a Greek tragic poet, a disciple of Socrates,
born at Athens, B.C. 448, and died about 401.

the Theban, Sophocles, Æschylus, Alcæus, all tragic poets, Aristophanes, Philemon, and many others, from all of whom Virgil took many ideas.

And having now spoken of certain Greek poets, he goes on to mention some Greek women well known to Statius.

> Quivi si veggion, delle genti tue
>   Antigone,* Deifile, ed Argia,   110
>   Ed Ismene sì trista come fue.
> Vedesi quella che mostrò Langia ;
>   Evvi la figlia di Tiresia e Teti,
>   E con le suore sue Deïdamia.

There are to be seen of thy personages, Antigone, Deiphile and Argia, and Ismene still sad as ever. There is seen she (Hypsipyle) who showed (the way to the river) Langia ; there is (Daphne) the daughter of Tiresias, and Thetis, and Deidamia with her sisters.

Scartazzini points out what a difficulty it has been to many commentators the apparent contradiction of Dante making Virgil say that the daughter of Tiresias is *quivi*, which is usually understood to mean in

---

* *Antigone* was daughter of Œdipus and Jocasta, and sister of Eteocles, Polynices and Ismene.

Ismene, her sister, is here represented as still mourning for the death of her betrothed.

Deipyle wife of Tydeus, and daughter of Adrastus, King of the Argives.

Argia, her sister, wife of Polynices.

Hypsipyle, who conducted Adrastus to the river Langia, when his soldiers were perishing with thirst on their march through Bœotia to Thebes.

Thetis, the mother of Achilles.

Deidamia, beloved by Achilles, one of the daughters of Deidamia, King of Scyros.

the *primo cinghio* of Hell, which is Limbo, whereas
the only daughter of Tiresias, mentioned by Dante, is
Manto (who is also introduced in the *Thebaid*), and
her Dante has placed in Hell among the soothsayers
in the fourth pit of the Malebolge.   It has generally
been taken for granted that this was a slip made by
Dante, and that he had taken a nap (*dormitat*).   But
Scartazzini asks, Is it so? was he asleep or awake?
He suggests a way of interpretation which would solve
the difficulty, and that is by referring *quivi* (verse 109),
vedesi (112) and *evvi* (113), not to Limbo (*il primo
cinghio*), but to Hell (*carcere cieco*).   According to
which interpretation, Virgil would say that all the
personages named by him, and by Statius introduced
into the *Thebaid*, are in Hell, leaving it uncertain in
what circle (*in qual vico*) their fate is laid, and the
contradiction disappears.   Scartazzini adds: " I do
not say that one *must*, but only that one *might* understand it so."

———

Division IV.   Benvenuto says that the Fourth and
concluding Division of this noble Canto is not less
curious and copious than the other three.   In it the
poets are made to reach the sixth cornice, in which
gluttony is punished.

> Tacevansi ambedue già li poeti,   115
>   Di nuovo attenti a riguardare intorno,
>   Liberi dal salire e da' pareti ;

Both the poets had now become silent ; being free
from the ascent and the walls, their attention was
awakened anew to look around.

Dante means that they had emerged from the stairway on to the sixth cornice.   He then, according to
custom, tells us what time it was.

> E già le quattro ancelle eran del giorno
>   Rimase addietro, e la quinta era al temo,
>   Drizzando pure in sù l' ardente corno :*   120

And by this time four of the handmaidens (hours)
of the day were left behind, and the fifth was at the
pole of the car [Benvenuto says, at the tiller], still
directing upwards its blazing point.

Dante now describes how, by the advice of Virgil,
and the assent of Statius, they turned as usual to the
right on emerging from the stairway.

> Quando il mio duca :—" Io credo ch' allo estremo
>   Le destre spalle volger ci convegna,
>   Girando il monte come far solemo."—†

---

* *l' ardente corno.*   Scartazzini quotes from Antonelli on this
passage: "Arrived at the summit of the stairway which led
into the sixth cornice we are informed what the time was, which
would be one hour before noon.   Dante had already, in Canto
XII, made us understand that the handmaidens of the day
were the hours, and allowing the hypothesis to be correct that
the sun rose at 6.30, if four of the handmaidens had remained
behind, and the fifth was at the pole, directing her blazing point
upwards (that is, not yet having reached the half of her course)
. . . . it follows that four and a half hours since sunrise were
nearly accomplished, and therefore it was not far from being
eleven o'clock."

The fifth hour is called *ardente*, because it was the nearest to
midday.

Compare *Purg.* XII, 79-81 :

> "Vedi colà un Angel che s' appresta
>   Per venir verso noi : vedi che torna
>   Dal servigio del dì l' ancella sesta."

† Compare *Purg.* XIX, 81 :

> "Le vostre destre sien sempre di furi."

R R

When my Leader: " I think we shall have to
turn our right shoulders to the outer edge, encircling
the mountain as we are wont to do."

By turning their right shoulders to the outer edge
of the mountain, they would of course turn to the right.
In the present cornice they do so without asking their
way, as previously.

> Così l' usanza fu lì nostra insegna,
>> E prendemmo la via con men sospetto   125
>> Per l' assentir di quell' anima degna.

Thus here custom was our guide, and we took the
way with less doubt, from having the assent of that
noble soul.*

Dante next tells us in what order they walked.

> Elli givan dinanzi, ed io soletto
>> Diretro, ed ascoltava i lor sermoni†
>> Ch' a poetar mi davano intelletto.

They (Virgil and Statius) walked on in front, and I
by myself after them ; and I listened to their discourse, which gave me inspiration for poesy.

Benvenuto says that Dante, having studied Virgil
and Statius constantly, and learned a great deal from

In Hell, on entering a circle, they had always turned to the
left.   See *Inf.* X, 133 :

"Appresso volse a man sinistra il piede."

* Statius having been liberated from further penance in Purgatory, was duly qualified to ascend to Heaven, and might
therefore be supposed to be guided by divine inspiration in his
way upwards.

† Compare *Ps.* CXIX, 130: " The entrance of thy words
giveth light ; it giveth understanding unto the simple," which,
in the *Vulgate*, is : " Declaratio sermonum tuorum illuminat :
et intellectum dat parvulis."

both of them, takes this opportunity of expressing his gratitude.

Dante next gives a detailed description of the punishment of the gluttonous in this cornice.

> Ma tosto ruppe le dolci ragioni   130
> Un arbor che trovammo in mezza strada,
> Con pomi ad odorar soavi e buoni.

But soon was the pleasant converse interrupted by (the sight of) a tree that we found midway in the path, with apples sweet and grateful to the smell.

Benvenuto admires the comparison in which Dante describes the shape of the tree.

> E come abete in alto si digrada
> Di ramo in ramo, così quello in giuso,
> Cred' io perchè persona su non vada.   135

And like as a fir tree tapers upwards from branch to branch, so did this tree (taper) downwards, I think in order that no one might climb up it.*

Dante having described the forbidden fruit, next mentions how the spirits had before their eyes a refreshing drink, but beyond their reach.

---

* Lubin is amused at the idea of the branches being too weak to support the weight of spirits.

Benvenuto explains the tree in a natural way, namely, that the foliage was abundant at the top, but that the branches diminished in the lower parts so as to offer no opportunity of access. But many of the old commentators, such as Lana, Landino, Petr. Dante, Vellutello, and others, actually believed that the tree was upside down with its roots in the air ! and the commentaries of Landino and Vellutello each contain an engraving so representing it. The illustration by Doré in the edition of Camerini shows an ordinary forest tree, of which the upper branches spread out widely, but are fewer as the tree tapers downwards.

Dal lato, onde il cammin nostro era chiuso,
Cadea dell' alta roccia un liquor chiaro,
E si spandeva per le foglie suso.

From the side, on which our path was closed, a
limpid water fell from the high cliff, and was thence
distributed all over the foliage.

In order to show in what way gluttony is to be
avoided, Dante then tells us how they heard a voice
proceeding from the tree, forbidding them to eat of
the fruit.

Li duo poeti all' arbor s' appressaro ;
Ed una voce per entro le fronde   140
Gridò :—" Di questo cibo avrete caro."—*

The two poets drew near to the tree, and a voice
from the midst of the leaves cried out : " Of this food
you will have scarcity."

Benvenuto says that the superabundance of food
which these spirits had formerly enjoyed, is now to be
atoned for by starvation. Gluttony is ever solicitous
to revive the sated appetite, that it may soften the
palate, dilate the stomach, and make the body the
abode of diseases and the receptacle of filth.

The voice in the tree continues, commending moderation as the contrast to gluttony and insobriety.

Poi disse :—" Più pensava Maria,† onde
Fosser le nozze orrevoli ed intere,
Ch' alla sua bocca, ch' or per voi risponde.

Then it said : " Mary thought more how to make

---

* *Caro.*   Blanc (*Vocabulario Dantesco*) says the word is used
for *carestia.*

† Compare *Purg.* XIII, 28-30 :

" La prima voce che passò volando,
Vinum non habent, altamente disse,
E dietro a noi l' andò reïterando."

the marriage festivities honourable and complete, than upon her own mouth, which answers now for you (that is to say, from her mouth proceed prayers to God on your behalf).

Benvenuto remarks that here, for fear that some might object that the Blessed Virgin being full of the Holy Spirit, her example would not apply to women with ordinary feelings and appetites, an instance is given, not of one, but of many abstemious women in heathen times. For the Roman ladies, as Valerius [*Factorum Dictorumque memorabil. lib.* II, c. 1, § 5] relates, used not to drink wine, lest they might be led into any breach of good manners. But in later days, in the time of the Emperors, things were changed, and Seneca complains that women now do not drink less than men, and also incite men to drink ; and that formerly baldness and gout were not prevalent among the Roman ladies, as is now the case. And therefore the voice from the tree spoke these words in addition.

> E le Romane antiche,* per lor bere 145
>   Contente furon d' acqua ; e Daniello†
>   Dispregiò cibo, ed acquistò savere.

---

* Compare St. Thomas Aquinas (*Summ. Theol.* p. II, 2^{æ} qu. CXLIX, art. 4) : "Sobrietas maxime requiritur in juvenibus et mulieribus, quia in juvenibus viget concupiscentia delectabilis propter fervorem ætatis ; in mulieribus autem non est sufficiens robur mentis ad hoc quod concupiscentiis resistant. Unde secundum Valerium Maximum mulieres apud Romanos antiquitûs non bibebant vinum."

† See *Daniel* I, 8 : "But Daniel purposed in his heart that he would not defile himself with the portion of the King's meat, nor with the wine which he drank : therefore he requested of the prince of the eunuchs that he might not defile himself." . . . v. 11. "Then said Daniel to Melzar, whom the prince of the

And the Roman women of old time for their drink were satisfied with water ; and Daniel despised food, and acquired wisdom.

Benvenuto says : " Would that the Florentine ladies nowadays were satisfied with one kind of wine ! " Daniel was an example of rigorous abstinence in the midst of the luxuries of the Chaldees.

The voice then alludes to the Golden Age which the ancients believed to have been while Saturn reigned over Crete ; when men lived soberly, without war, and without any artificially prepared food.

> Lo secol primo, quant' oro fu bello ;*
> Fe' savorose con fame le ghiande,
> E néttare con sete ogni ruscello.   150

---

eunuchs had set over Daniel, Hananiah, Mishael, and Azariah, Prove thy servants, I beseech thee, ten days ; and let them give us pulse to eat, and water to drink." . . . v. 17. " As for these four children, God gave them knowledge and skill in all learning and wisdom : and Daniel had understanding in all visions and dreams." . . . v. 20. " And in all matters of wisdom and understanding, that the King enquired of them, he found them ten times better than all the magicians and astrologers that were in all his realm."

  * Compare *Purg.* XXVIII, 139-144 :
> " Quelli che anticamente poetaro
>   L' età dell' oro e suo stato felice,
>   Forse in Parnaso esto loco sognaro.
> Qui fu innocente l' umana radice ;
>   Qui primavera sempre, e ogni frutto ;
>   Nettare è questo di che ciascun dice."

And Ovid, *Met.* I, 89-91 :
> " The golden age was first ; when man yet new,
>   No rule but uncorrupted reason knew,
>   And with a native bent, did good pursue."

being allowed to gain all the information he sought, as
to the cause of the earthquake, and the outburst of
song from the whole of the spirits in Purgatory. He
begins by showing that his thirst for knowledge was
only capable of being quenched by that water of Life,
of which our Lord told the Samaritan woman by
Jacob's Well.*

> La sete natural† che mai non sazia,
>> Se non con l' acqua onde la femminetta
>> Sammaritana dimandò la grazia,
> Mi travagliava,‡ e pungeami la fretta
>> Per la impacciata via dietro al mio duca,   5
>> E condoleami alla giusta vendetta.

The natural thirst (for knowledge), which never is

---

* *St. John* IV, 14, 15 : "Whosoever drinketh of the water that
I shall give him shall never thirst. ; . . . The woman saith unto
him, Sir, give me this water, that I thirst not, neither come hither
to draw."

Compare *Par.* XXX, 73 :

> "Ma di quést' acqua convien che tu bei,
> Prima che tanta sete in te si sazii."

† *La sete natural.* Compare *Convito* I, 1 : "Siccome dice il
Filosofo, nel principio della prima filosofi : tutti gli uomini
naturalmente desiderano di sapere. La ragione di che puote
essere, che ciascuna cosa, da provvidenza di propria natura
impinta, è inclinabile alla sua perfezione ; onde, acciocchè la
scienza è l' ultima perfezione della nostra anima, nella quale sta
la nostra ultima felicità, tutti naturalmente al suo desiderio
siamo suggetti."

‡ *Mi travagliava.* Compare St. Thomas Aquinas, *Summ.
Theol.* p. I, 2ᵃᵉ qu. III, art. 8 : "Homo non est perfecte beatus
quamdiu restat ei aliquid desiderandum et quærendum. . . . In
tantum procedit perfectio intellectus, in quantum cognoscit
essentiam alicujus rei. Si ergo intellectus aliquis cognoscat
essentiam alicujus effectus, per quam non possit cognosci
essentia causæ, ut scilicet sciatur de causa quid est, non
dicitur intellectus attingere ad causam simpliciter : quamvis

satisfied, except with that water for which the Samaritan woman requested the grace, was working upon me, and the speed at which I had to walk behind my leader over the pathway encumbered (with the reclining forms of the avaricious), was sorely trying me ; and I wept for pity for (those who were experiencing) the just vengeance (of God).

Benvenuto observes that in truth the penalty of these shades was a very bitter one, deprived as they were of the greatest benefits ; of light, for they could only see the earth, and of freedom in all their limbs. And Dante had three causes of trouble, first, his eager desire for knowledge ; secondly, the pace at which they were walking ; and, thirdly, compassion for the sufferers.

Dante now describes the sudden appearance of Statius. Benvenuto says : " Many wonder that the intensely Christian (*christianissimus*) Dante should

---

per effectum cognoscere possit de causa an sit. Et ideo remanet naturaliter homini desiderium, cum cognoscit effectum, et scit eum habere causam, ut etiam sciat de causa quid est : et illud desiderium est admirationis, et causat inquisitionem, puta si aliquis cognoscens eclipsim solis considerat quod ex aliqua causa procedit, de qua, quia nescit quid sit, admiratur, et admirando inquirit ; ex ista inquisitio quiescit, quousque perveniat ad cognoscendum essentiam causæ. Si igitur intellectus humanus cognoscens essentiam alicujus effectus creati non cognoscat de Deo nisi an est, nondum perfectio ejus attingit simpliciter ad causam primam, sed remanet ei adhuc naturale desiderium inquirendi causam ; unde nondum est perfecte beatus. Ad perfectam igitur beatitudinem requiritur quod intellectus pertingat ad ipsam essentiam primæ causæ. Et sic perfectionem suam habebit per unionem ad Deum sicut ad objectum, in quo solo beatitudo hominis consistit."

> Mele e locuste furon le vivande,
>> Che nudriro il Batista* nel diserto ;
>> Perch' egli è glorioso, e tanto grande
>> Quanto per l' Evangelio v' è aperto."—   154

The primal age was beautiful as gold ; it seasoned its acorns with hunger, and made every stream into nectar with thirst.   Honey and locusts were the nourishment that fed the Baptist in the wilderness ; and that is why he is so glorious and great, as is by the Gospel revealed unto you."

And v. 101-106 :
> " The teeming earth yet guiltless of the plough,
> And unprovoked, did fruitful stores allow :
> Content with food which nature freely bred.
> On wildings and on strawberries they fed ;
> Cornels and bramble-berries gave the rest,
> And falling acorns furnished forth a feast."

And Boœthius, *Consol. Philos.* II, *Metr.* V :
> " Felix nimium prior ætas,
>> Contenta fidelibus arvis,
>> Nec inerti perdita luxu ;
>> Facili quæ sera solebat
>> Jejunia solvere glande :
>> Nec Bacchica munera norat
>> Liquido fundere melle,
>> Nec lucida vellera serum
>> Tyrio miscere veneno."

† It should be remembered that the Baptist is the patron saint of Florence.

Compare *Inf.* XIII, 143 :
> " Io fui della città che nel Batista
>> Mutò il primo patrone."

END OF CANTO XXII.

CANTO XXIII.

THE SIXTH CORNICE (*continued.*)
PURGATION OF GLUTTONY.
FORESE DONATI.
THE WOMEN OF FLORENCE.

DANTE having, at the latter end of the previous
Canto, described the penance and purgation of the
gluttonous in general, in the present one treats the
same subject more in particular.

Benvenuto says that this Canto can be divided into
four parts, at the least.

In the First Division, from v. 1 to v. 36, Dante
gives an account of the spirits that are being purged
for gluttony.

In the Second Division, from v. 37 to v. 75, he
introduces the spirit of Forese Donati, well known in
life as gluttonous, and from him he gets an explanation of the punishment inflicted in this Cornice, which,
in the last Canto, was left somewhat obscure.

In the Third Division, from v. 76 to v. 111, Dante
asks Forese a certain question.

In the Fourth Division, from v. 112 to v. 133,
Dante informs Forese who he is, and who are his
guides.

Division I. Before beginning his description of
the chastisement of gluttony, Dante first tells us that
he is mildly reproved by Virgil for having been led,

from curiosity, to peer through the branches of the tree, in hopes of seeing from whom proceeded the mysterious voice.

> Mentre che gli occhi per la fronda verde
>   Ficcava io così, come far suole
>   Chi dietro all' uccellin sua vita perde,
> Lo più che padre mi dicea :—" Figliuole *
>   Vienne oramai ; chè il tempo che c' è imposto   5
>   Più utilmente compartir si vuole."—

While I was rivetting my eyes among the green leaves, as one is wont to do who wastes his time in looking after a little bird, he who was more than a father (Virgil) said to me : " My son, come on now, for the time that is allotted to us must be more usefully apportioned."†

Scartazzini observes that the word *perde* denotes censure, and shows the severe character of Dante's mind, to which bird-catching was a waste of time. Buti says that the life of a bird-catcher is of no purpose except for gluttony, and therefore Dante deservedly censures it. On hearing this admonition Dante leaves the tree, and joins Virgil and Statius.

> Io volsi il viso e il passo non men tosto
>   Appresso ai savi, che parlavan sìe,
>   Che l' andar mi facean di nullo costo.‡

---

* *Figliuole* is the Italianized form of *filiole*, the vocative case of *filiolus*. The literal sense here would be : " O my little son." We also find *scolare* for *scolaro; pensiere* for *pensiero*, &c.

† Compare Shakespeare (*As You Like It*, act II, sc. 7) :
>   " Under the shade of melancholy boughs
>   Lose and neglect the creeping hours of time."

† Lombardi quotes from the fragments of Publius Sirus (*De amicitia et concordia*) : " Comes facundus in via pro vehiculo est."

I turned my eyes and my steps not less quickly towards the Sages, who discoursed so well that they made my progress to be without fatigue.

As Dante approached this cornice he heard voices.

> Ed ecco piangere e cantar s' udìe :   10
> *Labia mea, Domine,** per modo †
> Tal che diletto e doglia parturìe.

And lo ! a lament and a chant were heard : "*Labia mea, Domine*," sung in such a fashion as gave birth both to joy and sorrow.

Delight at hearing such devotion, and grief out of compassion for those spirits suffering from hunger and thirst. The mouths that in life had ever been agape to eat and drink to excess, were only opened now to sing the praises of God, and penitential litanies for forgiveness.

Dante, according to his wont, asks Virgil for information.

> —"O dolce padre, che è quel ch' i' odo ?"—
> Comincia' io.   Ed egli :—"Ombre che vanno,
> Forse di lor dover solvendo il nodo."—‡   15

---

* *Psalm* LI, 15, "O Lord, open thou my lips ; and my mouth shall shew forth thy praise." This Psalm forms part of the service of Lauds for Tuesday, the day the present scene was supposed to be taking place.

† Compare *Purg.* VIII, 13-15 :
> " *Te lucis ante* sì devotamente
>   Le uscì di bocca, e con sì dolci note,
>   Che fece me a me uscir di mente."

‡ *solvendo il nodo.*   Compare *Purg.* XVI, 22-24 :
> —" Quei son spirti, maestro, ch' i' odo ?"—
>   Diss' io.   Ed egli a me :—" Tu vero apprendi ;
>   E d' iracondia van solvendo il nodo."—

" O gentle Father," I began : " What is that which I
hear ? " And he : " These are shades that go, perchance to unloose the knot of their debt." That is to
say, to perform the due expiation of their sins, tormented by the pangs of hunger and thirst.

Dante now relates how the spirits passed them.

> Sì come i peregrin pensosi fanno,
>> Giugnendo per cammin gente non nota,
>> Che si volgono ad essa e non ristanno ;
> Così diretro a noi, più tosto mota,
>> Venendo e trapassando, ci ammirava   20
>> D' anime turba tacita* e devota.

As pilgrims, who, rapt in thought, overtake on their
way people unknown, do turn round to them but
stay not ; even so a crowd of spirits, silent and
devout, came behind us at a more rapid pace (than
we), and passing by, gazed upon us with attention.

Benvenuto points out that the actions and demeanour of the shades of the gluttonous exactly
correspond with those of the pilgrims in his time,
who, if they passed other pilgrims whom they did
not know, would just glance back at them, but
would not interrupt their meditations by addressing
them.

Dante now describes the peculiar appearance of
the spirits.

---

* *Tacita.* It has been observed by Vellutello, but by no
commentator before him, that this word implies a contradiction
of v. 10, in which it says that the spirits were lamenting and
singing. But Lombardi justly points out that Dante never said
that they wept and sang unceasingly, but only when in their
circuit they approached the mysterious trees. But the Poets had
already passed the first tree, but not so far but what they could
hear the utterances of the spirits near it.

> Negli occhi era ciascuna oscura e cava,
>   Pallida nella faccia, e tanto scema,
>   Che dall' ossa la pelle s' informava.

Each in the eyes was dark and cavernous, pallid in the face, and so emaciated, that the skin took its outline from the bones.

Benvenuto says that Dante, by a very appropriate comparison, relates their extreme emaciation.

> Non credo che così a buccia estrema   25
>   Eresitone* fosse fatto secco,
>   Per digiunar, quando più n' ebbe tema.

I do not believe that Erysichthon, from starvation,

---

* Erysichthon ('Ερυσίκθων) was supposed to be the son of Triopas, King of Thessaly. Out of derision of Ceres, he cut down an oak in a forest sacred to the goddess. She punished him by perpetual hunger, and he at last gnawed his own flesh.

> " Straight he requires, impatient in demand,
>   Provisions from the air, the seas, the land ;
>   But though the land, air, seas, provisions grant,
>   Starves at full tables, and complains of want.
>   What to a people might in dole be paid,
>   Or victual cities for a long blockade,
>   Could not one wolfish appetite assuage ;
>   For glutting nourishment increased its rage.
>   As rivers poured from every distant shore
>   The sea insatiate drinks, and thirsts for more ;
>   Or as the fire, which all materials burns,
>   And wasted forests into ashes turns,
>   Grows more voracious as the more it preys,
>   Recruits dilate the flame, and spread the blaze :
>   So impious Erysichthon's hunger raves,
>   Receives refreshments, and refreshment craves.
>   Food raises a desire for food, and meat
>   Is but a new provocative to eat.
>   He grows more empty as the more supplied,
>   And endless cramming but extends the void."
>   —Ovid, *Met.* VIII. Vernon's Translation.

could have been withered up to such an extremity of mere skin, at the time that he had the most fear of it (starvation).

Dante having cited an instance of the hunger of one person goes on to relate that of many, and takes as his example the famine at Jerusalem when besieged by Titus.

> Io dicea fra me stesso pensando :—" Ecco
> La gente che perdè Jerusalemme,
> Quando Maria* nel figlio die' di becco."— 30

Thinking within myself, I said : " Behold the people who lost Jerusalem, when Mary thrust her beak into her own son."

> Parean l' occhiaje anella† senza gemme.
> Chi nel viso degli uomini legge *omo*,
> Ben avria quivi conosciuto l' emme.

The orbits appeared like gemless rings ; whoever in the faces of men can read *o, m, o,* could here without difficulty have distinguished the *m* (for the nose and cheekbones were conspicuously prominent).

It was a popular belief in olden times that the

---

* Josephus (*De Bello Jud.* lib. VI, cap. 3), in his account of the horrors of the siege of Jerusalem, relates how a noble lady, Mary, the daughter of Eleazar, maddened with hunger, killed her own little son and cooked and ate half of his body. Some robbers, attracted by the smell of cooked flesh, burst into the house and demanded the remainder of the meat, but on seeing the limbs of the child, and hearing the mother confess herself as his murderess, they fled in horror.

† Compare Shakespeare (*King Lear*, act V, sc. 3) :
> " And in this habit
> Met I my father with his bleeding rings,
> Their precious stones new lost."

letters °M° could be traced in the human face.*   The
o's are the two eyes; the *m* is formed by the nose
and eyebrows ; and *omo* is spelt.

And Dante adds, we are told by Benvenuto, that
he could not understand from what cause this extraordinary emaciation proceeded, for he could not have
imagined that it was caused by the tree.

> Chi crederebbe che l' odor d' un pomo
>   Sì governasse, generando brama,   35
>   E quel d' un acqua : non sappiendo como ?†

Who could believe that the smell of an apple, and
the (trickling) of a spring, could have such influence,
begetting craving, if they did not know why?

———

Division II.   In this Division Dante introduces
the spirit of Forese de' Donati, brother of his wife
Gemma, and his intimate friend, though certain
vituperative sonnets addressed to Dante, and attributed to Forese, if authentic, would show that their
friendship was not uninterrupted.   The brother of
Forese, Corso de' Donati, the celebrated Guelph
leader, was Dante's bitter foe.   He was the head of

---

* Brother Bertholdt, a Franciscan monk of Ratisbon in 1275,
alludes to this fancy in one of his sermons.

† *Como*, derived from the Latin *quomodo*, like *mo*, from *modo*.
Nannucci (*Anal. Crit.* page 80, note 3) says it was of very
frequent use among old Italian writers.

the Neri, by whom Dante was driven into banishment.
According to Francesco da Buti, Forese had an un-
enviable reputation for gluttony.

Dante now tells us how Forese recognised him.

> Già era* in ammirar che sì gli affama,
>> Per la cagione ancor non manifesta
>> Di lor magrezza e di lor trista squama ;†

I was still full of wonder at what so ahungered
them, by reason of there being no evident cause for
their emaciation and their miserable desquamation.

> Ed ecco del profondo della testa‡   4c
>> Volse a me gli occhi un' ombra, e guardò fiso,
>> Poi gridò forte :—" Qual grazia m' è questa ? "—

And lo ! a shade turned towards me his eyes (so
sunk in their sockets that they seemed to come) from
the innermost recesses of his head, and looked at me
attentively ; after which he cried with a loud voice :

" What grace to me is this ? "

---

* In *Purg.* XXV, 20-21, we find Dante asking Virgil to solve
this doubt for him, which Virgil does.   He asks :
> " Come si può far magro   ·
>> Là dove l' uopo di nutrir non tocca ?"

He could not understand how impalpable spirits, who have
no need of food, could grow thin from the lack of it.   Virgil's
answer is the leading feature in Canto XXV, showing how
bodily feelings are given to souls in Hell and Purgatory in order
that they may undergo their punishment.

† Blanc (*Vocabulario Dantesco*) says that *squama* only occurs
in this passage, and means dried-up skin (*pelle inaridita*).

‡ In verse 22 we read that—
> " Negli occhi era ciascuna oscura e cava,"

and now when he speaks of one of the shades moving his eyes
from the innermost cavities of his head, he paints with terrible
emphasis the hollowness of the eyes.

Dante had some difficulty in identifying his former friend, for he adds:

> Mai non l' avrei riconosciuto al viso ;
> Ma nella voce sua mi fu palese
> Ciò che l' aspetto in sè avea conquiso.   45

Never should I have recognised him by his face ; but that, which his aspect had suppressed within it, was made manifest to me by his voice.

Benvenuto, pointing out that Dante never would have known by the face that he was looking at Forese, observes that a prolonged indulgence in gluttony so changes a man's appearance, that Domitian, who had been a beautiful youth, grew ugly, bald, and fat, and in a letter told a friend that nothing was more short lived than beauty.

Dante had only recognised Forese's voice, and therefore adds:

> Questa favilla* tutta mi raccese
> Mia conoscenza alla cambiata labbia,
> E ravvisai la faccia di Forese.

This spark rekindled my recognition of his changed face (*lit.* lip) and I recalled the features of Forese.

Forese begs Dante not to heed the wreck of his face, but to tell him who he is, and who are his companions.

> —" Deh non contendere† all' asciutta scabbia,
> Che mi scolora (pregava) la pelle,   50
> Nè a difetto di carne ch' io abbia ;

---

* Others read *favella*, the voice, but Dante has just said *voce* in verse 44 ; and *favilla* means that the voice acted like a spark.

† Scartazzini has an elaborate note on *non contendere*, the meaning of which he says the commentators find obscure in this passage. Some, including Benvenuto, read *attendere*, and others

> Ma dimmi il ver di te, e chi son quelle
> Due anime che là ti fanno scorta :
> Non rimaner che tu non mi favelle."—

"Ah do not refuse (to recognise me)," was his prayer, "because of my face dried up as with leprosy, which makes my skin so pallid, nor at the want of flesh that I have, but tell me the truth about thyself, and who are those two souls yonder who are guiding thee : do not remain longer without speaking to me."

As we shall see by Dante's reply, he had been looking fixedly at Forese's altered countenance, hardly being able to recognise the once familiar features.

> —"La faccia tua, ch' io lagrimai già morta,   55
> Mi dà di pianger mo non minor doglia,*

---

intendere, but these readings he considers to be transcribers' corrections. Some again explain *contendere* in the sense of *attendere*. "Do not give heed to, &c." But the passage is quite clear to him. *Contendere* simply means, to deny, to forbid Forese was entreating that Dante should not refuse, or be too disgusted to satisfy his demands, on account of any disdain that his deformed features might have generated. He says : Do not deny me the truth on account of my discoloured skin. Do not refuse to my appearance the fulfilment of my prayer. Witte translates : "*Versage nicht dem dürren Aussatz....... Deine Antwort.*"

Scartazzini thinks there are only two interpretations ; either to explain *contendere* as *attendere* in the sense of giving heed, or in the sense of denying, refusing.

* I have followed a different reading from that in Scartazzini's text, for although, as he says, he gives the common reading *non minor doglia* in his text, yet he would naturally from the authority of the codices have preferred *minor la doglia*, in favour of which he argues at length. The celebrated Vatican MS., and others, give the latter reading, as well as one of the Chigi codices, and the ancient commentator Jacopo della Lana certainly did so, for he interprets : " I wept for thee in the first

(Risposi lui), veggendola sì torta.*
Però mi di', per Dio, che sì vi sfoglia ;
Non mi far dir mentr' io mi maraviglio,
Chè mal può dir chi è pien d' altra voglia."—   60

"Thy face," I answered him, "makes me now weep less bitterly, than when I bewailed it dead, though seeing it as I do so changed. Tell me then, for God's sake, what so denudes you; make me not speak while I am marvelling, for ill can he speak who is full of other longing."

Benvenuto remarks it is as though he would say : I am full of the desire to make thee speak thyself to gratify my curiosity, but am really not capable of answering thy questions rationally at this moment.

Forese concisely answers Dante's question as to his emaciation.

---

life when thou didst die, but now I do not grieve for thee thus, for I see thee not among the lost, but on the way to reach life eternal." The reading *mo minor doglia* is also found in a Riccardi MS., in the *Falso Boccaccio*, and in the early Mantua edition, and comes to the same signification.

* In Hell (*Inf.* XV, 82) Dante gave way to unbounded grief at seeing his old instructor Brunetto Latini among the lost, and with a face that was scorched (*cotto*) nearly beyond recognition. But there is a great difference in the condition of a soul supposed to be in Hell, from one in Purgatory. It is the contrast between eternal damnation and sure and certain hope of salvation. Brunetto's countenance would remain scorched to all eternity, but Forese's case is quite different. When Dante wept over his dead friend he knew not what was to be his future destiny. But now seeing him in Purgatory, he has full assurance that his sufferings are but for a while, and therefore tells him that his altered features (*faccia torta*) give him less cause for bitter weeping than when he mourned for him at his death.

Benvenuto interprets *torta tantum transmutatum ab illa.*

> Ed egli a me :—" Dall' eterno consiglio
> Cade virtù nell' acqua, e nella pianta
> Rimasa a dietro, ond' io sì m' assottiglio.

And he to me : " By the Eternal Will there descends into the water, as well as into the tree that is left behind us, a power whereby I become so extenuated.

The poets had evidently walked some distance beyond the tree. L' Ottimo says that the sight of the water and of the fruit sharpened the desire of the spirits, and the desire dried up their limbs.

Forese adds that not only he but all the others are similarly punished.

> Tutta esta gente che piangendo canta,
> Per seguitar la gola oltra misura,*   65
> In fame e in sete qui si rifà santa.†

All this multitude who while they lament sing, because they followed their appetite beyond measure, in hunger and thirst here are renewing their sanctification.

Benvenuto explains that *oltra misura* implies eating more than is necessary for the support of life, accord-

---

* Compare St. Thomas Aquinas (*Summ. Theol.* p. II, 2ᵃᵉ, qu. CXLVIII, art. 1) : " Gula non nominat (*Gregorius*) quemlibet appetitum edendi et bibendi, sed inordinatum. Dicitur autem appetitus inordinatus ex eo quod recedit ab ordine rationis, in quo bonum virtutis moralis consistit. . . . . Vitium gulæ non consistit in substantia cibi, sed in concupiscentia non regulata ratione. . . . . Hoc solum pertinet ad gulam quod aliquis propter concupiscentiam cibi dilectabilis excedat mensuram in edendo."

† *si rifà santa.* Compare *Purg.* II, 75 :
> " Quasi obbliando d' ire a farsi belle."

And *Purg.* XVI, 31 :
> " O creatura che ti mondi,
> Per tornar bella a Colui che ti fece. . . ."

ing to complexion, age, place, climate, the amount of work done, the part of the world lived in ; for what might be but a small quantity for one man, might be too much for another, like Milo, who used to kill a bull with a blow of his fist, and cook and eat it all up without feeling overloaded ; "whereas," says Benvenuto, "the foot of that bull would have done for me."

Forese now tells Dante the cause of their hunger and thirst.

> Di bere e di mangiar n' accende cura
> L' odor ch' esce del pomo,* e dello sprazzo
> Che si distende su per la verdura.

The odour that issues from the fruit, and from the spray which is diffused all over the verdure, enkindles in us the desire to eat and drink.

> E non pure una volta, questo spazzo   70
> Girando, si rinfresca nostra pena ;
> Io dico *pena*, e dovrei dir *sollazzo* ;†

---

* Dante uses *pomo* as a symbol of the highest good.

In *Inf.* XVI, 61, he says to the three Florentines "Lascio lo fele, e vo per dolci pomi." And as Virgil is taking leave of Dante at the entrance into the Terrestrial Paradise (*Purg.* XXVII, 115-117) he says to him :

—" Quel dolce pome, che per tanti rami
　　Cercando va la cura dei mortali,
　　Oggi porrà in pace le tue fami."—

And in *Purg.* XXXII, 73-74, Christ Himself is called :

　　　　　. . . "il melo,
　　Che del suo pomo gli Angeli fa ghiotti."

On the smell of the water, see *Job.* XIV, 9 :

　　" Yet through the scent of water it will bud,
　　And bring forth boughs like a plant."

† *sollazzo.*   Compare St. Thomas Aquinas (*Summ. Theol.* p. III, Supplem. Append. qu. II, art 2) : "Videtur quod illa poena

And not once only, as we encircle this path, is our penalty renewed : I say penalty and I ought to say solace.

Some commentators understand the renewal of torment to come from the return to the same tree again and again.   Others think that, as the shades go round the cornice, they meet with similar trees at different intervals.

And now, by way of testifying to their complete submission to the penance imposed upon them by God, Forese adds :

> Chè quella voglia all' arbore ci mena,
> Che menò Cristo lieto a dire : *Elì*,
> Quando ne liberò con la sua vena."—   75

For that same Will leads us to the tree, as led Christ rejoicing to say, *Eli*, when He freed us with His blood." (*lit.* vein).

Division III.   In the Third Division, which we now commence, Dante asks Forese a certain question. He had been told by Belacqua (*Purg.* IV, 130) that the souls of those who delayed their repentance till

---

sit voluntaria, quia illi qui sunt in purgatorio, rectum habent cor. Sed hæc est rectitudo cordis, ut quis voluntatem suam divinæ voluntati conformet, ut Augustinus dicit, conc. I, in psal. 32 a princ.   Ergo cum Deus velit eos puniri, ipsi illam pœnam voluntarie sustinent. Præterea, omnis sapiens vult illud sine quo non potest pervenire ad finem intentum.   Sed illi qui sunt in purgatorio, sciunt se non posse pervenire ad gloriam, nisi prius puniantur.   Ergo volunt puniri."

And *Rom.* v. 3 : " And not only so, but we glory in tribulations also."

death, had to remain in the Anti-Purgatorio for a
term equal in duration to the length of their lives on
earth, and as Dante knew that his friend Forese had
only died five years before, and probably knew also
that he had delayed his repentance until the very
end of his life, he is surprised to find him already in
one of the cornices of Purgatory proper. He asks
him the reason.

> Ed io a lui :—" Forese, da quel dì
>   Nel qual mutasti mondo a miglior vita,
>   Cinqu' anni non son vôlti infino a qui.

And I to him : " Forese, from that day when thou
didst change the world for a better life, five years have
not yet elapsed.

Lombardi remarks that they who are lost change
the world for a worse life.

> Se prima fu la possa in te finita
>   Di peccar più, che sorvenisse l' ora   80
>   Del buon dolor che a Dio ne rimarita,
> Come se' tu quassù venuto ?   Ancora
>   Io ti credea trovar laggiù di sotto,
>   Dove tempo per tempo si ristora."—

If the power of sinning any more was ended in thee,
before the hour surprised thee of the goodly sorrow
(repentance) which reweds us to God ; how is it that
thou art arrived up here?   I thought to find thee
still down there below (at the Gate of Purgatory),
where time (of penance) makes restitution for time
(wasted)."

Dante evidently knew that Forese had made some
sort of repentance, or else he would not have expected
to find him even in the Anti-Purgatorio, but in Hell
with Ciacco and the other gluttons.

Forese answers Dante, telling him that the inter-

cession of his wife Nella,* and her virtuous devout
life, have been efficacious in helping him to ascend
more speedily.

> Ond' egli a me :—"Sì tosto m' ha condotto   85
> A ber lo dolce assenzio† de' martíri
> La Nella mia col suo pianger dirotto.

Whereupon he to me : " It is my Nella with her
overflowing tears, who has brought me thus speedily
to drink the sweet wormwood of these torments.

> Con suo' prieghi‡ devoti e con sospiri
> Tratto m' ha della costa ove s' aspetta,
> E liberato m' ha degli altri giri.   90
> Tant' è a Dio più cara, e più diletta
> La vedovella mia, che tanto amai,
> Quanto in bene operare è più soletta ; ‖

---

* *La Nella* is the Florentine contraction of Giovanna,
Giovanella. It is a custom at Florence to attach the definite
article to the names of women—La Nella, L'Assunta, La Carla,
La Concetta.

It seems that Nella did all in her power to check Forese in
his excessive gluttony, and though she had to prepare the dishes
likely to tickle his fastidious palate, she never herself gave way
to excess, and after his death gave herself up to prayers for the
peace of his soul, and as we know from Canto IV, 134, that that
intercession would be listened to in heaven,

> " Che surga su di cor che in grazia viva,"

we may infer that, from her prayers having been heard, she was
known by Dante as a saintly woman.

† *assenzio*, from the Latin *absinthium*, wormwood. It is here
supposed to be bitter to the taste, but sweet to the intellect.
Likewise the torments of Purgatory are supposed to be bitter to
endure, but sweet to the soul, as they prepare it to enter into
life eternal.

‡ Compare *Rom.* VIII, 26 : " For we know not what we
should pray for as we ought : but the spirit itself maketh intercession for us with groanings which cannot be uttered."

‖ *soletta.* Scartazzini remarks that this word is the diminu-

By her pious orisons and by sighs, she has withdrawn me from the hill-side where one tarries (*i.e.,* Anti-Purgatorio), and has set me free from the other circles (*i.e.,* of pride, envy, &c.).   So much the more pleasing to God, the more beloved, is my widow, whom I tenderly loved, in proportion as she is the more single in good deeds.

Forese now draws an unpleasing picture of the dress and demeanour of the women of Florence, comparing that city to the district of Barbagia, in the Island of Sardinia, where the women had an evil reputation, both for the immodesty of their attire, and for their licentious morals.

> Chè la Barbagia* di Sardigna assai
>   Nelle femmine sue è più pudica,   95
>   Che la Barbagia dov' io la lasciai.

---

tive of *sola,* and is used with a certain tenderness to express the solitude of a beloved and modest woman.   Some have tried to make out that Dante, by saying that *Nella* was *soletta* in *bene operare* just before attacking the women of Florence, meant to cast a reproach on his own wife Gemma.   But it is not at all certain that Gemma was not already dead at the time these lines were written.

* *Barbagia* was a mountainous region of Sardinia, and took its name from the ancient Barbaricini, celebrated in the history of the Island for their idolatry and independent ways.   It lies in the heart of the principal chain of mountains, and is divided into Barbagia Superiore, Barbagia Centrale, and Barbagia Inferiore.   The Barbaricini are said to have been landed in Sardinia by the Vandals, and forthwith they took possession of the neighbouring mountains, and lived by robbery and plunder. St. Gregory (*Ep.* III, 26) says of them : *omnes ut insensata animalia vivunt.*   The Codice Cassinese says that in the Barbagia *mulieres vadunt seminude.*   Petr. Dante makes them worse : *ubi vadunt nudæ mulieres.*   The Codice Caetani : " In insula Sardinia est montana alta, quæ dicitur La Barbagia ; et

For the Barbagia of Sardinia is by far more modest in its women than the Barbagia where I left her.

He means that Florence was a second Barbagia. Then Forese tells Dante that he foresees a day of retribution on the Florentine women, when laws will have to be made to check the immodesty of their dress.

> O dolce frate, che vuoi tu ch' io dica ?
> Tempo futuro m' è già nel cospetto,
> Cui non sarà quest' ora molto antica,
> Nel qual sarà in pergamo* interdetto   100
> Alle sfacciate donne fiorentine
> L' andar mostrando con le poppe il petto.

---

quando Januenses (the Genoese) retraxerunt dictam insulam de manibus Infidelium, nunquam potuerunt retrahere dictam montanam, in qua habitat gens barbara et sine civilitate, e: fœminæ suæ vadunt indutæ subtili *pirgolato*, ita quod omnia membra ostendunt inhoneste ; nam est ibi magnus calor."

Benvenuto confirms this statement : "Nam pro calore et prava consuetudine vadunt indutæ panno lineo albo, excollatæ ita, ut ostendant pectus et ubera." It is said that even at the present day the costume of these women is somewhat scanty, but that although they are " sans peur," they are also " sans reproche."

* *pergamo*, a pulpit, is not to be confused, as some commentators have done, with *pergamena*, parchment. *Pulpito* is a desk, not pulpit. The words *in pergamo interdetto* may either mean the sermons that were preached against the gross immodesty of the women's dress, or better perhaps, the episcopal decrees, and canonical penalties which were proclaimed from the pulpit against such disgraceful habits. Scartazzini says that it is evident from verses 103-5 that Dante uses *interdetto* in the latter sense. Sacchetti (*Novelle*, 115 *and* 178) speaks at length on this subject. See also Napier, *Florentine History*, vol. II, p. 538.

O gentle brother, what wouldst thou have me say ?
A future time is already in my view, to which the
present hour will not be very old, when from the pulpit it shall be interdicted to the unblushing Florentine dames to go about displaying the breast with the
paps.

> Quai Barbare fur mai, quai Saracine,
>   Cui bisognasse, per farle ir coverte,
>   O spiritali o altre discipline ? *   105

What women of Barbary, what Saracens ever lived,
for whom either spiritual or other discipline was needed
to enforce their going about covered ?

---

* G. Villani (*Lib.* IX, c. 245) relates that in April, 1324,
"arbitri furono fatti in Firenze, i quali feciono molti capitoli e
forti ordini contra i disordinati ornamenti delle donne di Firenze."
He further relates (*Lib.* X, c. 11) that in December, 1326, Carlo,
Duke of Calabria, "a priego che le donne di Firenze aveano
fatto alla duchessa sua moglie, si rendè alle dette donne uno
loro spiacevole e disonesto ornamento di trecce grosse di seta
bianca e gialla, le quali portavano in luogo di trecce di capelli
dinanzi al viso, lo quale ornamento perchè spiacea ai Fiorentini,
perchè era disonesto e trasnaturato, aveano tolto alle donne, e
fatti capitoli contro a ciò e altri disordinati ornamenti."
Benvenuto speaks of this matter at great length, and thinks
the poet has most deservedly uttered his reproach against these
women.   No artificers in the world possess such varied ma-
chinery, divers instruments, or subtle contrivances for the
exercise of their handicraft, as the women of Florence for the
decoration of their persons.   For not content with natural
beauty, they ever strive to add to it, and are always arming
themselves against all defects with incredible art and sagacity.
They assist shortness of stature with a high patten (*cum planula
alta*); they whiten a dark skin ; they rouge a pallid face ; they
make their hair yellow, and their teeth like ivory; "Mamillas
breves et duras : et ut breviter dicam omnia membra artificiose
componunt."

In the middle ages all unbaptised persons except Jews were called Saracens.

Dante now puts into the mouth of Forese a prediction of the disasters that actually took place in Florence between 1300 and 1316.

> Ma se le svergognate fosser certe
>> Di quel che il ciel veloce loro ammanna,
>> Già per urlare avrian le bocche aperte.
> Chè se l' antiveder qui non m' inganna,
>> Prima fien triste, che le guance impeli   110
>> Colui che mo si consola con nanna.*

But if the shameless creatures only knew for certain of what swift Heaven has in store for them, they would already have their mouths wide open to howl. For, if my foresight here does not deceive me, they will become sad before that he who now is hushed with lullabies (*i.e.*, the infant) shall have put forth beard upon his cheeks.

Benvenuto says on this passage: "And note here, reader, that I have heard some say rashly, that this prognostication is a discredit to Dante (vituperium poetæ) since such a long time had elapsed, without those things taking place, which he seems to foretell as happening in so brief a space of time.   To which I reply, that the author speaks here of things that are past, and accomplished facts, and not merely of events about to take place.   But he appears to prophesy, because he looks at the supposed time of his vision,

---

*Jacopo della Lana comments : " He wishes here to mark the time that will elapse before such vengeance can take place ; and says that before the male child that is still in the cradle, and who is hushed to sleep with the (Italian nurse's lullaby) *Ninna Nanna*, shall have put forth a beard, this vengeance will have come to pass—*i.e.*, within the space of 20 years."

which was in MCCC., as has already been so often
said.   For great misfortunes did follow after that date,
such as intestine discords, civil wars, and the expulsion
of the factions, which things took place in the second
and third year following ; and in the fourth year the
Bianchi and Neri came again to arms against each
other.   And while the fury of war was raging, a fire
broke out, whether kindled by accident, or, as many
have said, the intentional work of a certain priest, Neri
degli Abati, who first set it going in his own house :
and in a short time the greater part of the city was
burned, more than two thousand houses being destroyed, with a damage beyond all estimation.   Nor
did they meanwhile cease from strife, but all the time
great pillage went on.   And in the fifteenth year
(1315) they (the Florentines) suffered a terrible
slaughter at Monte Catini at the hands of Uguccione
della Faggiuola."*

---

* Scartazzini says that Dante here alludes in the form of a
prophecy to all the calamities that befel Florence immediately
after the entry of Charles de Valois in November, 1302 (G.
Villani, *Lib.* VIII, *c.* 49) ; and in the following year the
massacres of which Fulcieri da Calboli was the author (G.
Villani, *Lib.* VIII, *c.* 59.)   See also Vol. I, p. 361, of this work,
on *Canto* XIV, 58-66.

> " Io veggio tuo nipote, che diventa
> >   Cacciator di quei lupi, in su la riva
> >   Del fiero fiume, e tutti gli sgomenta.
> Vende la carne loro, essendo viva ;
> >   Poscia gli ancide come antica belva :
> >   Molti di vita, e sè di pregiopriva.
> Sanguinoso esce della trista selva ;
> >   Lasciala tal, che di qui a mill' anni
> >   Nello stato primaio non si rinselva."

In this same year a great famine took place ; in the following

Division IV. In this concluding division of the
Canto Dante informs Forese how it happens that he,
being alive, has entered Purgatory, and tells him who
are the spirits with him.

Forese concludes his speech by asking Dante :

> Deh, frate, or fa che più non mi ti celi ;
>   Vedi che non pur io, ma questa gente
>   Tutta rimira là dove il sol veli."—*

O brother, now see that thou dost not any longer
conceal thyself from me ; see that not I alone, but all
this folk are gazing at that spot from which thou art
screening the sun."

Dante reminds Forese that during the time of their
friendship on earth, neither of them can have pleasing
recollections of their past sins.

> Perch' io a lui : —" Se ti riduci a mente   115
>   Qual fosti meco, e quale io teco fui,
>   Ancor fia grave il memorar presente.

Whereupon I to him : " If thou recall to thy mind
what thou wast in my company, and what I was in
thine, the present memory of it will be grievous still.

---

year the city was excommunicated by Cardinal da Prato (G.
Villani. *Lib.* VIII, *c.* 67), and the Ponte alla Carraja fell caus-
ing the death of a vast number of persons *con grande pianto
e dolore a tutta la cittade.* Villani says over and over again that
these misfortunes were sent as a punishment for the wickedness
of the citizens.

* *dove il sol veli.* Compare *Canto* III, 88-93.

> " Come color dinanzi vider rotta
>   La luce in terra dal mio destro canto,
>   Sì che l' ombra era da me alla grotta,
> Restâro, e trasser sè indietro alquanto,
>   E tutti gli altri che venieno appresso,
>   Non sapendo il perchè fenno altrettanto."

He then answers Forese's question :

> Di quella vita mi volse costui
>   Che mi va innanzi, l'altr' ier',* quando tonda†
>   Vi si mostrò la suora‡ di colui ;   120
> (E il sol mostrai).   Costui per la profonda
>   Notte menato m' ha da' veri morti,
>   Con questa vera carne§ che il seconda.‖

From that life he who goes in front of me (Virgil)
turned me the other day, when the sister (the moon)
of him up there, "and I pointed to the sun," showed
herself to you at the full.   He has guided me through
the profound darkness of those dead indeed (*i.e.* through
Hell) with this real flesh (*i.e.* my body) which is following him.

Having told how Virgil had led him down to Hell,
he next describes how he had conducted him up to
Purgatory.

> Indi m' han tratto su li suoi conforti,
>   Salendo e rigirando la montagna   125
>   Che drizza voi che il mondo fece torti.

From thence (Hell) his assistance has led me upwards,

---

* *l'altr' ier'.* L' altro ieri is properly speaking, "the day before
yesterday"; but all the commentators interpret it here, "the
other day," "a few days ago."

† Dante and Virgil had commenced their journey at the full
moon before Easter, 1300.

‡ *suora.* The ancients thought that the sun (Apollo) and the
moon (Diana or Luna) were the children of Jupiter and Latona.

§ *vera carne.* Compare *Purg.* II, 109, when Dante asking
Casella to sing, says to him :

> "Di ciò ti piaccia consolare alquanto
>   L' anima mia, che con la sua persona
>   Venendo qui è affannata tanto."

‖ *Che il seconda.* Compare *Inf.* IV.

ascending and encircling the mountain which makes straight(*i.e.* purges) you whom the world made crooked.

And he then speaks of the better hope he has to look to.

> Tanto dice di farmi sua compagna,
> Ch' io sarò là dove fia Beatrice ;
> Quivi convien che senza lui rimagna.

So far he says he will afford me his company until I am there beyond (these cornices), where Beatrice will be ; and there must I remain without him.

In conclusion, he tells Forese who are his two guides.

> Virgilio è questi, che così mi dice,   130
> (E additálo).   E quest' altro è quell' ombra
> Per cui scosse dïanzi ogni pendice
> Lo vostro regno che da sè lo sgombra."—

It is Virgil here who tells me so," and I pointed to him.   "And this other (Statius) is that shade for whom your kingdom (Purgatory), which is discharging him from itself, just now agitated all its slopes."

This refers to the last lines of Canto XX.

END OF CANTO XXIII.

CANTO XXIV.

THE SIXTH CORNICE (*continued*).
FORESE DONATI.
PICCARDA DONATI.
BONAGIUNTA OF LUCCA.
DEATH OF CORSO DONATI FORETOLD.
EXAMPLES OF INTEMPERANCE.
ASCENT TO THE SEVENTH CORNICE.

IN this Canto Dante continues the description of the penance and purgation of the gluttonous, introducing the spirits of many persons of modern times ; he also mentions wine-bibbers.

This Canto, says Benvenuto, cannot be divided into less than five parts.

In the First Division, from v. 1 to v. 33, Dante, continuing the conversation with Forese, that was broken off at the end of the last Canto, asks him about his sister Piccarda de' Donati, and about some persons notorious for gluttony.

In the Second Division, from v. 34 to v. 69, Bonagiunta of Lucca is introduced, who pays a graceful tribute of admiration to Dante's eloquence.

In the Third Division, from v. 70 to v. 99, Dante's conversation with Forese is resumed, and the latter predicts to Dante certain events that will befall him.

In the Fourth Division, from v. 100 to v. 129, an account is given of another tree, and a description follows of the checks that are used against gluttony.

In the Fifth Division, from v. 130 to v. 154, an Angel appears, who purifies Dante from the sin of gluttony, and points out to him the ascent to the seventh cornice.

Division I.   Benvenuto says that some people, when in conversation out walking, are in the habit of stopping their companion every time they speak ; and other persons, from the haste at which they are walking, either shorten their conversation, or omit parts of it.

Dante tells us how he and Forese neither slackened their speed, nor shortened their conversation.*

> Nè il dir† l' andar, nè l' andar lui più lento
> Facea ; ma ragionando andavam forte,
> Sì come nave pinta da buon vento.

Neither did our speech make our advance slower, nor did our advance shorten it (our speech); but as we talked we walked apace, like a ship impelled by a fair wind.

---

* It will be noticed however, in v. 91, that Forese did after all find Dante's speed too slow, and apologizes for leaving him behind.   Dante estimates the rate of their progress by what is given to man's powers.   The spirits not being burdened with *quel d' Adamo* (*Purg.* IX, 10), can naturally move much more rapidly.   It may be remembered that the fact of Dante being a bad walker was noticed in Vol. I, p. 267, in the note on Canto XI, 43-45, where Virgil says of him :

> " Chè questi che vien meco, per l' incarco
> Della carne d' Adamo, ond' ei si veste,
> Al montar su, contra sua voglia, è parco."

† Compare Ariosto (*Orl. Fur.* c. XXXI, st. 34) :

> " Non, per andar, di ragionar lasciando,
> Non, di seguir, per ragionar, lor via."

T T

Benvenuto compares Virgil and Statius walking in front to good pilots, who guide the ship in safety.

> E l' ombre, che parean cose rimorte,
>> Per le fosse degli occhi ammirazione   5
>> Traean di me, di mio vivere accorte.

And the shades, that seemed to be things twice dead, kept drawing in astonishment at me through the caverns of their eyes, having become aware of my living.

The spirits knew Dante was alive, both from seeing his shadow, and from his unstarved appearance.

Dante now resumes the sentence, which was broken off at the conclusion of the last canto. He had told Forese who Virgil was, and had said of Statius: *quest' altro è quell' ombra Per cui scosse dianzi ogni pendice Lo vostro regno.*

> Ed io, continuando il mio sermone,
>> Dissi :—" Ella sen va su forse più tarda
>> Che non farebbe, per l' altrui* cagione.

And I, continuing my speech, said : " It (that spirit) perchance walks on more slowly upwards than it would, for the sake of others.

---

* *per l' altrui cagione.* Scartazzini thinks this was solely for the purpose of talking with Virgil; but Benvenuto explains it to be for the sake both of Virgil and Dante, adding, that other- wise Statius would already have soared up to Heaven, "and thus see," observes Benvenuto, "how a real friend will for a while postpone his own comfort for a friend, as says the philosopher in the IXth book of the Ethics, and it is as though he (Dante) would say tacitly: ' I must hasten away from thee, lest we retard Statius who is going to Heaven, therefore tell me, I beseech thee, where is thy sister?' "

Virgil had adapted his speed to Dante's powers, and Statius his to Virgil's.

Dante then asks Forese if he can give him any information about his sister Piccarda, who was also a relation of Dante's wife, his interview with whom (Piccarda) in Heaven is described in *Par.* III., one of the most beautiful Cantos in the Divina Commedia.

> Ma dimmi, se tu sai, dov' è Piccarda*;   10
> Dimmi s' io veggio da notar persona
> Tra questa gente che sì mi riguarda."—

But tell me, if thou knowest, where is Piccarda; tell me if, among all these people who thus gaze at me, I see anyone to note."

Forese speaks in affectionate admiration of his sister's beauty and goodness.

---

* *Piccarda,* was the daughter of Simone de' Donati, and sister to Corso and Forese. She took the vows of the order of St. Clare, but was forcibly abducted from the cloister against her will, by order of Messer Corso her brother, and married to Rosellino della Tosa. She tells the tale herself in *Par.* III, 97-108.

> "¶Perfetta vita ed alto merto inciela
> Donna più su (mi disse), alla cui norma
> Nel vostro mondo giù si veste e vela,
> Perchè in fino al morir si vegghi e dorma
> Con quello spozo ch' ogni voto accetta,
> Che caritate a suo piacer conforma.
> Dal mondo, per seguirla, giovinetta
> Fuggi' mi, e nel suo abito mi chiusi,
> E promisi la via della sua setta.
> Uomini poi, a mal più ch' a bene usi,
> Fuor mi rapiron della dolce chiostra;
> E Dio si sa qual poi mia vita fùsi."

—" La mia sorella, che tra bella e buona,*
        Non so qual fosse più, trionfa lieta
        Nell' alto Olimpo† già di sua corona."—   15
    Sì disse prima, e poi :—" Qui non si vieta
        Di nominar ciascun, da ch' è sì munta,
        Nostra sembianza via per la dïeta.

"My sister, who betwixt beautiful and good I know
not which was most, already triumphs rejoicing in her
crown in high Olympus" (*i.e.* in Heaven). [Forese
now answers Dante's question as to whether there
were any notabilities among his companions.] Thus
said he first, and then: "Here there is no prohibition
to name each one, since by our diet our countenances
are so effaced (*lit.* milked away).

Forese means that, as the whole of the spirits
present are equally miserable in appearance, there can
be nothing invidious in naming any one specially, and
the more so, that otherwise, any recognition by a
stranger would be impossible. Dante had named
Piccarda, and Forese had in his answer said "my

---

* Petrarch (Part II, Sonnet LXXII) says of Laura :
    "Nè vivrei già, se chi tra bella e onesta,
        Qual fu più, lasciò in dubbio."

† *Nell' alto' Olimpo.* Scartazzini remarks that, according to
Dante, the heathen poets had a presentiment of the truth, and
their fancies are not mere fictions.
Piccarda was in the lowest sphere of Heaven, as she says
herself (*Par.* III, 49-51).
    "Ma riconoscerai ch' io son Piccarda,
        Che, posta qui con questi altri beati,
        Beata sono in la spera più tarda."
Benvenuto notices that Dante places the sister in Paradise,
the one brother, Forese, in Purgatory, and Corso, the other
brother, in Hell.

sister," and lest Dante should think that he wished to
reprove him, he hastens to reassure him, and names
several of his fellow penitents.

> Questi (e mostrò col dito) è Bonagiunta,*
>   Bonagiunta da Lucca ; e quella faccia†   20
>   Di là da lui, più che l'altre trapunta,

---

* *Bonagiunta degli Urbiciani* of Lucca, a notary and minor
poet, flourished about 1250. "He was a reciter of rhymes, and
very corrupt in the vice of gluttony," says Jacopo della Lana ;
and Benvenuto remarks : "*fuit maximus magister gulositatum,*'
. . . . and further on : "he was an honourable man, of the city
of Lucca, a splendid orator in his mother tongue, with much
facility in the matter of rhymes, but of greater facility in that of
wines."

† *quella faccia* : the idea of the intensity of the emaciation is
impressed on us by Dante saying "that face beyond him"
instead of "that spirit beyond him." He wishes his readers to
understand, that the sight of those cavernous eyes and hollow
cheeks so seized upon the attention of the beholder, that for the
time he would be unable to see anything but the faces. The
spirit in question is that of Pope Martin IV., a Frenchman, by
name Simon de Brion of Tours, who succeeded Nicholas III.
in 1281. G. Villani (lib. VII, ch. 58) says of him : "Di vile
nazione, ma molto fu magnanimo e di gran cuore ne' fatti della
Chiesa, ma per sè proprio per suoi parenti nulla cuvidigia ebbe :
e quand il fratello il venne a vedere papa, incontanente il
rimandò in Francia con piccoli doni e colle spese, dicendo
ch' e' beni erano della Chiesa e non suoi." He was a strong
partizan of Charles of Anjou, and an enemy of the Ghibellines.
He retired to Orvieto, where the rich wines of Orvieto and
Montefiascone, combined with the eels here mentioned, may
have given him the surfeit from which he is said to have died.
The Postillatore Cassinense tells us that, owing to his predi-
lection for eels, the following verses are said to have been written
on his tomb :

> "Gaudent anguillæ, quia mortuus hic jacet ille
>   Qui quasi morte reas excoriabat eas."

> Ebbe la santa Chiesa in le sue braccia :
> Dal Torso fu, e purga per digiuno
> Le anguille di Bolsena* e la vernaccia."†—

"This one here," and he pointed with his finger, "is Bonagiunta, Bonagiunta of Lucca, and that face beyond him, more extenuated than the others, once held the Holy Church in his embrace : from Tours was he (Pope Martin IV.) ; and he is expiating by abstinence the eels of Bolsena and the Vernaccia."

And he adds :

> Molti altri mi nomò ad uno ad uno ;   25
> E del nomar parean tutti contenti,‡
> Sì ch' io però non vidi un atto bruno.

---

* Lake *Bolsena* is near Viterbo, and said to abound in fish. It is in a most fertile district, but has an evil reputation for malaria.

† *Vernaccia:* from the Latin *vinaciola*, was produced from a thick skinned grape that imparted a sweet rough flavour to the wine, which Benvenuto says is excellent, and comes from the mountains near Genoa. He adds that he considers it to have been of special utility to that High Priest (meaning Martin IV) to have drunk of the wine in which eels had been slain ; for whoever drinks of wine so prepared straightway takes a disgust to all wine, as Albertus Magnus says, and Benvenuto himself saw the experiment succeed with a great bishop.

Chaucer mentions the wine in the Merchant's Tale :

> "He drinketh Ipocras, clarre, and vernage
> Of spices hot, to encresen his corage."

Longfellow quotes from Redi (*Bacchus in Tuscany*), Leigh Hunt's Trans. p. 30.

> "If anybody doesn't like Vernaccia,
> I mean that sort that's made in Pietrafitta,
> Let him fly
> My violent eye ;
> I curse him clean, through all the Alphabeta."

‡ *contenti :* Scartazzini says that the context shows that these spirits did not seek for renown in the world, and were not

Many others did he name to me one by one, and all seemed contented on hearing themselves mentioned, so that I did not for this (*però*) see one sombre gesture.

> Vidi per fame a vôto usar li denti*
> Ubaldin dalla Pila,† e Bonifazio‡
> Che pasturò col ròcco molte genti.   30

I saw Ubaldino dalla Pila in vain grinding his teeth

---

unduly elated, only not displeased at being mentioned by name. All they desired from the world was the prayers of the living.

* The phrase *usar li denti* is said to be derived from Ovid (*Metam.* VIII, 824-827) :

> "Petit ille dapes sub imagine somni :
> Oraque vana movet, dentemque in dente fatigat ;
> Exercetque cibo delusum guttur inani :
> Proque epulis tenues nequicquam devorat auras."

† *Ubaldin della Pila* : Benvenuto says he was a knight of the illustrious family of the Ubaldini, which gave birth to many other valiant men ; he was liberal and cultivated, and was brother of the Cardinal Ottaviano the magnificent, who once conducted the Pope, with his whole court, to enjoy his brother's hospitality at his castle on the mountains near Florence, and the Pope continued his guest for several months. Dante has the Cardinal placed in Hell among the Epicureans. It is he whom Farinata Degli Uberti mentions as a fellow sufferer in his fiery tomb (*Inf.* X. 118-120).

> "Dissemi : 'Qui con più di mille giaccio :
> Quà dentro è lo secondo Federico,
> E il cardinale.'"

‡ *Bonifazio* : This was the Archbishop of Ravenna, of the noble family of the Fieschi, Counts of Lavagna, in the Genoese territory ; he was nephew of Pope Innocent IV. He was appointed Archbishop by Gregory X at the time of the Council of Lyons in 1274. Honorius IV sent him as Nunzio to the Court of Philippe le Hardi, and afterwards to Philippe le Bel. The commentators speak of his gluttony, but this passage of Dante's is the only record of it.

for hunger, and Boniface too, who with his crozier governed many peoples.

Benvenuto explains this by saying that Dante describes Boniface by one of the chief insignia of his great dignity. The Archbishop of Ravenna is a great shepherd, who has under him many suffragan bishops from Rimini as far as Parma: and he says *col rocco*; for while the other shepherds (bishops) have the crooked pastoral staff, he (the archbishop) has the whole staff straight and round at the top like a castle at chess (ad modum calculi, sive rocchi). This word has been the cause of much disagreement. Some have tried to make out that *rocco* means a belfry, others a rochet, but Scartazzini asks: "How can an Archbishop rule with a part of his dress?" Scartazzini says: "It is derived, like *roque* in Spanish and Portuguese, and *roc*, Provençal and French, from the Persian *rokh*, and means neither more nor less than the castle in the game of chess. Now the ancient commentators have told us, that the crozier of the Archbishop of Ravenna has on the top a piece shaped like a castle at chess. *Col rocco* therefore signifies 'with his crozier,' and all the other interpretations are but dreams."

Benvenuto says that the Division concludes with the mention of another powerful man; and Dante passes from Ravenna to Forlì, where there are stouter drinkers and better wines.

> Vidi messer Marchese, ch' ebbe spazio
> Già di bere a Forlì con men secchezza,
> E sì fu tal che non si sentì sazio.

I saw Messer Marchese, who once had leisure for

drinking at Forlì with less thirst, and he was one who never felt sated.

Benvenuto is the only one of the commentators who gives trustworthy information about this personage, who was of the family of the Argugliosi of Forlì, *et pater dominæ Letæ, quæ fuit mater domini Bernardini de Podenta, qui fuit dominus Ravennatum.* He is said one day to have asked his secretary what was talked of him in the city. The secretary answered trembling: "My Lord, over the whole territory nothing else is said of you, than that you do nothing but drink;" to which the Marchese replied laughing : "And why do they not also say that it is because I am always thirsty ? "

Division II. In this second division of the Canto, Dante relates how he felt a strong inclination to converse with Bonagiunta of Lucca, whom Forese had pointed out to him before, as we read in v. 19-20. Bonagiunta addresses Dante, predicting that before long he will have reason to feel some interest in Lucca.

> Ma come fa chi guarda, e poi fa prezza
>> Più d' un che d' altro, fe' io a quel da Lucca,   35
>> Che più parea di me aver contezza.

But as he does, who looks about, [Benvenuto suggests, on entering a room, or an assemblage of people,] and then takes more special count of one than another, so did I to that (spirit) from Lucca, who most seemed to have knowledge of me.

Some read : *di me voler contezza, i.e.* seemed more

than the others to desire to make acquaintance with me.
Scartazzini says this last is by far the more intelligible
reading, and is confirmed by Dante telling Bonagiunta (v. 40) that he sees he wishes to speak with
him; but the great weight of MS. authority is in
favour of the reading *aver contezza.*

Bonagiunta murmurs some words to himself.

> Ei mormorava, e non so che *Gentucca*
> Sentiva ïo là ov' ei sentia la piaga
> Della giustizia che sì li pilucca.*

He was muttering; and I know not what methought
I heard (about) "Gentucca" from that place where he
was feeling the wound of the justice that so consumes
them.

The word of course issued from his mouth, between
his teeth, where he was most feeling the pangs of
starvation. Although Benvenuto interprets *là ove* as
above, he thinks it might also refer to the vicinity of
the tree and the sight of its fruit.

The above passage about *Gentucca* is, says Scartazzini, like many in the *Divina Commedia,* one that,
obscure in itself, has been rendered much more so by
the commentators. Out of seventy interpretations of
the word more than fifty take it to be a proper name.
Francesco da Buti says: "He formed an attachment to
a gentle lady called Madonna Gentucca, of Rossimpelo,
on account of her great virtue and modesty, and not
from any other love. Fraticelli says it was " A lady of
Lucca with whom Dante is supposed to have fallen in
love, when in 1314 he went to stay with his friend

---

* *li pilucca: piluccare* is akin to the German *pflücken*, to
pull grapes off a bunch one by one, whence it ⬛⬛⬛⬛ consume by slow degrees.

Uguccione della Fagiuola. Benvenuto and the Ottimo interpret the passage differently, making *gentucca* a common noun, and meaning *gente bassa*, low
people.

Scartazzini explains it categorically. Dante heard
Bonagiunta mutter something, and the only word he
caught was *Gentucca*. He thereupon begs him to
speak clearly, so that he can understand him.
Bonagiunta does so, telling him that a certain lady is
already born who will make him find Lucca pleasant,
though he had before uttered great abuse against it.
The inference then is, that Bonagiunta's statement
about the woman of Lucca is to explain what he had
muttered, when Dante had only heard *Gentucca*. If
so, Gentucca is the name of the woman. Some commentators contend however that it never was a
woman's name. But Troya (*Veltro di Dante*, p. 142)
tells us that, at that time, there really was living at
Lucca a lady so-called, wife of Bernardo Morla degli
Antelminelli Allucinghi. Carlo Minutoli (*Dante e il
suo secolo*, p. 228) says that it is proved by incon-
testible documents that, at the same time, there was
living in Lucca another lady of gentle blood, also
called *Gentucca*, much younger than the other one, to
whom she was related. This last Gentucca was the
wife of Buonaccorso di Lazzaro di Fondora, surnamed
after the fashion of those times *Coscio* or *Cosciorino*.
Scartazzini then says : " Let it be sufficient for us to
establish the following points : 1. *Gentucca* for *gen-
tuccia, gente bassa*, is not to be found in the works of
any writer. 2. It is proved by documents that, in the
time of Dante, there were living in Lucca two women,
not of low birth, of the name of *Gentucca*. 3. If *Gen-*

tucca was a proper name among the people of Lucca, then the assertion of some commentators, that the Lucchesi used the word *gentucca* to mean *gente bassa*, is most improbable. And therefore we may conclude that *Gentucca* is the name of a woman, who gained the affection of Dante when he was at Lucca in 1314." Scartazzini lays great stress on having purposely said *affection* and not *love*, for he is convinced that Dante's love for Gentucca was in no sense sinful, but a love that was platonic, pure, holy, and removed from even a thought that was not chaste and modest.

Dante now accosts Bonagiunta :

> "O anima (diss' io) che par sì vaga*   40
>   Di parlar meco, fa sì ch' io t' intenda,
>   E te e me col tuo parlare appaga."—

"O soul," said I, "that seemest so desirous to talk with me, do so that I can understand thee, and thereby make both thyself and me content."

Dante leaves one to suppose that Bonagiunta desired to speak with him to defend Lucca, his native place, from the bad repute in which Dante held it. Dante now says to him in so many words : " It may content thee to mutter through thy teeth, but I pray thee to content me also by speaking distinctly."

Bonagiunta answers him :

> " Femmina è nata, e non porta ancor benda,
>   (Comminciò ei), che ti farà piacere
>   La mia città, come ch' uom la riprenda.   45

"A woman is born, and wears not yet the wimple," (*i. e.*, is unwedded) he began, "who shall make

---

* *sì vaga di parlar meco* : compare *Par.* III, 34-5.
> "Ed io all' ombra, che parea più vaga
>   Di ragionar, drizza' mi, e comminciai."

my city (Lucca) please thee, howsoever men may blame it.

Some have thought that this is meant as a side hit at Dante, who had asserted that every man in Lucca was a fraudulent trafficker in public offices,* but Scartazzini says that in the year 1300, in which Dante pretends that his interview with Bonagiunta took place, he could not have put into the mouth of the latter words referring to the twenty-first Canto of the Inferno, for no one believes that that Canto had then been written. Buti thinks it is simply a censure spoken generally of the evil habits and words of the Lucchesi. And for fear his words should have been obscure he adds:

> Tu te n' andrai con questo antivedere ;
> Se nel mio mormorar prendesti errore,
> Dichiareranti ancor le cose vere.

Thou wilt now depart with this prediction ; if by my muttering thou wast led into error, the plain facts will hereafter make it clear to thee.

Benvenuto notices that, whereas Bonagiunta had first mentioned Dante's future love, he now speaks to him of his former love, for he knew that Dante had been wonderfully in love (*mirabiliter inamoratus*), and had composed noble love-songs.

> Ma di' s' io veggio quì colui che fuore

---

* See *Inf.* XXI, 38 :—
> " Ecco un degli anzian, di Santa Zita ;
> Mettetel sotto, ch' io torno per anche
> A quella terra ch' io n' ho ben fornita ;
> Ognun v' è barratier, fuor che Bonturo,
> Del no per li denar vi si fa ita."

Trasse le nuove rime,* cominciando :   50
Donne che avete intelletto d' Amore."—

But tell me if I here see him who produced those
new fashioned rhymes, which begin :
' Ladies, who of Love have knowledge.' "

Ed io a lui :—" Io mi son un che, quando
Amor mi spira, noto, ed a quel modo
Che dêtta dentro, vo significando."—†

And I to him : " I am one who, whenever Love in-
spires me, note, and, in that fashion that he (Love)
dictates within, set it forth."

Bonagiunta replies.

—" O frate, issa‡ veggio (disse) il nodo   55

---

* *le nuove rime:* Dante was the first to write sonnets in
which, instead of the conventional love of which other poets
had sung, he elevated love as one of the most noble, pure and
lofty feelings of the soul.   The line quoted here is the first
verse of a canzone in the *Vita Nuova.*   Dante evidently considered this to be one of his best canzoni, for he not only
quotes it here, but again in his *De Vulg. Eloq.* lib. II,
ch. 12.

† Compare Balaam's answer to Balak (*Numb.* XXII, 38).
" And Balaam said unto Balak, Lo, I am come unto thee :
have I now any power at all to say anything'; the word that
God putteth in my mouth, that shall I speak."

Also Chaucer, *Complaint of the Blacke Knight,* 194.

"But even like as doth a scrivenere,
That can no more tell what that he shall write,
But as his master beside dothe indite."

‡ *issa* stands for adesso, and is contracted from the Latin *in
ipsâ horâ.*   Compare *Inf.* XXIII, 7 :

" Che più non si pareggia *mo* ed *issa.*"
and *Inf.* XXVII, 20-21 :—

"che parlavi mo lombardo
Dicendo : *Issa ten va, più non t' adizzo.*"

> Che il Notaro,* e Guittone,† e me ritenne
> Di quà dal dolce stil nuovo ch' i' odo.

" O brother," said he, " now (*issà*) do I see the impediment (*lit.*, knot) that held back the notary, and Guittone and myself so far behind (*di qua*) that sweet new style which I hear.

> Io veggio ben come le vostre penne‡
> Diretro al dittator sen vanno strette,
> Che delle nostre certo non avvenne.   60

I see well how your pens follow closely after him (Love) who dictates ; and this certainly was not so with ours.

> E qual più a riguardar oltre si mette,
> Non vede più dall' uno all' altro stilo."—
> E quasi contentato si tacette.

And he who sets himself to look beyond this can no longer discern the slightest comparison between the one style and the other."   And, as if satisfied, he held his peace.

---

* *il Notaro :* This is Jacopo da Lentino, known as il Notajo. He is said to have been a Sicilian poet.   Although Dante seems here to censure his school, as antiquated, he did not the less give him the credit of being one of the most elegant poets of his time, and in *De Vulg. Eloq.* lib. I, ch. 12, he quotes a sonnet by Jacopo beginning : " *Madonna dir vi voglio.*"

† Fra Guittone d' Arezzo was one of the Frati Gaudenti mentioned in *Inf.* XXIII.   He first brought the Italian sonnet into the perfect form that it has since preserved, and he left behind him the earliest specimens of Italian letter writing.

‡ *le vostre penne :* Bonagiunta means the pens of the more modern sonneteers, such as Dante, Guido Cavalcanti, Cino da Pistoja and others, compared with whose style he felt that of himself and his contemporaries was indeed cold.   No one can write love-sonnets with any poetic fire, without experience of the passion.

Bonagiunta means that the later style adopted by Dante, Guido Cavalcanti, and the others was so vastly superior. Or the passage may be translated according to Buti : " cannot see any further difference between thy mode of writing and ours than this, namely, that thou followest closely the inspiration of the mind, and we take a much wider range."

Others read *a gradire oltre :* " Whoever sets himself to give greater pleasure in the world, in fact, to try and please everybody," but Scartazzini says that, whichever of the two readings one takes, the meaning must always remain doubtful and obscure. For the reading *a riguardar oltre,* there is the MS. authority of the Santa Croce, Berlin, Caetani, and Cassinese and other Codices, and the early editions of Foligno, Jesi, and Naples, of the commentaries of Lana, Buti, Landino, Vellutello, Brunone Bianchi, and Witte. For the reading *a gradire* there is the MS. authority of the Vatican and Vienna Codices, the printed editions of Mantua, Aldine, Crusca, and others, and of the commentators Anonimo Fiorentino, Daniello, Venturi, Lombardi, Costa, Camerini, and others. Benvenuto reads *a guardare.* Scartazzini says he hazards a conjecture that both readings may have been altered from a reading for which there is no authority, but which would remove all difficulty :

E qual più a gradire altri si mette

" And whoever any longer sets about pleasing others." He comments on this supposed reading by saying that the school of poets, previous to Guinicelli, was servilely Provençalesque, obeying the conventional, and being a perfect slave to the fashion. Dante has just told Bonagiunta that he, for his part, does not care for conventional poetry, but writes his poetry according to the inspiration of his heart, according to what Love dictates within it. And Bonagiunta would answer : " Now can I perceive the difference between your modern school and our ancient school. I see how far behind we were. Your pens followed the inspiration of Love, ours the fashion or tradition. And whoever any longer, after that you have entered upon this new way, sets about pleasing anyone else than Love who dictates, that is, whoever would continue to follow our older school would prove himself a fool, who did not know how to discern the differences between the one style and the other."

The alteration of *altri* into *oltre* in the Codices would have been quite easy.

Benvenuto thinks that Bonagiunta looked so pleased with himself, because he had so well explained the true state of the case. Dante, having now ended his conversation with Bonagiunta, describes the departure of the band of spirits, by one of his beautiful similes.

> Come gli augei* che vernan lungo il Nilo
> Alcuna volta di lor fanno schiera   65
> Poi volan più in fretta e vanno in filo ;

---

*Compare *Inf.* V, 40-47 :—

> " E come gli stornei ne portan l' ali
> Nel freddo tempo, a schiera larga e piena ;
> Così quel fiato gli spiriti mali
> Di quà, di là, di giù, di su gli mena ;
> Nulla speranza gli conforta mai,
> Non che di posa, ma di minor pena.
> E come i gru van cantando lor lai,
> Facendo in aër di sè lunga riga, &c.

Così tutta la gente che lì era,
   Volgendo il viso, raffrettò suo passo,
   E per magrezza e per voler leggiera.

As the birds (cranes), that winter along the Nile, at one time will form themselves into a flock, then will fly more in haste and go in file; so did all the folk that were there turn their heads round, and hurry on their steps, light both by leanness and by will.

———

Division III. In this division Dante resumes the conversation with Forese, which his interview with Bonagiunta had interrupted. Forese predicts the death of his own brother, Corso de' Donati.

Dante begins by telling us that Forese did not go on with the other shades, because he had been running for a long time before, and was tired. Benvenuto thinks he may have been out of breath with talking.

E come l' uom che di trottare è lasso   70
   Lascia andar li compagni, e sì passeggia
   Fin che si sfoghi l' affollar del casso ;*

———

Compare also in *Purg.* II, 124-132, the obedient departure of the spirits on the rebuke of Cato.

  "Come quando, cogliendo biada o loglio,
    Gli colombi adunati alla pastura,
    Queti senza mostrar l' usato orgoglio,
   Se cosa appare ond' egli abbian paura,
    Subitamente lasciano star l' esca,
    Perchè assaliti son di maggior cura."

* *l' affollar del casso: affollare* is derived from *follo,* a bellows; and the verb refers to the act of drawing in, and expelling the air from the lungs. *Casso* comes from the Latin *capsus* a receptacle, and here has the sense of the chest, thorax.

> Sì lasciò trapassar la santa greggia
>> Forese, e dietro meco sen veniva,
>> Dicendo:—"Quando fia ch' io ti riveggia?"— 75

And as a man who is wearied with running lets his companions pass on, and so walks until the heaving of his chest is allayed ; so did Forese allow that holy throng to pass before, and walked behind with me and said : "When shall I ever see thee again ?"

Dante tells Forese that the sooner the time comes for him to die, and pass into Purgatory, the better he will be pleased, foreseeing, as he does, the misfortunes that are hanging over Florence.

> —"Non so (rispos' io lui) quant' io mi viva ;
>> Ma già non fia il tornar mio tanto tosto,
>> Ch' io non sia col voler prima alla riva.

"I know not," answered I him, "how long I may live ; but anyhow my return here (after my death) cannot be so quick but that I shall reach the shore (of Purgatory) by my will still sooner."

He means that his desire to quit the world of vexation and sorrow was probably far in advance of the mandate of God for his departure. "And I said, Oh that I had wings like a dove! for then would I fly away and be at rest." (*Ps.* LV, 6)

> Però che il luogo, u' fui a viver posto,
>> Di giorno in giorno più di ben si spolpa, 80
>> E a trista ruina par disposto."—

Because the place, where I was set to live (*i.e.*, Florence) is day by day more deprived of good, and seems prepared for sad ruin."

By way of consoling Dante, Forese now tells him that the swift retribution of God will soon fall on him, who is the chief cause of this evil at Florence, meaning his own brother Corso de' Donati. Benvenuto says that, as the next few lines will appear to many very obscure, it must be understood that Corso, a soldier tried in arms, in skill and in bravery, had been restored to power in Florence, as chief of the *Neri*, by Charles de Valois (Sans Terre, *Carolum sine terra*). He had annihilated the *Bianchi*, at a time when they were at the zenith of their power and prosperity. His arrogance, however, and the state he kept, made him an object of suspicion to his colleagues in the Signorìa, and he fell into bad odour even among his own adherents, partly because they felt that he seemed more their lord than their comrade. Benvenuto has here an inconsistency, leaving it doubtful whether Corso was father-in-law or son-in-law of Uguccione della Faggiuola. First he says of Corso "*sed precipue odiosus populo, quia factus fuerat socer Ugucionis de fagiola domini Pisarum potentissimi hostis florenti-norum.*" Lower down, speaking of Corso's despair at the expected reinforcements from Uguccione not arriv-ing, he says : "*tandem destitutus sperato auxilio soceri, deseruit domos, etc.*" Benvenuto goes on to say that being captured and on his way back to Florence, he tried to escape by setting spurs to his horse, but that either by accident or design he let himself fall from the saddle, and was dragged a long way, till at last a soldier struck him on the head and killed him.

Giovanni Villani (*lib.* VIII, *c.* 96) tells the story somewhat differently from the account given by Dante. He says that, "being accused of treason, in less than an hour, without giving a longer time for the trial, Messer Corso was condemned as a rebel and traitor to the commonwealth, and the *priori* at once carried the standard of justice with the Podestà, the captain, and the executioner, ... to go to the houses inhabited by Messer Corso to carry out the execution." Corso defended himself all day like the gallant knight that he was, confiding in succour from Uguccione della Faggiuola, "and the battle lasted most of the day, and was so fierce that, notwithstanding all the power of the people, if the reinforcements expected from Uguccione and other friends in the district had arrived in time, the people of Florence would have had enough to do that day." But the succours did not arrive, and Corso was obliged to take to flight. "Messer Corso, departing quite alone, was overtaken and captured near Rovezzano by certain Catalonian troopers, and as they led him to Florence, when they drew near to San Salvi . . . . . Messer Corso, for fear of falling into the hands of his enemies, and being put to death by the people, suffering terribly as he was from gout in his hands and feet, let himself fall from his horse. The Catalonians seeing him on the ground, one of them thrust his lance through his throat, wounding him mortally and left him for dead : the monks of the said Monastery carried him into the Abbey, and some say that before dying he gave himself up to them in penitence, while others maintain that they found him dead, and the next day he was buried at San Salvi, with little honour and small attendance, as people were afraid of getting into bad odour with the authorities."

Scartazzini says that it is impossible to deny credence to the account of Villani, who, on the 15th September, when this occurred, was actually in Florence, and was to a certain extent an eye-witness of these events. Dante, on the other hand, was far away in exile, one does not know for certain where, and would receive the intelligence at second or third hand.   It is quite easy to suppose that the account of the simple fall of Corso from his horse, as related by Villani, would be magnified little by little into his having been dragged by the stirrup.   Dante must have written in perfect good faith, but from erroneous information.

> "Or va (diss' ei), chè quei che più n' ha colpa
> Vegg' io a coda d' una bestia* tratto
> In vêr la valle,† ove mai non si scolpa.

"Go thy way now," said he, "for I can see him, (Corso) who is most to blame for it (*i.e.* the misfortunes of Florence), dragged at the tail of a beast towards the valley, where never more can sins be forgiven.

The full meaning of this passage is : " I see the horse dragging Corso to his death, after which his soul will have to go to Hell, whence there is no redemption." The horse is dragging him to the Valley of the Shadow of Death.

---

* Benvenuto gives the following double interpretation : "*Vegg' io quel che più va' ha colpa,* scilicet, fratrem meum, *tratto a coda d' una bestia,* scilicet, ab equo, deinde a dæmone, *invêr la valle,* primo Arnalem, deinde infernalem."

Francesco da Buti also says that *bestia* must be understood in a double sense, literal and allegorical, *bestia* meaning the devil ; but Scartazzini takes *bestia* in the literal sense as the horse.

† *In vêr la valle:* This is the Valley of the Shadow of Death, or Hell.

See *Inf.* IV, 7-8:—   "in su la proda mi trovai
            Della valle d' abisso dolorosa."
and *Par.* XVII, 137:—
            "Nel monte, e nella valle dolorosa."

The description is continued :—

> La bestia ad ogni passo va più ratto, 85
> > Crescendo sempre, infin ch' ella il percuote,
> > E lascia il corpo vilmente disfatto.

The beast at every bound goes faster and faster, increasing his speed [understand *nel moto* after *crescendo*] until it tramples on him, and leaves the body hideously mutilated.

And he adds that this will soon take place.

> Non hanno molto a volger quelle ruote,
> > (E drizzò gli occhi al ciel) che ti fia chiaro
> > Ciò che il mio dir più dichiarar non puote. 90

Those spheres have not much to revolve," and he turned his eyes to the heaven, "before that which my speech no farther may explain will be made quite clear to you.

He means that many years will not elapse from 1300, the date of their supposed interview, and 1303, when Corso did actually die. Forese then explains to Dante that he can no longer accommodate his pace to Dante's, but must resume his penance of rapid running, which his conversation was interrupting.

> Tu ti rimani omai, chè il tempo è caro
> > In questo regno sì ch' io perdo troppo
> > Venendo teco sì a paro a paro."—

Now stay thou behind, for in this kingdom (Purgatory) time is so precious that I lose too much in going side by side with thee."

Forese's departure is described by a beautiful simile.

> Qual esce alcuna volta di galoppo
> > Lo cavalier di schiera che cavalchi, 95
> > E va per farsi onor del primo intoppo,

Tal si partì da noi con maggior valchi ;*
Ed io rimasi in via con esso i due,†
Che fûr del mondo sì gran maliscalchi.‡

Like a cavalier sometimes . issues at a gallop
from a troop of horsemen, and goes to do himself
honour at the first encounter, so did he (Forese) depart
from us with greater strides : and I was left in the
path with those two (Virgil and Statius), who were
such mighty marshals of the world.

Division IV. In this Division of the Canto Dante
describes a second tree, under which the gluttonous
have to suffer further pangs of hunger and thirst, but
first he tells us how Forese passed on out of sight.

E quando innanzi a noi entrato‖ fue   100
Che gli occhi miei si fêro a lui seguaci,
Come la mente alle parole sue,

---

* *valchi*: from *valco* or *varco* derived from *varcare, varicare,
valcare, valicare.* Akin to the English "walk" and the German
"wallen." *Valco* means a step, a pace.

† *con esso i due:* Blanc *(Voc. Dant.)* says "Sometimes this
pronoun *(esso)* seems to have no other duty than that of giving
greater precision to the image, and then it is always placed
between the preposition and the substantive without taking the
gender of the latter."

‡ *gran maliscalchi:* Great Masters, first in the matter of
knowledge. Marescalco means the governor of a province.
Blanc explains the word as *magister equorum,* from *mähre* a
mare and *schalk* a servant. In Danish and Norwegian too we
find *mær* a mare, and *skalk* a rogue.

‖ *Entrare innanzi* is the same as *passare oltre,* and is used
in that sense by Boccaccio, in the *Decameron,* g. V, nov. 7 :
" Pietro che giovane era, e la fanciulla similemente avanzavano

> Parvermi i rami gravidi e vivaci
> > D' un altro pomo, e non molto lontani,
> > Per esser pure allora vôlto in làci.   105

And when he (Forese) had passed on so far in front of us, that my eyes had to go in pursuit of him as my mind did of his words, there appeared to me the laden and luxuriant boughs of another fruit tree, and not very far off, for I had only just then turned in that direction.

It must be remembered that the poets were walking in circles round the cornices, so that, as they rounded the base of the cliff, they found this new tree quite close to them.

Benvenuto says that the shades of the gluttonous are punished between these two trees, but the second tree seems to give more torment than the other, perhaps because the first tormented them as to quantity, and the second as to the quality of the food and water that tempted their appetites (forte quia prima punit in quanto, secunda in quali); or, because the first punished the eaters, and the second the drinkers, who, being the greater sinners, have the greater torment, as will now be seen.

> Vidi gente sott' esso alzar le mani,
> > E gridar non so che verso le fronde,
> > Quasi bramosi fantolini* e vani,

---

nello andare la madre di lei e l' altre compagne assai . . . . et essendo già tanto entrati innanzi alla donna et agli altri che appena si vedevano," &c.

* *fantolini:* compare Purg. XXX, 43-5 :—

> "Volsimi alla sinistra col respitto
> > Col quale il fantolin corre alla mamma,
> > Quando ha paura o quando egli è afflitto."

> Che pregano, e il pregato non risponde ;
>> Ma per fare esser ben la voglia acuta,   110
>> Tien alto lor disio e nol nasconde.

Beneath it I saw folk raising their hands, and crying I know not what towards the branches, just as little children are wont to beg eagerly and in vain, and he to whom they pray answers not; but, in order to sharpen the edge of their wish, he holds on high (the object of) their desire, and conceals it not.

Benvenuto says that gluttonous people are like children in their senseless eagerness for some new food, and if they do not get what they want, they at once suffer acutely, and indeed appear to suffocate and die like pregnant women.

> Poi si partì sì come ricreduta ;
>> E noi venimmo al grande arbore ad esso,*
>> Che tanti prieghi e lagrime rifiuta.

Then they departed as if undeceived; and we straightway came up to the great tree, which is deaf to . so many prayers and tears.

From this tree also a voice is heard.

> *Trapassate oltre senza farvi presso;*   115
>> *Legno è più su che fu morso da Eva,*
>> *E questa pianta si levò da esso.*

---

* *ad esso*: from the Latin *ad ipsum* scilicet tempus. Scartazzini remarks that some, being ignorant of the true force of this word among old writers, altered it into *ad esso*. But *Rosa Morando* (*Div. Com.* Venez. 1757, vol. III, Append. p. 34), shows this to be a false reading, and remarks that were it to be adopted the word *esso* would be used twice as a rhyme, and adds that the same words cannot be repeated in rhyme when bearing the same sense except in cases like that in *Purg.* XX, 65, where the repetition, three times over, of the sentence *per ammenda* gives much greater force and fiery eloquence to the irony.

> Sì tra le frasche non so chi diceva ;
> Per che Virgilio e Stazio ed io ristretti,
> Oltre andavam dal lato che si leva.   120

"Pass on your way without approaching; higher up (in the Terrestrial Paradise) there is the tree that was eaten of by Eve,* and this plant was reared from it." Thus spoke, I know not who, among the boughs : whereupon Virgil and Statius, and I, drawing close together, went further on the side that rises.

They passed to the left of the tree, on that side of the way where was the perpendicular side of the mountain. The voice continues to give further instances of gluttony.

> —" Ricordivi (dicea) dei maledetti
> Nei nuvoli formati, che satolli
> Tésëo combattêr coi doppi petti ;
> E degli Ebrei ch' al ber si mostrâr molli,
> Per che non gli ebbe Gedeon compagni,   125
> Quando invêr Madián discese i colli."—

"Bethink ye," said (the voice), "of the accursed

---

* It was in the original Terrestrial Paradise that the first law of abstinence was placed, and it was broken. These examples are uttered here as checks upon gluttony ; of which the first example is that of Eve, who, from the desire of eating an apple, brought death upon the human race. The first tree announced the example of the temperance of Mary (*Purg.* XXII, 142) ; this second tree cites the intemperance of Eve. Compare *Purg.* XXIX, 23-27 :—

> " onde buon zelo
> Mi fe' riprender l' ardimento d' Eva,
> . Che, là dove ubbidia la terra e il cielo,
> Femmina sola, e pur testè formata,
> Non sofferse di star sotto alcun velo."

ones (the Centaurs), formed in the clouds, who inebriate fought against Theseus with their double breasts.*

[Having given an example of the evil effects of immoderate drinking, Dante introduces a story from Jewish History of the men who drank immoderately of water, as a lesson that moderation is to be practised even in those things that are not of themselves hurtful.]

And (bethink ye) of the Hebrews who showed themselves luxurious in drinking (*i.e.*, lay flat down to

---

* The Centaurs are said to have been the progeny of Ixion and the cloud Nephele, to whom Jupiter had given the appearance of Juno, beloved by Ixion. They were half men and half horses, for which reason Dante speaks of their double breasts. Being invited by their neighbours, the Lapithæ, to the nuptials of Pirithous and Hippodamia, and becoming drunk, they attempted to carry off the bride, and the other women. They were opposed by Theseus and the Lapithæ, who defeated them and slew a great number of them. The battle is described by Ovid (*Met.* XII, 219-229), Dryden's trans.

" For one, most brutal of the brutal brood,
  Or whether wine or beauty fired his blood,
  Or both at once, beheld with lustful eyes
  The bride ; at once resolved to make his prize
  Down went the board ; and fastening on her hair,
  He seized with sudden force the frighted fair.
  'Twas Eurytus began : his bestial kind
  His crime pursued ; and each, as pleased his mind,
  Or her whom chance presented, took : the feast
  An image of a taken town expressed.
      The cave resounds with female shrieks ; we rise,
  Mad with revenge, to make a swift reprise :
  And Theseus first, ' What frenzy has possessed,
  O Eurytus,' he cried, ' thy brutal breast,
  To wrong Pirithous, and not him alone,
  But, while I live, two friends conjoined in one ? ' "

drink), on which account Gideon* would not have them for companions, when he descended the hills towards Midian."

> Sì, accostati all' un de' due vivagni,
>   Passammo, udendo colpe della gola,
>   Seguite già da miseri guadagni.

Thus closely skirting one of the two edges (*i.e.*, the inside one), we passed on, hearing of the faults of gluttony, which are already followed by a woeful retribution (*lit.* wretched gains).

Division V. In the Fifth and concluding Division of the Canto, Dante relates how an Angel purified him from the sin of gluttony.

The three poets are walking on side by side, but apart, in profound meditation and silence.

> Poi, rallargati† per la strada sola,   130
>   Ben mille passi e più ci portâr oltre,
>   Contemplando ciascun senza parola.

---

* *Gedeon.* See *Judges* VII, 5-6 : " So he brought the people down unto the water : and the Lord said unto Gideon, Every one that lappeth water with his tongue, as a dog lappeth, him shalt thou set by himself; likewise every one that boweth down upon his knees to drink. And the number of them that lapped, putting their hand to their mouth, were three hundred men : but all the rest of the people bowed down upon their knees to drink water."
Scartazzini denies this to be a happy example of immoderate drinking, and says he does not think that his profound reverence for the lofty Bard forbids him making such a criticism.

† *rallargati:* Blanc (*Voc. Dant.*) says of this word, that it is only used as a participle in this one passage in the *Divina*

Then, spreading out along the lonely road, we advanced a good thousand and more paces further, each in contemplation, without a word.

Benvenuto thinks that their meditations were to prepare their minds for the subject they were about to discuss in Canto XXV, which is very profound, so that to elucidate it, the three worked together, Virgil representing the natural, Statius the moral, and Dante the divine intelligence. Benvenuto adds : " In the whole Commedia you will find but few cantos more difficult to understand (than Canto XXV)."

Their contemplations are interrupted by a new voice.

—" Che andate pensando sì voi sol tre ? "—
    Subita voce disse ; ond' io mi scossi,
    Come fan bestie spaventate e poltre.*   135

" What go ye three alone thus thinking about ? "

Commedia, and it means : " One who finds himself at large on a road not restrained by any obstacle." Benvenuto explains the full force of the word by showing that, before, they had been obliged to walk close along the edge of the cliff, but, now that they had left the tree behind them, they could again walk freely in the middle of the cornice. Fraticelli says that *rallargati* means " walking with a certain space between each pair of them," and that they were no longer *ristretti insieme.*

* Benvenuto takes *poltre* to be for *polledre* (*idest, pullæ*), and translates " like fools," adding that the comparison is exceedingly appropriate, for it is as though Dante would avow himself to be young and inexperienced, whereas his companions were men of years (*antiqui*) and of vast experience. Most commentators, however, take *poltre* in the sense that *poltro* is the positive of the comparative *poltrone*, lazy, sleepy, torpid, and the passage would imply that animals are suddenly startled, *mentre poltriscono*, while in a torpid state. Compare the fol-

said a voice suddenly ; whereat I started, as do terrified and timid beasts.

Dante looks up and sees that it is an Angel who has addressed them.

> Drizzai la testa per veder chi fossi ;*
> 　　E giammai non si videro in fornace
> 　　Vetri o metalli sì lucenti e rossi,
> Com' io vidi un che dicea :—" Se a voi piace
> 　　Montare in su, qui si convien dar volta ;　　140
> 　　Quinci si va chi vuole andar per pace."—

I raised my head to see who this might be ; and never in a furnace were there seen glass or metals so glowing and so ruddy, as one I beheld, who said : " If it is your pleasure to mount upward, it is here that one must turn ; this way passes he who would go after peace."

They have now come to the end of the Sixth

---

lowing two passages from Ariosto. In the first (*Orl. Fur.* XXIII, st. 90), he takes *poltra* in the sense of *polledra*.

> " La bestia ch' era spaventosa e poltra,
> 　　Senza guardarsi ai piè, corre a traverso."

In the second (*Sat.* IV, ad Annibale Malaguzzo, v. 49, &c.) he gives the sense of *poltrone.*

> " E più mi piace di posar le poltre
> 　　Membra, che di vantarle che à gli Sciti
> 　　Sian state, a gl' Indi, a gli Etiopi, ed oltre."

* *Fossi :* In early times the third person singular of the imperfect subjunctive, which ends in *e* ended in *i.* Comp. *Inf.* IV, 64 :—

> " Non lasciavám l' andar perch' ei *dicessi.*"

and IX, 60 : —

> " Che con le sue ancor non mi *chiudessi.*"

and *Vita di Cola di Renzo*, Cap. XXXVII : "Vestiva panni come *fussi* un asinino tiranno." Therefore Scartazzini maintains that it is not a poetical license taken by Dante to suit the rhyme, but a regular termination of the time, now obsolete.

Cornice, and this shining one is the Angel pointing out to them the stairway leading to the Seventh. Dante is so dazzled by the radiance of the Angel, that his eyes refuse their office, and he is obliged to have recourse to his guides.

> L' aspetto suo m' avea la vista tolta :
>> Per ch' io mi volsi retro a' miei dottori,
>> Com' uom che va secondo ch' egli ascolta.

His aspect had bereft me of my sight : wherefore I turned round behind to my Teachers, as does a (blind) man, that goes according as he hears (*i.e.* guides himself by sound).

Dante now describes his purification by the Angel.

> E quale, annunziatrice degli albóri,*   145
>> L' aura di maggio muovesi, ed olezza :
>> Tutta impregnata dall' erba e dai fiori ;
> Tal mi sentii un vento dar per mezza
>> La fronte, e ben sentir muover la piuma,
>> Che fe' sentir d' ambrosïa l' orezza.†   150

And as, a herald of the dawn, the breeze of May moves, and breathes out a fragrance all impregnated by the herbage and by the flowers ; so did I feel a wind on the middle of my forehead, and I distinctly felt the movement of the pinions that made me aware of the odour of ambrosia.

---

* *degli albóri* : The *Anonimo Fiorentino* interprets this : "Vuol dire che, innanzi che si lievi l' alba, comincia a trarre uno venticello, che si chiama aura, et questa aura, cioè questo vinticello, che si lieva da' fiori et dall' erbe odorifere, rende odore et soavità."

† Dante's notions of ambrosia were derived from Virgil. See *Georg.* IV, 415 :—

"Hæc ait et liquidum ambrosiæ diffundit odorem."
and *Æn.* I, 403 :—

   "Ambrosiæque comæ divinum vertice odorem
      Spiravere."

Dante concludes the Canto by adding :

> E sentii dir : *Beati cui alluma*
> *Tanto di grazia, che l' amor del gusto*
> *Nel petto lor troppo disir non fuma,*
> *Esuriendo sempre quanto è giusto.*

And I heard (the Angel) say : "Blessed are they whom so large a measure of grace doth illuminate, that the love of taste does not make too great desire to smoke in their breasts, (but) hungering always so far as is just."

.

END OF CANTO XXIV.

,

CANTO XXV.

THE SEVENTH CORNICE.
THE MYSTERIES OF MAN'S FIRST AND SECOND
    BIRTHS.
THE CORPOREAL SHAPES OF SOULS IN PUR-
    GATORY.
PUNISHMENT OF THE LUXURIOUS IN FIRE.
EXAMPLES OF CHASTITY.

IN the last Canto Dante completed his description
of the purgation of Gluttony in the sixth cornice.   In
this one he treats a very perplexing subject which had
arisen out of the previous conversation.

Benvenuto divides the Canto into four principal parts.

In the First Division, from v. 1 to v. 30, Dante
proposes to Virgil a question of much difficulty, and
Virgil answers him in general terms.

In the Second Division, from v. 31 to v. 60, Statius
at the request of Virgil proceeds to explain at length
how it is that the soul, when separated from the body,
is able to suffer physical punishment, and he describes
the generation of the embryo.

In the Third Division, from v. 61 to v. 108,
Statius describes how the soul is developed in the
embryo; how it gets separated from the body; and its
sensitive powers.

In the Fourth Division, from v. 109 to v. 139,
Dante enters upon the subject of Luxury, and describes
its punishment in the seventh cornice.

Division I.   When the canto opens, the three poets
are still in the sixth cornice, but are standing at the
entrance to the new stairway, just where Dante had
felt the angel's wing erase the last P but one from his
brow.

He first tells what time it was.

> Ora era onde il salir non volea storpio,
>> Chè il sole aveva il cerchio di merigge*
>> Lasciato al Tauro e la notte allo Scorpio.

It was an hour in which the ascent brooked no
delay, because the Sun had left its meridian circle to
Taurus, and night to the Scorpion.

Dr. Moore (*Time References*, 107), says: "This is
one of the passages on which I think some superfluous
astronomical ingenuity has been expended, the point
being whether we are to make allowance for the retro-
cession of the Equinox and the error in the Calendar,
and so take the Sun's true astronomical position, or
whether we are to be guided by the ordinary popular
notion that the Sun is in Aries for a month from
March 21st onwards. The difference of the result is
absolutely immaterial, as it is only a question between
about 12.30 and 2 p.m., either hour here being quite
arbitrary and fictitious. Here again I think it is more
probable that Dante adopts the sense in which ordinary people would be most likely to understand his

---

* Compare *Purg.* II, 1 :—

> " Già era il sole all' orizzonte giunto,
>> Lo cui meridïan cerchio coverchia
>> Jerusalem col suo più alto punto :
> É la notte che opposta a lui cerchia,
>> Uscia di Gange fuor colle bilance,
>> Che le caggion di man quando soverchia."

words, just as we popularly refer to the indications of
the compass as it stands, without allowing for the
magnetic variation, though we are quite aware that in
England it amounts to a no less serious difference than
about 23 degrees. If this be the way to interpret the
passage, the Sun being now rather backward in Aries,
the time when Taurus is on the meridian of Noon, and
the opposite sign of Scorpio on that of midnight, as
here described, would be generally understood to be
about 2 p.m., though, as each constellation covers
many degrees of space, the indication is only an
approximate one."

We may therefore proceed on the assumption that
in Purgatory it was about 2 p.m., and in Europe about
2 a.m.

Dante now describes their progress by an appropriate simile.

> Per che, come fa l' uom che non s' affigge,*
> Ma vassi alla via sua, checchè gli appaja,   5
> Se di bisogno stimolo il trafigge ;
> Così entrammo noi per la callaja,†
> Uno innanzi altro, prendendo la scala
> Che per artezza i salitor dispaja.

Wherefore, as does the man who does not stop, but
goes his way, no matter what presents itself to him, if
the goad of necessity transfixes him; thus did we
enter through the gap, one before the other taking the

---

* *s' affigge : si ferma,* stands still. Compare *Purg.* XXX, 7:—
> " Fermo si affisse."
and XXXIII, 106-7 :—
> " Quando s' affisser, sì come s' affigge
> Chi va dinanzi a gente per iscorta."
† Blanc says that *callaja* is the opening in a hedge.

stairway, which by its narrowness divides (*lit.* dispairs) climbers.

Benvenuto remarks that Virgil was walking first, Statius second, and Dante third, and now, by a very intelligible comparison, Dante shows what an intense desire there was in his mind to put a certain question to his leaders, but that he lacked the courage to begin speaking. He is burning to know how it is possible for aërial forms, which have no need of food, to suffer from emaciation.

> E quale il cigognin che leva l' ala   10
>   Per voglia di volare, e non s' attenta
>   D' abbandonar lo nido, e giù la cala ;
> Tal era io, con voglia accesa e spenta
>   Di dimandar, venendo infino all' atto
>   Che fa colui ch' a dicer s' argomenta.*   15

And like the young stork, that spreads its wing with the will to fly, and yet does not venture to leave the nest, but lets it (the wing) droop again; such was I, with my desire of asking kindled, and (at the same time) quenched (for fear of saying anything displeasing), getting as far as the movement (of the lips) which he makes who prepares himself to speak.

Benvenuto says the comparison is appropriate in all its parts; for the great tragic poets, Virgil and Statius, may be compared to storks building their nests on the lofty roofs of houses, and Dante, as a junior poet, may well be likened to the fledgeling. And as the young stork desires to spread its wings before the fitting time,

---

* Compare Shakespeare (*Hamlet*, Act I, Sc. II, near the end):—
    "Answer it made none : yet once methought
     It lifted up its head and did address
     Itself to motion, like as it would speak."

but, feeling itself powerless to fly, lets them droop again, so did Dante, after walking for a mile in silence, feel keenly desirous of moving his tongue to propound a question on a very elevated subject; but, doubting whether he ought to fly before the fitting season, he repressed his desire until he had obtained the leave of his elders.

He did not have to wait long, for, just as Beatrice* on a subsequent occasion saw through his thirst for information, and ordered him to send forth the flame of his desire, so here does Virgil intuitively divine what is in his mind, and commands him to come out with it.

> Non lasciò, per l' andar che fosse ratto,
> Lo dolce padre mio, ma disse :—" Scocca
> L' arco del dir che insino al ferro hai tratto."—

My gentle father (Virgil) did not abstain (from speaking) for all that our pace was rapid, but said: "Let fly the bow of speech which thou hast drawn up to the barb."

Benvenuto remarks that speech flies as lightly and irrevocably as an arrow, and penetrates into the depth of the heart.

Virgil's words encourage Dante.

> Allor sicuramente aprii la bocca,
> E cominciai :—" Come si può far magro   20
> Là dove l' uopo di nutrir non tocca ?"—

Then I opened my mouth in all confidence, and

---

* See *Par.* XVII, 7-12 :—

> " Per che mia donna :—' Manda fuor la vampa
> Del tuo disio '—mi disse,—' sì ch' ella esca
> Segnata bene della interna stampa ;
> Non perchè nostra conoscenza cresca
> Per tuo parlare, ma perchè t' aúsi
> A dir la sete, sì che l' uom ti mesca.' "

began: "How can one grow lean there, where the need of nourishment applies not?"

Benvenuto observes that it was high time that Dante put this question, for all, that had been said in Hell and Purgatory of such wonderful varieties of punishment, would seem to be worth nothing, unless it were in some way made clear that the soul, when separated from the body, could by natural means be affected by hunger, thirst, or any other liability to suffering.

Virgil, in answer to Dante, tries to give him some sort of idea of the subject in question, by an example taken from mythology, and with a natural simile; he then turns to Statius, and begs him to solve the problem fully, and so satisfy Dante's craving for explanation.

    "Se t' ammentassi come Meleagro*

---

* *Meleagro*: Meleager was said to have been the son of Æneus, king of Calydon and Althæa. At his birth the Fates predicted: Clotho, that he would be brave; Lachesis that he would be strong; and Atropos that his life would last as long as a log, thrown upon the fire at the moment of his birth, remained unconsumed. As soon as the fates had departed Althæa snatched the brand from the fire, and preserved it carefully. See Ovid *Met.* VIII.

    "There lay a log unlighted on the hearth,
      When she was labouring in the throes of birth
      For the unborn chief: the fatal sisters came,
      And raised it up, and tossed it on the flame;
      Then on the rock a scanty measure place
      Of vital flax, and turned the wheel apace;
      And turning sung, 'To this red brand and thee,
      O new born babe, we give an equal destiny;'
      So vanished out of view. The frighted dame
      Sprung hasty from her bed, and quenched the flame.

Si consumò al consumar d' un stizzo,*
Non fora† (disse) questo a te sì agro.

" If thou wouldst call to mind," said he, "how Meleager wasted away during the consuming of a firebrand, this would not be so difficult (*lit.* sour) to thee (to understand.)

Benvenuto says that Althæa is put figuratively for every mother who bears a child, at whose birth the planets, according to the astrologers, at once prescribe the allotted period of life. The firebrand is a figure for the natural caloric of the body, and, as long as it lasts, life endures. Benvenuto adds that many persons had often asked him what possible connection there was between the history of Meleager, and the proposition we are ·considering ; and that he had always replied that no history could be more to the purpose ;

The log, in secret locked, she kept with care,
And that, whilst thus preserved, preserved her heir."

Meleager distinguished himself in the Argonautic expedition, and afterwards slew the wild boar of Calydon ; but a dispute having arisen between himself and his two uncles, Plexippus and Toxeus, Althæa's brothers, for the possession of it, he slew them both. Althæa, enraged at the slaughter of her brothers, threw the fatal log on the fire, and Meleager perished as it consumed.

* *stizzo* : compare *Inf.* XIII, 40-42 :—
    " Come d' un stizzo verde, che arso sia
        Dall' un de' capi, che dall' altro geme,
        E cigola per vento che va via."

† *fora :* for *sarebbe,* compare *Purg.* VI, 90 :—
        " Senz' esso fora la vergogna meno."
and *Par.* III, 73-75 :—
        " Se disiassimo esser più superne
            Foran discordi gli nostri disiri
            Dal voler di colui che qui ne cerne."

for, as Meleager gradually wasted away according to the wasting of the firebrand, so here did the spirits in the sixth cornice become lean in proportion to the amount of perfume from the fruit-tree, and the water trickling over its branches. And, as Meleager was consumed from an extrinsic cause, that is, the influence of the planets, so here do the spirits become emaciated from an extrinsic cause, namely, by the will of God. Some however have argued that the death of Meleager was brought about by magic art ; and this would be much to the purpose, for then he argues *a minori*, as Augustine rightly does in his book *De Civitate Dei*, where he says, that if necromancers are able to imprison the spirit in an aerial body, how much more can the Power of God confine the soul in corporeal fire.

And now Virgil brings forward a second example applicable to his proposition, and this is the reflected image, which moves in accordance with the body, as the body is reflected in the mirror.

> E se pensassi come al vostro guizzo   25
>   Guizza dentro allo specchio vostra image,
>   Ciò che par duro ti parrebbe vizzo.*

And if thou wouldst think how, at every movement (*lit.* quivering) on your part, your image moves within the mirror, that which seems hard would appear to thee easy.

"And now mark," says Benvenuto, "that this comparison seems to be very much to the point; for, as an image without substance moves in a mirror which has substance, so the unsubstantial soul is tormented in sub-

---

* *vizzo* according to Blanc is of uncertain origin, but implies whatever is the opposite of hard.

stantial air ; and as the reflection comes from without,
so suffering or power of feeling comes into the soul ·
from without." As there is need for discussing the
subject more closely, Virgil refers Dante to Statius.

> Ma perchè dentro a tuo voler t' adage,
> Ecco qui Stazio, ed io lui chiamo e prego,
> Che sia or sanator delle tue piage."—*   30

But in order that thou mayest get to the very depth
of the subject, to the full measure of thy desire, behold
here is Statius, and I call on him, and pray him, to be
now the healer of thy wounds."

Benvenuto says that it has puzzled many why Virgil
should leave this question to be solved by Statius.
He thinks it is because Virgil was a follower of Plato,
and held that souls were created from Eternity, and
descended from the planets into mortal bodies, and
after death returned to those planets : but that, as such
ideas were repugnant to Christianity, Dante makes
Virgil call upon Statius who was a Christian poet, and
who touches on these subjects in accordance with
philosophy and faith. Besides, Statius is at this time
qualified for heaven, having completed his purgation,
and may be supposed to know more of these matters
than Virgil, who will soon have to return to Limbo.

———

Division II. In this second division Dante tells
us how Statius makes a graceful admission, that he
cannot refuse any request from Virgil, although it is a
rash and hazardous thing to speak in his presence, and
he then answers and explains, at considerable length,

* *piage :* for *piaghe,* latin *plagæ.*

the difficult question that Dante had put, describing
the generation of the human embryo.

> " Se la veduta* eterna gli dislego,
>   (Rispose Stazio) là dove tu sie,
>   Discolpi me non poter' io far niego."—

" If I unfold to him," replied Statius, "the insight
into these eternal matters there where thou art
(present), let my not being able to deny thee anything
be my exculpation."

Benvenuto says that it is as though Statius said to
Virgil : " I am so much in the habit of taking every
word of thine as a precept, that I must perforce do
whatever thou askest me."

Statius now turns to Dante and, with much kindness of manner, tells him that, if he will give him
his attention, he will clear away his doubts.

> Poi cominciò : " Se le parole mie
>   Figlio,† la mente tua guarda e riceve,‡   3:
>   Lume ti fieno al come che tu die.||

He then began : " My son, if thy mind will contem-

---

* *veduta* is the reading of the large majority of the MSS., but
vendetta is not an uncommon reading, and, if adopted, the
passage would signify : " If I unfold to him the penalty imposed
by the Eternal God on the souls that are being purged."

† *figlio :* Benvenuto remarks that Statius would say : " O Son,
who hast two fathers here present, Virgil and myself.

‡ *guarda e riceve :* compare Prov. II, 1-5 :—
" My Son, if thou wilt receive my words, and hide thy commandments with thee . . . . . then shalt thou understand the
fear of the Lord, and the knowledge of God."

|| *die :* for *dici,* from which when the *c* was omitted was
obtained *dii,* and Nannucci (*Anal. crit.*) says that by the termination in *e,* which was formerly given to the second person
singular of the indicative present, the word *dii* was altered in *die.*

plate and receive my words, they will be to thee a light for the 'How' that thou sayest."

My words fully explain thy difficulty, and answer thy question : " How can one grow lean there where the need of nourishment applies not ? " Statius now proceeds to develop the theory of generation and the formation of the body with the vegetative and sensitive soul. And the words which Dante here puts into his mouth, may be found also in the *Convito* IV. ch. 21.*

---

* It will be well before studying the speech of Statius, to read the whole of chapter 21 of *Convito* IV, and compare Dante's own words there with what he says here : " In prima è da sapere che l' uomo è composto d' anima e di corpo ; ma dell' anima è quella, siccome detto è che è a guisa di semente della vertù divina . . . . . E però dico che quando l' umano seme cade nel suo recettacolo, cioè nella matrice, esso porta seco la vertù dell' anima generativa e la vertù del cielo, e la vertù degli alimenti legata, cioè la complessione del seme. Esso matura e dispone la materia alla vertù formativa, la quale diede l' anima generante ; e la vertù formativa prepara gli organi alla vertù celestiale, che produce della potenzia del seme l' anima in vita ; la quale incontanente produtta, riceve dalla vertù del motore del cielo lo intelletto possibile ; il quale potenzial mente in sè adduce tutte le forme universali, secondochè sono nel suo produttore e tanto meno quando più è dilungato dalla prima Intelligenzia. Non si maravigli alcuno, s' io parlo sì, che pare forte ad intendere ; chè a me medesimo pare maraviglia, come cotale produzione si può pur conchiudere e collo intelletto vedere : e non è cosa da manifestare a lingua, lingua dico veramente volgare . . . . . E perocche la complessione del seme può essere migliore e men buona; e la disposizione del seminato può essere migliore e men buona ; e la disposizione del cielo a questo effetto puote essere buona e migliore e ottima, la quale si varia nelle costellazioni, che continovamente si trasmutano ; incontra che dell' umano seme e di queste vertù più e men pura anima si produce : e seconda la sua purità discende in esso la vertù intellettuale possibile, che detta è e come detto è. E s' elli avviene che per la

> Sangue perfetto, che mai non si beve
> Dalla assetate vene, e si rimane*
> Quasi alimento che di mensa leve,
> Prende nel cuore a tutte membra umane   40
> Virtute informativa, come quello
> Che a farsi quelle per le vene vàne.

purità dell' anima ricevente, la intellettuale vertù sia bene astratta e assoluta da ogni ombra corporea, la divina bontà in lei multiplica, siccome in cosa sufficiente a ricevere quella : e quindi si multiplica nell' anima di questa intelligenzia, secondochè ricever può . . . . . Poichè la somma deità, cioè Iddio, vede apparecchiata la sua creatura a ricevere del suo beneficio, tanto largamente in quella ne mette, quanto apparecchiata è a riceverne."

According to Longfellow, Varchi (*Lezioni sul Dante, Firenze,* 1841) admires the dissertation in this Canto so much, that he says it is sufficient to prove Dante to have been a physician, philosopher and theologian, of the highest order: " I not only confess, but I swear, that as many times as I have read it, which day and night are more than a thousand, my wonder and aston- ishment have always increased, seeming every time to find therein new beauties and new instruction, and consequently new difficulties." The subject is also discussed by St. Thomas Aquinas, *Sum. Theol.* I, quæst. c. XIX, art. 2., *De propagatione hominis quantum ad corpus ;* but Scartazzini says that above all the treatise of Aristotle (*De. Gen. Animal.* Lib. I. ch. 19) should be studied, and the appendix of Tommaseo added to his com- mentary of this Canto.

* Varchi writes : " When the veins have sucked up a sufficient quantity of nourishment to restore the waste of the body, they do not suck up any more, just as a modest and temperate man, after eating what is necessary, leaves the remainder of his food, and therefore the expression *e si rimane quasi alimento,* that is, remains over and above just like food. . . . . . The idea con- veyed in Dante's words seems to me something like this, that like as the blood, that has not become semen, receives from the heart the power of becoming all the different members respect- ively, as is the case in nourishment ; for the bones change the

Blood in its perfect state, which never is drunk up by the thirsty veins, and remains like food that thou removest from the table, receives in the heart a virtue informative (*i.e.* creative power) for all the human members, like that (blood) which to be changed into these members runs through the veins.

Benvenuto remarks upon the appropriateness of this comparison ; for as, from that food set before a king or lord, that which remains, and is carried from the table, is as good as that which has been eaten, for it is of the same composition, so it is with the blood given to the heart ; for that which remains after a meal has been eaten, and the blood distributed through the veins, is as good as that which becomes nutrition (*in alimentum*).

Statius continues his physiological description.

> Ancor digesto, scende ov' è più bello
> Tacer che dire ; e quindi poscia geme
> Sovr' altrui sangue in natural vasello.*   45

Digested yet again, it descends (to those vessels) whereof it is better to be silent than to speak ; and from these afterwards it trickles upon another's blood in nature's vase.

---

blood into bones, the veins into veins, the flesh into flesh, and so on with all the others after the same fashion ; now just in the same way, after the perfect blood has been converted into semen, it has the power of forming all the members, operating upon the powers of the soul."

* *natural vasello* : Compare St. Thomas Aquinas, *Sum. Theol.* P. III, qu. XXXII, art. 4., "Fœmina ad conceptionem prolis materiam ministrat (quæ est sanguis menstruus), ex qua naturaliter corpus prolis formatur." And *Sum. Theol.* P. III, qu. XXXIII, art. 1, "Ad formationem corporis . . . . . requirebatur motus localis quo sanguines . . . . . ad locum generationi congruum pervenirent."

Ivi s' accoglie l' uno e l' altro insieme,
  L' un disposto a patire e l' altro a fare,*
  Per lo perfetto luogo onde si preme ; †
E, giunto lui, ‡ comincia ad operare,
  Coagulando prima, e poi s' avviva   50
  Ciò che per sua materia fe' constare.‖

Therein the (blood of the) one and the other mingle
together, the one (the female) prepared to be passive,

---

* *L' un disposto a patire e l' altro a fare.*
Compare St. Thomas Aquinas, *Sum. Theol.* P. III, qu. XXXII,
art. 4 : "In generatione distinguitur operatio agentis et
patientis. Unde relinquitur quod tota virtus activa sit ex parte
maris, passio autem ex parte fœminæ."

† *si preme :* Scartazzini explains this : "the blood of the male,
disposed to give form to the human members, issues as if
expressed from the heart."

‡ *giunto lui :* Scartazzini has no doubt of *lui* meaning *a lei*,
and having the signification : the blood of the male being conjoined to (mingled with) the blood of the female, &c.

‖ *fe' constare :* Compare St. Thomas Aquinas, *Sum. Theol.* P.
III, qu. XXXIII, art. 1 : "Formatio corporis fit per potentiam
generativam, non ejus qui generatur, sed ipsius generantis ex
semine, in quo operatur vis formativa ab anima patris derivata."
And P. III, qu. XXXII, art. 4 : "Potentia generativa in
fœmina est imperfecta respectu potentiæ generativæ quæ est in
mare. Et ideo sicut in artibus ars inferior disponit materiam,
ars autem superior inducit formam, ita etiam virtus generativa
fœminæ præparat materiam, virtus autem activa maris format
materiam præparatam."
Benvenuto says of *fe' constare :* "id est, remanere, *per sua
matera,* scilicet sanguinem menstruum quod fecit consistere ibi
pro sua materia, in quam imprimit suam formam : et bene dicit ;
nam communiter non fluit sanguis hic a muliere post impregna-
tionem ; unde habent istud commune signum conceptionis : et
non vult aliud dicere nisi quod generatur anima vegetativa in
fætu qualis est in arboribus."

and the other (the male) to be active, by reason of the perfect source (the heart) from which each respectively flowed; and (the male blood) being conjoined to it (the female blood) begins to operate, first by coagulating, and then gives life to that which, as substance necessary for its operation, it has made to take consistence.

And now Statius touches upon the generation of the sensitive soul, after the generation of the vegetative soul, each of which is evolved out of the potentiality of substance, and is not brought in from without, as is the rational soul, about which he speaks farther on.

Anima fatta la virtute attiva,*

---

* *Virtute attiva:* compare St. Thomas Aquinas, l.c.   P. I. qu. CXVIII, art. I:—

"Quia generans est simile generato, necesse est quod naturaliter tam anima sensitiva, quam aliæ hujusmodi formæ producantur in esse ab aliquibus corporalibus agentibus transmutantibus materiam de potentia in actum per aliquam virtutem corpoream quæ est in eis . . . . . Ex anima generantis derivatur quædam virtus activa ad ipsum semen animalis, vel plantæ . . . . . In animalibus perfectis, quæ generantur ex coitu, virtus activa est in semine maris ; materia autem fœtus est illud, quod ministratur a fœmina : in qua quidem materia statim a principio est anima vegetabilis, non quidem secundum actum secundum, sed secundum actum primum, sicut anima sensitiva est in dormientibus ; cum autem incipit attrahere alimentum, tunc jam actu operatur.   Hujusmodi igitur materia transmutatur a virtute quæ est in semine maris, quousque perducatur in actum animæ sensitivæ . . . . . Postquam autem per virtutem principii activi quod erat in semine, producta est anima sensitiva in generato quantum ad aliquam partem principalem, tunc jam illa anima sensitiva prolis incipit operari ad complementum proprii corporis per modum nutritionis et augmenti."

Qual d' una pianta,* in tanto differente,
Che quest' è in via, e quella è già a riva,
Tanto ovra poi che già si muove e sente, 55
Come fungo marino ;† ed indi imprende
Ad organar le posse ond' è semente.

---

* *Qual d' una pianta:* Scartazzini says that it is needless to
point out that Dante in this passage conforms to the doctrines
of St. Thomas Aquinas, and that it will be well to refer to what
he says on the succession of the souls—the vegetative, the sensitive, and the intellectual, in the formation of man.

See l.c. P.I. qu. CXVIII, art. 2. "Anima præexistit in
embryone, à principio quidem nutritiva, postmodum autem
sensitiva, et tandem intellectiva. Dicunt ergo quidam, quod
supra animam vegetabilem quæ primo inerat, supervenit alia
anima, quæ est sensitiva : supra illam iterum alia, quæ est
intellectiva. Et sic sunt in homine tres animæ, quarum una est
in potentia ad aliam, quod supra improbatum est. (Compare
Purg. IV, 1 et seq.). Et ideo alii dicunt quod illa eadem anima,
quæ primo fuit vegetativa tantum, postmodum per actionem
virtutis quæ est in semine, perducitur ad hoc ut ipsa eadem fiat
sensitiva, et tandem ad hoc ut ipsa eadem fiat intellectiva, non
quidem per virtutem activam seminis, sed per virtutem superi-
oris agentis, scilicet Dei deforis illustrantis. . . . . . Sed hoc
stare non potest . . . . . Et ideo dicendum est quod cum gene-
ratio unius semper sit corruptio alterius, necesse est dicere, quod
tam in homine, quam in animalibus aliis, quando perfectior forma
advenit, fit corruptio prioris ; ita tamen quod sequens forma
habet quidquid habebat prima, et adhuc amplius : et sic per
multas generationes et corruptiones pervenitur ad ultimam
formam substantialem tam in homine quam in aliis animalibus.
Et hoc ad sensum apparet in animalibus ex putrefactione gene-
ratis. Sic igitur dicendum est, quod anima intellectiva creatur
a Deo in fine generationis humanæ, quæ simul est et sensitiva
et nutritiva, corruptis formis præexistentibus."

† *si muove e sente come fungo marino :* spontaneous movement and feeling are essential characteristics of animal life, to
which Statius says the fœtus arrives.

Compare Ozanam (*Dante et la philos. cathol.* p. 111): " Cette

The active virtue (the male) having become a soul, as that of a plant, but in this much differing from it, that this one (the human life) is only on the way (*i.e.* has only reached the first stage), and that one (the plant) has already arrived (*i.e.* has reached perfection), it then works so much that already it moves and feels, as does a sea-fungus; and after that it undertakes to organize the powers of which it is the germ.

And Statius concludes this portion of his dissertation by saying to Dante.

> Or si spiega, figliuolo, or si distende
> La virtù ch' è dal cuor del generante,
> Dove natura a tutte membra intende :   60

Now, my son, the power which is (derived) from the heart of him who generates, at one time dilates, and at another time extends itself, in which (heart) nature is intent on (forming) all the members.

Both Benvenuto and Talice da Ricaldone translate the passage :

"Now it is explained to thee, now it is declared or made clear to thee, my son, from what has been said before, that nature has given so much power to the heart, that it is able to give forth that blood from which all the members are formed."

Division III. In this third division of the Canto, Statius explains how the embryo, from being a mere animal, becomes endowed with a rational soul.

------

vie, végétale d'abord, mais progressive, se développe par son propre exercice ; elle fait passer l'organisme de l'état de plante à celui de zoophyte, pour parvenir ensuite à la complète animalité."

In treating this difficult subject, Dante shows that he rejected the theory of *Traducianism* as taught by Averrhoës, Tertullian and others, who maintained that the human soul is generated at the same time as the body. Dante evidently adopted the theory of *Creationism*, and closely followed the teaching of St. Thomas Aquinas and the mediæval theologians, who held that the rational soul comes directly from God, Who, as soon as the organism of the brain has reached its full development, breathes into it a divine afflatus, and this attracts to it the principle of activity, with which it in its turn is brought in contact, when it unites with the embryo, and thus becomes a living soul, by the three acts of plant life, animal life, and rational life.

> Ma, come d' animal divenga fante,
>> Non vedi tu ancor : quest' è tal punto
>> Che più savio di te fe' già errante ;
> Sì che, per sua dottrina, fe' disgiunto
>> Dall' anima il possibile intelletto,*   65
>> Perchè da lui non vide organo assunto.

But, how from animal it becomes rational (*lit.* endowed with speech) thou canst not yet discern, for

---

* *intelletto possibile.* Compare St. Thomas Aquinas, *Summ. Theol.* P. I. qu. LXXIX, art. 10 : "Quandoque enim ponunt quatuor intellectus, scilicet intellectum agentem, possibilem, et in habitu, et adeptum ; quorum quatuor intellectus agens et possibilis sunt diverse potentiæ, sicut et in omnibus est alia potentia activa et alia passiva ; alia verò tria distinguuntur secundùm tres status intellectûs possibilis ; qui quandoque est in potentia tantùm, et sic dicitur possibilis ; quandoque autem in actu primo, qui est scientia, et sic dicitur intellectus in habitu ; quandoque autem in actu secundo qui est considerare, et sic dicitur intellectus in actu, sive intellectus adeptus."

this is the point—that it has already made one (Averrhoës), more learned than thou, to err so that in his teaching he separated the possible intellect from the soul, because he could see no organ appropriated by it (*i.e.* the possible intellect).

Averrhoës did not see in the human body any organ specially assigned to the intellect, as are the ears for hearing, the eyes for seeing, and so on with the other senses.

Ozanam (*Le Purgatoire de Dante, page* 418), writes : " Averrhoës, en commentant Aristote s'efforce d'établir que l'intellect qu'Aristote appelle possible est une substance séparée du corps quant à l'être, et qui lui est unie quant à la forme, et de plus que l'intellect possible est unique pour tous. Or, étant détruite la diversité d'intellect possible qui est seul immortel, il s'ensuit qu'après la mort il ne reste rien des âmes humaines que l'unité de l'intellect, et ainsi on supprime les peines et les recompenses. Albert le Grand ajoute que, distinguant l'âme sensible de l'âme intellectuelle, les péripatéticiens font naître la première du sang du père ; mais l'âme intellectuelle, ils la conçoivent séparée et rayonnant sur l'âme sensible comme le soleil sur le milieu transparent, et de même que si l'on ôte les objets illuminés il ne reste que la lumière du soleil, de même, les hommes périssant, il ne reste qu'une seule intelligence perpétuelle et impérissable."

In the language of the Schools, the potential intellect, is the faculty which receives impressions through the senses, and forms from them pictures or phantasmata in the mind. The active intellect draws from these pictures various ideas, notions, and conclusions. The two represent the Understanding and the Reason.

Statius is very anxious that Dante should be fully aware of the great difficulty of the above passage to render him forearmed against any incorrect explanations of it.   Benvenuto says that after having thus condemned the opinions of Averrhoës about the rational soul, he goes on to give the true opinion of the Catholic Church, namely, that the soul is given by the First Giver, God, and he begs Dante to take in fully and to retain the true doctrine.

> Apri alla verità che viene il petto,
>> E sappi che, sì tosto come al feto
>> L' articolar nel cerebro è perfetto,
> Lo Motor primo a lui si volge lieto*   .70
>> Sovra tanta arte di natura, e spira
>> Spirito nuovo di virtù repleto,
> Che ciò che trova attivo quivi tira
>> In sua sustanzia, e fassi un' alma sola,†
>> Che vive e sente, e sè in sè rigira.‡   75

---

* *lieto* : compare Purg. XVI, 88-90 :—

> " L' anima semplicetta, che sa nulla,
>> Salvo che, mossa da lieto fattore,
>> Volontier torna a ciò che la trastulla,"

and Psalm CIV, 31 : " The Lord shall rejoice in His works."

† *sola* : see *Purg.* IV, 5-6 :—

> " E questo è contra quello error, che crede
>> Che un' anima sovr' altra in noi s' accenda."

Scartazzini quotes from St. Thomas Aquinas on this (*Summ. Theol.* P. I, qu. LXXVI, art. 3) :—

" Sic ergo dicendum quod eadem numero est anima in homine, sensitiva et intellectiva et nutritiva. . . . . Prius embric habet animam quæ est sensitiva tantum : qua ablata, advenit perfectior anima, quæ est simul sensitiva et intellectiva."

‡ *sè in sè rigira* : reflecting within itself it acquires the conscience of its own existence.   Compare Boetius (*Phil. Cons.* lib. III, *Poes.* IX, 15 etc.) :—

Open thy breast to the truth which comes to thee, and know that as soon as the articulation of the brain is perfected in the embryo, the primal Mover turns to it, rejoicing at such great skill in nature, and breathes into it a new-born spirit replete with power, which draws into its own substance whatever it finds active in it (the embryo), and forms itself into one single soul, which lives, and feels, and revolves within itself.

The new-born rational soul draws in the vegetative and sensitive souls, and identifies them with its own substance and with itself and then forms one single soul having three powers, the vegetative, the sensitive, and the intellectual.

Benvenuto remarks on *sè in sè rigira*, that perhaps the meaning is that the movement of reason proceeds from the Creator, to the created thing; and thence from the created thing to the Creator as it were in a circle (*circulariter*).

"Quæ (*anima*) cum secta duos motum glomeravit in orbes,
  In semet reditura meat mentemque profundam
  Circuit et simili convertit imagine cælum."

Scartazzini says that, although Boetius is here speaking of the universal soul—the soul of the world, yet the expression *in semet reditura meat* might equally apply to the human and rational soul, inasmuch as the latter has, according to the Platonists, a double conversion, to intellectual matters and to sensitive matters, *i.e.*, that it resolves itself into two circles, one the external and greater, formed of the intelligible powers of the soul, the other internal and lesser, and contrary to the first, formed from the knowledge that the senses infuse into it, by means of which the soul revolves to the things of the world. And, because this movement forms a double circle of conversion, therefore the soul returns into itself; it being the property of the circle to revolve upon itself, or, as Aristotle (*Phys.* book VIII) says, to unite both beginning and end.

> E perchè meno ammiri la parola,
> Guarda il calor del sol che si fa vino,*
> Giunto all' umor che dalla vite cola.

And that thou mayest the less wonder at my speech, look at the heat of the sun, which gets turned into wine when combined with the juice that distils from the vine.

Benvenuto remarks upon the beauty and appropriateness of this comparison ; for, as the sun by its heat makes the wine, whose results are either the best or the worst, and to such an extent that some compare the nature of wine to the power of the gods, in like manner the Sun Eternal, in His beneficence, creates the rational soul, whose deeds will be either the best or the worst. So that the nature of the soul is almost divine, for it is as the result of the eternal light, and is indeed, as Themistocles says, nearly all things.

Statius, having established the production of the rational soul, now explains its mode of existence after the death of the body, and how it is that aerial bodies can suffer from leanness. He first describes, by a poetical figure, the separation of the soul from the body.

> E quando Lachesìs non ha più lino,
> Solvesi dalla carne, ed in virtute   80
> Ne porta seco e l' umano e il divino.

And when Lachesis has no more thread (*i.e.*, when man's life is run), it loosens itself from the flesh, and by its innate power (*in virtute*) bears away with itself

---

* Compare Redi (*Bacco in Toscana*, v. 15-16) :—
    " Sì bel sangue è un raggio acceso
    Di quel sol che in ciel vedete."

both the human (or corporeal) and the divine (intellectual faculties).

Statius next shows what the separated soul casts off and what it retains.

> L' altre potenzie tutte quante mute ;
>   Memoria, intelligenza, e volontade,*
>   In atto molto più che prima acute.

All the other faculties (that are not intellectual faculties from their representative organs being destroyed) are mute (*i.e.* inoperative) ; memory, intelligence, and will (which are spiritual faculties), are, in action more acute than before.

Being inorganic, these can be better exercised without the impediment of the body.

Benvenuto says that just as a sailor is not necessarily destroyed by the destruction or wearing out of his ship, so the soul, liberated from the body, has its own powers, and although it may not use them mechanically, it still retains its intellectual powers in greater perfection than before.

---

* Compare St. August. (*De Trinit.* lib. X, ch. 18): "Hæc igitur tria, memoria, intelligentia, voluntas, quoniam non sunt tres vitæ, sed una vita : non tres mentes, sed una mens : consequenter utique nec tres substantiæ sunt sed una substantia."

And St. Thomas Aquinas (*Summ. Theol.* P. I, qu. LXXVII, art. 8): "Omnes potentiæ animæ comparantur ad animam solam sicut ad principium. Sed quædam potentiæ comparantur ad animam solam sicut ad subjectum, ut intellectus et voluntas ; et hujusmodi potentiæ necesse est quod maneant in anima, corpore destructo. Quædam vero potentiæ sunt in conjuncto sicut in subjecto, sicut omnes potentiæ sensitivæ partis et nutritivæ. Destructo autem subjecto, non potest accidens remanere. Unde corrupto conjuncto, non manent hujusmodi potentiæ actu, sed virtute tantum manent in anima sicut in principio vel radice."

Statius next tells Dante whither goes the soul, thus separated from the body, and states that it immediately passes either into Hell or into Purgatory.

> Senza arrestarsi, per sè stessa cade   85
>   Mirabilmente all' una delle rive ;*
>   Quivi conosce prima le sue strade.†

Without delay, it falls spontaneously and in wondrous fashion upon one of the two shores ; here for the first time it learns its (allotted) path.

This means that the soul immediately after the death of the body, in obedience to divine impulse, instinctively wings its way to the bank of Acheron, if doomed to Hell, or to the bank of the Tiber, if to be transported to Purgatory, and not until it reaches one of these shores does it know on which of the two roads it will have to travel.

---

* *all' una delle rive* : compare *Purg.* II, 100-105 :—
>   " Ond' io che era ora alla marina volto,
>   Dove l' acqua di Tevere s' insala,
>   Benignamente fui da lui ricolto
>   A quella foce, ov' egli ha dritta l' ala :
>   Però che sempre quivi si ricoglie,
>   Qual verso d' Acheronte non si cala."

In *St. Luke* XVI, 22-3, we read : " the rich man also died, and was buried ; and in Hell he lift up his eyes, being in torments and seeth Abraham afar off, and Lazarus in his bosom."

† Scartazzini points out that no one seems to have noticed that Dante here contradicts what he has said elsewhere, that a Devil came to take the soul of Guido da Montefeltro as soon as ever it was loosed from the body (*Inf.* XXVII, 112 *et seq.*), and an Angel for that of Buonconte da Montefeltro, likewise at the instant of his death (*Purg.* v. 104 *et seq.*). So both of these souls knew their allotted paths before falling upon one of the two shores.

Benvenuto remarks that in either case the soul has to go by water.

Statius then describes how the soul, when it reaches its appointed shore, is turned to its allotted punishment.

> Tosto che luogo lì* la circonscrive,
> La virtù formativa raggia intorno,
> Così e quanto nelle membra vive ;   ' 90

So soon as the place (either Purgatory or Hell) circumscribes it, the formative virtue radiates around it in the same manner and measure as upon the living members (of the body to which it formerly was united).

Scartazzini prefers referring *così* to the form and features, and *quanto* to the measurement, so that the poet would mean to tell us that the soul shedding

---

* *lì* : Dante means that the soul puts on an aërial body as soon as ever it has lighted on one of the shores and is contained by the spot. Compare St. Thomas Aquinas (*Summ. Theol.* P. III, Suppl. qu. LXIX, art. 1):—

"Quamvis substantiæ spirituales secundum *esse* suum a corpore non dependeant, corporalia tamen a Deo mediantibus spiritualibus gubernantur, ut dicit Augustinus . . . . et Gregorius . . . . et ideo est quædum convenentia spiritualium substantiarum ad corporales substantias per congruentiam quamdam, ut scilicet dignioribus substantiis digniora corpora adaptentur . . . . Quamvis autem animabus post mortem non assignentur aliqua corpora, quorum sint formæ, vel determinati motores, determinantur tamen eis quædam corporalia loca per congruentiam quamdam secundum gradum dignitatis earum, in quibus sint quasi in loco, eo modo quo incorporalia esse possunt in loco . . . . Incorporalia non sunt in loco modo aliquo nobis noto, et consueto, secundum quod dicimus corpora proprie in loco esse ; sunt tamen in loco modo substantiis spiritualibus convenienti, qui nobis plene manifestus esse non potest."

forth its active power into the air, forms itself into a body, identical in form and features, and in the measurement or size of the human body that it animated in the world.

Statius next shows the new disposition which the soul acquires.

> E come l' aere, quando è ben piorno,
>> Per l' altrui raggio che in sè si riflette,*
>> Di diversi color diventa adorno,
> Così l' aër vicin quivi si mette
>> In quella forma che in lui suggella,   95
>> Virtualmente, l' alma che ristette.†

And as the air, when full of watery vapours from the effect of the rays of another (the Sun) which are reflected in it, becomes adorned with divers colours (of the rainbow), thus here does the air near (the place) shape itself into that form on the soul that has lighted there, gives its impress by innate power.

Benvenuto translates *virtualmente :* " quæ habet potentiam imprimendi talem formam." Scartazzini explains it " imprime in esso per propria virtù opera-

---

* *si riflette :* Scartazzini quotes from Antonelli that though *ri-flette* now means "reflect," in the time of Dante it also meant "re-fract," and thus one may see that Dante was in a fair way towards understanding the nature of the rainbow.

† *ristette :* The soul has the power of operating on matter, and impressing upon the surrounding air the shape which it animated in life, forms for itself an aërial vesture. Ozanam (*Purg.* p. 423) says : " Dante se fait une opinion moyenne. Il emprunte à St. Thomas la notion de l'âme séparée qui recueille ses puissances intellectuelles plus actives que jamais, sa sensibilité comme endormie ; à St. Augustin, à Origène, la notion de l'ombre ou du corps subtil." See also Dante, *Conv.* tr. II, c. 9.

trice," or "per effetto della conservata *virtù infor-
mativa.*"

Statius then shows what is the power of the soul in
its new garb. Benvenuto remarks that the comparison of the incorporeal soul to fire, which is a subtile
spiritual body, is very appropriate, for indeed some
have thought the soul to be fire.

> E simigliante poi alla fiammella
>> Che segue il fuoco là 'vunque si muta,
>> Segue allo spirto sua forma novella.

And thenceforth, after the manner of a little flame
which follows the fire wheresoever it shifts, so does
the new shape accompany the spirit.

The soul acquires a new name.

> Però che quindi ha poscia sua paruta,   100
>> È chiamata ombra ; e quindi organa poi
>> Ciascun sentire infino alla veduta.

And because from this (aërial form) it (the soul)
has hereafter its appearance (*i.e.,* becomes visible), it
is called a shade ; and from this it supplies an organ
to every one of the senses, even to sight.

Benvenuto says that some persons will have it that
the passions and feelings of the body do not remain
in the soul after its separation from the body, but
rather something else that resembles them, like as a
mechanic, who lacks both tools and materials, still
has their shapes and forms before him. For, since the
soul is naturally the perfection of the body, there remains in it, and in its powers of action, habits and
passions which follow the movements of the body,
just as in the mind of the sailor there remain the
thoughts and imaginations of his ship, after he has
been separated from it.

At last Statius brings his long discourse to a conclusion by establishing his principal proposition,
namely, that by these arguments the soul is shown to
be able to suffer in different ways, as though it had
been seated in a body.

> Quindi parliamo, e quindi ridiam noi,
>> Quindi facciam le lagrime e i sospiri
>> Che per lo monte aver sentiti puoi.　　　　105

From this (form) we speak, from it we laugh, from
it we produce the tears and the sighs which thou
mayest have heard in traversing the mountain.

> Secondo che ci affiggon li disiri
>> E gli altri affetti, l' ombra si figura,
>> E questa è la cagion di che tu miri."—

According as the desires and other passions make
an impression upon us, so does the shade figure itself,
and this is the cause of what thou wonderest at."

That is the reason why the soul, when separated
from the body, can endure suffering, about which Dante
was enquiring from Virgil, before he asked Statius to
explain it.*

---

* Virgil's own ideas on the subject are very clearly expressed
in *Æn.* VI, 723, *et seq.* (Conington's Transl.) :—

> " Know first, the heaven, the earth, the main,
>> The moon's pale orb, the starry train,
>>> Are nourished by a soul,
>> A bright intelligence, which darts
>> Its influence through the several parts,
>>> And animates the whole.
>> Thence souls of men and cattle spring,
>> And the gay people of the wing,
>> And those strange shapes that ocean hides
>> Beneath the smoothness of his tides.
>> A fiery strength inspires their lives,
>> An essence that from heaven derives

Division IV. Here begins the fourth division of
the Canto.

While holding their profound conversation, the

> Though clogged in part by limbs of clay,
> And the dull ' vesture of decay.'
> Hence wild desires and grovelling fears,
> And human laughter, human tears :
> Immured in dungeon-seeming night,
> They look abroad, yet see no light.
> Nay when at last the light has fled,
> And left the body cold and dead,
> E'en then there passes not away
> The painful heritage of clay ;
> Full many a long contracted stain
> Perforce must linger deep in grain.
> So penal sufferings they endure
> For ancient crime, to make them pure :
> Some hang aloft in open view
> For winds to pierce them through and through,
> While others purge their guilt deep-dyed
> In burning fire or whelming tide.
> Each for himself, we all sustain
> The durance of our ghostly pain ;
> Then to Elysium we repair ;
> The few, and breathe this blissful air :
> Till, many a length of ages past,
> The inherent taint is cleansed at last,
> And nought remains but ether bright,
> The quintessence of heavenly light.
> All these, when centuries ten times told
> The wheel of destiny have rolled,
> The voice divine from far and wide
> Calls up to Lethe's river side,
> That earthward they may pass once more
> Remembering not the things before,
> And with a blind propension yearn
> To fleshly bodies to return."

three poets have been ascending the staircase from
the sixth Cornice to the one above, and, as Statius
uttered the concluding words of his long discourse,
they seem to have stepped on to the seventh Cornice,
the last one of all in Purgatory, wherein the sins of
Lust or Luxury are being purged.

> E già venuto all' ultima tortura*
>   S' era per noi,† e vôlto alla man destra,‡   110
> Ed eravamo attenti ad altra cura.

And now we had arrived at the last turning, and
had bent to the right hand, and were intent on
another care.

They had been in deep speculation as to how
spirits can grow thin, but now they will have to turn
to the more practical question of how to avoid the
flames on this new Cornice.

---

* *tortura*: this word is interpreted by Jacopo della Lana,
Anonimo Fiorentino, Benvenuto, Post. Cassinese, Danielli, and
others of the older commentators in the sense of "turning"
(*torcimento*), and that interpretation has been adopted by the
Accademici della Crusca, but a great number of commentators have preferred to attach to it the sense of "torture."
Scartazzini, however, points out that *tortura* in the sense of
"torment" did not enter into the Italian language till much
later. In *Conv.* tr. IV, c. 7, Dante writes : "Per suo difetto
il cammino, che altri senza scorta ha saputo tenere, questo
scôrto erra, e *tortisce* per li pruni e per le ruine."

† *per noi*: the expression *venuto s' era per noi* is the rendering of the Latin *ventum erat ad* = we had come to ; comp.
Virg. *Æn.* VI, 45 : Ventum erat ad limen. And *Georg.* III,
98 : Ad prælia ventum est.

‡ *alla man destra*: as usual they turned to the right on
entering a new cornice. Comp. *Purg.* XIX, 80-81 :—

> " E volete trovar la via più tosto,
>   Le vostre destre sien sempre di furi."

A short explanation of what follows may not be out of place. As in the other cornices, so in this one, the pathway, from about 12 to 15 feet broad, runs right round the mountain between the high rocky cliff (*la ripa*) and the edge of the precipice below. The spirits who are being punished for incontinence stand against the rock, from which issue flames to torment them, but a wind, blowing from the contrary direction, that is, from the edge of the precipice, blows back the flames, and keeps them against the rock, so that a narrow pathway remains between the edge of the flames, and the edge of the precipice, and on this alone can the Poets walk without being burned.

> Quivi la ripa fiamma in fuor balestra,
>   E la cornice spira fiato in suso,
>   Che la riflette, e via da lei sequestra.

Here the cliff darts forth a flame outwards, and the cornice sends a blast upward, which turns it (the flame) back, and drives it away from it (the cornice).

Benvenuto interprets *sequestra* as separating the flame in two, so as to leave a narrow footway, as it were, between two walls of fire, but the interpretation I have followed, which is that of Fraticelli and Scartazzini, seems preferable, for the next three verses show very distinctly that the fire is on one side and the precipice on the other.

> Onde ir ne convenía dal lato schiuso   115
>   Ad uno ad uno, ed io temeva il fuoco
>   Quinci, e quindi temeva cadere giuso.

On this account we had to walk one by one on the open side (*i.e.* on the unprotected edge of the precipice), and I was in fear of the fire on the one side, and on the other of falling headlong.

Virgil now gives Dante some timely warning.

> Lo duca mio dicea :—" Per questo loco
> Si vuol tenere agli occhi stretto il freno,
> Perocch' errar potrebbesi per poco."— 120

My leader said : " Along this place one will have to keep a tight rein on the eyes ; for one might easily make a false step."

Benvenuto and others tell us that the allegorical meaning of this passage is that the eyes ought to be curbed, for otherwise one may easily fall into the sin of concupiscence.*

And as in each of the other cornices they have heard the voices of the penitents chanting the praise of the virtue opposed to the particular sin they are purging, so now do they hear the spirits of the sinners in lust chanting a hymn in praise of chastity.

> *Summæ Dëus clementiæ*,† nel seno
> Al grande ardore allora udii cantando,
> Che di volger mi fe' caler non meno.

---

* Compare Propertius (II, xv, 16) :—
> " Oculi sunt in amore duces."
and *Psalm* CXIX, 37 : " Turn away mine eyes from beholding vanity ; and quicken thou me in thy way."

† *Summæ Deus clementiæ :* the opening words of the hymn that the spirits in the flames were singing. There is only one hymn in the Breviarium Romanum that begins with these words, and that is in the service of Lauds on the Festival of our Lady of the Seven Sorrows ; but the words of that hymn have nothing to do with the sins purged in the Seventh Cornice. The principal commentators explain, however, that Dante was quoting from the hymn sung at the service of Matins on Saturday, which we are told was in Dante's time somewhat differently worded, and was remodelled at a later period. It runs as follows :—

"*Summæ Deus clementiæ*," I then heard them singing in the bosom of that great burning, which made me give my thoughts to turning round (towards them) not less (than taking heed to my footing).

Benvenuto explains it is as though Dante would say: "I had at first turned my eyes to look after my footing, as Virgil had enjoined me, but now I turned them with no less care towards the fire, when I heard the sacred chant."

Dante now directs his attention to the shades whom up till now he had not remarked.

> E vidi spirti per la fiamma andando ;
> Perch' io guardav' a' loro, ed a' miei passi,   125
> Compartendo la vista a quando a quando.

And I saw spirits going through the flame ; where-

"Summæ *Parens* clementiæ,
   Mundi regis qui machinam,
   Unius et substantiæ,
   Trinusque personis Deus
      Nostros pius cum canticis
   Fletus benigne suscipe :
   Ut corde puro sordium
   Te perfruamur largius.
      Lumbos, jecurque morbidum
   Flammis adure congruis,
   Accincti ut artus excubent
   Luxu remoto prossimo.
      Quicumque ut horas noctium
   Nunc concinendo rumpimus,
   Ditemur omnes affatim
   Donis beatæ patriæ.
      Præsta pater piissime,
   Patrique compar Unice.
   Cum Spiritu Paraclito
   Regnans per omne sæculum.
            Amen."

upon I looked at them from time to time dividing my
gaze with my footsteps.

Dante next tells how he heard the spirits crying
aloud the words of the Blessed Virgin to the Archangel
Gabriel, " I know not a man " (*St. Luke* I, 34). As we
have seen in the other cornices, so we find here an
example from the life of the Virgin contrasted with the
sin being purged.

> Appresso il fine ch' a quell' inno fassi,
>> Gridavano alto : *Virum non cognosco;*
> Indi ricominciavan l' inno bassi.

After the conclusion which is made to that hymn,
they cried with a loud voice : *Virum non cognosco;*
then they recommenced the hymn in low tones.

They are recording examples of the virtue of chastity, the opposite to sins of lust. They proclaim the
examples aloud, as if to remind themselves of the
reproof to their own sins given by these holy incidents,
but when they recommence singing the other stanzas
of the hymn " Summæ Deus clementiæ," they do so
with bated breath, because they are uttering a humble
prayer to God.

The next example given is that of Helice.*

---

* Helice, sometimes called Callisto, was supposed to have
been the daughter of Lycaon, King of Arcadia. She was one of
the attendant nymphs of Diana, who discarded her on account of
an amour with Jupiter, and Juno turned her and her child Arcas
into bears. Jupiter then changed them again into the constellations of the Great and Little Bear. The tale-is told in Ovid,
Met. II (Addison's translation). After Callisto had been changed
into a bear her son, not yet transformed, finds her.

> " But now her son had fifteen summers told,
> Fierce at the chase, and in the forest bold ;
> When, as he beat the woods in search of prey,
> He chanced to rouse his mother where she lay.

> Finitolo, anche gridavano : *Al bosco*   130
> *Si tenne Diana, ed Elice caccionne*
> *Che di Venere avea sentito il tosco.*

This done, they cry out anew: " Diana stayed in the wood and drove from it Helice who had felt the poison of Venus."

Benvenuto says that Diana, the moon, whose influence was thought to be favourable to maidenhood, is supposed to go forth with her virgin nymphs to the chase for the purpose of destroying wild beasts, that is, to promote the mortification of the lusts of concupiscence, which lacerate and wound the soul and body worse than any wild beast.

In conclusion Dante describes another song in praise of chaste men and women.

> Indi al cantar tornavano ; indi donne
> Gridavano, e mariti che fur casti,
> Come virtute e matrimonio imponne.   135

Then they turned to their singing ; then they proclaimed wives and husbands who were chaste, according as virtue and wedlock ordain.

Benvenuto and Buti read " indi donne *gridavano i mariti che fur* casti," which would be translated : "after this, women took up the cry, and proclaimed the virtues of husbands who were chaste." But if this were the

---

She knew her son, and kept him in her sight,
And fondly gazed : the boy was in a fright,
And aimed a pointed arrow at her breast,
And would have slain his mother in the beast ;
But Jove forbad, and snatched them through the air
In whirlwinds up to heaven, and fixed them there ;
Where the new constellations nightly rise,
And add a lustre to the northern skies."

correct reading we should not have been told what the men were proclaiming. We may also take for granted that all the spirits in the cornice of either sex must have · been guilty of the sin of lust, and would have enough to do in purging their own sins, without thinking of what was profitable for the souls of the other sex.

Dante concludes the Canto by saying :

> E questo modo credo che lor basti
> Per tutto il tempo che il fuoco gli abbrucia ;
> Con tal cura convien, con cotai pasti
> Che la piaga dasezzo* si ricucia.   139

And this habit, I believe, suffices them for the whole of the time that the fire burns them ; with such a cure, with such a diet, is it necessary that the last wound (*i.e.*, the last of the seven P's) should be healed, (*lit.*, sewn up).

Benvenuto says this is a beautiful and appropriate metaphor ; for, as the physician sews up an extensive wound, and sometimes burns it with fire that it may not putrefy, so does the Eternal Physician here purge away the sin of Luxury by fire, that it may not introduce poisonous matter into the soul.

---

* *La piaga dasezzo :* Blanc interprets " Da sezzo " or " das-sezzo " as " alla fine, finalmente, da ultimo."

END OF CANTO XXV.

CANTO XXVI.

—

The Seventh Cornice.
Purgation of Incontinence (*continued*).

THIS Canto is so exceptional as to the subjects treated in it, that I think it desirable to abstain from the close explanation that I have endeavoured to give elsewhere. I am compelled to translate the text as written by Dante, whose meanings and intentions (often greatly misinterpreted and misunderstood) can be studied in Scartazzini's notes.

We read in the concluding division of the preceding Canto, the description of the penance of those who have yielded to the sin of incontinence. In this Canto Dante continues the subject.

Benvenuto divides the Canto into three parts.

In the First Division, from v. 1 to v. 51, Dante introduces two bands of penitents, and one of the shades in the first band addresses a certain question to Dante.

In the Second Division, from v. 52 to v. 102, Dante answers the question, tells the spirits who he is, and desires those in both bands to tell him their names.

In the Third Division, from v. 103 to v. 148, he speaks with great praise of a shade who in life had been famed for writing verses, both in the Provençal as well as in the mother-tongue, and he also names other authors and troubadours, both in France and Italy, who

were celebrated at the time, and among them Arnauld
Daniel, a Provençal poet and troubadour.

Division I. Virgil again warns Dante to beware
how he walks.

> Mentre che sì per l' orlo, uno innanzi altro,
>> Ce n' andavamo, e spesso il buon maestro
>> Diceva :—" Guarda ; giovi ch' io ti scaltro,"*—

While we thus wended our way along the edge (of
the cornice), one before the other, the good master
(Virgil) kept saying often to me : "Take heed, and
let my warning profit thee."

We learn from verses 16 and 17 that Dante was
walking behind Virgil and Statius. Benvenuto has a
long digression here showing that Virgil was warning
Dante against the sin of incontinence, when he used
the above words.

Dante now tells us what was the hour.

> Feriami il Sole in su l' omero destro,
>> Che già, raggiando, tutto l' occidente   5
>> Mutava in bianco aspetto di cilestro ;

Striking me on the right shoulder was the sun, who,
darting forth his rays, was already changing the whole
west from its azure colour into white.

On this passage let us again turn to Dr. Moore
(*Time References*, 108) :—

" In XXVI, 4-6, they are on the 7th and last cornice,
where lust is punished, and the time is apparently
about 4 or 5 p.m., since the sun is getting low in the
west. This is indicated by two circumstances : (1)
the blue of the western sky is turned pale by his light,

---

* *ti scaltro :* Blanc says of *scaltrire*, that it is from the Latin
callere, to instruct, to draw attention to anything.

and (2) his rays strike them on the shoulder, which indicates a low altitude. Note the continuation of this beautiful passage. Dante's body does not cast a shadow here, as so often elsewhere in his passage through Purgatory, falling as it does on the burning flame in which those spirits are being purified. The only effect produced by it is that the flames appear more ruddy where it intercepts the sun's rays. Observe the words '*pure a tanto indizio*,' v. 8. Some of my readers may remember that these few lines are quoted by Mr. Ruskin (*Mod. Painters* II, p. 259), as probably the finest description in literature of intense heat. He maintains that in these few very simple, and in some sense common-place, touches, Dante '*with no help from smoke or cinders*' has produced a more vivid effect than Milton has secured in ten lines of elaborate description and varied imagery. Dante's few words suggest, as Ruskin says, '*lambent annihilation.*' I wish I had space to illustrate further this splendid and unequalled power in Dante, of piercing at once to the very heart of things, and revealing, as it were, a whole world of scenery, or of emotion, or of passion at a flash, and as often as not by a flash of silence, that is more eloquent than any words."

Dante now describes the first band of the spirits of the incontinent ; but first shows how they pondered over his having a living body, which cast a shadow to his left.

> Ed io facea con l' ombra più rovente
> Parer la fiamma ; e pure a tanto indizio
> Vidi molt' ombre, andando, poner mente.

And I with my shadow caused the flames to appear more ruddy ; and even to this sign (of my being alive)

I perceived that many of the shades, as they passed, gave heed.

The only way that on this occasion Dante could be seen to have a shadow was, that where it was projected on the flames they showed redder, which fire always does when seen in the shade.

> Questa fu la cagion che diede inizio 10
> Loro a parlar di me ; e cominciârsi
> A dir :—" Colui non par corpo fittizio."—*

This was the occasion that gave them an opening to speak about me ; and they began saying one to the other: "That does not seem to be a fictitious body (like ours)."

On hearing this wonderful intelligence the other spirits all flocked towards Dante.†

> Poi verso me, quanto potevan farsi,‡
> Certi si feron, sempre con riguardo
> Di non uscir dove non fossero arsi. 15

---

* Blanc (*Voc. Dant.*) says that *fittizio* is the opposite of *reale*, real.

† Compare *Purg.* II, 67-75 :—

> " L' anime che si fur di me accorte,
> Per lo spirar, ch' io era ancor vivo,
> Maravigliando diventaro smorte ;
> E come a messaggier, che porta olivo,
> Tragge la gente per udir novelle,
> E di calcar nessun si mostra schivo ;
> Così al viso mio s' affisar quelle
> Anime fortunate tutte quante,
> Quasi obbliando d' ire a farsi belle." ·

‡ *farsi avanti* is a well-known Tuscan idiom, meaning to step forward. *Farsi verso uno*: to approach any one. Compare *Purg.* VIII, 52 :

> " Vêr me si fece, ed io vêr lui mi fei :"

Then certain of them came towards me, as near as they could, always with heed not to come forth to where they would not be burned.

They would not for one single instant interrupt their penance. It must be noticed that in Purgatory the spirits not only submit willingly to the chastisement imposed upon them, but they actually love it. In *Purg.* XI, 73, Oderisi begs Dante to walk stooping beside him ; in XIV, 124, Guido del Duca begs him to depart as he is more desirous of weeping than of talking ; in XVI, 142, Marco Lombardo will not listen any more to him for fear of leaving the pitchy smoke ; in XVIII, 115, the penitents beg him not to ascribe it to any discourtesy if they leave him, but only to their wish to move on; in XIX, 139, Pope Adrian begs Dante to pass on and not retard his penitent weeping; in XXIV, 91, Forese leaves him because he says that in that kingdom the time is too precious ; and here the penitents take heed to keep within the flames.

One of the spirits now addresses Dante. We shall see that it was Guido Guinicelli.

—"O tu che vai, non per esser più tardo,
       Ma force reverente, agli altri dopo,
       Rispondi a me che in sete e in fuoco ardo :*

"O thou, who goest behind the others, not from being slower, but perchance out of reverence (for thy companions), answer me, who am burning in thirst and fire.

---

* Compare *Inf.* XXVII, 22-24 :—
    " Perch' io sia giunto forse alquanto tardo,
        Non t' incresca restare a parlar meco.
        Vedi che non incresce a me, ed ardo."

And he confirms his words by an appropriate comparison.

> Nè solo a me la tua risposta è uopo ;
>> Chè tutti questi n' hanno maggior sete   20
>> Che d' acqua fredda Indo o Etiópo.

Nor is it by me alone that thine answer is needed ;
for all of these (the penitent) have a thirst for it
greater than an Indian or an Ethiop for cold water.

He supposes that dwellers in the hottest parts of
the earth are those, who would most suffer from thirst

> Dinne com' è che fai di te parete
>> Al sol, come se tu non fossi ancora
>> Di morte entrato dentro dalla rete ? "—

Tell us how it is that thou makest thyself a wall
to the sun, as though thou hadst not yet entered
into the net of death ? "

Benvenuto says the simile is very appropriate, for
death casts its net into the great sea of mortals, and
lays hold of every species of living being.

> Sì mi parlava un d' essi ; ed io mi fora   25
>> Già manifesto, s' io non fossi atteso
>> Ad altra novità ch' apparse allora ;

Thus did one of them address me; and I should
straightway have made myself known, had I not given
my attention to another new thing, which then appeared.

We learn from v. 92 that the speaker was Guido
Guinicelli, of whom Benvenuto relates that he was a
knight of a very illustrious family of Bologna, banished
for their imperialist sympathies by a civil sedition.
Guido himself was a prudent, eloquent man, who composed beautiful sonnets in his mother tongue, and was
not only of a mercurial temperament in his genius and
his speech, but also in his amorous susceptibilities.

Benvenuto expresses his regret to think of how many men, virtuous in other ways, have been marred by a disposition to licentiousness.

Dante now tells us that the new thing that caught his attention was the arrival of a fresh band of spirits.

> Chè per lo mezzo del cammino acceso
> Venne gente, col viso incontro a questa,
> La qual mi fece a rimirar sospeso.　　　30

For, through the middle of the fiery path, there came a people with their faces turned the opposite way to those (of the first company), which (people) made me stop to gaze.

> Lì veggio d' ogni parte farsi presta
> Ciascun' ombra, e baciarsi una con una
> Senza restar, contente a breve festa.

There (where they met) I saw every shade advance from either side, and one by one kiss each other without staying, content with a brief exhibition of affection.

Dante compares the two companies to a swarm of ants.

> Così per entro loro schiera bruna
> S' ammusa l' una con l' altra formica,*　　　35
> Forse ad espiar† lor via e lor fortuna.

---

* *formica*: compare Virg. *Æneid*, IV, 404 (Conington's trans.)
> " E'en as when ants industrious toil
> Some mighty heap of corn to spoil,
> And mindful of the cold to come
> Convey their new worn beauty home :
> There moves the column long and black,
> And threads the grass with one thin track :
> Some labouring with their shoulders strong
> Heave huge and heavy grains along :
> Some force the stragglers into file :
> The pathway seethes and glows the while."

† *espiar*: Blanc says that *spiare* is akin to the German *spähen*, to investigate.

Thus within their dusky battalions one ant meets another muzzle to muzzle, perchance to espy their path and their luck.

The ants give each other information, as to the path to be pursued, and as to the good or bad fortune they have had in finding food.

Dante now tells us what the spirits said to one another.

> Tosto che parton l' accoglienza amica,
>> Prima che il primo passo lì trascorra,
>> . Sopragridar ciascuna s' affatica ;
> · La nuova gente : *Soddoma e Gomorra;*
>> E l' altra : *Nelle vacca entra Pasife,*
>> *Perchè il torello a sua lussuria corra.*

As soon as they terminate their friendly greeting, before ever the first footstep passes away from that spot, each (spirit) vies with the other in crying the loudest ; the newly (arrived) company : *Sodom and Gomorrah;* and the other : *Into the* (effigy of the) *cow Pasiphae enters, in order that the bull may run to her lust.*

Dante then, by a simile, describes the departure of the spirits.

> Poi come gru,* ch' alle montagne Rife
>> Volasser parte, e parte invêr le arene,
>> Queste del giel, quelle del sole schife :   45

Then, like the cranes, of which one flock should fly towards the Rhiphæan mountains,† and the other flock

---

* It is remarkable that the word "*gru*" only occurs twice in the *Divina Commedia,* and both times as a simile connected with those punished for incontinence. The other instance is in *Inf.* v. 46.

† The Rhiphæan mountains were supposed to be situated in the North of Scythia, but the name was applied to any cold mountain in a northern country.

towards the sands (the Libyan deserts), the one
portion fighting shy of the ice, and the other of the
(heat of the) sun.

> L' una gente sen va, l' altra sen viene,
> E tornan lagrimando a' primi canti,
> Ed al gridar che più lor si conviene.

The one company goes, the other comes, and with
tears they return to the chants they were singing
before, and to the cry which is most adapted to them.

Their chant was *Summæ Deus clementiæ*, their cry
was one of the examples of chastity which best con-
veyed the lesson of the contrary to their special sin.
Benvenuto says that it is more honourable to chant
and cry out the names of the All Merciful God and
the Virgin Mary, than to cry out Sodom and Gomorrah and the like.

Dante next tells us that the shades turned to the
edge of the flame awaiting his answer.

> E raccostârsi a me, come davanti,
> Essi medesmi che m' avean pregato,   50
> Attenti ad ascoltar ne' lor sembianti.

And those same (spirits), who had entreated me (to
speak) drew near to me, as (they had done) before
(the other band interrupted them), showing in their
countenances great attention to listen.

———

Division II. We here commence the second division
of the Canto, in which Dante, in answer to the
questions put to him, states his own identity, and gets
from both bands of spirits information as to themselves.

> Io, che due volte avea visto lor grato,
>   Incominciai :—" O anime sicure
>   D' aver quando che sia di pace stato,
> Non son rimase acerbe nè mature   55
>   Le membra mie di là, ma son qui meco
>   Col sangue suo e con le sue giunture.

I, who had twice perceived what they desired (*lor grato*) began : " O souls, sure of attaining a state of peace, whenever it may be, (know that) my limbs have not remained yonder (on earth) either tender or ripe, but are here with me now with their blood and all articulations.*

He means that he had neither died when young nor when old, but that his body was present as well as his soul. Benvenuto explains that this means that Dante was not only alive, but of middle age.

And now, because with the petition the spirits had made to Dante, they had at the same time assured him that they did not think that it was from any slothful lack of zeal that he was walking last of the three poets, he therefore, who, as Benvenuto points

---

* Aristotle taught that man was the body unformed by the soul. Plato held man to be the soul alone disjoined from the body. Dante here follows the doctrine of his master St. Thomas Aquinas, that man is neither the body alone, nor the soul alone, but the two together. See *Summ. Theol.* P. I, qu. LXXV, art. 4. : " Nam ad naturam speciei pertinet id quod significat definitio. Definitio autem in rebus naturalibus non significat formam tantum, sed formam et materiem. Unde materia est pars speciei in rebus naturalibus, non quidem materia signata, quæ est principium individuationis, sed materia communis. Sicut enim de ratione hujus hominis est quod sit ex anima, et carnibus, et ossibus; oportet enim de substantia speciei esse quidquid est communiter de substantia omnium individuorum sub specie contentorum."

out, sought not praise, but purgation of his sins, answers humbly, confessing his negligence and ignorance.

> Quinci su* vo per non esser più cieco :
> Donna è di sopra che n' acquista grazia,†
> Per che il mortal pel vostro mondo reco.   60

Up here (on this mountain) am I going, so as to be no longer blind (to God's grace): there is above (in Heaven) a Lady (the Blessed Virgin) who wins grace for us (*ne*), in virtue of which (grace) I bear the mortal part of me through your world.

He then begs both these shades, as well as those in the other band, to tell him their names.

> Ma, se la vostra maggior voglia sazia
> Tosto divenga, sì che il ciel v' alberghi,
> Ch' è pien d' amore e più ampio si spazia,
> Ditemi, acciò che ancor carte ne verghi
> Chi siete voi, e chi è quella turba   65
> Che se ne va diretro a' vostri terghi ? ''—

But as I pray that your greater longing may soon become satisfied, so that that Heaven may house you,

---

* *quinci sù :* Scartazzini is very positive that this means *quassù,* "here," but not "to heaven," only "on this mountain."

† *Donna è di sopra che n' acquista grazia :* Some commentators pass over this passage, others take it for granted that Beatrice is the lady meant, but Scartazzini contends very reasonably that it refers to the lady in heaven who sent Lucia to Virgil ; see *Inf.* II, 94-96 :—

> "Donna è gentil nel ciel, che si compiange
> Di questo impedimento ov' io ti mando,
> Sì che duro giudicio lassù frange."

He lays great stress on *n' acquista grazia,* who wins grace *for us* men, and says that even conceding that it was Beatrice who won grace for Dante, no one can make out that Dante would mean that she acquires grace for all men.

which is full of love and is of widest extent (*i.e.* the Empyrean, which encircles all the other heavers) ; tell me, in order that I may hereafter record it on paper, who are ye, and who are that multitude that go thus behind your backs."

Dante describes the effect of his answer, and relates how the spirits, when they heard of his being alive, were struck dumb with astonishment.

> Non altrimenti stupido si turba
> > Lo montanaro, e rimirando ammuta,
> > Quando rozzo e salvatico s' inurba,
> Che ciascun' ombra fece in sua paruta ;   70
> > Ma poi che furon di stupore scarche,
> > Lo qual negli alti cuor tosto s' attuta,
> —" Beato te, che delle nostre marche,"—
> > Ricominciò colei che pria m' inchiese,
> —" Per <u>viver</u> meglio esperienza imbarche !   75

Not otherwise is the mountaineer stupidly bewildered, and is speechless as he looks around, when rough and rustic he comes into the town, than each one of the shades became in its appearance ; but when they had got over (*lit.* were disburdened) their amazement, which in elevated minds is quickly subdued : " Blessed art thou," began again the same one who first had made his request to me, " who art embarking experience (which will enable thee) to live better.

Some read *per morir meglio*, but *viver* seems to be the reading generally preferred. Scartazzini in his note criticizes Benvenuto, but makes it evident that he must have taken Benvenuto's opinion from the unfaithful translation by Tamburini in 1830. Scartazzini says that Benvenuto most inaptly reads *Per morte meglio*, quoting Benvenuto in Italian. In the original

Latin, however, Benvenuto's words are: "*'per viver meglio.' Nec dubito quod poeta melius vixit, et melius mortuus est per compilationem hujus operis.*" "Nor do I doubt that the poet did live a better life, and qualified himself for a better death by the compilation of this work." So that Benvenuto may have known both readings, and while preferring the one may have made his remarks deal with both.

Guido Guinicelli now gives Dante the information he asks about both bands of spirits, and tells him of the sin of the other company with much plainness of speech.

> La gente che non vien con noi, offese
> Di ciò per che già Cesar, trionfando,
> *Regina*, contra sè, chiamar s' intese ;
> Però si parton *Soddoma*, gridando,
> Rimproverando a sè, com' hai udito,   80
> Ed ajutan l' arsura vergognando.

The people that come not with us (*i.e.* those that walk in the opposite way), were guilty of that, on account of which in former days (Julius) Cæsar, at one of his triumphs, heard himself called "Queen," as a term of reproach. That is why they part from us crying "Sodom" in self vituperation, as thou hast heard, and by (the glow of) their shame assist the burning.

> Nostro peccato fu ermafrodito ;*
> Ma perchè non servammo umana legge,
> Seguendo come bestie l' appetito,

---

* I do not offer any opinion on this much disputed passage, further than this, that whereas the company that cried Sodom and Gomorrah turned to the left, that in which Guido Guinicelli was turned to the right—a very marked indication that Dante implied that they had been less sinful than the others.

> In obbrobrio di noi, per noi si legge, 85
> Quando partiamci, il nome di colei
> Che s' imbestiò nell' imbestiate schegge.

Our sin was hermaphrodite (*i.e.* we were guilty of perfectly unbridled depravity) ; but because we violated the laws of humanity, following our appetites like brute beasts, therefore, to our own shame, is cried out by us (*si legge*), when we part company, the name of her that wore a brute's form in the wickerwork beast.

And now Guido excuses himself from naming any one but himself.

> Or sai nostri atti, e di che fummo rei :
> Se forse a nome vuoi saper chi semo,
> Tempo non è da dire, e non saprei. 90
> Farotti ben di me volere scemo ;
> Son Guido Guinicelli,* e già mi purgo
> Per ben dolermi prima ch' allo stremo."—

Now thou knowest our deeds, and of what we were guilty : if perchance thou desirest to know by name who we are, there is no time to tell (for it was near evening), nor should I know (among so many). I will indeed satisfy thy wish (*lit.* make thee desire less) as regards myself ; I am Guido Guinicelli, and I am already purging myself, because I deeply repented before my extreme hour."

---

* *Guido Guinicelli*, the best of the Italian poets before Dante, flourished in the first half of the thirteenth century. He was a native of Bologna, but of his life nothing is known. His most celebrated work is a canzone on the nature of Love, which goes far, says Longfellow, to justify the warmth and tenderness of Dante's praise. Dante speaks of him in the *De Volgari Eloquio* as the greatest of the Bolognese poets, and in one of his canzoni says :—
> " Al cor gentil ripara sempre Amore."

Dante's delight on finding that the speaker was Guido Guinicelli is so great, that he compares it to that of the twin brothers Thoas and Eunius, on recognizing their mother Hypsipyle.

> Quali nella tristizia di Licurgo*
>> Si fêr duo figli a riveder la madre,   95
>> Tal mi fec' io (ma non a tanto insurgo)
> Quand' i' odo nomar sè stesso il padre†
>> Mio, e degli altri miei miglior, che mai‡
>> Rime d' amore usâr dolci e leggiadre : ‖
> E senza udire e dir pensoso andai,   .   100
>> Lunga fïata rimirando lui,
>> Nè per lo fuoco in là più m' appressai.

Such as the two sons became when they again saw their mother, during the grief of Lycurgus, such became I, but without going so far (as to rush forward

---

* Lycurgus, King of Nemea, was about to put to death Hypsipyle, to whose negligence he attributed the death of his infant son Opheltes, who had died by the bite of a serpent. As she was being led to execution she was recognised by her twin sons, Thoas and Eunius, who rushed forward and delivered her. See Statius, *Thebaid* V, 721 *et seq.*

† *il padre mio* : compare *Inf.* XV, 82-85 :—

> " Chè in la mente m' è fitta, ed or mi accora,
>> La cara e buona imagine paterna
>> Di voi, quando nel mondo ad ora ad ora
>> M' insegnevate come l' uom s' eterna."

These words are addressed to Brunetto Latini, his former master in science, as Guido Guinicelli was in poetry. Curiously enough both are undergoing chastisement for the same offence.

‡ *miei miglior* : Contrast with *Purg.* XI, 97-99:—

> " Così ha tolto l' uno all' altro Guido
>> La gloria della lingua ; e forse è nato
>> Chi l' uno e l' altro caccerà di nido."

‖ *dolci e leggiadre* : compare Horace, *Ars. Poet.* 99 :—.

> " Non satis est pulchra esse poemata ; dulcia sunto."

as they did), when I heard him (Guido Guinicelli)
name himself, who was the father (in poesy) to me,
and to the others, my betters, who have ever turned
sweet and graceful rhymes of love ; and I walked on
in thought for a long time without hearing or speaking,
gazing on him the while, yet on account of the flames
I did not approach him nearer.

———

Division III.   Here commences the third and concluding division of the Canto, in which Dante speaks
in warm praise of Guido Guinicelli for his noble
poetry, and also mentions incidentally several French
and Italian troubadours and poets.

> Poi che di riguardar pasciuto fui,
>> Tutto m' offersi pronto al suo servigio,
>> Con l' affermar che fa credere altrui.   105

As soon as I was satiated with gazing, I offered
myself as quite ready for his service, with that affir-
mation that makes others believe.

He invoked God to witness the promise that he
would speak up for Guido's good name, and would
have prayers offered up for him.   Verse 109 shows
that Dante swore to do so.

Guido, in reply, tells Dante that he has already
done him service in perpetuating his fame.

> Ed egli a me :—"Tu lasci tal vestigio,
>> Per quel ch' i' odo, in me, e tanto chiaro,
>> Che Lete nol può torre nè far bigio.

And he to me : " Thou leavest such a trace, and so

distinct in me, from what I hear, as Lethe cannot efface, nor make obscure.

We shall see in Canto XXXI, 91-104, that souls before passing from Purgatory into Paradise are immersed in Lethe. Guido means, by his words, that as long as Dante's books are renowned so will be his (Guido's) fame.

He then asks Dante the reason of his affection for him.

> Ma, se le tue parole or ver giuraro,
> > Dimmi che è cagion per che dimostri   110
> > Nel dire e nel guardare avermi caro ? "—

But, if thy words just now sware the truth, tell me the reason why both in thy speech and in thy looks thou showest that I am dear to thee?"

Dante tells him why, addressing him in the plural.

> Ed io a lui :—"Li dolci detti vostri
> > Che, quanto durerà l' uso moderno,
> > Faranno cari ancora i loro inchiostri."—

And I to him : "Those sweet lays of yours which, as long as the modern use (of writing poetry in the vulgar tongue) shall endure, will make ever dear to me their very ink."

Like Oderisi d' Agobbio,* Guido at once gives the greater honour to another.

> —"O frate (disse), questi ch' io ti scerno   115
> > Col dito (e additò uno spirto innanzi),
> > Fu miglior fabbro del parlar materno.

"O my brother," said he, "this one that I indicate

---

* See *Purg.* XI, 82-84 :—

> "'Frate'"—diss' egli, —"' più ridon le carte
> Che pennelleggia Franco Bolognese :
> L' onore è tutto or suo, e mio in parte.'"

to thee with my finger"—and he pointed out a spirit in front—"was a more skilful composer (than I) in the mother tongue.

The shade that he thus introduces is that of Arnaud Daniel, a Provençal poet.*

Guido confirms what he said by adding:

> Versi d' amore e prose di romanzi
> Soverchiò tutti; e lascia dir gli stolti
> Che quel di Lemosì† credon ch' avanzi.   120

(Of those who wrote) songs of love and prose of romance he surpassed all‡; and let the idiots talk who believe that he of Limoges (Giraud de Borneil) excels him.

Benvenuto observes that in his days there have come from Limoges many Popes, Cardinals, and

---

.* Arnaud Daniel flourished between 1180 and 1200. Very little is recorded of him by the earlier commentators, but Petrarch speaks of him as one of the foremost poets of his time. He lived in Provence in the time of Raymond Berenger (the Good) Count of Provence. He is said to have died about 1189 according to Nostradamus. He was the inventor of the Sestina, a song of six stanzas of six lines each, with the same rhymes repeated in all, arranged in intricate order.

Benvenuto says that, although the Provençal tongue is not beautiful, yet it is difficult, and Arnaud's thoughts were so well expressed, that Dante might have said of them what Virgil is supposed to have said of Ennius:

> "Lego aurum in stercore Ennii."

† *quel di Lemosì:* this is Giraud de Borneil. He was born at Excideul near Limoges. Dante, in the *De Volgari Eloquio,* lib. II, c. 2, speaks of him as "a poet of righteousness."

Arnaud was a poet of love, and of higher merit in the estimation of Dante.

‡ See interesting letter by Mr. Paget Toynbee in *Academy,* April 13th, 1889.

Bishops, whose morals were unworthy of the Church of Christ, and it is well for them to be purged in that fire.

Guido goes on to say, that it is only from the acclamations of the vulgar, that there could arise any question of comparing Giraud de Borneil to Arnaud Daniel.

> A voce più ch' al ver drizzan li volti,
>   E così ferman sua opinione
>   Prima ch' arte o ragion per lor s' ascolti.

They (the idiots) turn their countenances to common report more than to the truth, and so establish their opinion, before art or reason is heard by them.

Benvenuto remarks on the above : " And note well here the most true opinion of our Poet, who so justly satirises the insane vulgar herd. For in every profession we have seen it occur, that many men make false and vain assertions : and when examined by persons of experience, as to whether they be acquainted with such an art, or if they really have any opinion on the subject about which they speak so positively, they do not know what else to say than, ' Everybody says so ; ' and thus they make use of the judgment of the ignorant multitude as their shield."

And now Dante, having censured rumour for preferring the French to the Provençal poet, proceeds to exclude from the first place an Italian one, Fra Guittone d' Arezzo, who had a great popular reputation, and quotes him as an instance of misplaced praise. What he says in effect is that, just as public opinion in Provence was fallacious in the matter of Giraud de Borneil of Limoges, so did public opinion at Florence go astray about Fra Guittone d' Arezzo, until, through the opinions of experts, the real truth was arrived at. Guittone expressed beautiful thoughts, but his style was not happy.

> Così fêr molti antichi di Guittone,
>   Dì grido in grido pur lui dando pregio,   125
>   Fin che l' ha vinto il ver con più persone.

Thus did many in olden time with Guittone, giving applause to him alone from mouth to mouth, until the truth gained the day with more persons.

Dante now briefly tells us that Guido Guinicelli, while gratefully declining to avail himself of Dante's offer to celebrate his fame beyond what he had already done, asks him all the same to utter a short prayer for him.

> Or se tu hai sì ampio privilegio,
>   Che licito ti sia l' andare al chiostro,
>   Nel quale è Cristo abate del collegio,
> Fàgli per me un dir di paternostro,   130
>   Quanto bisogna a noi di questo mondo,
>   Dove poter peccar non è più nostro."—

Now if thou hast such ample privilege, that it is granted to thee to enter that cloister (*i.e.* Paradise), in which Christ is the Abbot of the college, repeat to Him a Paternoster on my behalf, as far as is needful for us in this world (of spirits), where the power to sin is no longer ours."

We may remember in Canto XI, 23, the shades of the proud are described as not omitting from the Lord's Prayer the sentence about leading into temptation, but explaining that they use it for the sake of those who remain behind them in the world.

Dante now relates how Guido Guinicelli disappeared.

> Poi, forse per dar luogo altrui, secondo
> Che presso avea, disparve per lo fuoco,
> Come per l' acqua* pesce andando al fondo.   135

Then, perchance to give place to the other who was
just behind him, he disappeared through the flame, like
a fish going to the bottom through the water.

Dante now draws near to Arnaud.

> Io mi feci al mostrato innanzi un poco,
> E dissi ch' al suo nome il mio desire
> Apparecchiava grazioso loco.

I moved a little towards him who had been pointed
out, and said that my desire was preparing an honourable place for his name.

Scartazzini explains this : I told him that my desire
to know him was so great, that I should receive his
name with especial affection.

Arnaud replies in the Provençal tongue.

> Ei cominciò liberamente a dire :
> *Tan m' abelis vostre cortes deman,*   140
> *Que ieu no-m puesc ni-m vueil a vos cobrire.*
> *Ieu sui Arnaut, que plor e vau cantan :*
> *Car, sitot vei la passada folor,*
> *Eu vei jausen lo jorn, qu' esper, denan.*
> *Ara vos prec per aquella valor,*   145
> *Que us guida al som de l' escalina*
> *Sovegna vos a temps de ma dolor.*
> Poi s' ascose nel fuoco che gli affina.   148

He began freely to say : " Your courteous demand
so pleases me, that I neither can nor will hide myself
from you. I am Arnaud, who weep and go singing ;

---

* *Come per l' acqua pesce* : compare the disappearance into
the mist of Piccarda de Donati, *Par. III,* 121 :—

> "Così parlommi ; e poi cominciò : Ave,
> Maria, cantando ; e cantando vanìo,
> Come per acqua cupa cosa grave."

for when I see the folly of my past life, I can still behold in exultation the hoped-for day (of salvation) before me.   Now, I implore you by that power, which is guiding you up to the summit of the stairs, be mindful in due time of my suffering."   He then hid himself in the fire that purifies.

Arnaud was anxious that Dante should repeat a Paternoster for him also, when he fulfilled his promise of doing so for Guido.

END OF CANTO XXVI.

CANTO XXVII.

THE SEVENTH CORNICE (*continued*).
THE PASSAGE THROUGH THE FIRE.
THE LAST ASCENT.
FAREWELL OF VIRGIL.

FROM the ninth Canto, until the close of the scene
last described, Dante has been describing Purgatory
proper, divided into seven Cornices, in which the
seven capital sins are purged in different ways.   From
now to the end of the Cantica, we shall have the
description of the Post Purgatorio, wherein is situated
the Paradise of Delights, figurative of the Church
Militant.

Benvenuto divides the Canto into four Parts.

In the First Division, from v. 1 to v. 45, Dante
describes the appearance of an Angel, who purges
him from the seventh and last sin, of Lust, and invites
him, with the assistance of Virgil, to pass through the
fire into the Terrestrial Paradise.

In the Second Division, from v. 46 to v. 87, he
describes his passage through the fire.

In the Third Division, from v. 88 to v. 108, he
relates how night came upon the poets, how they slept
on the stairway, and Dante's dream.

In the Fourth Division, from v. 109 to v. 142, is
contained Virgil's farewell exhortation to Dante.

Division I.   Before speaking of the Angel, Dante
describes the hour of the day by the position of the

Sun. According to the Cosmography of the time, when the sun is first dawning on Mount Sion, it is midday (the beginning of the Nones) at the Ganges ; and consequently at Purgatory, which is the Antipodes to Jerusalem, the sun is about to set.   If the sun is at the Ganges in Aries at midday, the night would naturally be at the Ebro in Libra at midnight.

> Sì come quando i primi raggi vibra
>   Là dove il suo Fattore il sangue sparse,
>   Cadendo Ibero * sotto l' alta Libra,
> E l' onde in Gange da nona riarse ;
>   Sì stava il sole ; onde il giorno sen giva,   5
>   Quando l' Angel di Dio lieto ci apparse.

As when he (the sun) throws his earliest rays on that place where his Maker shed His blood, while Ebro is sinking under the lofty Libra, and the waters of the Ganges have been scorched since noon ; so stood the sun ; wherefore the day was departing, when God's Angel, joyful, appeared to us.

This means that Dante, towards sunset, saw the Angel of God appear to him, rejoicing that Dante had

---

* In the time of Dante, to use the expression "from the Ebro to the Ganges," was equivalent to saying "from one end to the other of the inhabited world."   Compare Juvenal (*Sat.* X, 1):—

> "Omnibus in terris, quæ sunt a Gadibus usque
>   Auroram et Gangem."

Compare also a passage, nearly identically similar to these opening lines of the Canto, in *Purg.* II, 1-6:—

> "Già era il Sole all' orizzonte giunto,
>   Lo cui meridian cerchio coverchia
>   Jerusalem col suo più alto punto :
> E la notte, che opposita a lui cerchia,
>   Uscìa di Gange fuor colle bilance,
>   Che le caggion di man quando soverchia."

accomplished his last purification, that is, from the vice of lust.*

The Angel showed in his face the joy that there is among the Angels of God over one sinner that repenteth, and possibly (Scartazzini thinks) in order that his countenance might cheer the wayfarers onwards.

> Fuor della fiamma stava in su la riva,
> E cantava : *Beati mundo corde*,
> In voce assai più che la nostra viva.

He was standing outside the flame on the edge (of the cornice), and chanted : " Blessed are the pure in heart," in a voice (that seemed) far more living than ours.

These are the words of the Beatitude (*St. Matt.* V, 8) especially appropriate to the occasion, for Dante and Statius, not Virgil alas ! having now been purged from the seven mortal sins, have qualified themselves to ascend to the Terrestrial Paradise, where they will have a vision of Christ, and thence ascend still higher.

The Angel now invites them to pass on, but says that they must first go through the flames.

> Poscia :—" Più non si va, se pria non morde,   10
> Anime sante, il fuoco.   Entrate in esso,
> Ed al cantar di là non siate sorde."—

---

* In this circle alone are there two Angels, one on each side of the flames; this one is the usual guardian of the Cornice—the Angel of Purity. Scartazzini thinks the other must be the Angel warder of the Terrestrial Paradise. See Pietro Dante on this passage : " In principio noctis quando ut plurimum committitur et incalescit vitium et crimen luxuriosi ignis, fingit se mitti et duci ab Angelo, id est ab judicio conscientiæ, et a Virgilio, id est ab judicio rationis, codem tempore in flammam et incendium conscientiæ et reprehensionis talis vitii."

Then (the Angel added): "No one can advance farther, O sanctified souls, if first the fire does not bite (*i. e.* torment); enter into it, and be not deaf to the chant beyond."

> Sì disse come noi gli fummo presso :
> Perch' io divenni tal, quando lo intesi,
> Quale è colui che nella fossa è messo.   15

Thus said he when we had drawn near to him; whereat I became, when I heard it, as one who is placed in the grave (or, Scartazzini prefers, like him who is buried alive head downwards).*

Dante is paralysed with fear; and all the terrible scenes he has witnessed, of sufferers executed at the stake, recur to his mind with horror in all their hideous details.

> In su le man commesse mi protesi,
> Guardando il fuoco, e imaginando forte
> Umani corpi già veduti accesi.

I extended my clasped hands turning them upwards, and, as I looked at the flames, I vividly recalled the human bodies of yore seen perishing at the stake.

It may be noticed, moreover, that Dante had himself been condemned by contumacy to be burnt alive. Virgil and Statius turn to him in kindness and sympathy, and Virgil reminds him how he escorted him through all kinds of danger in Hell, and urges Dante to trust to him now.

---

* Scartazzini thinks it is evident that Dante here describes his fear as being fear of death, but of present death, such as that of malefactors buried alive head downwards in the trench. Compare *Inf.* XIX, 49 :—

> " Io stava come il frate che confessa
> Lo perfido assassin che, poi che è fitto,
> Richiama lui perchè la morte cessa."

Volsersi verso me le buone scorte,
     E Virgilio mi disse :—" Figliuol mio,   20
     Qui può esser tormento ma non morte.*
Ricordati, ricordati . . . e, se io
     Sovr' esso Gerïon † ti guidai salvo,
     Che farò ora presso più a Dio ?

The good conductors turned them towards me, and
Virgil said to me : " My Son, here there may be torment, but not death.   Remember, remember . . . and
if I was able to guide thee safely even on Geryon,
what will I (not) do now so much nearer to (the Paradise of) God ?

He further encourages him by demonstrating to
him that the fire will only burn, but not consume him.
Let him try it with his hands, and on his clothes.
He will emerge from it like the three Hebrew youths,
who yielded their bodies to the fiery furnace.

---

* *non morte.*   The fire of Purgatory is quite different from
that in our world, for it burns without consuming.   The fire on
this cornice signifies the chastisement of the flesh, abstinence
and prayer, by means of which our flesh is mortified and consumes, as it were, on the altar of God.   As, therefore, the
abstinence on earth afflicts and mortifies the flesh, but does not
destroy, so does the fire of purification burn without consuming.
See St. Gregory (*Mor.* lib. XXVII, c. 3) : " Dum carnalis vita
corrigitur, et usque ad abstinentiæ atque orationis studium a
perficientibus perveniretur, quasi jam in altari caro incenditur :
ut inde omnipotentis Dei sacrificium redoleat, unde prius culpa
displicebat."

   † *Sovr' esso Gerïon.*   Scartazzini renders it thus :—
          "persino sul dosso di Gerïone."
It must be remembered that *sovr' esso* has a much more emphatic signification than merely *upon*.   For Geryon, see *Inf.*
XVII, 91, *et seq.*

> Credi per certo che, se dentro all' alvo 25
> Di questa fiamma stessi ben mill' anni,
> Non ti potrebbe far d' un capel calvo.

Believe for certain that, if thou wert even to remain within the bosom of this flame for full a thousand years, it could not make thee bald of a single hair.

Benvenuto says baldness is caused by natural heat, but the power of spiritual fire only has influence upon spiritual substance.

> E se tu credi forse ch' io t' inganni,
> Fàtti vêr lei, e fàtti far credenza *
> Con le tue mani al lembo de' tuoi panni. 30

And if thou thinkest perchance that I am deceiving thee, step forward towards it, and bring conviction to thy mind with thine own hands on the hem of thy garments.

> Pon giù omai, pon giù ogni temenza,
> Volgiti in qua, e vieni oltre securo."—
> Ed io pur fermo, e contra coscīenza.

Put away now, put away all terror; turn this way, and come further on in all security." And still I stood motionless, in spite of conscience.

His conscience was telling him to perform what his Leader prescribed for him.

Virgil now, with knowledge of the soft side of Dante's nature, has recourse to an artifice to get round him and urge him forward.

> Quando mi vide star pur fermo e duro,†
> Turbato un poco, disse :—" Or vedi, figlio ! 35
> Tra Beatrice e te è questo muro."—

---

* Brunone Bianchi says that *far la credenza* was an expression used in former days about one who tasted the victuals at the table of a prince, to insure their not being poisoned.

† *duro.* Compare St. Thomas Aquinas (*Summ. Theol.* p. III, Suppl. qu. I, art. 1): "Ille qui in suo sensu perseverat, rigidus

When he saw me still standing fast and stubborn, in some vexation, he said : " Now look, my son, between Beatrice and thee is this wall."

Dante shows how Virgil's reasoning overcame him.

> Come al nome di Tisbe * aperse il ciglio
> Piramo, in su la morte, e riguardolla,
> Allor che il gelso † diventò vermiglio ;

---

et *durus* per similitudinem vocatur ; sicut *durum* in materialibus dicitur quod non cedit tactui ; unde et frangi dicitur aliquis quando a suo sensu divellitur."

* *Tisbe.* This alludes to the well known story of Pyramus and Thisbe, two lovers in Babylon, whose tragic death at the foot of the mulberry tree, which up to that time had borne white fruit, caused it thereafter for evermore to bear purple fruit. See Ovid, *Met.* IV, 145-6 :—

> " Ad nomen Thisbes oculos jam morte gravatos
> Pyramus erexit, visaque recondidit illa."

Benvenuto sees close analogy between the loves of Pyramus and Thisbe, and those of Dante and Beatrice. Both couples loved each other (according to Benvenuto) from early childhood.

Dante says in Canto XXX, 41-42 :—

> " L' alta virtù che già m' avea trafitto
> Prima ch' io fuor di puerizia fosse."

Both couples were separated by death. If Thisbe wished to follow her beloved Pyramus into death, so did Dante wish to follow his beloved Beatrice when she died, and become blessed in her company.

† *il gelso diventò vermiglio.* This is described in Ovid (*Met.* IV.) Eusden's translation:—

> " The Pray'r, which dying Thisbe had preferr'd,
> Both Gods, and Parents, with compassion heard.
> The Whiteness of the Mulberry soon fled,
> And rip'ning, saddened in a dusky Red ;
> While both their Parents their lost Children mourn,
> And mix their Ashes in one golden Urn."

Così, la mia durezza fatta solla,*   40
    Mi volsi al savio duca, udendo il nome
    Che nella mente sempre mi rampolla.

As, at the name of Thisbe, Pyramus, at the point of
death, opened his eyes and looked upon her, at the
time when the mulberry was changed into purple ; so,
all my stubbornness being softened, I turned to my
wise guide, when I heard that name (*i.e.* Beatrice)
which is ever sprouting up in my mind.

    Ond' ei crollò la fronte, e disse :—"Come !
    Volemci star di qua ?"—Indi sorrise,
    Come al fanciul si fa ch' è vinto al pome.   45

On which he shook his head, and said : "Well ! are
we going to remain on this side?" Then he smiled,
as one does to a child who has been conquered at the
(promise of an) apple.

<hr/>

Divison II. Dante now relates his successful passage through the dreaded flames. He first tells us
how Virgil, to obviate the possibility of any further
want of decision on his part, walked into the fire in
front of him, and begged Statius to bring up the rear.
Up to that moment Virgil had been walking first,
Statius second, and Dante third. As soon however

<hr/>

  * *solla*, the same as *cedevole* (yielding) ; or *arrendevole*
(flexible, supple).
  Compare *Inf.* XVI, 28 : *Esto loco sollo*, this yielding sandy
spot.
  And *Purg.* V, 18 :—
    " Perchè la foga l' un dell' altro insolla."

as they enter the Terrestrial Paradise, it is Dante who
leads the way.

> Poi dentro al fuoco innanzi mi si mise,
> Pregando Stazio che venisse retro,
> Che pria per lunga strada ci divise.

He then entered into the fire in front of me, begging
Statius that he would come behind, who for a long
way before had been between us (*lit.* divided us).

Dante describes his terror and his suffering.

> Come fui dentro, in un bogliente vetro
> Gittato mi sarei per rinfrescarmi,   50
> Tant' era ivi lo incendio senza metro.

As soon as I was in it (the fire), I would (willingly)
have cast myself into molten glass to cool me, so
immeasurable was the burning there.

Benvenuto says that Dante has well imagined so
intense a fire being necessary to purge out so much
wickedness. Glass at white heat was supposed to be
the greatest heat imaginable; and that, says Scartazzini, was in Dante's estimation as cold water compared to that of the fire in Purgatory.

Virgil endeavours to distract his attention from the
flames by speaking to him of Beatrice.

> Lo dolce padre mio, per confortarmi,
> Pur di Beatrice ragionando andava,
> Dicendo :—" Gli occhi suoi * già veder parmi."—

---

* *gli occhi suoi.* Francesco da Buti says : " Li occhi di
Beatrice sono le ragioni sottilissime et efficacissime e l' intelletti
sottilissimi, che anno avuto li Teologi in considerare e con-
templare Iddio et insegnare a considerarlo e contemplarlo."

In Canto XXXI, 109, the four Maidens who represent the
Cardinal Virtues say to Dante :—

> " Merrenti agli occhi suoi ; ma nel giocondo
> Lume ch' è dentro aguzzeranno i tuoi
> Le tre di là, che miran più profondo."

My gentle Father (Virgil), to encourage me, spoke
of nothing but Beatrice as we walked along, saying :
" Already I almost fancy I see her eyes."

As Beatrice represents Theology, the observation
may remind one of the supplication in the Book of
Common Prayer, that " in all our sufferings here upon
earth, we may steadfastly look up to Heaven."   Virgil,
symbol of human science, tacitly acknowledges the
insufficiency of earthly means to comfort and sustain
man in times of great sorrow and suffering.

The poets are now so enveloped in flames, that
they cannot see their way, but an angelic song guides
their steps.

> Guidavaci una voce che cantava   55
>> Di là ; e noi, attenti pure a lei,
>> Venimmo fuor, là ove si montava.

A voice that was singing* on the far side (of the

In *Convito*, tr. II, cap. 16, Dante says : " Gli occhi di questa
donna sono le sue dimostrazioni, le quali dritte negli occhi dello
intelletto, inamorano l' anima."

On the power of her eyes, see *Par.* XV, 32-36.

> " Poscia rivolsi alla mia donna il viso,
>> E quinci e quindi stupefatto fui ;
> Chè dentro agli occhi suoi ardeva un riso
>> Tal, ch' io pensai co' miei toccar lo fondo
>> Della mia grazia e del mio paradiso."

* Cesari compares this distant chant guiding the penitents
through the flame to boats on the Lago di Garda, which, during
the fogs that are prevalent there, have bells on their prows,
to help them to avoid collisions.

Scartazzini observes that whereas in the other cornices it had
always been an angel who effaced one of the seven P's from
Dante's brow, in this cornice there is no such mention, and we
are left to infer that the last P, signifying the sin of Lust, is
burnt out while he is in the fire.   This is commented on by

fire) guided us ; and we, intent only to it, issued forth where the ascent began.

The Angel had enjoined them in v. 12, *al cantar di là non siate sorde*, meaning that when in the fire they were to listen to the chant on the far side of it. The voice is, as we shall gather from v. 58-63, that of another Angel, who is doubtless the Guardian of the Terrestrial Paradise. Unlike the two with flaming swords placed there by God to drive away whoever should approach, this one, the Angel of Purity, invites all the pure in heart to enter.

They now approach a light of such dazzling radiance that Dante says that he could not gaze upon it.

> *Venite, benedicti patris mei,*
> Sonò dentro ad un lume, che lì era,
> Tal che mi vinse, e guardar nol potei.   60

"Come, ye blessed of my Father," sounded from the interior of a light that was there, so (brilliant) that it overcame me, and I could not gaze upon it.*

The Angel though invisible, addresses them.

Pietro di Dante : " Et nota auctorem in hoc vitio fuisse multum implicitum, ut nunc ostendit de incendio quod habuit in dicta flamma in reminiscentia conscientiæ." In none of the cornices of Purgatory, and not even in Hell, has Dante had to suffer so much as in this cornice of the Lustful. In *Purg.* XIII, 133-138, he says that he fears he will have *after death* to do penance among the proud and envious, but he now finds that for a few moments he has to suffer the torments of the lustful even before his death.

* Scartazzini points out that, as the Angel Warder at the entrance of Purgatory takes the functions of St. Peter, so does the Angel at the exit from Purgatory take the functions of Jesus Christ, pronouncing the great sentence that will be repeated on the Day of Judgment.

—" Lo sol sen va (soggiunse), e vien la sera ;
        Non v' arrestate, ma studiate il passo,
        Mentre che l' occidente non s' annera."—

" The sun is sinking fast," added (the voice), "and the night cometh ; tarry not, but press on your steps before the West shall become darkened by night."

We learnt from Canto VII, ⸹2, that, as soon as the night falls in Purgatory, all progress is arrested. And therefore the Angel advises their not delaying on the very threshold of the Terrestrial Paradise, as though he would say, " Life is short, Death is at hand."

Benvenuto draws attention to the fact that up to this point the road had been winding round the circuit of the mount ; but here, as in the Anti-Purgatorio, it diverges and ascends through a hollow way straight up to the summit. This path Dante now proceeds to describe, and Benvenuto thinks he wishes, by an allegory, to speak of the path of virtue.

        Dritta salía la via per entro il sasso
            Verso tal parte, ch' io toglieva i raggi   65
            Dinanzi a me * del sol ch' era già basso.†

---

* Benvenuto interprets *dinanzi a me* as *reverberantes in faciem meam*, and *verso tal parte* towards the west ; but Jacopo della Lana, Francesco da Buti, Scartazzini, Fraticelli and others, are very positive that it means towards the east, and Scartazzini quotes from Antonelli expressing the opinion that this last stairway was lighted by the rays of the sun just setting ; and that the Poet as he ascended it would have before him the shadow of his own body. The stairway then was seen from the west, and led towards the east. Buti adds to this that it is an appropriate and allegorical fiction, to describe the ascending to Paradise as ascending towards the east, whence the Sun is first manifested to the world, the Sun, which signifies the Salvation of God.

† Some read *lasso*, weary of his long course.

The passage ascended straight up through the rock, in such wise, that before me I impeded the rays of the Sun, which was already low.

He next describes the sunset.

> E di pochi scaglion' levammo i saggi,
>> Che il sol corcar, per l' ombra che si spense,
>> Sentimmo dietro ed io e li miei saggi.

And we had made essay of but few steps, before both I and my wise (Leaders) perceived that the sun was set behind us, by reason of the shadow (of me) disappearing in front of us.

As it was now night, they could ascend no higher.

> E pria che in tutte le sue parti immense   70
>> Fosse orizzonte * fatto d' un aspetto,
>> E notte avesse tutte sue dispense,
> Ciascun di noi d' un grado fece letto ;
>> Chè la natura del monte ci affranse
>> La possa del salir, più che il diletto.†   75

---

* Tommaseo says that Dante almost personifies the horizon by giving it without the definite article.

Dr. Moore (*Time References*, p. 110) tells us that in this passage we have the coming on of darkness, in lines 89-90 the shining out of the stars clearer and larger than their wont. This brings us to the end of the third day, Tuesday, April 12th, and the poets have now reached the end of Purgatory proper. The dawn of the fourth day is beautifully described in lines 109, etc.; the Earthly Paradise is entered, and Virgil takes his leave in the splendid passage with which this Canto ends, in the course of which (in line 135) he points to the now fully risen sun.

Longfellow quotes here from Dr. Furness's *Hymn* :—

> " Slowly by God's hand unfurled,
> Down around the weary world
> Falls the darkness."

† *il diletto*. Giuliani is quoted by Scartazzini as saying, that Virgil had to enter the fire of purification to render himself worthy of passing the threshold of the Terrestrial Paradise ; and

And ere that the horizon was become of one un-
varied hue in all its boundless parts, and night had
equally diffused its darkness all over it, each of us
made a bed of a stair, for the nature of the mountain
took away from the power of ascending more than
the desire.

Benvenuto says that Dante probably means that
he gave himself up to nocturnal meditation with
Statius, a poet of moral science, and with Virgil, a poet
of natural science, before proceeding to describe the
elevated matter that is to follow.

Dante next describes their respective positions.

> Quali si fanno ruminando manse
>   Le capre, state rapide e proterve
>   Sopra le cime, avanti che sien pranse,
> Tacite all' ombra, mentre che il sol ferve,
>   Guardate dal pastor che in su la verga   £o
>   Poggiato s' è, e lor poggiato serve ;*

Statius, because he would naturally do so before ascending to
God. Dante had to go through that trial and torment as though
to mortify the spirit of the flesh as a holocaust to God.

Scartazzini thinks that Virgil and Statius had to pass through
the flames, for the simple reason that there was no other way to
ascend. They lay themselves down on a step to obey the law
of the holy mountain, which cannot be ascended by night.
They do not sleep, not being subject to the imperfections of the
flesh, but, like the shepherds, watch all night, while Dante alone,
from having the flesh of Adam (*quel d' Adamo*) was overcome
by sleep.

* Boccaccio, in his *Vita di Dante*, relates that he wrote two
very beautiful Eclogues, in answer to some verses sent to him
by his friend Maestro Giovanni del Virgilio, a poet of Bologna
(Bolognese allora famosissimo e gran Poeta, e di Dante singo-
larissimo amico), who himself wrote an epitaph on Dante after

Just as the goats become quiet while ruminating, which had been agile and venturesome upon the mountain tops before they took their meal, resting hushed in the shade, while the sun is hot, watched by their shepherd who leans upon his staff, and leaning watches them.

Others read "*e lor di posa serve*" "and resting while they rest causes them to rest also," but the former reading has an overwhelming weight of MS. authority.

Benvenuto says : Like as the goats ascend the high hill tops, and gather the most succulent branches, shrubs and leaves, and, when satiated, are led by the shepherd to ruminate in the shade, so Dante's spirit soars to more lofty themes, to feed on more elevated thoughts, which he can think out and discuss with his guides, at a time well fitted for contemplation of the new and sublime matter of which he will now have to treat.

> E quale il mandrïan * che fuori alberga,
>> Lungo il peculio† suo queto pernotta,

---

his death.   In the second Eclogue (verses 7-15) there is a passage resembling this one of the goats:—

> "Tityrus hæc propter confugit et Alphesibœus
> Ad silvam, pecudumque suique misertus uterque,
> Fraxineam silvam, tiliis platanisque frequentem :
> Et dum silvestri pecudes mistæque capellæ
> Insidunt herbæ, dum naribus aëra captant,
> Tityrus heic annosus enim, defensus acerna
> Fronde, soporifero gravis incumbebat odori,
> Nodosoque piri vulso de stirpe bacillo
> Stabat subnixus, ut diceret Alphesibœus."

* *mandrïano* is a herdsman rather than a shepherd, *pastore*, and has charge rather of large animals than of sheep.

† *Peculio* is said to be a mixed flock of sheep and goats. Compare Virgil (*Georg.* IV, 433-436) :—

> " Ipse velut stabuli custos in montibus olim,

> Guardando perchè fiera non lo sperga ;
> Tali eravamo tutti e tre allotta, 85
> Io come capra, ed ei come pastori
> Fasciati quinci e quindi d' alta grotta.

And as the herdsman, who lives in the open, watches by night beside his resting flock, keeping guard that no wild beast scatter it ; such, at that hour, were we three, I like a goat, and they like shepherds, hedged in on either side by lofty rock.*

Benvenuto explains that while ascending the winding road, like those striving after virtue, they might have slipped over the edge of the cornice, but having once arrived at an abode of bliss, there is no more falling away.

Division III. We now enter upon the Third Division of the Canto, in which Dante describes a dream, but first he indicates the hour in which he fell asleep.

> Poco potea parer lì del di fuori ;

> Vesper ubi e pastu vitulos ad tecta reducit
> Auditisque lupos acuunt balatibus agni,
> Considit scopulo medius numerumque recenset."

In Dryden's translation :—

> " Himself, their herdsman, on the middle mount,
> Takes of his mustered flocks a just account.
> So, seated on a rock, a shepherd's groom
> Surveys his evening flocks returning home,
> When loving calves and bleating lambs, from far,
> Provoke the prowling wolf to nightly war."

* Scartazzini misquotes Benvenuto here as reading *d' alta* instead of *dalla*, which is the reading Benvenuto adopts. I have more than once noticed inaccuracies as to Benvenuto in Scartazzini, who has probably made use of Tamburini's spurious translation.

> Ma per quel poco vedev' io le stelle,
> Di lor solere e più chiare e maggiori.*   90

(Of the sky) outside but little could be seen; but in that little I beheld the stars more brilliant and larger than their wont.

They were reposing on the steps in a deep hollow way or cutting, and consequently could see but little on either side of them, as one in a well can only see a small portion of the sky.

> Sì ruminando, e sì mirando in quelle,
> Mì prese il sonno; il sonno che sovente,
> Anzi che il fatto sia, sa le novelle.†

---

* Antonelli says that the increased brilliancy of the stars would be due to the intensely pure and rarefied air of that elevated region; and, as regards their appearing larger, it is probable that Dante wished to convey to his readers that he had reached such an altitude, as to be appreciably nearer to the starry sphere, so that the stars would actually seem larger; and, according to the theories prevailing at that time as to the distance of the stars, there would be nothing absurd in such an idea.   Benvenuto quite confirms this conception in these words: "Stellæ videbantur clariores sibi et majores solito, quia erat vicinior cœlo et in loco puro a nubibus: distantia enim loci facit stellas videri minimas, quæ sunt in se maximæ."

† Dreams prophetic of things really about to happen were supposed to be those dreamt in the morning before waking.   Comp. *Inf.* XXVI, 7: "Ma se presso al mattin del ver si sogna,
> Tu sentirai di qua da picciol tempo
> Di quel che Prato, non ch' altri t' agogna."
and *Purg.* IX, 13:
> "Nell' ora, che comincia i tristi lai
> La rondinella presso alla mattina,
> Forse a memoria de' suoi primi guai,
> E che la mente nostra, peregrina
> Più dalla carne, e men da pensier presa,
> Alle sue visïon quasi è divina;
> In sogno mi parea, &c."

So ruminating, and so gazing upon them (the stars), sleep came over me, the sleep that, oftentimes before the fact occurs, has intelligence of it.

Dante dreamt what he had thought out, ruminating while he rested in the dark, like a goat plucking the choicest shoots in the shade. These thoughts now formed the subject of his dream, which he now relates, and which we may infer took place a couple of hours before the dawn.

> Nell' ora credo, che dell' oriente
>> Prima raggiò nel monte Citerea,* 95
>> Che di fuoco d' amor par sempre ardente,
> Giovanet† e bella in sogno mi parea
>> Donna vedere andar per una landa
>> Cogliendo fiori. E cantando dicea :
> —" Sappia, qualunque il mio nome dimanda, 100

---

* The Planet Venus has a peculiar lustrous twinkling, which was popularly supposed to be the throbbing of the fire of love. Compare *Purg.* I, 19 :—

> " Lo bel pianeta che ad amar conforta,
>> Faceva tutto rider l' oriente."

† Leah did not die young, but St. Thomas Aquinas (*Summ. Theol.* p. III, qu. XLVI, art. 9) states that " Omnes resurgent in ætate juvenili," and she therefore is seen by Dante, as it were in the prime of life, in the form in which she would be supposed to rise again. Benvenuto has a very long note upon Leah, and says that this noble fiction is usually explained all wrong, and that Dante here wishes to speak of the Countess Matelda of Canossa, in the State of Reggio. I cannot follow his views of the matter and prefer to take those of Scartazzini, to which I will refer in the next Canto, when we are brought into contact with the real Matelda, of whom Leah is but the symbol seen in a dream.

Ch' io mi son Lia, e vo movendo intorno
Le belle mani a farmi una ghirlanda.

About the hour, I think, when first Venus beamed
from the East upon the mountain (of Purgatory), who
ever seems to burn with the fire of love, in a dream
methought I saw a young and beautiful Lady walking
over a plain, gathering flowers.   And in song she was
saying, " Let whoever may demand my name know
that I am Leah, and I go moving round my fair hands
to make myself a garland.

Per piacermi allo specchio qui m' adorno ;
Ma mia suora Rachel mai non si smaga
Dal suo miraglio, e siede tutto giorno.   105
Ell' è de' suoi begli occhi veder vaga,
Com' io dell' adornarmi con le mani ;
Lei lo vedere, e me l' ovrare appaga."—

To please myself at the mirror (*i. e.* God) I here
adorn myself ; but my sister Rachel never departs
from her looking-glass, and sits at it all day.   She is
as eager to gaze upon her beauteous eyes, as I to
adorn myself with my hands ; contemplation satisfies
her, and work satisfies me."

Scartazzini says that, to understand better the difficulties in the lines from 94 to 108, it will be well to
consult passages from St. Thomas Aquinas.

In *Summ. Theol.* p. II, 2, qu. CLXXIX, art. 1,
"Quia quidam homines precipue intendunt contem-
platione veritatis, quidam vero intendunt principaliter
exterioribus actionibus, inde est quod vita hominis
convenienter dividitur per activam et contemplativam."
Again, *Summ. Theol.* p. II, 2, qu. CLXXIX, art. 2,
" Istæ duæ vitæ significantur per duas uxores Jacob :
activa quidem per Liam, contemplativa vero per

Rachelem ; et per duas mulieres quæ Dominum hos-
pitio receperunt : contemplativa quidem per Mariam,
activa vero per Martham. . . Divisio ista datur de
vita humana ; quæ quidem attenditur secundum intellectum.   Intellectus autem dividitur per activum et
contemplativum, quia finis intellectivæ cognitionis vel
est ipsa cognitio veritatis, quod pertinet ad intellectum
contemplativum ; vel est aliqua exterior actio, quod
pertinet ad intellectum practicum sive activum."
Again, *Summ. Theol.* qu. CLXXXII, art. 2 : " Deum
diligere secundum se est magis meritorium quam diligere proximum. Vita autem contemplativa directe
et immediate pertinet ad dilectionem Dei ; vita autem
activa directius ordinatur ad dilectionem proximi.
Et ideo ex suo genere contemplativa vita est majoris
meriti quam activa."   In *Convito* tr. II, cap. 5, Dante,
in accordance with the teaching of St. Thomas Aquinas,
contends that the contemplative life is the one which
most resembles God, and is more loved by Him. [The
Terrestrial Paradise, into which Dante is just entering,
is a figure of the happiness of this contemplative life ;
the Celestial Paradise symbolizes the blessedness of
Life Eternal. At the entrance of the Terrestrial Paradise, Dante in a dream sees Leah, who represents the
perfection of the active life that must follow after
expiation of sins, and is but a step to the contemplative life, a link between Purgatory and Heaven, between
politics and religion, between Virgil and Beatrice.
Leah speaks to Dante of her sister Rachel, who fore-
casts to him the sight of Beatrice, the two latter both
symbolizing the contemplative life.

Dante's dream therefore is intended to show him
the double life of man when purified, and at the same

time shows him by anticipation what he will see when in Paradise. Longfellow remarks that his vision is a foreshadowing of Matelda and Beatrice in the Terrestrial Paradise. In the Old Testament Leah is the symbol of the Active Life, and Rachel of the Contemplative: as Martha and Mary are in the New Testament, and Matelda and Beatrice in the Divine Comedy.

Ruskin (*Mod. Painters* III, 221,) says, " This interpretation appears at first straightforward and certain ; but it has missed count of exactly the most important fact in the two passages which we have to explain. Observe : Leah gathers the flowers to decorate *herself*, and delights in *Her Own* Labour. Rachel sits silent, contemplating herself, and delights in *Her Own* Image. These are the types of the Unglorified Active and Contemplative powers of Man. But Beatrice and Matilda are the same powers, Glorified. And how are they Glorified? Leah took delight in her own Labour; but Matilda, in operibus *manuum Tuarum—in God's Labour :* Rachel, in the sight of her own face ; Beatrice, in the sight of *God's face.*"

———————

Division IV. Here we commence the Fourth and concluding Division of the Canto, in which, after Dante awakes from his dream, Virgil takes leave of him, giving him much comfort, and wholesome advice.

The dawn of the fourth day in Purgatory, Wednesday, April 13th, 1300, is beautifully described.

> E già per gli splendori antelucani,
>> Che tanto ai peregrin' surgon più grati,   110
>> Quanto tornando albergan men lontani,*
> Le tenebre fuggían da tutti i lati,†
>> E il sonno mio con esse ; ond' io levámi,
>> Veggendo i gran maestri già levati.

And already through the brightness that precedes
the dawn, which arises to wayfarers all the sweeter,
the less distant they lodge as they return, the darkness
was flying away on every side, and my slumbers with
it ; whereupon I arose, seeing the great Masters already
risen.

Dante now shows how Virgil kindles his desire to
get forward, by showing him the reward he had been
in quest of through so many toils.

---

* *men lontani* or *più lontani* : Of these two much disputed
readings the one most commonly adopted is *men lontani*, which
is that found in the early editions of Jesì and Mantua, and is
also followed by Benvenuto, Buti and all succeeding commentators.   Even Scartazzini, who accepts the reading *più* on account
of its MS. authority, says he prefers *men*, besides which he says
the idea of *men lontani* is to be found elsewhere in Dante's own
works.   In *Convito*, tr. III, c. 10, Dante writes : "Quanto la
cosa desiderata più s' appropinqua al desiderante, tanto il
desiderio è maggiore."   And *De Mon.* lib. I, c. 11 : "Omne
diligibile tanto magis diligitur, quanto propinquius est diligenti."
Dante is comparing himself to a returning wayfarer who beholds
the dawn with increasing delight, as day by day he gets nearer
and nearer to his longed-for home.   The sense of the reading
più lontani is that, the farther off one is from the desired object,
the more eagerly does one gird oneself to the daily task of
diminishing the distance.

† *Le tenebre fuggían.*   Compare *Purg.* II, 55-57 :—
> " Da tutte parti saettava il giorno
>> Lo sol, ch' avea colle saette conte
>> Di mezzo il ciel cacciato il Capricorno."

—" Quel dolce pome che per tanti rami   115
  Cercando va la cura dei mortali,
  Oggi porrà in pace le tue fami."—
Virgilio inverso me queste cotali
  Parole usò, e mai non furo strenne
  Che fosser di piacere a queste eguali. 120

" That sweet fruit (*i. e.* The Supreme Good), of which
the care of mortals goes in pursuit in so many ways
(*lit.* through so many branches), will this very day
appease thy hungerings." Virgil used these words to
me, and never were there guerdons which were, for
pleasure, equal to these.

Virgil says in effect, " Blessed are they that do
hunger and thirst after righteousness," and then he
would add, " To-day thou wilt see Beatrice and the
whole Church Militant ; to-morrow thou wilt ascend
into Paradise."

Benvenuto notices the great change that these words
of Virgil produced·in Dante, who thereupon became
more happy and morè bold.

Tanto voler sovra voler mi venne
  Dell' esser su, che ad ogni passo poi
  Al volo mi sentia crescer le penne.*

Such longing upon longing came upon me to be
above, that at every step thereafter I felt wings growing upon me.

---

* From the intensity of his joy Dante felt so light that he
could almost fly. See *Par.* XV, 71-72 :—
   " . . . ed arrisemi un cenno
  Che fece crescer l' ale al voler mio."
And lines 79-81 :—
  " Ma voglia ed argomento nei mortali,
   Per la cagion che a voi è manifesta,
   Diversamente son pennuti in ali."

And now we reach the time when Virgil, knowing that Dante is about to enter into the presence of Beatrice, Divine Science, and that the companionship of himself, Human Science, will no longer be necessary, addresses his last farewell to Dante, in noble and touching words. We may infer that these words are spoken on the very threshold of the Terrestrial Paradise, and although we see him continue to be Dante's silent companion over the Debateable Land, yet as soon as Beatrice appears he vanishes for ever.*

> Come la scala tutta sotto noi
> > Fu corsa, e fummo in su il grado supemo,　125
> > In me ficcò Virgilio gli occhi suoi,
> E disse :—" Il temporal fuoco e l' eterno
> > Veduto hai, figlio, e sei venuto in parte
> > Dov' io per me più oltre non discerno.†

When the whole of the stairway had been passed over (and was left) below us, and we were on the topmost step, Virgil fastened his eyes upon me, and said, " My Son, thou hast beheld both the temporal fire (of Purgatory), and the eternal fire (of Hell), and art

---

* Benvenuto thinks that Virgil vanished after concluding his address, but that is manifestly an error, for Virgil is twice spoken of afterwards. See *Purg.* XXVIII, 145-7 :—

> " Io mi rivolsi addietro allora tutto
> > A' miei poeti, e vidi che con riso
> > Udito avevan l' ultimo costrutto."

And again *Purg.* XXIX, 55-57 :—

> " Io mi rivolsi d' ammirazion pieno
> > Al buon Virgilio, ed esso mi rispose
> > Con vista carca di stupor non meno."

† Compare *Purg.* XVIII, 48 :—

> " Ed egli a me :—' Quanto ragion qui vede
> > Dir ti poss' io ; da indi in là t' aspetta
> > Pure a Beatrice ; ch' è opra di fede.'"

come to a place where I can no longer see clearly of myself.

He means that purer eyes than his are required to guide Dante through the mysterious beauties of the Terrestrial Paradise.

> Tratto t' ho qui con ingegno e con arte ; *   130
>   Lo tuo piacere omai prendi per duce :
>   Fuor sei dell' erte vie, fuor sei dell' arte.

I have led thee thus far with intellect and with art; henceforth take for thy guide thine own pleasure; thou art now beyond the steep paths, beyond the narrow ones.

Before bringing his words to a conclusion, Virgil points out the way to Dante.

> Vedi là il sol che in fronte ti riluce ;
>   Vedi l' erbetta, i fiori e gli arbuscelli,
>   Che qui la terra sol da sè† produce.   135

Behold there the sun which is shining on thy brow‡ ; behold the soft grass, the flowers, and the shrubs, which yonder region (the Terrestrial Paradise) of itself alone produces.

---

* Francesco da Buti says of *ingegno e con arte* : " Ingegno chiamano li autori lo naturale intendimento che l' uomo ha ; et arte è quella che ammaestra l' uomo con regole e con ammaestramenti ; sicchè vuol dire : Io t' abbo tirato infin qui tra per lo ingegno che hai avuto sottile e buono e disciplinevile, e tra per l' arte che t' ha ammaestrato."

† *la terra sol da sè produce.* Virgil here wishes Dante to understand that, where the soil is not in need of man's labour, man will not need the guidance of another man.

‡ Dante's brow is now healed from the seven wounds traced on it by the Angel's sword, and is therefore fitted more worthily to receive the light of God, which Virgil implies will now shine upon Dante and be his guide.

> Mentre che vegnan lieti gli occhi belli,
>   Che lagrimando a te venir mi fenno,
>   Seder ti puoi e puoi andar tra elli.

Until in joy come to thee the beauteous eyes (of Beatrice), which in sorrow caused me to come to thee,
thou canst sit down (on the grass), and canst walk
among them (the flowers and shrubs).

> Non aspettar mio dir più, nè mio cenno,
>   Libero,* dritto e sano è tuo arbitrio,   140
>   E fallo fora non fare a suo senno ;
> Perch' io te sovra te corono e mitrio." —

Expect no further speech or sign from me, thy will
is released, upright, and sound, and thou wouldst err
greatly not to act upon its impulses ; I therefore crown
and mitre thee (as sovereign) over thyself."

Dean Plumptre says ; " The most natural interpretation is that Dante now takes his place among those
who are kings and priests unto God (1 *Pet.* II, 9 ;
Rev. I, 6 ; *Rev.* V, 10). Difficulties have been raised
on the ground that the mitre was used in the Roman
ritual for the coronation of an emperor. Otho is described as both *coronatus et mitratus,* and hence Scartazzini urges that both words refer to civil and not to
ecclesiastical functions. On the other hand this may

---

* *Libero.* Dante writes in the *De Monarchia,* lib. I, c. 12 :
" Primum principium nostræ libertatis est libertas arbitrii, quam
multi habent in ore, in intellectu vero pauci. Veniunt namque
usque ad hoc, ut dicant liberum arbitrium esse, liberum de
voluntate judicium. Et verum dicunt . . . . . Si judicium moveat
omnino appetitum, et nullo modo præveniatur ab eo, liberum
est ; si vero ab appetitu, quocumque modo præveniente, judicium moveatur, liberum esse non potest."

be traversed by the fact that the word *corona* was used
as an equivalent to *mitra*, so that both the words might
refer to the Episcopate."

Benvenuto does not seem to attach any ecclesiastical
sense to the words, but translates : "Fatio te super te
regem et dominum."

END OF CANTO XXVII.

CANTO XXVIII.

THE EARTHLY PARADISE.
THE RIVER LETHE.
MATELDA.
THE WIND AND THE WATER IN THE TERRES-
 TRIAL PARADISE.

IN the last Canto Dante described how he and his companions had at length reached the summit of the Mountain of Purgatory, where they find the Terrestrial Paradise, of which the present Canto is a description.

Benvenuto divides it into four principal parts.

In the First Divison, from v. 1 to v. 33, he describes the freshness and luxuriance of the herbage and trees ; the wind, the water, and the birds.

In the Second Division, from v. 34 to v. 84, he speaks of meeting a beautiful and illustrious Lady.

In the Third Division, from v. 85 to v. 120, Dante puts a question to the beautiful Lady as to the reason of water and wind existing in a region placed higher than the Gate of Purgatory, and she answers him respecting the wind.

In the Fourth Division, from v. 121 to v. 148, the beautiful Lady completes her answer to Dante's question, by explaining to him whence comes the water which irrigates this holy spot.

Benvenuto adds that the whole of this Canto is figurative and allegorical. Were we not to look at it under this aspect, it would lack any real meaning or import.

Division I. Dante wishes to describe the happy condition of man, so far as is compatible with the misfortunes of human life, in a state of perfect virtue. He accordingly figures him to be in an extremely elevated spot, secure from all changes, where no evil can befall him, and living in the midst of bliss.*

Fraticelli says that, in order to understand the description that follows, the reader should recall to his mind a few leading particulars about the Mountain of Purgatory. Dante has pictured it at a great altitude above the Earth. The lower part alone, which the Commentators have styled the Antipurgatorio, rose so high above it, that it was supposed to reach up to the highest level of the atmosphere, and it is at

---

* St. Thomas Aquinas teaches that the Terrestrial Paradise is situated in the Eastern parts of the earth, which are the more noble. See *Summ. Theol.* p. I, qu. CII, art. I : "Cum autem Oriens sit dextera cœli . . . dextera autem est nobilior quam sinistra: conveniens fuit ut in orientali parte paradisus terrenus institueretur a Deo . . . Quidam autem dicunt, quod paradisus pertingebat usque ad lunarem globum," and "locus ille seclusus est a nostra habitatione aliquibus impedimentis vel montium, vel marium, vel alicujus æstuosæ regionis, quæ pertransiri non potest."

St. Isidore, *Etym.* lib. XIV, c. 3, writes : "*Paradisus* est locus in Orientis partibus constitutus, cujus vocabulum ex Græco in Latinum vertitur *hortus*: porro Hebraice *Eden* dicitur, quod in nostra lingua *deliciæ* interpretatur. Quod utrumque junctum facit *hortum deliciarum;* est enim omni genere ligni et pomiferarum arborum consitus, habens etiam lignum vitæ ; non ibi frigus, non æstus, sed perpetua veris temperies."

this point that Dante places the Gate of Purgatory, which he supposes to be placed on the very lowest edge of the Sphere of Fire. The Antipurgatorio was subject to rain, heat and cold, earthquakes and other convulsions of nature ; not so the Purgatorio proper. Landino calls the Terrestrial Paradise the Post Purgatorio. It was situated, according to Dante, above the uppermost cornice or circle of Purgatory proper ; and no spirit could enter therein until purged of all its sins.

Dante paints the Paradise of Delights in the most glowing colours.*

> Vago già di cercar dentro e dintorno
>> La divina foresta spessa e viva,
>> Che agli occhi temperava il nuovo giorno,
> Senza più aspettar lasciai la riva,†
>> Prendendo la campagna lento lento‡   5
>> Su per lo suol che d' ogni parte oliva.‖

---

* Among the best known descriptions of ideal landscapes may be mentioned the following :—

Homer, *Odyssey*, V, description of the visit of Mercury to the Island of Calypso.

Sophocles, *Œdipus Coloneus*, description of the wood of Colonos.

Tasso, *Gerusalemme Liberata*, XVI, Garden of Armida.

Spenser, *Faerie Queen*, VI, X, 6, Mount Acidale.

Milton, *Par. Lost*, IV, 214-270, The Terrestrial Paradise.

† *la riva* : Dante and his guides have just surmounted the last step of the stairway and are standing on the edge of the plateau or table land at the summit. Dante now quits this edge and walks inland.

Scartazzini explains *riva*, " l' estremità di quel piano."

‡ Benvenuto says of *lento lento* that Dante was entering upon a sacred and, to him, unknown country with fear and trembling ; and he also wished to show the difficulty of the new and lofty matter upon which he was entering.

‖ *oliva* is derived from the Latin *olebat*. Contrast the soft

(By Virgil's words rendered) eager already to explore within and about the heavenly wilderness, which, luxuriant and evergreen, made the new-born day tempered to my eyes, without longer waiting, I left the edge (of the mountain) and very slowly roamed across the plain, over the soil that everywhere breathes fragrance.

Dante's delight in this beautiful region is such that he cannot hurry over any part of it. He goes on to describe the soft wind wafted through the forest.

> Un aura dolce, senza mutamento
>   Avere in sè, mi feria per la fronte
>   Non di più colpo che soave vento ;
> Per cui le fronde, tremolando pronte,   10
>   Tutte quante piegavano alla parte
>   U' la prim' ombra gitta il santo monte :

A fragrant breeze, subject to no variations in itself, smote me on the brow, with no heavier stroke than that of a light wind ; by which the boughs, in tremulous accord, one and all were bent down towards that quarter (the West) whereon the holy mountain (of Purgatory) casts its first shadow.

Benvenuto says, that the moral Dante wishes us to deduce from this passage is that, however much man, in a state of virtue, may find light winds, *i.e.*, slight

---

beauty here related, and the aromatic perfume of the soil with the ghastly description of the City of Dis, and the fetid atmosphere there.   See *Inf.* X, 133-6 :—

> "Appresso volse a man sinistra il piede :
>   Lasciammo il muro, e gimmo in vêr lo mezzo
>   Per un sentier che ad una valle fiede
> Che in fin lassù facea spiacer suo lezzo."

Here, too, Dante quitted the wall of circumference and walked inland.

troubles, come upon him, yet they do not hinder him
from performing his allotted duties any more than, in
the Terrestrial Paradise, they crush or overthrow the
trees that are in it. Although the branches bend where
the wind strikes upon them, yet he tells us that the
little birds are not prevented from resting upon them,
and filling the wood with their songs.

> Non però dal lor esser dritto sparte
>   Tanto, che gli augelletti per le cime
>   Lasciasser d' operare ogni lor arte ;   15
> Ma con piena letizia l' ôre prime,*
>   Cantando, ricevièno intra le foglie,
>   Che tenevan bordone† alle sue rime,
> Tal, qual di ramo in ramo si raccoglie
>   Per la pineta in sul lito di Chiassi,‡   20

---

* *l' ôre prime :* Scartazzini censures those commentators who
have interpreted *ore* here as "hours," whereas he agrees with
others who hold that the word stands for *aure.* He quotes from
Petrarch, sonnet 143 :—

> " Parmi d' udirla, udendo i rami, e l' *ore*
>   E le fronde, e gli augei lagnarsi, &c."

Benvenuto says that, by the birds, Dante here means to
express wise and virtuous men, who soar to the summits of the
virtues, and sing the praises of God with joy.

† *bordone* in its literal sense is the large cord of a violin, or
other stringed instrument.

‡ *Chiassi,* now *Classe.* Scartazzini feels certain that, although
in ancient times the name was Classis, and in modern times
Classe, yet in Dante's time it must have been called Chiassi, for
both Buti and Landino speak of it by that name without explaining that it stood for Classe. In the middle ages it was on the
sea shore, though in modern times the sea has receded, and
left it far inland, and now it is a dreary, pestilential, marshy
plain, untenanted save by the magnificent early Christian Church
of Sant' Apollinare in Classe, which Benvenuto informs us was

Quand' Eolo Scirocco fuor discioglie.*

Yet not, however, so far diverted from their upright position, but what the little birds upon their tops can continue the practice of every art of theirs ; but, with holy exultation singing their matin song, they received the first breezes of the day amid the leaves, which kept up such an accompaniment (*bordone*) to their warbling, such as one may hear gathering up, and running from branch to branch through the pine wood on the shore of Chiassi (Classe), when Eolus unlooses the Scirocco.

Dante now describes the water that irrigated the Terrestrial Paradise.

---

built by Justinian, but much damaged by Luitprand, King of the Lombards.   It was the port of Ravenna, and was called Classis because Augustus used to keep his fleet there for the protection of the Adriatic.   One can well imagine Dante, during his exile at Ravenna, often walking on the sea shore of Classe, roaming in deep thought through the lovely woods, and treading on the soft carpet of verdure, amid the twittering of the birds, in the once far famed, but now, alas, extinct Pineta.

* *Eolo.*   Æolus was king of the Lipari Isles, and resided at Stromboli.   The inhabitants of those isles used to imagine that they could, by the nature of the flames sent forth by the volcano, foretell the kind of winds that might be expected.   Eolus was supposed to have kept the winds imprisoned in bags of skin. The Scirocco is the S.E. wind.

See Virgil's description (*Æn.* I, 52, &c.) of the cave of Æolus, and his loosing the winds from it :—

> " Æoliam venit.   Hic vasto rex Æolus antro
>   Luctantis ventos tempestatesque sonoras
>   Imperio premit ac vinclis et carcere frenat."

Già m' avean trasportato i lenti passi
    Dentro alla selva antica* tanto, ch' io
    Non potea rivedere ond' io m' entrassi :†
Ed ecco più andar mi tolse un rio,   25
    Che invêr sinistra con sue picciole onde
    Piegava l' erba che in sua ripa uscìo.

Already had the slow pace (I was walking) carried me so far into the ancient wood, that I could no longer · see (when I turned back) the place where I had entered : and behold a little stream checked my further progress, which, with its light ripple, bent the herbage that sprouted on its bank towards the left hand.

This is the river of Lethe, which is supposed to gird the Terrestrial Paradise on the one side, while the river Eunoe girds it on the other, just as the Garden of Eden was bounded by the Tigris and Euphrates. Lethe is the water of Oblivion, which implies that the soul, which desires to attain to a state of innocence, must forget and cast behind it all those sins and failings that it has either committed or known, in order to attain to simplicity of mind, and to remove every incentive to sin. The waters of Oblivion flow towards the left, because they carry away the memory of evil, which is always figured as on the left hand. The sheep on the right, the goats on the left. Eunoe (from εὔνοος, favourable,) is the contrast to Lethe, and im-

---

* *antica*. The Garden of Paradise is one of the oldest things in man's history, seeing that our first parents were placed there.

† *ond' io m' entrassi.* Compare *Inf.* XV, 13-15 :—
    " Già eravam dalla selva rimossi
        Tanto, ch' io non avrei visto dov' era
        Perch' io indietro rivolto mi fossi."

plies the memory of all the good that the soul has effected or known, that it may have good knowledge of all virtue.

Dante now describes the purity of the water.

> Tutte l' acque che son di qua più monde,
>   Parrieno avere in sè mistura alcuna,
>   Verso di quella che nulla nasconde.   30
> Avvegna che si muova bruna bruna
>   Sotto l' ombra perpetua, che mai
>   Raggiar non lascia sole ivi nè luna.*

All the waters, that are the most limpid here (in the world), would seem to have in themselves some impurity compared with these, which conceal nought, though the current moves of a deep brown colour beneath the everlasting shade, that never allows a single ray of sun or of moon to penetrate it.

---

* Scartazzini does not share the opinion of Buti and some other commentators, that there is a deep allegory concealed in the above six lines. He thinks that Dante, in describing the holy forest, had in his mind some of the passages in Scripture that describe the New Jerusalem. See *Rev.* XXI, 23: "And the city had no need of the sun, neither of the moon, to shine in it; for the glory of God did lighten it, and the Lamb is the light thereof."

Tasso has a passage in the *Gerusalemme Liberata* (Canto XV, st. 56) which is almost copied from the one here :—

> "Ma tutta insieme poi tra verdi sponde
>   In profondo canal l' acqua s' aduna ;
>   E sotto l' ombra di perpetue fronde
>   Mormorando sen va gelida e bruna ;
>   Ma trasparente sì che non asconde
>   Dell' imo letto suo vaghezza alcuna :
>   E sovra le sue rive alta si estolle
>   L' erbetta, e vi fa seggio fresco e molle."

Division II. In this division Dante describes meeting a beautiful Lady by the side of the stream, who is gathering flowers and singing.

Benvenuto wishes us to mark that Dante now beholds in reality the same lady whom, in the last Canto, he fancied he saw in a dream, in the same dress, and employed in the same occupation. Benvenuto thinks she is figured as being here to warn the purified souls that they cannot ascend to Heaven, without having passed through the hosts of the Church Militant, or without having been previously washed in the waters of Lethe.*

Dante now speaks of her first appearance.

> Coi piè ristetti e con gli occhi passai
> Di là dal fiumicello, per mirare   35
> La gran variazion dei freschi mai :†
> E là m' apparvet (sì com' egli appare
> Subitamente cosa che disvia
> Per maraviglia tutt' altro pensare)

---

* We see Matelda thus engaged, just as, at the entrance of the Antipurgatorio, we saw Cato preparing the souls by a preliminary washing of the face to ascend the mountain of Purgatory.

† *Maio* properly signifies a branch, covered with leaves, which peasants plant on the 1st of May before the houses of their sweethearts, hanging upon it cakes, fruit, &c. It is thus described by Allegri (*Prose e Rime*, 160) :—

> "E voglio — —
> Dinanzi all' uscio un dì ficcarti il majo,
> Il qual di berricuocoli e ciambelle,
> Di melarance dolci e confortini
> Farò gremito, e d' altre cose belle."

but Scartazzini thinks that here *Majo* simply means any branch of a tree loaded with blossoms.

‡ *E là m' apparve* . . . . *donna soletta.* Only in *Purg.* XXXIII, 119, do we learn that this beautiful Lady is *Matelda.*

Una donna soletta, che si gia   40
   Cantando, ed iscegliendo fior da fiore,
   Ond' era pinta tutta la sua via.

I stood still with my feet on the bank of the little
stream, but with my eyes I passed beyond it, to gaze
with wondering delight on the great variety of the
fragrant shrubs. And there (on the opposite bank)
there appeared to me, even as there appears quite
suddenly, something which from very wonder drives
all other thoughts aside, a Lady all alone, who went
along singing, and selecting flower from flower with
which her path was all enamelled.

What Matelda she was, seems to afford room for much difference
of opinion. Benvenuto is very positive that she is the celebrated
Countess of Canossa, and, in commenting on Dante's dream in
Canto XXVII, in a very lengthy paragraph attempts to prove
that Leah is identical with her. Fraticelli, however, disagrees
with Benvenuto, and thinks it highly improbable that Dante, a
Ghibelline Poet, would have so much extolled a woman who was
the ally of the Popes, and was always warring against the
Empire. Scartazzini has a special digression devoted to the
subject. He considers that the Matelda of Dante was some
Florentine lady, probably the *donna gentile* mentioned in the
Vita Nuova, a friend of Beatrice, and also of Dante. He
concludes by saying " Suppose that the Matelda in the holy
forest is historically the *gentil donna* who was the shelter of
Dante's love—and suppose her allegorically to figure the ecclesiastical ministry (of the Church) and then the *donna soletta* is no
longer a mysterious personage, but she is Matelda disclosed (*La
Matelda svelata.*)" There can be no doubt that Dante is now
supposed to see the verification of his dream, though the person
is different. In the dream it was Leah, now it is Matelda. It
is like Dante's dream related in *Purg.* IX, 19, *et seq.*, when the
eagle was seen in the dream instead of Lucia. Dante here has
been dreaming of Leah and Rachel, when he awakes he finds
neither of them, but Matelda and Beatrice.

Dante felt like one, who, having a thought in his head, is on a sudden struck by something wonderful, which causes him to forget it entirely. In the next six terzine Dante represents how he addressed himself to Matelda, and how she, to converse with him, drew near to the margin of the rill. Being now purified, Dante has an intense longing to be brought nearer to the works of virtue that are represented by Matelda, so he says :

—" Deh, bella donna, ch' ai raggi d' amore
    Ti scaldi, s' io vo' credere ai sembianti,*
    Che soglion esser testimon' del core,   45
Vegnati voglia di trarreti avanti
    (Diss' io a lei) verso questa riviera,
    Tanto ch' io possa intender che tu canti.

" Ah beautiful Lady, who dost warm thyself in the rays of love, if I may trust to the look of thy features, which are usually the witnesses of the heart, let the will come to thee," I said to her, "to draw so far forward towards this bank of the stream, that I may understand what thou sayest.

---

* *sembianti* : Blanc says the word *sembiante* means features, and especially here so because in the plural. Compare *Inf.* XXIII, 145-6 :—

    " Appresso il duca a gran passi sen gì
        Turbato un poco d' ira nel sembiante."

Scartazzini says of *sembianti* that the principal features are the eyes and the smile, and quotes Dante's own words in the Canzone that begins, "Amor che nella mente mi ragiona." *Str.* IV, v. 1, *et seq.*

    " Cose appariscon nello suo aspetto,
        Che mostran de' piacer del paradiso ;
        Dico negli occhi e nel suo dolce riso ;
        Che le vi reca amor com' a suo loco."

Tu mi fai rimembrar, dove e qual era
　　Proserpina nel tempo, che perdette   50
　　La madre lei, ed ella primavera." *—

Thou makest me remember where and what was
Proserpine, at the time her mother lost her, and she
(Proserpine lost) the flowers of Spring (*lit.* lost the
spring)."

Dante means that Matelda looked as did Proser-

---

* Dr. Moore feels very strongly that *primavera* here means
the flowers of Spring that Proserpine had been gathering, chiefly
on the ground that the imitation of Ovid, *Met.* V, by Dante
seems conclusive.　The following is from Maynwaring's translation :—

　　"Here, while young Proserpine, among the maids,
　　　Diverts herself in these delicious shades ;
　　　While like a child with busy speed and care
　　　She gathers lilies here and violets there ;
　　　While first to fill her little lap she strives,
　　　Hell's grisly monarch at the shade arrives ;
　　　Sees her thus sporting on the flowery green,
　　　And loves the blooming maid, as soon as seen.
　　　His urgent flame impatient of delay,
　　　Swift as his thought he seized the beauteous prey,
　　　And bore her in his sooty car away.
　　　The frighted goddess to her mother cries,
　　　But all in vain, for now far off she flies.
　　　Far she behind her leaves her virgin train ;
　　　To them too cries, and cries to them in vain.
　　　And while with passion she repeats her call,
　　　The violets from her lap, and lilies fall :
　　　She misses them, poor heart ! and makes new moan ;
　　　Her lilies, ah ! are lost, her violets gone."

Scartazzini notices that in Tuscany that flower which is one
of the first to show in Spring, a kind of daisy, is called *primavera.*　Dante, in *Par.* XXX, 62-3, says :

　　". . . intra due rive
　　Dipinte di mirabil primavera."

pine, when Pluto first saw her gathering flowers in
Sicily, at the time Ceres, her mother, lost her, and
Proserpine lost the bright world, and the joy of the
Spring flowers.

Benvenuto considers that Dante wished to express
to Matelda : " Thou seemest to me like a goddess,
beautiful and modest as Diana the goddess of chastity." Diana was called Luna on earth, and Hecate
or Proserpine in Hell ; Diana being properly her
name in Olympus.

Dante next tells us how Matelda complied with his
request.

> Come si volge, con le piante strette
>   A terra ed intra sè, donna che balli,
>   E piede innanzi piede appena mette,
> Volsesi in sui vermigli ed in sui gialli   55
>   Fioretti verso me, non altrimenti
>   Che vergine, che gli occhi onesti avvalli ;
> E fece i preghi miei esser contenti,
>   Sì appressando sè, che il dolce suono
>   Veniva a me co' suoi intendimenti.   60

Like as a dame who, when dancing, turns herself
with feet together pressed and just grazing the
ground, and hardly puts one foot before the other, so
she (the beautiful Lady) turned towards me, (moving)
over the vermilion and yellow flowers, not otherwise
than a maiden who casts down her modest eyes ; and
made my entreaties to be content by approaching me
so near, that the sweet song came to me, and with it
its meaning.

Not only did the sound of her voice now reach Dante,
but he could also plainly distinguish her words. As
soon as Matelda's feet touch the spot, where the grass
is washed by the waters of Lethe, she gladdens

Dante's heart by raising her beauteous eyes to his.
This seems to have made a deep impression upon
him, notwithstanding his earnest longing to behold
Beatrice.

> Tosto che fu là dove l' erbe sono
> Bagnate già* dall' onde del bel fiume,
> Di levar gli occhi suoi mi fece dono.
> Non credo che splendesse tanto lume
> Sotto le ciglia a Venere trafitta   65
> Dal figlio,† fuor di tutto suo costume.

As soon as she had reached even to˙ (*già*) where
the grass is bathed by the waters of the fair stream,
she did me the grace to raise her eyes. I do not believe that such a radiance shone under the eye-lids of
Venus when transfixed by her own son, quite contrary
to his wont (for he wounded her accidentally).

---

* Giuliani says that *già* here serves to denote a determined
distance of place (*determinato spazio di luogo*).

† *Venere trafitta dal figlio* : The fable here alluded to is
taken from Ovid, *Met.* X, v. 525, *et seq.*, Eusden's translation :—

> " For Cytherea's lips while Cupid press'd,
> He with a heedless arrow razed her breast.
> The goddess felt it, and with fury stung,
> The wanton mischief from her bosom flung :
> Yet thought at first the danger slight, but found
> The dart too faithful, and too deep the wound.
> Fired with a mortal beauty, she disdains
> To haunt the Idalian mount, or Phrygian plains.
> She seeks not Cnidos, nor her Paphian shrines,
> Nor Amathus, that teems with brazen mines :
> Even Heaven itself with all its sweets unsought,
> Adonis far a sweeter Heaven is thought."

The simile means to show that in Matelda, emblem of the
active life, and whose eyes are full of Divine Love, reason and
intellect are brighter than in the eyes of Venus, who was the type
of pleasure in the things of this world.

> Ella ridea dall' altra riva dritta,
>   Traendo più color con le sue mani,
>   Che l' alta terra senza seme gitta.

Standing upright upon the opposite bank she smiled, gathering into her hands (flowers of) many hues which that elevated spot throws up without seed.

Benvenuto says that this was the highest place in the world.   Dante now tells us that his desire of passing across the stream to join the unknown Lady was so great, that, although the rill was only three paces wide, he took as great a dislike to it as Leander did to the Hellespont, which separated him from his beloved Hero.

> Tre passi* ci facea il fiume lontani ;   70
>   Ma Ellesponto, là 've passò Serse,
>   Ancora freno a tutti orgogli umani,
> Più odio da Leandro non sofferse,
>   Per mareggiare intra Sesto ed Abido,
>   Che quel da me, perchè allor non s' aperse.   75

The stream kept us three paces apart; but the Hel-

---

* *Tre passi.* Scartazzini says that these three paces, which separate Dante from Matelda, remind one of the three steps at the threshold of Purgatory. (See *Purg.* IX, 94, *et seq.*)   Dante will surmount these three obstacles by three acts of confession, repenting of his former aberrations from the faith.   Scartazzini feels sure that it is only for shortcomings as to faith that Dante's purgation is not otherwise completed.   He thinks that between the top of the stairway and Lethe is the Ante-Terrestrial Paradise, which Virgil may enter but not go on further.   The Terrestrial Paradise on the side of the earth is bounded by Lethe, which takes away from the soul every memory that is only earthly, and unfitted for the Kingdom of Heaven ; on the side of Paradise the Terrestrial Paradise is bounded by Eunoè, which restores to the soul the memory of any good deeds that it wrought, which may have made for it treasures in Heaven.

lespont, there where passed Xerxes, still (remembered
as) a check to human pride, did not endure greater
hatred from Leander, because its waters flowed between
Sestos and Abydos, than this (little stream) was hated
by me, because it did not at once cleave asunder.

Benvenuto says that Dante compares himself to
Leander, Matelda to Hero, and the little stream to
the Hellespont.   Leander hates the sea, Dante hates
the rill.

And now Dante describes how Matelda, at length,
addressed him and his companions, and it would seem
by her words, that the three were greatly astonished
that she should be laughing in so sacred a spot.

> —" Voi siete nuovi, e forse perch' io rido,"—
>   Cominciò ella,—" in questo luogo eletto
>   All' umana natura per suo nido,
> Maravigliando tienvi alcun sospetto ;
>   Ma luce rende il salmo *Delectasti,**   80
>   Che puote disnebbiar vostro intelletto.

She began (addressing Dante, Virgil, and Statius):
" Ye are new comers : and perchance some doubts
may keep you marvelling as to why I smile in this
place, elected to the human race to be its nest; but the
Psalm *Delectasti* affords a light that may clear your
intellect of all haze.

Matelda tells the poets how the words of the Psalm
will make them understand that, in this sacred place,
she can be glad and rejoice.   Her laughter is pure and
holy, because inspired by the sweet loveliness around

---

* *Psalm* XCII, 4 : " For Thou, Lord, hast made me glad
through thy work : I will triumph in the works of thy hands.
O Lord, how great are thy works ! and thy thoughts are very
deep."

her ; nor can sin, that was first committed here, and
which caused humanity to be driven forth from it,
disturb it in any way.

Matelda addresses herself to Dante personally,
having noticed that he is now in front of the group,
whereas before he was walking behind.

> E tu, che sei dinanzi, e mi pregasti,
> > Di' s' altro vuoi udir ; ch' io venni presta
> > Ad ogni tua question, tanto che basti."—

And thou (Dante) that standest foremost, and didst
entreat me to approach thee, if thou wouldst hear
more, tell me what thou dost require ; as I have come
ready (to answer) every one of thy questions, so far
as may suffice."

Division III.   In the Third Division of the Canto
Dante puts to Matelda a question about the wind and
the water, the existence of which seems to him almost
impossible in a place which is situated at a higher elevation than the Gate of Purgatory.

> —" L' acqua (diss' io) e il suon della foresta,   85
> > Impugna dentro a me novella fede
> > Di cosa, ch' io udii contraria a questa."—

" The water," said I, " and the sound of (the rustling
of) the forest, militate within me against the new belief
of a thing that I heard (totally) opposed to this."

Statius had told him that, on the Mountain of Purgatory, there was neither wind, nor rain, nor frost, nor
dew, nor snow, nor clouds, nor lightning.*

---

* He refers to the words of Statius in Canto XXI, 40-57 :—

> " . . . Cosa non è che sanza
> Ordine senta la religïone
> Della montagna, o che sia fuor d' usanza.

Matelda promises to solve his doubts.

> Ond' ella :—" Io dicerò come procede
> Per sua cagion ciò ch' ammirar ti face,
> E purgherò la nebbia che ti fiede.   90

Whereupon she : " I will tell thee how by its cause proceeds that which makes thee to wonder (*i.e.* the wind and the water), and I will clear away the mist which strikes upon thee.

> Lo sommo Ben,* che solo esso a sè piace,
> Fece l' uom buono, e a bene, e questo loco
> Diede per arra a lui d' eterna pace.

The Supreme Good (*i.e.* God), only delighting in Himself, created man good and destined him for a good (end) ; and bestowed on him (the joys of) this

---

> Libero è qui da ogni alterazione ;
> Di quel che il ciel da sè in sè riceve
> Esserci puote, e non d' altro, cagione
> Perchè non pioggia, non grando, non neve,
> Non rugiada, non brina più su cade,
> Che la scaletta dei tre gradi breve.
> Nuvole spesse non paion, nè rade,
> Nè corruscar, nè figlia di Taumante,
> Che di là cangia sovente contrade.
> Secco vapor non surge più avante
> Che al sommo dei tre gradi ch' io parlai,
> Ov' ha il vicario di Pietro le piante.
> Trema forse più giù poco od assai ;
> Ma, per vento che in terra si nasconda,
> Non so come, quassù non tremò mai."

† *Lo sommo Ben.*   See St. Thomas Aquinas, *Summ. Theol.* p. I, qu. VI, art. 2 : " Deus est summum bonum simpliciter, et non solum in aliquo genere vel ordine rerum. . . . Oportet quod cum bonum sit in Deo sicut in prima causa omnium non univoca, quod sit in eo excellentissimo modo ; et propter hoc dicitur summum bonum."

spot (*i.e.* the Terrestrial Paradise) as an earnest of eternal peace.

Benvenuto remarks that our first parents had quiet rest without toil, safety without fear, peace without war, health without fatigue, freedom without slavery, and, more than all, life without death : but the more happy they were before their fall, the more unhappy were they after it.

> Per sua diffalta qui dimorò poco ;
> > Per sua diffalta in pianto ed in affanno   95
> > Cambiò onesto riso e dolce giuoco.

On account of his own default he dwelt here but a short time ; on account of his own default he changed innocent joys and gentle pastimes into weeping and trouble.

According to Francesco da Buti, the theologians supposed Adam and Eve to have only remained in a state of innocence for five hours, and in Paradise itself only for seven hours.* God was thought to have placed Adam in Paradise at the third hour, and gave him His commandments, and presented the animals to him, for Adam to give them names ; He then caused a deep sleep to fall upon him, and formed Eve out of his rib, the serpent then came and tempted Eve, and after the ninth hour they ate of the forbidden fruit, and were driven out of Paradise.

> Perchè il turbar, che sotto da sè fanno
> > L' esalazion dell' acqua e della terra,
> > Che, quanto posson, dietro al calor vanno,

---

* See *Par.* XXVI, 139, where Adam says :—

> " Nel monte, che sì leva più dall' onda,
> > Fu' io, con vita pura, e disonesta,
> > Dalla prim' ora a quella che seconda,
> Come il sol muta quadra, l' ora sesta."

All' uomo non facesse alcuna guerra,　　　100
　　Questo monte salìo vêr lo ciel tanto ;
　　E libero n' è d' indi, ove si serra.

In order that the disturbance, which the exhala-
tion of sea and land cause below the level (of the Gate
of Purgatory), and which, as far as possible, go after
the heat, in order that this should not give any annoyance to man, this mountain was made to ascend
to so great an elevation towards heaven ; and is free
from them (*i.e.* from those disturbing influences) from
that spot where (the entrance) is closed (by the
Angel).

The meaning is that, from the Gate of Purgatory up
to the Terrestrial Paradise, all atmospheric influences
are inoperative.　Fraticelli says the ancients were
ignorant of the gravity of the air which causes the
lightest vapours to ascend upwards, and they believed
that these had a natural tendency to go to the Sun.

Up to this point Matelda has confirmed what Dante
had already heard from Statius, and she now proceeds
to explain to him the origin of the breeze that moves
the foliage, and of the water of the river Lethe.

Benvenuto thinks that Dante practically says : " O
beautiful Lady, thou hast sufficiently explained to me
why our winds from Earth do not extend as far as
these altitudes, but that is not what I ask, I want to
know the origin of this wind up here that causes the
leaves to rustle."

Matelda answers Dante—
　　Or, perchè in circuito* tutto quanto

---

* Scartazzini writes that, according to the astronomical
notions that prevailed in the time of Dante, the earth remains
fixed in the centre of the universe.　The air revolves with *la*

L' aer si volge con la prima vôlta,
Se non gli è rotto il cerchio d' alcun canto ;   105
In questa altezza, che tutta è disciolta
Nell' aer vivo, tal moto percote,
E fa sonar la selva perch' è folta ;

Now seeing that the whole atmosphere revolves round in a circle, together with the first (Heaven) that revolves, if the gyration meets with no interruption at any point; on this height, that is altogether disengaged in the pure air, such motion strikes, and makes the forest resound because it is thick set.

He means that this elevated plateau, on which the forest is situated, is open and not locked in by other mountains, and the wind which exists here, is nothing else than a movement of the air.

Matelda next shows him how fruits are generated by means of the wind.

---

prima vôlta, i.e. with the *Primo Mobile*, and with all the heavens beneath it from East to West, for the revolution of the *Primo Mobile* causes the air below it to revolve also. The vapours that form the wind often impart to the air down here a different motion than from East to West. Up there vapours do not rise: therefore the air up there is always gyrating in accordance with the *Primo Mobile*, unless it be intercepted anywhere by any extraneous force. Therefore the air moving from East to West finds resistance up there in the density of the forest, and that produces the sound of which Dante begged Matelda to tell him the cause. Scartazzini says that all the many commentators he has consulted interpret *la prima vôlta* as the *Primo Mobile*. Antonelli alone thinks it means the Sphere of Fire, but Scartazzini observes that Dante adheres to the Ptolemaic system, according to which the ninth sphere, or the *Primo Mobile*, revolves with the greatest velocity round the earth in twenty-four hours, and communicates its motion to the eight other lower spheres contained within it.

E la percossa pianta tanto puote,
　　Che della sua virtute l' aura impregna,   110
　　E quella poi girando intorno scuote :
E l' altra terra, secondo ch' è degna
　　Per sè e per suo ciel, concepe e figlia
　　Di diverse virtù diverse legna.

And the forest* when struck has such power that
with its properties it impregnates the air, and that
again, in its revolution around, shakes them (the properties or seeds) off: and the other earth (*i.e.* that inhabited by man), according as it is fit, either by itself
or by its climate (*lit.* sky), conceives and produces different trees possessing different properties.

Benvenuto says that the same thing is to be seen in
Nature constantly; for some odoriferous trees impreg-
nate the surrounding air with their aroma, and some
winds can convey that aromatized air to some country
fit to conceive such a tree, and there it spontaneously
shoots forth, and sometimes the wind will carry the
seed of the tree to some far distant land, like as we
may find at times a purely domestic tree growing in
the forest, or a sylvan tree growing in a garden.

Non parrebbe di là poi maraviglia,   115
　　Udito questo, quando alcuna pianta
　　Senza seme palese vi s' appiglia.

It would not then on earth appear a marvel, if this
were known, whenever any plant takes a root there
without any manifest seed.

Benvenuto comments on this by saying that, when
men see a phenomenon, they marvel if they know not
the cause ; but when they know the cause, they cease
to do so: and therefore Dante need no longer marvel,

---

* I follow Benvenuto in taking *pianta* to mean the forest.

now that he knows that the movement of the air causes the generation of the trees.

> E saper déi che la campagna santa,
> Ove tu sei, d' ogni semenza* è piena,
> E frutto ha in sè, che di là non si schianta.† 120

And thou must know that the holy country where thou now art, is full of every seed, and has within itself fruit that is never gathered yonder (on earth).

Benvenuto takes *ogni semenza* to be virtues and virtuous works.

Division IV. Matelda, having enlightened Dante as to the origin of the wind in the Terrestrial Paradise, proceeds to tell him about the water.

> L' acqua che vedi non surge di vena
> Che ristori vapor, che giel converta,
> Come fiume ch' acquista e perde lena ;
> Ma esce di fontana salda e certa,
> Che tanto dal voler di Dio riprende, 125
> Quant' ella versa da due parti aperta.

The water which thou seest does not well up from any spring (*lit.* vein), that the vapour condensed by cold can replenish, as rivers which wax and wane ; but (this water) issues from a sure and unfailing source which receives back again, by the will of God, as much as it pours away when divided into two streams.

---

* Scartazzini says it is evident that by *semenza* Dante meant trees, since they have *frutto in sè* and the fruit is gathered (*si schianta*) from the tree, and not from the seed.

† *non si schianta :* Not only fruits known on earth can be gathered there, but also those unknown. Some think that Matelda means to allude to the Tree of Life, which remained in Paradise, and was not allowed to bear fruit on Earth as long as Death exists there.

Matelda then describes how the two diverging streams have different names, and different operations, which tend however to one and the same end.   The water of Lethe, when drunk, causes the oblivion of past sin ; while that of Eunoe commemorates what is good and strengthens virtue.

> Da questa parte con virtù discende,
>   Che toglie altrui memoria del peccato ;
>   Dall' altra, d' ogni ben fatto la rende.

On this side (the left) it descends with the faculty which takes away from a man the memory of sin ; on the other (the right) it restores that of every good deed.

And observe, says Benvenuto, that two things are necessary to the man who aims at happiness ; in the first place, forgetfulness of what is evil, so that it may no longer come into his mind to sin : and secondly, remembrance of what is good, which will not allow him to sin any more.

Matelda then tells Dante the names of the two streams.

> Quinci Letè, così dall' altro lato   130
>   Eunoè si chiama, e non adopra,
>   Se quinci e quindi pria non è gustato.

Here (on the left) Lethe, so upon the other (the right) side it is called Eunoe ; and it is not operative (*i.e.* does not produce its beneficial effect), if it is not first tasted on this side and then on that.

It is not only necessary to forget past sins and abstain from present ones, but also is it necessary to work active good.

> A tutt' altri sapori esto è di sopra ;

> Ed avvegna ch' assai possa esser sazia
> La sete tua,* perch' io più non ti scuopra,   135
> Darotti un corollario† ancor per grazia,
> Nè credo che il mio dir ti sia men caro,
> Se oltre promission‡ teco si spazia.

This (water) has a savour above all others ; and although perchance thy thirst is sufficiently slaked without my making any further revelations to thee, I will in addition in token of favour give thee a corollary ; nor do I think my speech will be less prized by thee, if it extends beyond the explanation which I promised to give thee.

Matelda, in explaining her corollary, relates how the ancient poets imagined the Golden Age, possibly divining this realm.

> Quelli che anticamente poetaro
> L' età dell' oro e suo stato felice,   140
> Forse in Parnaso esto loco sognaro.

Those who in ancient times celebrated in song the

---

* *La sete tua :* compare *Purg.* XXI, 1 :—
   " La sete natural che mai non sazia," &c.

† *Corollario :* compare Boethius, *Phil. Consol.* lib. III, Pros. X. " Super hæc, inquit, igitur, veluti geometræ solent, demonstratis propositis, aliquid inferre, quæ πορίσματα ipsi vocant, ita ego quoque tibi veluti corollarium dabo . . . . .

Et pulchrum, inquam, hoc, atque pretiosum, sive πόρισμα, sive corollarium vocari mavis."

Benvenuto says that a *corollario* is the final conclusion, which is given after others as the conclusion of conclusions. The word is derived from *corolla*, a little crown, which, in disputations was given to the victor.

‡ *Oltre promission :* Matelda had only promised Dante to explain to him the origin of the wind and the water in the Terrestrial Paradise.

Golden Age and its happy state, perchance dreamed of this place on Parnassus.

In conclusion, she speaks of the happiness of the Terrestrial Paradise.

> Qui fu innocente l' umana radice ;
>> Qui primavera sempre, ed ogni frutto ;
>> Nettare* è questo di che ciascun dice."—

Here (Adam and Eve), the root of mankind, lived in innocence ; here there is perpetual spring, and every fruit ; this (rill) is the nectar of which every one speaks."

Dante evidently thought that Matelda's corollary rather applied to Virgil and Statius, who more than himself *poetaron dell' età dell' oro*, and he looks round to see what impression the last words had made upon them.

> Io mi rivolsi addietro allora tutto   145
>> A' miei poeti, e vidi che con riso
>> Udito avevan l' ultimo costrutto :
> Poi alla bella donna tornai il viso.   148

I thereupon turned quite round towards my poets, and I noticed that they had heard (Matelda's) concluding words with a smile : I then turned my eyes back to gaze on the beautiful Lady.

This is the last time but one that Dante sees Virgil's face. He only looks upon it once more. See Canto XXIX, 55 *et seq.*

---

* Benvenuto gravely explains that nectar was wine flavoured with spices.

END OF CANTO XXVIII.

CANTO XXIX.

___

THE CHURCH MILITANT.

IN the last Canto Dante described the beauties of the Terrestrial Paradise, which Matelda pointed out to him, explaining at the same time the phenomena peculiar to it.   He now tells us how a Mystic Procession passes before him, which we find is figurative of the whole of the books of the Old and New Testament.

Benvenuto divides the Canto into four parts.

In the First Division, from v. 1 to v. 30, Dante relates how Matelda moved on, bidding him to follow her, and how she drew his attention to a great light that suddenly shone in the forest.

In the Second Division, from v. 31 to v. 60, he describes the Seven Golden Candlesticks, the standards of the approaching Church Militant.

In the Third Division, from v. 61 to v. 105, he describes the glorious Army of the Church Militant with its Leaders.

In the Fourth Division, from v. 106 to v. 154, he tells us of the Triumphal chariot, of the Gryphon who drew it, and of those that accompanied it.

Division I.   Matelda, having given Dante the explanation he sought, as to the causes of the wind and the water in this sacred region, recommences her singing.   In v. 80 of the last Canto we read that she was singing the Psalm *Delectasti,* and broke off to listen to Dante's doubts.   She now resumes with another psalm.

E E E

Cantando come donna innamorata,*
Continuò col fin di sue parole :
Beati, quorum tecta sunt peccata.†

Singing like a lady in love, at the end of her words
(recorded in the last Canto) she went on with, *Blessed
are they whose sins are covered.*

Matelda, who is emblematical of the doctrine of
Holy Scripture, enamoured of virtuous deeds, rejoices
in the purification of Dante, and having said at the
end of the preceding Canto, the words *qui fu innocente
l'umana radice,* she continues by singing *Beati quorum
tecta sunt peccata,* words most appropriate to the occasion, as Dante is about to pass through the river that

---

* *donna innamorata:* I find in a note of Scartazzini that
Dante, in the description of his meeting with Matelda, has
imitated a sonnet of his friend Guido Cavalcanti addressed to a
shepherdess:—

    "In un boschetto trovai pastorella,
      Più che stella—bella al mio parere.
    Capegli avea biondetti e ricciutelli,
      E gli occhi pien d' amor cera rosata :
      Con sua verghetta pasturava agnelli ;
      E scalza, e di rugiada era bagnata :
      Cantava come fosse inamorata,
      Era adornata—di tutto piacere.
    D' amor la salutai immantinente,
      E domandai se avesse compagnia :
      Ed ella mi rispose dolcemente
      Che sola sola per lo bosco gia," &c.

† "Blessed is he whose transgression is forgiven, whose sin
is covered." This is verse 1 of the Penitential Psalm XXXI,
which is one of the Psalms for Matins in the Roman Breviary.
It may well follow on to *Delectasti* (which is in verse 5 of Psalm
XCI in the Vulgate), as rightly indicating the joy of which the
latter Psalm is the utterance. "Quia delectasti me, Domine, in
factura tua : et in operibus manuum tuarum exsultabo."

takes away the memory of sin.   It is as though she
would say to him : " O happy thou who hast been
found worthy to behold this state of blessedness."

Dante now describes Matelda's mode of walking
away.

> E come ninfe che si givan sole
>> Per le selvatiche ombre, disiando   5
>> Qual di veder, qual di fuggir lo sole,
> Allor si mosse contra il fiume, andando
>> Su per la riva, ed io pari di lei,
>> Picciol passo con picciol seguitando.

And like unto the Nymphs, who were wont to roam
in solitude through the forest shades, some desirous to
avoid, others to behold the sun, so did she (Matelda)
then begin to move up the stream going along the
bank, and I (moved) evenly with her, following her
short steps with short steps.

Benvenuto remarks that the poets, by the Nymphs
or water-goddesses, wished to portray the various
wonderful powers of God over the waters, shown in so
many ways, as we are taught by science and by experience, while, according to other authors, they represent figuratively wise and good men, and are thus a
fair type of Matelda and Dante advancing with slow
and dignified steps up the course of the stream, under
the shadow of the lofty trees.

Dante next tells us how the rill took a sudden
bend, so that he found himself facing the East.

> Non eran cento tra i suo' passi e i miei,   10
>> Quando le ripe igualmente diêr volta,
>> Per modo ch' a levante mi rendei.*

---

* Antonelli observes that Dante, when he reached the top of
the stairway, had the East facing him. Being *vago di cercar
dentro e dintorno,* it is natural to suppose that, as he penetrated

There were not a hundred steps between her's and mine (*i.e.,* we had not walked more than fifty paces each), when both the banks took a sudden turn (*i.e.* remained equally distant) in such a manner that I found me turned towards the East.

In the next eighteen verses Dante imagines that Matelda, now that he is turned to the East, causes him to see and comprehend the wonderful things belonging to God.

> Nè anco fu così nostra via molta,
>   Quando la donna* tutta a me si torse,
>   Dicendo :—" Frate mio, guarda ed ascolta."—   15

Nor had our way (the distance we had walked) been even so much (as fifty paces), when the Lady turned completely round to me, saying, " My brother, look and listen."

Benvenuto explains this to mean that they had not yet walked far beyond the bend the river had taken.

He says also that Dante now begins to describe the Church Militant, and points out that theologians

---

into the depths of the holy forest, he should turn in different directions. He walked upstream along the bank of Lethe, which flowed from its source towards the West, but with many bends ; the part up which he had last been walking had a bend towards the North, and Dante had been therefore facing the South, and now a sudden turn to the left brings him back to face the East.

* Nearly all the best authorities read *la donna tutta a me si torse.* Some read *Quando la donna mia a me si torse;* but this does not seem nearly so good a reading as the first, as Dante has never elsewhere called Matelda " *la donna mia,*" but " *la donna,*" or " *la bella donna.*" " *La donna mia*" could only refer to Beatrice, just as in *Inf.* v. 123 : " Ciò sa il tuo dottore " refers to Virgil and not to Boethius.

always distinguish between the Church Militant, which is ever fighting against the Church's enemies, and the Church Triumphant, which rejoices in Heaven over the victories obtained.

> Ed ecco un lustro subito trascorse
> Da tutte parti per la gran foresta,
> Tal che di balenar mi mise in forse.*

And behold a bright lustre suddenly ran through the great forest on every side, so brilliant that it set me to doubt of (whether it were) lightning.

Dante thought it might be a flash of lightning, until he perceived that it was not followed by thunder.

> Ma perchè il balenar, come vien, resta,
> E quel, durando, più e più splendeva,   20
> Nel mio pensar dicea : *Che cosa è questa?*

But since lightning disappears as quickly as it comes, and this kept getting more and more brilliant, within my thought I said, "What thing is this?"

The light Dante saw proceeded from the seven candlesticks, carried at the head of the procession, and emblematical of the Sevenfold Holy Spirit. A soft sweet strain fell on his ear, the song of the Prophets, Apostles, Martyrs, Confessors, Doctors, and Saints, who, filled with the grace of the Holy Spirit, were chanting their prophecies, prayers, psalms, and orations. The scene, with its glorious accessories, so enchanted Dante, that he could not repress an outburst

---

* *mi mise in forse:* compare *Inf.* VIII, 109-111 :—
> " e quivi m' abbandona
> Lo dolce padre, ed io rimango in forse ;
> Chè il sì e il nò nel capo mi tenzona."

of indignation against Eve, on thinking of the fatal
effects to man of her fall.

> Ed una melodia dolce correva
> Per l' aër luminoso ; onde buon zelo
> Mi fe' riprender l' ardimento d' Eva,*

---

* Scartazzini notices that, whereas in this passage Dante censures Eve, in *Purg.* XXXII, 37, we read that the Mystic Procession censures Adam. But St. Thomas Aquinas (*Summ. Theol.*
P. II, 2ᵃᵉ, qu. CLXIII, art. 4) demonstrates that the sin of the
woman was greater than that of the man.

"Videtur quod peccatum Adæ fuerit gravius quam peccatum
Evæ. Dicitur enim 1 ad. Tim. II, 14, quod *Adam non est
seductus, mulier autem seducta in prævaricatione fuit;* et sic
videtur quod peccatum mulieris fuerit ex ignorantiâ, peccatum
viri ex certâ scientiâ. . . . Si consideremus conditionem personæ
utriusque, scilicet mulieris et viri, peccatum viri est gravius, quia
erat perfectior muliere. Sed quantum ad ipsum genus peccati
utriusque peccatum æqualitur dicitur, quia utriusque peccatum
fuit superbia. . . . Sed quantum ad speciem superbiæ gravius
peccavit mulier, triplici ratione. Primo quidem quia major ela-
tio fuit mulieris quam viri : mulier enim credidit verum esse
quod serpens suasit, scilicet quod Deus prohibuerit ligni esum,
ne ad ejus similitudinem pervenirent ; et ita dum per esum ligni
vetiti Dei similitudinem consequi voluit, superbia ejus ad hoc se
erexit quod contra Dei voluntatem aliquid voluit obtinere. Sed
vir non credidit hoc esse verum : unde non voluit consequi divi-
nam similitudinem contra Dei voluntatem ; sed in hoc super-
bivit, quod voluit eam consequi per seipsum. Secundo, quia
mulier non solum ipsa peccavit, sed etiam viro peccatum sug-
gessit : unde peccavit et in Deum et in proximum. Tertio, in
hoc quod peccatum viri diminutum est ex hoc quod in peccatum
consensit amicabili quâdam benevolentiâ, quâ plerumque fit ut
offendatur Deus, ne homo ex amico fiat inimicus, quod eum facere non debuisse divinæ sententiæ justus exitus indicavit, ut
Augustinus dicit (II Super. Gen. ad. litt., cap. ult., à med). Et
sic patet quod peccatum mulieris fuit gravius quam peccatum
viri."

Che, là dove ubbidia la terra e il cielo,   25
     Femmina sola,† e pur testè formata,
     Non sofferse di star sotto alcun velo ;
Sotto il qual, se divota fosse stata,
     Avrei quelle ineffabili delizie
     Sentite prima, e più lunga fiata.   30

And a sweet melody was borne along through the
illumined air, whereat a righteous indignation made
me rebuke Eve's temerity, who there, where Earth and
Heaven were obedient (to the Divine Will), she, a
woman, and alone, but newly formed, could not endure
to remain under any veil (*i.e.*, in ignorance), under the
which, if she had devoutly stayed, I should sooner
have enjoyed those unspeakable delights (*i.e.*, from my
birth), and afterwards for a long time (*i.e.*, eternally).

Dante was full of anger at Eve not having had the
patience and submission to have her understanding
overshadowed by the slightest secret, or that any
fact should be concealed from her. Dante makes
out Eve's fault to be greater because she was a woman,
and as such ought to have been less bold, because as
yet she was the only woman, and rashness comes more
from consultation and connivance with other companions, and, being newly formed, she could not lay
claim to any experience.

Division II. Here begins *the Second Division of
the Canto*, in which Dante describes the approach of
the seven golden candlesticks, the standards of the

----

† *Femmina sola :* Scartazzini explains this by saying that
being alone, the only woman, she could not have the excuse of
being tempted by emulation, or the desire to excel over other
women.

Church Militant, and emblematical of the Sevenfold
Holy Spirit, or, according to others, of the Seven
Sacraments of the Roman Church.

> Mentr' io m' andava tra tante primizie
> Dell' eterno piacer, tutto sospeso,
> E disïoso* ancor a più letizie,
> Dinanzi a noi, tal, quale un fuoco acceso,
> Ci si fe' l' aer, sotto i verdi rami,   35
> E il dolce suon per canto era già inteso :

While I was walking along among such (wonderful)
first-fruits† of the eternal happiness, all enrapt, and
eager for (the sight of) still more bliss, the air glowed
before us like an enkindled fire under the green
branches, and the sweet sound could now be heard to
be a chant.

And now Dante, before attempting to describe a
lofty and important theme, invokes the favour and aid
·of the Muses.

> O sacrosante Vergini, se fami,‡

---

* Dante had heard frequently from Virgil that, as soon as he
reached the top of the mountain, he should behold Beatrice (see
Purg. VI, 46, *et seq.*).   Therefore his suspense may be understood, expecting, as he does, to see her appear at any moment.

† The Terrestrial Paradise is a foretaste of the Celestial.
The blessedness of this life is a first-fruit of the blessedness of
Life Eternal.

‡ *se fami, &c:* In Filippo Villani's *Vita Dantis* the following
passage occurs : " Tanto pernoscendæ poesis amore flagravit,
ut dies noctesque nil aliud cogitaret."

In *Convito*, tr. III, c. 1, Dante writes himself, " O quante notti
furono, che gli occhi dell' altre persone chiusi dormendo si po-
savano, che li miei nell' abitacolo del mio amore fisamente mira-
vano."

And Boccaccio (*Vita di Dante*) writes : " Non curando nè
caldo, nè freddo, nè vigilie, nè digiuni, nè niuno altro corporale

Freddi o vigilie mai per voi soffersi,
Cagion mi sprona, ch' io mercè ne chiami.
Or convien ch' Elicona* per me versi,   40
Ed Urania† m' aiuti col suo coro,
Forti cose a pensar, mettere in versi.

O most holy Virgins (divine Muses), if for you I
have ever suffered hunger, cold, or vigils, necessity
constrains me to claim my reward for them from you.
Now it is fitting that Helicon should pour forth (its
waters) for me, and that Urania aid me with her choir,
to put into verse things of great concept.

Dante, having now uttered this invocation to the

disagio, con assiduo studio divenne a conoscere della divina
essenzia e delle altre separate intelligenze quello che per umano
ingegno quì se ne può comprendere."

* Helicon was a spur of Mount Parnassus, whereon theory
and science were studied, and here was the fount Castalia ; but
Dante here takes Helicon as the fountain of the Muses. The
waters of Helicon were supposed to give poetical inspiration.

Compare the invocation to the Muses with that at the beginning of the Purgatorio, and *Inf.* II, 7.

† Urania, the Muse of Astronomy, or things celestial, is represented as crowned with stars and robed in azure. See Milton,
Par. Lost, VII, 1 :—

" Descend from Heaven Urania, by that name
If rightly thou art called, whose voice divine
Following, above the Olympian hill I soar,
Above the flight of Pegasean wing !
The meaning, not the name I call : for thou
Nor of the Muses nine, nor on the top
Of old Olympus dwell'st ; but, heavenly-born,
Before the hills appeared, or fountain flowed
Thou with Eternal Wisdom didst converse,
Wisdom thy sister, and with her didst play
In presence of the Almighty Father, pleased
With thy celestial song."

Muses, at once enters upon the divine subjects he has
to describe. In the next fifteen lines, from v. 43 to
v. 57, he explains what it was that caused the light
to shine forth so brilliantly, and what were the voices
heard singing.

> Poco più oltre* sette alberi d' oro†
> Falsava nel parere il lungo tratto
> Del mezzo, ch' era ancor tra noi e loro ;   45

---

* Scartazzini explains that Dante's vision of the Mystic Procession in the Terrestrial Paradise may be divided into two
principal parts. *The first* (XXIX-XXX, 33) shows how the
Church, as a divine institution, or the ideal of the Church,
comes to meet the penitent sinner, who is earnestly seeking
salvation, and does so as the depositary of divine mysteries and
means of grace.

In the second part (from XXXII, 16, to XXXIII, 12) Dante
beholds in the vision the vicissitudes of the Church from its origin
up to the time of the transfer of the seat of the Papacy to Avignon,
and he endeavours further (XXXIII, 34-78), through the mouth
of Beatrice, to predict the future destiny of the Church. Midway in the vision there occurs a great scene of a personal
character; namely, Dante's final penitence and his reconciliation
with Beatrice. In that part of the great vision Dante shows
what must be done by the man who desires to obtain salvation.
The Church comes to meet the sinner, seeks for him so to
speak, as the good Shepherd for the lost sheep, gathers him
into her bosom, and administers to him the means of grace :
the sinner in his turn goes to meet the Church, and submits
himself voluntarily to perform whatever she may require from
him ; repentance of sins, XXX, 78, XXXI, 64 ; regeneration,
XXXI, 91 *et seq.* ; practice of virtue, XXXI, 103 *et seq.*

† *Sette alberi d' oro: Seven* was a sacred number. St. Thomas
Aquinas (*Summ. Theol.* p. I, 2ᵃᵉ, qu. CII, art. 5) writes, " Sep-
tenarius numerus universatem significat." Seven is composed
of *three*, the number of the Trinity, and *four*, which is the
number of the world. The union of *three* and *four* into the
single number *seven* is a figure of the union of God and the

> Ma quando fui sì presso di lor fatto,
>> Che l' obbietto comun, che il senso inganna,
>> Non perdea per distanza alcun suo atto ;
> La virtù che a ragion discorso ammanna,
>> Sì com' elli eran candelabri apprese, 50
>> E nelle voci del cantare, *Osanna.*

A little further on, the wide space which intervened between us and them gave a false illusion of their being seven golden trees ; but when I had drawn so near to them that the general form, that deceives the sense of vision, lost none of its features by distance (*i.e.* when we were near enough to distinguish details) the (discerning) faculty, which prepares for reason its powers of judgment, began to apprehend that they were candlesticks, and in the words of the chant (it distinguished) the word " Hosannah !"

He had at first, before getting near enough to the

---

world in general concord and harmony. Scartazzini thinks Dante certainly took the idea of the seven candlesticks from *Rev.* I, 12, and *Rev.* IV, 5 ; the name from the first, and the signification from the second. The seven candlesticks signify therefore the Sevenfold Holy Spirit, Who is Sevenfold, not for what He is in God, but as He exists in the world as an instrument of divine government. Like as the Sevenfold Spirit of God moved upon the face of the waters, after a fashion preceding the work of the creation, so that same Spirit, in the vision of Dante, precedes the Mystic Procession which represents the work of Salvation. These seven candlesticks being the Sevenfold Spirit of God, we must not take them, as many commentators have done, for the Seven Gifts of the Holy Spirit, for gift and giver are not the same thing.

Dante tells us that the twenty-four Elders followed these lights *come a lor duci.* The writers of the Books of the Old Testament cannot be said to have been guided by the Gifts of the Holy Spirit, but by that Sevenfold Spirit Itself. The Gifts of the Holy Spirit are rather the *sette liste* mentioned in v. 77.

objects advancing to meet him, been deceived by that confusing similitude of things to one another which objects acquire by distance, and which deludes the sense of sight. Here it was a certain resemblance between a tree with branches and a candlestick with branches. The seven candlesticks were very large, and appeared like small trees.

And now Dante, having shown how he had been able to discern that the seven objects were candlesticks, tells us how he recognized that light proceeded from them.

> Di sopra fiammeggiava il bello arnese*
>   Più chiaro assai, che luna per sereno
>   Di mezza notte nel suo mezzo mese.

On the summit (of the candlesticks) flamed the fair equipment (of lamps) more brilliant than the moon, in clear weather at midnight, in the middle of her month.

The moon is lighted by the sun, and the candlesticks receive their light from God, the Eternal Sun, and shine in the clear air of this pure region, like the moon in a clear sky.

Dante turns round full of wonder and, for the last time, looks at Virgil, but finds that the latter (the symbol of human knowledge) is as much awed as himself.

---

* Scartazzini calls special attention to *arnese* being in the singular, as showing that the seven lamps were on one candlestick, and says it shows that, without doubt, Dante wished his readers to understand that the seven candlesticks symbolize a sevenfold unity, which also demonstrates the accuracy of his (Scartazzini's) interpretation.

> Io mi rivolsi* d' ammirazion pieno   55
>   Al buon Virgilio, ed esso mi rispose
>   Con vista carca di stupor non meno.

I turned me round full of admiration to the good
Virgil : and he replied to me with a look not less
charged with stupor.

Benvenuto thinks he gave a shrug of the shoulders,
as all Italians do when a thing is beyond their comprehension.   Virgil's look of awe signified to Dante
that these divine mysteries were beyond the pene-
tration of human science.

Dante then turns round again to gaze at the candlesticks that are advancing towards him, so slowly, that
their forward movement is even slower than that of a
bashful maid approaching the Altar.

> Indi rendei l' aspetto all' alte cose,
>   Che si movièno incontro a noi sì tardi,
>   Che foran vinte da novelle spose.   60

I then turned back my gaze to those lofty things,

---

* A few minutes afterwards Dante turns round again to look
at Virgil, when Beatrice first appears, but finds him no longer
behind him.   See *Purg.* XXX, 40-51 :—
> " Tosto che nella vista mi percosse
>   L' alta virtù, che già m' avea trafitto
>   Prima ch' io fuor di puerizia fosse,
> Volsimi alla sinistra col rispitto
>   Col quale il fantolin corre alla mamma,
>   Quando ha paura o quando egli è afflitto,
> Per dicere a Virgilio :—' Men che dramma
>   Di sangue m' è rimaso che non tremi ;
>   Conosco i segni dell' antica fiamma.'
> Ma Virgilio n' avea lasciati scemi
>   Di sè, Virgilio, dolcissimo padre ;
>   Virgilio a cui per mia salute diémi."

which were moving towards us at a pace so slow, that they would not be surpassed by (the hesitating advance of) young brides.

————

Division III. We now commence the Third Division of the Canto, in which Dante gives a magnificent description of the Army of the Church Militant, which, with its leaders, was following after the golden candlesticks, like a host follows after the standards.

Matelda reproves Dante for confining his attention to the candlesticks, and for not seeing what comes after them. She reminds him that his mind must take a bold wide grasp of the whole scene, and not fritter itself away on any single detail, however important.

> La donna mi sgridò :*—" Perchè pur ardi
> Sì nell' affetto delle vive luci,
> E ciò che vien diretro a lor non guardi ?"—

The Lady reproved me : " Why art thou so ardent in thine affection for these brilliant lights, and regardest not what comes behind them ?"

————

* Compare *Purg.* XXXII, 1-9 :—

> " Tanto eran gli occhi miei fissi ed attenti
> A disbramarsi la decenne sete,
> Che gli altri sensi m' eran tutti spenti.
> Ed essi quinci e quindi avean parete
> Di non caler, così lo santo riso
> A sè traéli con l' antica rete ;
> Quando per forza mi fu vôlto il viso
> Vêr la sinistra mia da quelle Dee,
> Perch' io udia da loro un : *Troppo fiso.*"

Beatrice herself makes a similar reproof to Dante in *Par.* XXIII, 70-72 :—

> " Perchè la faccia mia sì t' innamora,
> Che tu non ti rivolgi al bel giardino
> Che sotto i raggi di CRISTO s' infiora."

Dante obeys Matelda.

> Genti vid' io allor, come a lor duci,
>> Venire appresso, vestite de bianco ; *   65
>> E tal candor di qua giammai non fúci.

I then beheld a company approaching behind (the candlesticks) as though after their leaders, clothed in white, and of such whiteness as never existed in our world.

This purity is a symbol of their faith : such faith as has never been found since.

He next describes, as a sight of increasing perfection, the purity of the water, when struck by so heavenly a light.

> L' acqua splendeva dal sinistro fianco,
>> E rendea a me la mia sinistra costa,
>> S' io riguardava in lei, come specchio anco.

The water was glittering (from the light of the candlesticks) upon my left hand, and moreover reflected back to me my left side even as a mirror.

As Dante was going to the right, his left side was of course nearest to the rill.   This was the side of his heart, and Francesco da Buti thinks that the allegorical sense would show that Lethe is the emblem of the purity and innocence that causes oblivion of sin, and makes the heart known to one's self-perception, if we seek to see ourselves as we are.

---

* *Genti*: the company were the four-and-twenty elders.   See *Rev.* IV, 4:—"And round about the throne were four-and-twenty seats : and upon the seats I saw four-and-twenty elders sitting, clothed in white raiment.

And *Rev.* VII, 14.   "These are they which came out of great tribulation, and have washed their robes, and made them white in the blood of the Lamb."

He places himself so that he can the better contemplate the vision.

> Quand' io dalla mia riva ebbi tal posta,   70
>   Che solo il fiume mi facea distante,
>   Per veder meglio ai passi diedi sosta,

When I had (gained) such a position on the bank
on my side, that the stream alone kept me apart
(from the procession), in order to see better, I gave a
halt to my steps.

As he stops, the candlesticks pass on beyond
him.

> E vidi le fiammelle andar davante,
>   Lasciando dietro a sè l' aer dipinto,
>   E di tratti pennelli avean sembiante ;   75
> Sì che lì sopra rimanea distinto
>   Di sette liste,* tutte in quei colori,
>   Onde fa l' arco il sole, e Delia il cinto.

And I saw the flamelets pass on in front, leaving
behind them the air streaked with colour (*lit.* painted) ;
and they had the semblance of strokes of a painter's
brush ; so that there (the air) overhead, remained distinct with seven bands, all of the colours of which the

---

* The seven long streaks of light, which stream behind the
seven golden candlesticks, are, as we take the latter to be, the
Sevenfold Spirit of God, undoubtedly the effects of that Holy
Spirit, His Sevenfold Gift to man of the Virtues which are often
called the Seven Gifts of the Holy Spirit.   These are said to be :

Piety, as opposed to		Envy.
Fear of God	„	Pride.
Knowledge	„	Anger.
Fortitude	„	Sloth.
Counsel	„	Avarice.
Intellect	„	Luxury.
Wisdom	„	Gluttony.

Some read *Sicchè di sopra*, and others, *Sì ch' egli sopra.*

sun forms the rainbow, and Delia (the moon) her girdle (*i. e.* halo).

He then defines the dimensions of the bands of light.

> Questi ostendali dietro eran maggiori,
> Che la mia vista ; e, quanto al mio avviso,   80
> Dieci passi* distavan quei di fuori.

These standards to the rearward were extended · beyond where my eye could reach ; and, as far as I could estimate, the two on the outer sides were but ten paces apart.

Dante now describes in detail the chiefs or leaders of the Mystic Army.   He tells us that they were twenty-four in number, representing the twenty-four Elders mentioned in *Rev.* IV, 4, who symbolize the twenty-four books of the Old Testament.†

---

* *Dieci passi.* Many interpretations are given to these words, most commentators taking the ten paces to be the ten commandments. Scartazzini however says : " A much better interpretation than this can be obtained if we remember that *the number ten* is a symbolic number, and that, just for the fact of the symbolism of that number, the commandments also are ten. As it concludes the series of radical numbers, and contains them all within itself, the number ten represents a complete and perfect being, and is a symbol of completeness and perfection. The number ten in this passage appears to have the same allegorical sense, so that the meaning of the passage would be, that the Sevenfold Virtue of the Holy Spirit, which extends over the Church, illumines and sanctifies it completely and perfectly."

See also *Vita Nuova*, XXX.   Ten, the Perfect Number.

Francesco da Buti reads : *Dieci passi distavan quei dai fiori*, meaning that the height of the candlesticks above the flowery turf was only ten paces.

† The twenty-four books are accounted for by counting the two books of Samuel, the two books of Kings, and the two books

> Sotto così bel ciel com' io diviso,
>   Ventiquattro seniori, a due a due,
>   Coronati venian de fiordaliso.*

Under so beautiful a sky as I describe, came four-and-twenty Elders, two and two, all crowned with flower-de-luce.

Benvenuto seems to use *diviso* in the sense of *divide, quale ego distinguo in septem listas mirabiles*, which one might translate: "Under so beautiful a heaven, divided, as I have described, into seven won-drous bands or streaks of rainbow hues."

Dante adds that the Elders are singing a hymn of praise to the glory of Beatrice, symbol of divine wisdom, who is shortly expected to descend in triumph.

> Tutti cantavan : *Benedetta tùe* †   85
>   *Nelle figlie d' Adamo ! e benedette*
>   *Sieno in eterno le bellezze tue !*

---

of Chronicles as one book each.   Some think the four-and-twenty Elders are composed of the twelve Patriarchs and the twelve Apostles.

* The four-and-twenty Elders are crowned with lilies to signify the purity of Holy Writ.

† *Benedetta tùe, etc.*   The words of the salutation of the Angel Gabriel to the Virgin Mary (Luke I, 28) : "Blessed art thou among women."   Scartazzini seems in great doubt as to whether the person saluted here is Beatrice or the Virgin Mary. He says, however, that if one considers that in the following Canto (XXX, 11) Beatrice is hailed in the words " *Veni sponsa de Libano cantando*," and (XXX, 19), " *Benedictus qui venis*," and if one considers that it is Beatrice and not Mary, who will shortly appear and will sit upon the Car of the Church, one may believe that Beatrice is the person referred to here, the more so that, in the *Vita Nuova*, § 43, Dante distinctly states that he will say of Beatrice what was never yet said of woman before.

All were singing: "Blessed art thou (Beatrice) among the daughters of Adam; and blessed for evermore be thy beauties."

Having now described the books of the Old Testament in the persons of the four-and-twenty Elders, Dante passes on to the New Testament.

> Poscia che i fiori e l' altre fresche erbette,
>> A rimpetto di me dall' altra sponda,
>> Libere fûr da quelle genti elette,   90
> Sì come luce luce in ciel seconda,
>> Vennero appresso lor quattro animali,
>> Coronati ciascun di verde fronda.

As soon as the flowers and other tender herbage on the other bank opposite to me had been left clear by that band of the elect; even as in the heavens one star rises immediately after another star, so there followed after them (the Elders) four Living Beings, each of them crowned with verdant foliage.*

He then describes how they were fashioned.

> Ognuno era pennuto di sei ali,
>> Le penne piene d' occhi; e gli occhi d' Argo,   95
>> Se fosser vivi, sarebber cotali.

Each one was plumed with six wings; the feathers were full of eyes; and the eyes of Argus, were they living, would be such.

The six wings were to enable them to soar up to

---

* Benvenuto remarks upon the great appropriateness of this simile, for as in the heavens by night one star follows hard upon another, so did the ancient books of the Old Testament appear in a time of spiritual darkness, and were followed during a period of grace by the greater books of the New Testament.

The four Living Beings are generally interpreted as the Four Evangelists, of whom the four mysterious animals in Ezekiel are regarded as symbols.

high heaven, and symbolized the rapid spread of the
Gospel ; and the eyes in their wings, which looked
all ways, were to show their knowledge alike of the
past and the present, and to exercise untiring vigi-
lance to maintain the Church doctrines pure in the
future.

Dante excuses himself for not more fully describing
these wondrous beings.

> A descriver lor forme più non spargo
> Rime, lettor ; ch' altra spesa mi strigne
> Tanto, che a questa non posso esser largo.

To describe their forms, reader, no more of my poesy
do I waste ; as another debt engrosses me so much,
that in this I cannot be diffuse.

Benvenuto says that Dante has to describe the
leader of this army, and he does not wish to dwell too
long over the followers, lest it should diminish the importance of the Lord and Master. The account of the
coming of the four living creatures from the cold north
may be read in Ezekiel, who gives a more lengthened
description of them than does St. John.

> Ma leggi Ezechïel,* che li dipigne　　　　　　　100
> Come li vide dalla fredda parte
> Venir con vento, con nube e con igne ;

---

* *Ezekiel*, I, 4-7. "And I looked, and behold, a whirlwind came
out of the north, a great cloud, and a fire infolding itself, and a
brightness was about it, and out of the midst thereof, as the colour
of amber, out of the midst of the fire. Also out of the midst
thereof came the likeness of four living creatures. And this was
their appearance ; they had the likeness of a man. And every
one had four faces, and every one had four wings. And their
feet were straight feet ; and the sole of their feet was like the
sole of a calf's foot ; and they sparkled like the colour of bur-
nished brass."

> E quai li troverai nelle sue carte,
>   Tali eran quivi, salvo ch' alle penne
>   Giovanni è meco,* e da lui si diparte.   105

But read Ezekiel, who depicts them as he saw them
come from the cold quarter with whirlwind, with
cloud and with fire ; and such as thou shalt find them
in his pages, such were they here, save that in the
matter of wings the account of John tallies with mine,
and differs from him (Ezekiel).

St. John's description of the four beasts with six
wings agrees better with what Dante saw, than the
account of Ezekiel, who only speaks of four wings.

———

Division IV. And now we reach the Fourth and
last Division of the Canto, in which Dante describes
the triumphal chariot with the leader of the Church
militant. ^ A Gryphon drew it

He tells us how he sees a chariot on two wheels, by
which he means to express the Church (or, according
to some, the Pontifical Court), resting on the Old and
New Testaments, and drawn by a fabulous animal,
called a Gryphon, of a twofold nature, typifying our
Lord Jesus Christ, God and Man. The Gryphon was
supposed to be partly man, and partly eagle or lion.

> Lo spazio dentro a lor quattro contenne
>   Un carro, in su due ruote,† trionfale,
>   Ch' al collo d' un grifon tirato venne.

* St. John says in *Rev.* IV, 8 : "And the four beasts had
each of them six wings about him ; and they were full of eyes
within."

† The triumphal chariot is the Church Universal. Scartazzini points out that Dante, in his other works, speaks of the
chariot as the Church Universal, and not the Papal seat. In

Ed esso tendea in su l' una e l' altr' ale *
　　Tra la mezzana e le tre e tre liste,　　　　　110
　　Sì ch' a nulla fendendo facea male.

The space intervening between those four (living
beings) contained a triumphal chariot on two wheels,
which came on, drawn by the neck of a Gryphon.
And he extended both his wings aloft between the
middle band and the three and three (bands of light

De Monarch. lib. III, c. 3, Dante writes : " *Ecclesia dicit,*
loquens ad Sponsum : Trahe me post te ! " The Gryphon draws
the chariot behind him ; therefore he is the bridegroom and the
chariot is the Church.　In *Convito,* tr. II, ch. 6, Dante expressly
says that "the bride" of the Canticles is the Church.　But
Scartazzini thinks that the following passage is quite decisive,
from the letter Dante wrote to the Italian Cardinals a short
time before he wrote the *Purgatorio.*　(§ 4)　"Vos equidem,
Ecclesiæ militantis veluti primi præpositi pili, per manifestam
orbitam Crucifixi currum Sponsæ regere negligentes, non aliter
quam falsus auriga Phæton exorbitastis, et, quorum, sequentem
gregem per saltus peregrinationis hujus illustrare, intererat,
ipsum una vobiscum ad præcipitium traduxistis.　Nec ad
imitandum recensio vobis exempla quum dorsa, non vultus, ad
Sponsæ vehiculum habe."　That the two wheels have an allegorical signification is proved by the passage in Canto XXXII,
131-139, but, as to what they symbolize, has been much disputed
by the commentators.　Some think they signify the active and
the contemplative life ; some the Old and New Testaments, the
New on the right and the Old on the left, and this is the interpretation more generally accepted.　Some have tried to prove
them to be the Greek and Latin Churches.　Some Justice and
Mercy ; but Justice already has its place as one of the four
Cardinal Virtues.　Others interpret them as the clergy and the
laity.　Witte thinks they are the conventual and secular orders
of the clergy, and Scartazzini inclines most to this view.

　　* Note that *ale* is here in the singular.　*Ale* singular, *ali*
plural ; or *ala* singular, *ale* plural.

from the candlesticks), so that he did harm to none
by cleaving it.

The Gryphon was moving partly behind the candlesticks and partly among them, he had three on either
side of him, and extended his wings so as not to
cleave any of the bands of prismatic light.

Dante then speaks of the twofold nature of Christ
in one body.

> Tanto salivan, che non eran viste ;
>> Le membra d' oro avea, quanto era uccello,
>> E bianche l' altre di vermiglio miste.*

So high did they (the wings) reach, that they were
lost to sight : (the Gryphon, *i.e.*, Christ) had His limbs
of gold in so much of Him as was bird, and the rest
white mixed with vermilion.

The wings of gold indicate His incorruptibility, and
the white mingled with red, the purity of His human
nature, yet stained with the blood of the Passion.

He then dilates on the splendour of the chariot.

> Non che Roma di carro così bello   115
>> Rallegrasse Affricano,† o vero Augusto ;
>> Ma quel del Sol saría pover con ello ;
> Quel del Sol, che sviando fu combusto,
>> Per l' orazion della Terra devota,
>> Quando fu Giove arcanamente giusto.   120

Not only did Rome never honour Africanus or
(Cæsar) Augustus with so splendid a chariot, but even

---

* Scartazzini says that the colours are suggested by Canticle V,
10-11 : " My beloved is white and ruddy ; the chiefest among
ten thousand. His head is as the most fine gold ; his locks are
bushy, and black as a raven."

† Publius Cornelius Scipio Africanus, the conqueror of
Hannibal, was honoured by the Romans after his victory at
Zama, B.C. 202, with the surname of Africanus and a magni-
ficent triumph.

that of the Sun would be poor beside it; that of the
Sun, which, when driven awry, was burned in answer
to the prayer of suppliant earth, when Jove was just
in his mysterious purpose.*

Dante now describes seven maidens who accompany the car, and who represent the four cardinal and
the three theological virtues, and Benvenuto says that,
after describing the seven gifts of the Holy Spirit and
the seven Sacraments, it is very appropriate to describe the seven virtues.

> Tre donne in giro, dalla destra ruota,
> Venian danzando; l' una tanto rossa,†
> Ch' a pena fora dentro al fuoco nota:

---

* Ovid (*Met.* II, 107) describes the magnificence of the
chariot of the sun :—

> "A golden axle did the work uphold,
> Gold was the beam, the wheels were orbed with gold;
> The spokes in rows of silver pleased the sight,
> The seat with party-coloured gems was bright;
> Apollo shined amid the glare of light."

and further on, verse 304 :—

> "Jove called to witness every power above,
> And e'en the god whose son the chariot drove,
> That what he acts he is compelled to do,
> Or universal ruin must ensue.
> Straight he ascends the high ethereal throne,
> From whence he used to dart his thunder down,
> From whence his showers and storms he used to pour,
> And now could meet with neither storm nor shower:
> Then aiming at the youth, with lifted hand,
> Full at his head he hurl'd the forky brand,
> In dreadful thunderings. Thus th' almighty sire
> Suppressed the raging of the fires with fire."

† Charity is represented red to denote burning love.

> "Hope ever fresh and green.
> Faith ever pure, like newly fallen snow."

> L' altra era come se le carni e l' ossa
> Fossero state di smeraldo fatte ;   125
> La terza parea neve testè mossa :

Three ladies (Faith, Hope, and Charity or Love) came onward dancing in a circle at the right wheel of the chariot (the New Testament) ; one so ruddy, that within the flames scarce could she have been perceived ; the second was as if her flesh and bones had all been fashioned out of emerald ; the third appeared as new driven snow.

> Ed or parevan dalla bianca tratte,
> Or dalla rossa ; e dal canto di questa
> L' altre toglién l' andare e tarde e ratte.

And now they seemed as led by her in white, and now by her in red: and to the melody of her who was in advance, the other two timed their movement quick or slow.

It must be either Love or Faith who leads ; Hope can only follow.

He next describes the four maidens who represent the four cardinal or moral virtues.

> Dalla sinistra quattro facean festa,   130
> In porpora vestite, dietro al modo
> D' una di lor, che avea tre occhi in testa.

On the left side (*i.e.*, on that of the Old Testament) there were four (maidens) who were rejoicing in purple vestments (*i.e.*, Justice, Prudence, Fortitude, Temperance): following the measure of one of them with three eyes in her head.

Prudence is represented with three eyes, as looking at the past, the present and the future, and is therefore the leader of the group. One cannot have any virtue, says Benvenuto, without prudence, but one may well have prudence without the other three virtues.*

He then depicts two old men as coming next, whom nearly all the commentators agree in taking for St. Luke and St. Paul, the former as representing the book of the Acts of the Apostles, and the latter the books of his Epistles.† Benvenuto thinks the former is St. Peter, but Jacopo della Lana, Francesco da Buti, Fraticelli, Philalethes, Lubin, Longfellow, Pollock and Lamennais, all agree that the former is intended to represent St. Luke.

One of these, St. Luke, is dressed as a physician ; the other, St. Paul, has a sword in his hand.

> Appresso tutto il pertrattato nodo,
>   Vidi due vecchi in abito dispari,
>   Ma pari in atto, ed onesto e sodo.   135
> L' un si mostrava alcun de' famigliari
>   Di quel sommo Ippocrate, che natura
>   Agli animali‡ fe' ch' ella ha più cari.

Behind all this group that I have treated of, I beheld two old men, unlike in habit, but alike in de-

---

* Pietro Dante says, on this passage : "Quatuor a sinistra, id est circa peginam veteris testamenti, sunt quatuor virtutes cardinales, Justitia, Fortitudo, Temperantia, et Prudentia. Et quia, ut ait Seneca de formula honestatis : 'si prudeus est animus tuus, tribus temporibus dispensetur : præsentia ordina, et futura prævide, et præterita recordare' ; et alibi :—

'Judico prudentem, prius, et nunc, postque videntum'; ideo ipsam justitiam nunc fingit auctor cum tribus occulis."

† This seems the more evident, in that all the other personages in this procession represent not men, but the different books of the Old and New Testaments.

‡ In *Convito*, tr. III, c. 2, Dante says : "L' uomo è divino animale da' filosofi chiamato."

meanour, dignified and grave. The one (St. Luke) showed himself as one of the familiars of that sub.ime Hippocrates, whom Nature made for those living creatures whom she holds most dear (*i.e.*, the human race).

> Mostrava l' altro la contraria cura
>> Con una spada* lucida ed acuta,   140
>> Tal che di qua dal rio mi fe' paura.†

The other (St. Paul) showed an opposite intent, with a sword so shining and sharp that, even on this hither side of the river, it caused me fear.

St. Luke, as a physician, had the thought of saving men's lives ; St. Paul is represented with a sword in his hand to show how he persecuted Christians before the time of his conversion. He next describes four of a humble aspect, and after them an aged solitary.

> Poi vidi quattro‡ in umile paruta,
>> E diretro da tutti un veglio solo
>> Venir dormendo, con la faccia arguta.

---

* Mrs. Jameson (*Sacred and Legendary Art*, vol. I, page 188) states that the sword was not attributed to St. Paul before the end of the eleventh century. " When St. Paul is leaning on his sword, it expresses his martyrdom ; when he holds it aloft, it expresses also his warfare in the cause of Christ ; when two swords are given to him, one is the attribute, the other the emblem ; but this double allusion does not occur in any of the old representations."

† We may here again notice how Dante, who had fought as a brave soldier at the battle of Campaldino when he was 24 years old, never fails to depict himself as totally devoid of courage, when in presence either of the horrors of Hell, or the exalted supernatural mysteries of Purgatory.

‡ Benvenuto thinks the four are St. Augustine, St. Jerome, St. Ambrose, and St. Gregory ; and that the aged Solitary is

After that I saw four in humble apparel, and in the rear of all an aged man alone, walking asleep with his face inspired.

By this is meant St. John, as representing the Apocalypse. He appears to be asleep, as if he were in the Spirit on the Lord's Day, and heard behind him the great voice as of a trumpet. Or perhaps the allusion may be to the belief of the early Christians that St. John did not die, but tarries in sleep till his Lord's reappearance. Anyhow it is a fact that St. John survived all his contemporaries, and lived on into a generation which had not known them, and it is said, that it was to supply this new generation with additional information concerning the incidents of our Lord's life and ministry on earth, that St. John wrote his Gospel. It is therefore a beautiful and most appropriate idea of Dante to depict him as an old man, of very great age, walking all alone, the sole survivor of the brethren whom he had known in his youth.

Dante next points out wherein their attire was identical with that of the patriarchs who passed first, and wherein it was different.

> E questi sette col primaio stuolo   145
>   Erano abituati ; ma di gigli
>   Dintorno al capo non facevan brolo,*

Bernard, but I certainly prefer the view of nearly all the other Commentators that these five are the natural concluding sequence of the books of the New Testament.

* Brolo is the Lombard for a garden in which there is verdure. In the Romagnole dialect there occurs the word "*Broi*," a nursery ground : and as the Romagnoles habitually clip their terminations, we may suppose it to be an abbreviation. See Ainsworth's Latin Dictionary under the heading "*Vocabula*

Anzi di rose e d' altri fior' vermigli :
    Giurato avria poco lontano aspetto,
    Che tutti ardesser di sopra dai cigli.* 150

And these seven (viz., the two in v. 134, the four in
mean attire in v. 142, and the *veglio solo* in v. 143)
were apparelled like those in the first group (in white
raiment) ; but they did not wear thick coronals of
lilies about their heads, but rather of roses and other
vermilion flowers: only, to look at them from a short
distance, one might have sworn that they were all on
fire above their brows.

He finally tells us how the whole army, having displayed itself before him, was brought to a halt.

---

in Jure Anglicano municipali occurrentia," where one finds
"*Bruilletus:*" a small coppice or wood. Dr. Moore calls it a
most curious and difficult word, and believes it means thicket,
so that the idea is not so much that of a brilliant garden-like
look of the flowers, but a thicket or bush, referring to their
quantity. And the best translation is to say that the seven who
came last "did not, like those in the first rank, wear a forest
(or rather a thicket) of lilies on their heads," the idea being an
unlimited mass, and luxuriant amount.

There are two places named *Broill* near Chichester. Also
Brailsford in Derbyshire, perhaps from the same root. Brill
near Oxford. The two Broills in Sussex are respectively named
in the old charters "Bruillum Regis" and "Bruillum Depe-
marsh."

* *Ardesser di sopra dai cigli:* Biagioli says the red crowns
were signs of their martyrdom, but if we take all these personages as representing the books of the Old and New Testaments, which I much prefer, we may well take the view that the
red, flame-coloured garlands, on the heads of the later writers of
the New Testament, showed that they were more burning with
the fire of Christian Love than their predecessors.

E quando il carro a me fu a rimpetto,
　　Un tuon s' udì ; e quelle genti degne
　　Parvero aver l' andar più interdetto,
　Formandos' ivi con le prime insegne.　　　154

And as soon as the chariot was opposite to me a
clap of thunder was heard ; and all that divine throng
appeared to have their progress interdicted, halting
there behind their leading standards (*i.e.*, the candlesticks).

Benvenuto thinks that Dante would show, that God
had done him the wondrous favour of letting him see
these things himself, so that he might in turn describe
them to others.

END OF CANTO XXIX.

CANTO XXX.

APPEARANCE OF BEATRICE.
DISAPPEARANCE OF VIRGIL.
DANTE SEVERELY CENSURED BY BEATRICE.

WHEREAS, in the last Canto, Dante gave a figurative description of the Militant Church of God, so, in the present one, he introduces Beatrice, who represents Divine Theology, and who teaches and instructs both churches, in order that she may, by first showing Dante the Church Militant, prepare his mind for gazing, later on, upon the Church Triumphant.

Benvenuto divides the Canto into four parts.

In the First Division, from v. 1 to v. 21, Dante relates how the army of the Church Militant came to a halt.

In the Second Division, from v. 22 to v. 57, the appearance of Beatrice, her attire and demeanour, are minutely described, while Virgil is found to have disappeared.

In the Third Division, from v. 58 to v. 99, Dante tells how Beatrice sharply reproves him for not having remained faithful to her after her death, and he also tells us the effect upon himself that her censure produced.

In the Fourth Division, from v. 100 to v. 145, she begins by praising his early life of promise, and goes on to show how great was his fall from

it, and the necessity that had arisen for her interposition.*

Division I. The seven candlesticks having come
to a halt, and, consequently, the whole procession as
well, the four-and-twenty elders turn themselves round
so as to face the chariot; and one of them, Solomon,
as though he had been specially deputed to do so by
divine command, cries three times aloud to Beatrice
to appear; and at the sound of his voice a hundred
angels, who are mentioned as ministers and messengers of Life Eternal, rise up upon the chariot, all
of them chanting and strewing flowers on and around
it.

> Quando il settentrion del primo cielo,
>   Che nè occaso mai seppe nè òrto,
>   Nè d' altra nebbia, che di colpa, velo,
> E che faceva lì ciascuno accorto
>   Di suo dover, come il più basso face   5
>   Qual timon gira per venire a porto,
> Fermo si affise, la gente verace,†
>   Venuta prima tra il grifone ed esso,
>   Al carro volse sè, come a sua pace.‡

---

* Scartazzini says that those, who desire to grasp the full
meaning of this Canto and the succeeding one, had better begin
to read the *Vita Nuova* of Dante over again from the beginning
to the end.

† *la gente verace*: the truthful company, are supposed to represent or personify the books of the Old Testament, in which
the deepest truth is contained.

‡ As the four and twenty Elders had been walking they had
the chariot directly behind them, but as they stopped they turned
themselves round and faced it, as though the goal and object of
all their desires was before them, in the form of the Gryphon
(Jesus Christ) and the chariot (His Church).

When the Septentrion of the Highest Heaven,—
which never knew setting or rising, or any other
clouding than the veil of sin, and which was making
each person there (in the Earthly Paradise) acquainted
with his duty, just as that lower one (the Constellation of the Great Bear) makes whoever turns the helm,
to come into port,—halted, then all that truthful
company (the Elders) turned towards the chariot, as
to their peace.

The word Septentrion in its literal sense means the
sevenfold group of stars in the Constellation of the
Great Bear.   The Septentrion of the Highest Heaven
here implies the Sevenfold Holy Spirit, which, with
Its sevenfold benefits, is ever ready, as It has ever
been, to receive all who make themselves worthy.

Dante now describes the holy festival that took
place round the chariot, but before doing so he introduces one of the Elders.

> Ed un di loro, quasi da ciel messo,*   10
>   *Veni, sponsa, de Libano*, cantando,
>   Gridò tre volte ; e tutti gli altri appresso.

And one of them (the four and twenty Elders),
as though sent from Heaven, cried out three times in
song " *Veni, sponsa, de Libano !* "†

Benvenuto tells us that Dante, after relating the
manner in which (the so-called) Solomon and the
other Elders had sung the praises of the Church, now

---

* *un di loro, etc.*: Scartazzini says that this does not mean
Solomon, as most of the Commentators explain, but the book of
the Canticles personified by one of the four and twenty Elders.

† Veni de Libano, sponsa mea, veni de Libano" (Vulgate).
" Come with me from Lebanon, my spouse, with me from Lebanon." *Canticles*, IV, 8.

introduces a multitude of the Heavenly Host, singing
the praises of the Bridegroom, and he says that these
angels suddenly rose from the chariot, just as the
Blessed will rise from their sepulchres at the sound of
the last trump.

> Quali i beati al novissimo bando*
>   Surgeran presti ognun di sua caverna,
>   La rivestita voce alleluiando,†   15
> Cotali, in su la divina basterna,‡
>   Si levâr cento, *ad vocem tanti senis,*
>   Ministri e messaggier' di vita eterna.

---

* Blanc says that *bando,* akin to the German *Bann,* and *ban*
in English, has two meanings :—

(1) The extension of the jurisdiction, the district (hence " *ab-
bandonare* ") whence comes also exile from the district ; *uscir
di bando, Purg.* XXI, 102, means to return from exile, and (2)
the publication, the edict, proclamation, and here *il novissimo
bando,* the summons to the Universal Judgment.

† *Rivestita voce:* Compare St. Paul, II *Cor.* v. 2 :—
" Earnestly desiring to be clothed upon with our house which is
from Heaven." Francesco da Buti puts it very well : " Reas-
sumptis organis corporalibus ; " the body in which the voice
once resided is again restored to it. The voice reclothed with
its body. Compare *Inf.* XIII, 103-105, where poor Pier delle
Vigne tells Dante what will be the ultimate fate of himself and
his companions in doom.

> " Come l' altre verrem per nostre spoglie,
>   Ma non però ch' alcuna sen rinvesta ;
>   Chè non è giusto aver ciò ch' uom si toglie."

Others read *La rivestita carne alleviando,* making light and
active (*levia*) through immortality the bodies which they have
again assumed, but the reading *alleluiando* is much to be preferred. There has, however, been much controversy about
the two readings.

‡ *Basterna :* Benvenuto says that *basterna* is a vehicle for
travelling, so called from *vesterna,* because it was spread over

As the Blessed, at the last summons, will rise ready, each from his sepulchre, singing Hallelujah with the voice again clothed (with the body), in like manner at the voice of that old man of so great wisdom, there rose up upon the heavenly litter a hundred ministers and messengers of eternal life.*

It may be taken for granted that Dante meant angels, for in verse 82 he says: *Ella si tacque. E gli angeli cantaro, etc.*, clearly showing that he was speaking of the angels having been previously introduced as having appeared. Otherwise he would not have said *Gli Angeli.*

The song, which was now taken up by the Heavenly Choir, was from the words of the Canticle for Palm Sunday, and, as they scattered flowers over and around the chariot, they also sang one of the most beautiful lines of Virgil's Æneid.

> Tutti dicean : *Benedictus qui venis,*
>> E, fior gittando di sopra e d' intorno :   20
>> *Manibus o date lilia plenis.*

They all exclaimed " *Blessed Thou that comest,*" and

---

with soft garments, and drawn by two beasts, being used for carrying noble ladies. He thinks the metaphor appropriate, for the chariot here is drawn by an animal of a twofold nature, and in it a most noble lady, Beatrice, is carried.

* Compare *Hebrews*, I, 7 : " And of the angels he saith, Who maketh his angels spirits and his ministers a flame of fire," and in v. 14 : " Are they not all ministering spirits, sent forth to minister for them who shall be heirs of salvation?" Scartazzini imagines that the angels were in the chariot, but only sprang into view at the call of Solomon, just as the chariots and horses of fire, which surrounded the town of Dothan, were invisible to mortal eyes, until Elisha prayed that the eyes of his servant might be opened to behold them. II *Kings*, vi, 17.

casting flowers from above and round (the chariot, they added) " *Bring lilies here, in handfuls bring.*"

It was as if they wished their praise not only to be in laudation of saints, but also to take in the praise of mortal man.

I venture to offer the opinion that this is the moment when Virgil vanishes, just when Beatrice is about to come into view, and that, as he himself wrote of scattering lilies over the glorious tomb of the young Marcellus, so Dante quotes the choicest line in the choicest passage of Virgil's great work, by way of figuratively throwing flowers in sorrow and regret over the grave that is to separate them for ever. Anyhow it is singular that, immediately before he misses Virgil from his side, the words that he hears sung are words, written by Virgil himself, to honour the tomb of a deeply-mourned young warrior of the Augustan family.*

————

Division II. Here commences the Second Division of the Canto, in which Dante describes how Beatrice first appeared to him.

———————————————————

* We read in the Sixth book of the *Æneid* that Æneas, conducted by the Sybil into the Infernal Regions, finds his father Anchises in a beautiful spot, and surrounded by the shades of illustrious men whom he points out to his son. He also shows him the great Romans who were to descend from his stock, among whom was the young Marcellus. When Virgil read the magnificent lines which compose this passage, Augustus could not restrain his tears ; Octavia, the mother of Marcellus, swooned away at the words *Tu Marcellus eris*, but afterwards presented Virgil with ten sesterces for every verse in praise of her son, the whole equivalent to £2000 English.

Io vidi già, nel cominciar del giorno,
    La parte oriental tutta rosata,*
    E l' altro ciel di bel sereno adorno ;
E la faccia del sol nascere ombrata,   25
    Sì che per temperanza di vapori,
    L' occhio la sostenea lunga fïata.

I have seen ere now, at break of day, the East all
of one rosy tint, and the other parts of the heavens
decked in tranquil beauty ; and the face of the sun
rising clouded, so much so that, through being tempered by vapours, the eye could bear to gaze upon it
for a long time.

Benvenuto remarks on the appropriateness of this
simile : for Beatrice is as the sun that illumines the
chariot, and like as the human eye cannot endure the
rays of the sun, except through the medium of
vapours, so the human intellect cannot contemplate
the glory of Beatrice, except through the showers of
flowers falling over the chariot.

---

* *rosata :* Scartazzini gives the following illustrations : Ovid
Metam. VI, 47-48 :—
                    " Ut solet aer
    Purpureus fieri, cum primum aurora movetur."
And Petrarch (*Rime in Morte di Laura. Son.* XXIII.)
    " Quand' io veggio dal ciel scender l' Aurora
    Con la fronte di rose, e co' crin d' oro."   .
And Tasso (*Ger. Lib.* VIII, st. 1)
    " E l' Alba uscia della magion celeste
    Con la fronte di rose, e co' piè d' oro."
And Ariosto (*Orl. Fur.* XLIII, st. 54)
    " . . . . . e già il color cilestro
    Si vedea in Oriente venir manco,
    Che, votando di fior tutto il canestro,
    L' Aurora vi faceva vermiglio e bianco."

Così d' entro una nuvola di fiori,
　Che dalle mani angeliche saliva,
　　E ricadea in giù dentro e di fuori,　　　　30
Sovra candido vel* cinta d' oliva
　Donna m' apparve, sotto verde manto,
　　Vestita di color di fiamma viva.

So within a cloud of flowers, which were thrown upwards from the hands of the angels, and fell down again both within and around (the chariot), crowned with olive (leaves) over a white veil, there appeared to me a Lady, vestured in colour of living flame under a green mantle.

The white represents Faith ; the green, Hope ; and the crimson, Love. The Olive is a symbol of wisdom (see v. 68), and perhaps also of peace.

Benvenuto says that the cloud of flowers figures the books of the Old Testament, coming from the hands of learned writers who had angelic intellects, and that

---

* *velata:* compare Milton, *Par.* Lost, IX, 424-5.
　　"..... Eve separate he spies,
　　Veiled in a cloud of fragrance, where she stood."
And Thomson's *Spring,* l. 4.
　　"..... veil'd in a shower
　　Of shadowing roses, on our plains descend."
Beatrice appears to Dante veiled, as he is not as yet sufficiently purified and reconciled to her to be thought worthy of looking upon her face.

In the *Vita Nuova,* § 2, Dante says : " She (Beatrice) appeared clothed in a most noble colour, a modest and becoming crimson, garlanded and adorned in such wise as befitted her very youthful age."

And in § 3 : " This admirable lady appeared before me clothed in purest white ...... She seemed to me to be wrapped lightly in a blood red cloth."

it is a beautiful idea to make Beatrice, Divine Theology, to appear through the midst of such flowers.

Dante now tells us how an instinct within him made him recognize Beatrice (who had been dead ten years), though he could not see her face.

> E lo spirito mio, che già cotanto
> > Tempo era stato che alla sua presenza   35
> > Non era di stupor, tremando, affranto,
> Senza degli occhi aver più conoscenza,
> > Per occulta virtù che da lei mosse,
> > D' antico amor sentì la gran potenza.*

And my spirit, that had already now been so long a time without having been broken down, trembling with awe, in her presence, without having any more knowledge of her by my eyes, yet, from the

---

* Fully to understand and feel what is expressed in these lines, we ought to read the Second Section of the *Vita Nuova* and also Sections 11, 14, 24. Benvenuto, at this point, quotes from the *Vita Nuova* the episode of Dante's first meeting with Beatrice, and says that from the facts there mentioned one can understand that Dante, in speaking of his Beatrice, mentions some circumstances in their literal sense, as they actually occurred, while others are to be taken in an allegorical sense.

The last paragraph in the *Vita Nuova* (Section XLIII) shows how Beatrice's influence made Dante write the *Divina Commedia*.

"After this sonnet, a wonderful vision appeared to me, in which I saw things which made me resolve to speak no more of this blessed one, until I could more worthily treat of her. And to attain to this, I study to the utmost of my power, as she truly knoweth. So that, if it shall please Him through whom all things live that my life shall be prolonged for some years, I hope to say of her what was never said of any woman. And then may it please Him, who is the Lord of Grace, that my soul may go to behold the glory of its lady, namely, of that blessed Beatrice, who in glory looketh upon the face of Him *qui est per omnia sæcula benedictus.*"

occult virtue that emanated from her, I felt the mighty influence of bygone love.

Dante now says that, finding himself in sore perplexity, his first impulse prompted him to turn to Virgil, as he had been wont to do during the whole of his passage through Hell and Purgatory.

> Tosto che nella vista mi percosse　　　　　　40
> 　L' altra virtù,* che già m' avea trafitto
> 　Prima ch' io fuor di puerizia fosse,
> Volsimi alla sinistra col rispitto†
> 　Col quale il fantolin corre alla mamma,
> 　Quando ha paura o quando egli è afflitto,　　45

---

* *nella vista mi percosse l' altra virtù:* There appears to be some difficulty in explaining how a vivid impression, a sublime influence, could strike upon Dante's vision, but Dante did not recognise Beatrice at first through her veil; he only says that the *appearance* of the veiled Lady made the same impression upon him as that of Beatrice had done in his early youth.

† *rispitto:* Scartazzini quotes all the different interpretations given of this word by commentators, but thinks the best is to understand that Dante turned to his left hand to get comfort and help from Virgil. He thinks *rispitto* is derived from the Provençal word *rispicit*, which means trust, confidence, hope; and he says that Nannucci gives that interpretation in his book (*Voci e locuzioni italiane derivate dalla lingua provenzale*), We may note here that the very last words in the poem, which Dante addresses to Virgil, are words of Virgil's own in *Æn.* IV, 23, where Dido says to Anna: "Agnosco veteris vestigia flammæ."

> " E' en in these ashen embers cold,
> 　I feel the spark I felt of old."

Scartazzini remarks upon the inconsistency of Beatrice visiting the gates of death to induce Virgil to go and succour Dante, and yet, in the Terrestrial Paradise, Virgil vanishes on Beatrice's appearance without their exchanging a word.

> Per dicere a Virgilio :—" Men che dramma
> Di sangue m' è rimaso, che non tremi ;
> Conosco i segni dell' antica fiamma."—

So soon as on my vision smote that sublime influence, which had already pierced me before I had ceased to be a boy, I turned round towards my left, with that trust with which a little child runs towards its mother when he is in fear, or when he is in grief, to say to Virgil, " I have less than a single drop (*lit.* drachm) of blood remaining in me which is not in tremor ; I recognize the symptoms of the ancient flame (of love)."

Dante's hopes of aid and counsel from Virgil are disappointed, he turns round, but his father in poetry has vanished from his sight for ever.

> Ma Virgilio n' avea lasciati scemi
> Di sè, Virgilio, dolcissimo* padre ;   50
> Virgilio a cui per mia salute diémi:

But Virgil had left us deprived of his company, Virgil, my most beloved father (in poesy), Virgil, to whom I gave myself up for my salvation.

Overflowing with affection Dante repeats in three consecutive verses the name of Virgil,† and then, notwithstanding the bliss of that sacred spot, he cannot restrain his tears.

---

* Scartazzini remarks that Dante always called Virgil *dolce padre*, but, now that he finds he has lost him, he calls him *dolcissimo.* The words *dolcissimo amico* are a common expression in Italy, and occur frequently in Leopardi's and Giusti's letters.

† Here Dante imitates a passage in the *Georgics*, Book IV, 525-527, where the name of Eurydice is three times repeated.

> " . . . . . Eurydicen vox ipsa et frigida lingua,
> Ah, miseram Eurydicen, anima fugiente vocabat :
> Eurydicen toto referebant flumine ripæ."

Nè quantunque perdeo l' antica madre,
Valse alle guance nette di rugiada,*
Che lagrimando non tornassero adre.†

Nor did all that our ancient mother Eve lost (*i. e.,* the Terrestrial Paradise) avail my cheeks (that had been by Virgil) cleansed with dew, to prevent their again becoming soiled from weeping.

Beatrice on coming forward is indignant at Dante's tears, and shows him in her first words that he will soon have to undergo greater grief than for the departure of Virgil.

—" Dante,‡ perchè Virgilio se ne vada,   55
Non pianger anco ; non pianger ancora ;
Chè pianger ti convien per altra spada."—

" Dante, because Virgil is gone, weep not any longer

---

* *guance nette di rugiada:* " cheeks free from the moisture of tears " ; or, " cheeks that had been washed in the morning dew on the shores of the Antipurgatorio."—*Purg.* I, 124-129.

Benvenuto says Dante's grief is not to be wondered at.   He had loved Virgil in his writings even from a child.

† *adre* is the same as *atre, oscure, fosche.*

‡ *Dante:* This is the only mention of Dante by name throughout the *Divina Commedia,* though some Commentators have tried to prove that the words *Da te,* in *Par.* XXVI, 104, ought to be *Dante,* but Scartazzini says that their arguments have not much weight, whereas in verses 62-63 of the present Canto he says :

" . . . . mi volsi al suon del nome mio,
Che di necessità qui si registra."

showing the exceptional circumstance under which he mentions his name, and modestly apologizing for doing so.

In the *Convito,* Tr. I. Cap. II, Dante says : " Non si concede per li rettorici, alcuno di sè medesimo sanza necessaria cagione parlare."

(at all events), weep not yet, for thou wilt soon have to weep for another wound (*lit.* sword)."

He will have to weep for the follies of which Beatrice is about to remind him, namely, for not only having loved Virgil too much, but also for having been guilty of forgetting Beatrice for others after her death.

Division III. We now enter upon the Third Division of the Canto, and Dante compares Beatrice to an admiral who goes round to inspect the ships under his flag.

Scartazzini thinks that the dignity of the office of admiral in the simile strongly marks the dignified nobility of Beatrice.

> Quasi ammiraglio, che n poppa e in prora
>> Viene a veder la gente che ministra
>> Per gli altri legni, ed a ben far la incuora,   60
> In su la sponda del carro sinistra,
>> Quando mi volsi al suon del nome mio,
>> Che di necessità qui si registra,
> Vidi la donna, che pria m' apparío
>> Velata, sotto l' angelica festa,   65
>> Drizzar gli occhi vêr me di qua dal rio.

Even as an admiral that on poop and prow comes to inspect the people that are serving throughout the other ships, and encourages them to be smart, (in like dignified manner,) when I turned at the sound of my own name, which of necessity is recorded here, I saw, on the left hand edge of the chariot, the Lady who had first appeared to me veiled, under that angelic festival (of flowers), direct her eyes towards me on my side of the stream.

He sees Beatrice, who, on her first appearance, was only to be discerned with some difficulty, amid the clouds of flowers that fell upon her from the ministering angels, standing on the left hand border of the chariot, *i. e.,* on the side of the Old Testament. She looks steadily at him, as he is standing on the Purgatory side of Lethe. Dante shows great ingenuity in the modest way he introduces his own name, making Beatrice only utter it for purposes of disparagement. His description of her demeanour is fully in keeping with the dignity of the subject.

> Tutto che il vel che le scendea di testa,
>   Cerchiato dalla fronde di Minerva,
>   Non la lasciasse parer manifesta ;
> Regalmente, nell' atto ancor proterva   70
>   Continuò, come colui che dice,
>   E il più caldo parlar dietro si serva :
> —" Guardaci ben : ben sem, ben sem Beatrice !
>   Come degnasti d' accedere al monte ?
>   Non sapei tu, che qui è l' uom felice ? "—   75

Although the veil that descended from her head, which was wreathed with the leaf of Minerva, did not let her be seen distinctly, yet, standing in an attitude that was royally majestic, she continued as one who speaks, and keeps his strongest argument in reserve : " Look well upon us ; we are, we are in sooth Beatrice ! How condescendedst thou to climb up the mountain ? Didst thou not know perchance that here (alone) man is happy ? "

I follow Scartazzini's reading in making Beatrice speak in the royal plural.*

---

* The whole speech, when disconnected from Dante's description of the scene, runs thus : " Dante, because Virgil has disappeared, do not weep any longer, or at all events not just at

Dante then relates the burning shame that he felt
at her words of reproof.

> Gli occhi mi cadder giù nel chiaro fonte ;
> Ma veggendomi in esso, i* trassi all' erba,
> Tanta vergogna mi gravò la fronte.

My eyes fell down into the limpid stream, but seeing
myself reflected in it, I turned them (my eyes) on to
the grass, such shame was weighing on my brow.

Scartazzini asks the question very appropriately :
" Shame for what ? "   It could not be for any of the
sins of the Antipurgatorio, or of the seven circles of
the Purgatorio itself, because as each of the seven P's
was erased from Dante's brow, so he was perfectly
absolved, and would no longer have occasion for being
in sin.   Therefore we must conclude that he felt shame
for some sin or error, not yet remitted to him.   And,
Scartazzini says, that pride of philosophic doubt of
things concerning the faith is not actually atoned for
in any of the circles of Purgatory.

---

present, but thou wilt soon have to weep to some purpose for a
very different kind of wound.   Look well at me, look, I *am*, yes,
I *am* Beatrice ! How camest thou to deign to ascend this mountain ? Didst thou not know that here alone man is truly happy ? "

Scartazzini has a long note on the line *Come degnasti*, etc.,
which he says must be interpreted very differently from the
description of Benvenuto.   He says the verse is, " oscuro e di
difficile interpretazione," and that the question asked by Beatrice
reminds him of that of the Psalmist, " Who shall ascend into
the hill of the Lord ? " to which the answer is : " Even he that
hath clean hands and a pure heart, that hath not lift up his
mind unto vanity," as Dante himself confesses to Beatrice in
XXXI, 34-36.

* *I trassi all' erba : i* means *gli occhi*, " *i* " being the Provençal
for " *gli*."

Benvenuto remarks that Dante shows in the next three lines how profitable for him was the wrath of Beatrice, because it sprung, not from hate, but from love.

> Così la madre al figlio par superba,
>> Com' ella parve a me ; per che d' amaro   80
>> Sente il sapor della pietate acerba.

So to her son the mother seems haughty, as she appeared to me, because the savour of stern pity has a somewhat bitter taste.

Dante knew that Beatrice loved him, and, from the fact of her loving him, her displeasure, expressed in ironical words, cut him to the very quick. The angels, sweet ministers of comfort to the mourning sinner, suddenly burst out into song.

> Ella si tacque.   E gli Angeli cantaro
>> Di subito : *In te, Domine, speravi ;*
>> Ma oltre *pedes meos* non passaro.*

She ceased, and the angels suddenly sang : "*In te Domine, speravi,*" but they did not go beyond (the words), "*pedes meos.*"

He tells us that their gentle intercessions so touched his heart that he burst into tears.

> Sì come neve, tra le vive travi,†   85

---

* The words are taken from *Psalm* XXXI, 1, *et seq.* "In thee, O Lord, do I put my trust; let me never be ashamed." They sang this, in order that Dante should not despair, but ceased at the words in v. 8, "Thou hast set my feet in a large room."

† *Vive travi :* compare Virgil, Æn. VI, 181 :—
   "Fraxineæque trabes, cuneis et fissile robur
      Scinditur."

Per lo dosso : The Apennines are almost like the spine of Italy.

Dennistoun (*Mem. of the Duke of Urbino I,* 4,) says : "On the

Per lo dosso d' Italia si congela
Soffiata e stretta dalli venti schiavi,
Poi liquefatta in sè stessa trapela,
Pur che la terra, che perde ombra,* spiri,
Sì che par fuoco fonder la candela ;   90
Così fui senza lagrime e sospiri
Anzi il cantar di que' che notan sempre
Dietro alle note degli eterni giri.

Like unto snow that, on the leafless trees (*lit.* living beams) on the backbone of Italy (*i.e.* the Apennines), congeals when blown upon and bound up by the Sclavonian winds, and afterwards dissolving filters through itself (*i.e.* through the snow below, which thaw only takes place), provided that the land which loses shadow breathes, so that it seems a fire that melts a taper : thus was I deprived of tears and sighs before (I heard) the song of those, who always tune their notes after (the harmony) of the eternal spheres.

He means the singing of the angels.

---

summit grew those magnificent pines, which gave to the district of Massa the epithet of Trabaria, from the beams which were carried thence for the palaces of Rome, and which Dante calls

'. . . . the living rafters
On the back of Italy.' "

The Mount of Purgatory is compared to the beautiful Apennines. The trees of the Apennines are compared to Dante born among the Apennines. The snow like the purified soul. The fierce North Wind, the Bora, is compared to Beatrice, harsh, but penetrating the heart for Dante's good. The hot South Wind, which brings rain, is compared to the song of the angels which melts Dante's heart into tears.

* *la terra, che perde ombra* : This means Africa, or the tropics, where, at midday, the Sun is so exactly overhead that it sends down its rays quite perpendicularly ; and is therefore a land that loses its shadows.

Ma poi che intesi nelle dolci tempre
    Lor compatire* a me, più che se detto   95
    Avesser :—" Donna, perchè sì lo stempre ? "—
Lo giel che m' era intorno al cor ristretto,
    Spirito ed acqua fessi, e con angoscia
    Per la bocca e per gli occhi uscì del petto.

But when I heard in the sweet melodies (of the
Angels) their sympathy for me, more (expressive)
than if they had said : " Lady, why dost thou so mortify him ? " then, the ice that had congealed round my
heart, dissolved itself into sighs and tears (*lit.* air and
water), and issued from my heart through my mouth
and through my eyes.

Division IV. We now enter upon the Fourth Division of the Canto, in which Beàtrice, after highly
commending Dante's early life of promise, reproves
him for his fall from it, and points out the necessity
that had arisen for her interposition.

Ella, pur ferma in su la detta* coscia   100

-----

   * *Lor compatire a me :* Compare St. Thomas Aquinas (*Summ.
Theol.* P. III, Suppl. qu. XCIV, art. 2):—

" Peccatores . . . . quamdiu sunt in hoc mundo, in tali statu
sunt, quod sine præjudicio divinæ justitiæ possunt in beatitudinem transferri de statu miseriæ et peccati. Et ideo compassio
ad eos locum habet et secundum electionem voluntatis (prout
Deus, angeli et beati eis compati dicuntur, eorum salutem vo-
lendo), et secundum passionem, sicut compatiuntur eis homines
boni in statu viæ existentes."

   * *In su la detta coscia :*—

We have here a very important difference of reading, about
which the principal authorities are pretty equally divided.

     " Ella, pur ferma in su la *detta* coscia
       Del carro," etc.

> Del carro stando, alle sustanzie pie
> Volse le sue parole così poscia :

She, still standing unmoved on the afore-mentioned side of the chariot, thereafter addressed her words to the holy beings (*i.e.* the angels) thus :

> —" Voi vigilate nell' eterno dìe,
> Sì che notte nè sonno a voi non fura
> Passo,* che faccia il secol per sue vie ;   105

" Ye watch in the eternal day, so that neither the night nor sleep robs from you a step which time may make in its revolutions.

These celestial intelligences can see all things in the Divine Light of God, nothing that Time can operate in its revolutions can escape them.   All is manifest to them, for they see all in God.

> Onde la mia risposta è con più cura,
> Che m' intenda colui che di là piagne,
> Perchè sia colpa e duol d' una misura.

Wherefore my reply is (*i.e.*, shall be given) with greater care, that he, who is weeping yonder (on the farther bank) may hear me, in order that his fault and his remorse (for it) may be of equal measure.

---

which reading I take here ; or

> " Ella, pur ferma in su la *destra* coscia
> Del carro," etc.

which Benvenuto adopts ; and which would imply that Beatrice had changed her position, and passed over to the right, or New Testament side of the car.   The word *pur* speaks in favour of the former reading.   Beatrice was *still* standing on the aforementioned side of the car.

* *non fura passo:* Compare St. Thomas Aquinas (*Summ. Theol.* P. I, qu. LVII, art. 1):—

" Sicut Deus per suam essentiam materialia cognoscit, ita Angeli ea cognoscunt per hoc quod sunt in eis per suas intelligibiles species."

Dante's penitence must be proportioned to his errors.

Beatrice now enlarges on the early promise of Dante's young life.

> Non pur per ovra delle ruote magne,
>> Che drizzan ciascun seme ad alcun fine,   110
>> Secondo che le stelle son compagne ;
> Ma per larghezza di grazie divine,
>> Che sì alti vapori hanno a lor piova,
>> Che nostre viste là non van vicine,
> Questi fu tal nella sua vita nuova*   115
>> Virtualmente, ch' ogni abito destro
>> Fatto averebbe in lui mirabil pruova.

Not only by the working of the mighty spheres, which mark each seed to some end, according as the stars accompany (*i.e.* influence it), but through the gift of the Divine Graces which fall in showers from such lofty clouds (*lit.* which have such lofty vapours for their rain), that our (human) sight comes not near them, this man was in his early youth potentially such (*i.e.* of such great promise) that every good quality would have had in him a marvellous example.

From this Beatrice concludes that, from Dante having made a bad use of Divine Grace, it turned to his injury.

> Ma tanto più maligno e più silvestro
>> Si fa il terren col mal seme e non colto,
>> Quant' egli ha più del buon vigor terrestro.   120

But all the more unprofitable and rank does soil become, with bad seed, and (when) untilled, the more it (the soil) has of good earthly vigour.

Scartazzini thinks that only a just measure of reproof should be understood here. The meaning is,

---

* Some interpret this as referring to Dante's *Vita Nuova*, which he wrote in his youth, and regretted in middle age.

that a nature with great powers of good is just the
one to be the greatest for evil, if not guided and
governed by religion. There is no idea here of ac-
cusing Dante of profligate habits, but only of want of
faith.

Beatrice now speaks historically and allegorically
of their early acquaintance.

> Alcun tempo il sostenni col mio volto*;
> Mostrando gli occhi giovinetti a lui,
> Meco il menava in dritta parte vôlto.

---

* Scartazzini points out that the Commentaries of Jacopo
della Lana and the Anonimo Fiorentino fully confirm his opinion,
that Beatrice is only reproving Dante for his philosophical
aberrations. Witte (*Ueber das Missverständniss Dantes* re-
printed in *Dante-Forschungen*) also holds the same view. Witte
says that, even in childhood, the innocent heart of Dante was
inflamed with love, so pure that it is impossible to say whether
it was caused by one of the daughters of earth, or whether the
youth did not typify his affection for a Heavenly Father in his
Beloved Beatrice. "The *Vita Nuova* is the book of a boyish
love and of piety undisturbed by doubt, that knew no wish save
for a perpetual and beatifying contemplation of the wonders in
which the grace of God beams and is reflected; and the fulness
of the tender secret was guarded deeply in his breast as one
which a single strange glance would profane. Certain *Rime*
are joined to it. When, in the meanwhile, Dante had reached
complete manhood Beatrice was snatched away from him.
Long he lamented for her as for lost innocence, but at last he
was enticed away by new charms. In the glance of a gracious
maiden he thought he found again the love and commiseration
of Beatrice; she promised him consolation, and soon the light
of her eyes dispossessed the memory of the departed, and she
took his whole heart. She is Philosophy. The *Amoroso con-
vivio* is devoted to this sorrow-laden love. Unquiet is it and
full of torment, since the peace of childish resignation has for-
saken his breast. More impetuously desired he ever a new
grace from the beloved one, who often turned herself unwillingly

For some time (*i.e.* for sixteen years) I sustained him with my countenance, showing him my young eyes, I led him with me turned in the right way.

In the *Vita Nuova*, Dante relates that the mere sight of Beatrice was sufficient to extinguish in him every depraved appetite, and to nourish in his breast a flame of love and humility.

> Sì tosto come in su la soglia fui
> > Di mia seconda etade,* e mutai vita,   125
> > Questi si tolse a me, e diessi altrui.

So soon as I was on the threshold of my second age (*i.e.* about 25 years old), and changed life (for death), then he left me, and gave himself to others.

---

from him, and then he gave himself up to loud lament ; at times also he felt that his affection could never bring lasting comfort into his heart. Thus was Dante led to speculate on everything that came under his view. He explored the nature of justice, valour, magnanimity ; he developed his principles of state-administration ; explored the signification of the great events of his time ; and devoted his life to the bringing into practice of all he held to be true. During this epoch of his life fell the portion that he gave up to public life in the city of his birth, and when most probably he perfected his views on language and poetry" (I, 58, &c.). Troubled, however, by earthly cares he turned to philosophy, which unveiled to him that side of her usually unseen by mortals. He attempted to ascend the steepest paths of speculation by the aid of natural reason, and, bewildered by philosophic pride, was for a time drawn away from the religion of Christ. At last, however, divine grace was rekindled in his heart, and he returned to his first love for Beatrice.

* In the *Convito*, Tr. IV, c. 24, Dante divides human life into four ages, the first age ending at 25 years; so he rightly speaks of Beatrice as just about to enter upon her second age when she died, which she did in 1290, at the age of 24 years and 3 months.

Benvenuto takes this passage in its literal sense, implying that, when Beatrice married, Dante forgot her and thought of others, and eventually, at the solicitation of his friends, took a wife, but he adds that many explain it allegorically, that *gli occhi giovi-netti* would be the first elements of Theology, that *si tolse a me e diessi altrui* would be that he took to other and secular sciences, and that, when Beatrice died, his wife made him enter into public, municipal, and diplomatic affairs. Scartazzini thinks that *altrui*, taken in its literal sense, refers to *la donna gentile* mentioned in the *Vita Nuova*, 30-39, and, allegorically, the philosophic speculation to which he gave himself up, after abandoning his faith, but that, whoever *la donna gentile* may have been, she was in no way un-worthy, either morally or socially, of the pure affection and holy love of a great mind like that of Dante.

Beatrice continues her narrative.

> Quando di carne a spirto era salita,
>> E bellezza e virtù cresciuta* m' era,
>> Fu' io a lui men cara e men gradita ;†
> E volse i passi suoi per via non vera,   130
>> Imagini di ben seguendo false,
>> Che nulla promission rendono intera.‡

---

* Scartazzini says that the soul of the just is beautiful and vigorous, but when confined in the body is not able to manifest all its beauty and vigour; in Paradise it is full of beauty and life.

† Beatrice does not say that Dante altogether ceased to love her, but that his love for her grew lukewarm, and that, moreover, just when he ought to have loved her most.

‡ *Che nulla promission rendono intera* : compare Boet. *Phil. Cons.* lib. III, pr. 8 : "Nihil igitur dubium est, quin hæ ad beati-tudinem viæ devia quædam sint, nec perducere quemquam eo

When I was risen up from flesh into spirit, and beauty and virtue had increased in me, I became to him less precious and less dear ; and he turned his steps into a way that was untrue (*i.e.* philosophic speculations), following after deceptive semblances of good, that never fulfil what they seem to promise.

And then Beatrice, by way of censuring Dante still more severely, points out his obstinate persistence in these paths of error.

> Nè l' impetrare spirazion mi valse,
> Con le quali ed in sogno ed altrimenti
> Lo rivocai ; sì poco a lui ne calse.   135

Nor did it avail me to obtain inspirations, with which, both by means of dreams and in other ways, I recalled him (Dante into the right path) ; so little recked he.

Dante doubtless alludes here to the visions related by him in the *Vita Nuova*, §§ 40 and 43. Scartazzini thinks that his confessions in the last Cantos of the Purgatorio are a supplement or complement of what he related in the *Vita Nuova*.

Beatrice goes on.

> Tanto giù cadde, che tutti argomenti
> Alla salute sua eran già corti,
> Fuor che mostrargli le perdute genti.

He fell so low (in the condition of his soul) that all means would have been insufficient for his salvation, except by showing him the lost (in Hell).

---

valeant, ad quod se perducturas esse promittunt." And lib. III, pr. 9 : "Hæc igitur vel *imagines veri boni* vel imperfecta quædam bona dare mortalibus videntur : verum autem atque perfectum bonum conferre non possunt."

> Per questo visitai l' uscio dei morti,
>> Ed a colui che l' ha quassù condotto,   140
>> Li prieghi miei, piangendo,* furon porti.

For this purpose I (Beatrice) visited the gate of the dead, and to him (Virgil), who has brought him up hither, my prayers with tears were addressed.

The whole of this episode is recounted in the Second Canto of the Inferno, and is often referred to in other passages.

Benvenuto says that Beatrice's concluding words are addressed as an answer to the question of the angels, *Donna, perchè si lo stemfre?*

Beatrice concludes :

> Alto fato† di Dio sarebbe rotto,

---

* *Piangendo:* Compare *Inf.* II, 115-117 :—

> " Poscia che m' ebbe ragionato questo,
>> Gli occhi lucenti lagrimando volse,
>> Perchè mi fece del venir più presto."

Morti : Dead in the second death.

Inf. I, 117 : " Che la seconda morte ciascun grida."

Fraticelli thinks that *uscio de' morti* means Limbo, placed just above the boundary of Hell.

In *Purg.* XXIII, 121-123, Dante says :—

> " . . . Costui per la profonda
>> Notte menato m' ha de' veri morti,
>> Con questa vera carne che il seconda."

† *Alto fato :* Scartazzini says that *l' alto fato di Dio* is God's justice, and he refers to Boet. *Phil. Cons.* lib. IV, pr. 6 :—

" Nam providentia est ipsa illa divina ratio in summo omnium principi constituta quæ cuncta disponit : fatum vero inhærens rebus mobilibus dispositio per quam providentia suis quæque nectit ordinibus.   Providentia namque cuncta pariter quamvis diversa quamvis infinita complectitur, fatum vero singula digerit in motum locis formis ac temporibus distributa : ut hæc temporalis ordinis explicatio in divinæ mentis adunata prospectum

Se Lete si passasse, e tal vivanda
Fosse gustata senza alcuno scotto†
Di pentimento che lagrime spanda."—   145

The lofty decrees of God would be infringed, if
Lethe were passed (by Dante), and such living water
were tasted without some sort of penitence which
may (cause him to) pour forth tears."

---

providentia sit, eadem vero adunatio digesta atque explicata
temporibus fatum vocetur."

And St. Thomas Aquinas(*Summ. Theol.* P. I, qu. CXVI, art. 2):
"Causaliter Dei potestas vel voluntas dici potest fatum."

† *scotto* : (=*Angl.* scot) is properly the food one consumes
in taverns, and also the reckoning that is paid for such food.

END OF CANTO XXX.

CANTO XXXI.

——

TERRESTRIAL PARADISE (*continued.*)
BEATRICE REPROVES DANTE.
HIS PENITENCE AND FORGIVENESS.
THE PASSAGE OF LETHE.
BEATRICE UNVEILS HERSELF.

IN the last Canto we read of the severe reprehension of Dante by Beatrice in general terms. In the present Canto her reproaches go more into particulars.

Benvenuto divides the Canto into four parts.

In the First Divison, from v. 1 to v. 42, Beatrice compels Dante to confess his past errors, and their causes.

In the Second Division, from v. 43 to v. 75, she convinces him that he had no valid excuse to offer for straying from the right path.

In the Third Division, from v. 76 to v. 111, after Dante's manifestation of sincere repentance, he is immersed by Matelda in the waters of Lethe, and led up to the four Nymphs.

In the Fourth Division, from v. 112 to v. 145, Beatrice, at the request of the four Nymphs, unveils herself, and allows Dante at last to contemplate her features.

Division I. We left Dante in the preceding Canto, after lamenting the departure of Virgil, being reproved by Beatrice for doing so, with the warning that he

would soon have to weep for a more serious cause
(*piangere . . . convien per altra spada,* v. 57).   In
her reply to the Angels, beginning with the words
" *Voi vigilate nell' eterno die,*" (v. 103) she made good
her words, though as yet only assailing Dante with
the edge of her sword; but now in this Canto she begins at once to attack him with the point; that is
much more vigorously, making her words go home,
forcing him fully and freely to avow his faults, and to
confirm by his own admission the justice of her
censure.

> —" O tu, che sei di là dal fiume sacro,"—
>   Volgendo suo parlare a me per punta,
>   Che pur per taglio m' era paruto acro,
> Ricominciò seguendo senza cunta,*
> —" Di', di',† se questo è vero.   A tanta accusa   5
>   Tua confession conviene esser congiunta."—

"O thou that art standing on the far side of the
sacred stream (of Lethe)" she recommenced, continuing without a pause, turning on me the point of
her discourse, which even with its side blow had
seemed to me so keen, " Say, say, if this be true.   To
such a charge thine own confession must be joined
(if thou wouldst merit absolution)."

Beatrice's remarks in the last Canto had been addressed to the attendant handmaidens around her
chariot, but now she addresses her discourse directly
to Dante (*per punta*).

Dante is suffocated with shame.   For a moment
he is unable to utter a word.

---

* *cunta:* from the Latin *cunctari,* to delay.

† *Di', di':* This is a conduplication expressing vehemence of
speech.

> Era la mia virtù tanto confusa,
>> Che la voce si mosse e pria si spense,
>> Che dagli organi suoi fosse dischiusa.

My faculties were so confounded, that my voice started (as if to speak) and then died away before it had been unlocked from its organs.

Beatrice follows up her attack.

> Poco sofferse, poi disse :—" Che pense ?*   10
>> Rispondi a me ; chè le memorie triste
>> In te non sono ancor dall' acqua offense."—†

She suffered (my silence) awhile, then said: "What thinkest thou? Answer me: for the unhappy recollections (of thy sins) have not as yet been effaced by the water (of Lethe)."

Dante admits his errors by a monosyllabic confession.

> Confusione e paura insieme miste
>> Mi pinsero un tal sì fuor della bocca,
>> Al quale intender fur mestier le viste.   15

Confusion and terror mingled together forced out of my mouth such a (low-toned) " yes," that eye-sight was requisite for it to be understood.

Benvenuto remarks that Dante's answer was like that of a bride, when asked by the priest if she will take the bridegroom to be her husband, her words can only be read from the lips, but rarely heard by the ear.

Dante now gives way to an outburst of grief.

---

* " *Che pense ?*" Virgil roused Dante from his compassionate meditation on the sorrows of Francesca da Rimini and Paolo Malatesta with the same words.—See *Inf.* V, 111.

† *offense* is for *offese* = *spente, scancellate.*

Come balestro frange, quando scocca
    Da troppa tesa, la sua corda e l' arco,
    E con men foga l' asta il segno tocca ;
Sì scoppia' io sott' esso grave carco,
    Fuori sgorgando lagrime e sospiri,   20
    E la voce allentò* per lo suo varco.

Like as a crossbow, when it is discharged after too
much tension, shivers both its string and the bow,
and the arrow in consequence strikes the mark with
diminished force; so did I burst forth under this
heavy burden (of confusion and fear) pouring out
tears and sighs, and my voice flagged upon its passage.

Scartazzini explains that the voice nearly died on
the lips, which are the passage of the voice.

Beatrice continues her reproaches, and presses Dante
to show, if he can, any just cause or excuse for his
having gone astray.

Ond' ella a me :—" Per entro i miei disiri,
    Che ti menavano ad amar lo Bene,
    Di là dal qual non è a che† si aspiri,

---

* *allentò:* compare Virgil, *Æneid*, XI, 150 :—

            ". . . hæret lacrimansque gemensque
            Et via vix tandem voci laxata dolorest."

† *a che:* In *Convito*, tr. IV, c. 22, Dante writes : " Dio è
nostra beatitudine somma." See also Boet., *Phil. Cons.*, lib. III,
pros. 10 : " Deum rerum omnium principem bonum esse communis humanorum conceptio probat animorum ; nam cum nihil
Deo melius excogitari queat, id quo melius nihil est bonum esse
quis dubitet ? Ita vero bonum esse Deum ratio demonstrat, ut
perfectum quoque in eo bonum esse convincat. Nam ni tale sit
rerum omnium princeps esse non poterit : erit enim eo praestan-
tius aliquid perfectum possidens bonum, quod hoc prius atque
antiquius esse videatur : omnia namque perfecta minus integris
priora esse claruerunt. Quare ne in infinitum ratio prodeat,

Quai fosse attraversate o quai catene   25
    Trovasti, per che del passare innanzi
    Dovessiti così spogliar la spene?*
E quali agevolezze o quali avanzi
    Nella fronte degli altri si mostraro,
    Per che dovessi lor passeggiare anzi?"—   30

Whereupon she to me: "Amidst thy love for me, which led thee on to love that Good (*i.e.*, God), than to attain Whom man cannot have any higher aspira-tion, what trenches across thy path, or what chains (to impede thy bark) didst thou find, that thou shouldest thus strip thyself of the hope of passing onward? And what attractions (*lit.* facilities) or what advantages showed themselves on the forehead of the others (*i.e.* temporal goods), that thou shouldest have walked (astray) towards them?"

Benvenuto remarks that Beatrice's argument here is most subtle and ingenious, and may be taken in the allegorical sense that, however difficult the study of holy things may be, as it requires faith in matters that cannot be known to our natural reason, yet, when the Supreme Good was the Instructor of Dante, leading him on to the knowledge of God, every fatigue in acquiring experience of holy things ought to have seemed easy to him. Although the secular sciences have the greatest charm outwardly, yet they are in substance vain and hurtful, because they tend to vain glory, and often lead to covetousness.

---

confitendum est summum Deum summi perfectique boni esse plenissimum : sed perfectum bonum veram esse beatitudinem constituimus : veram igitur beatitudinem in summo Deo sitam esse necesse est."

   * *spene:* Blanc (*Voc. Dant.*), derives the word from the Latin *spe*, and says it is an ancient poetic form of *speranza.*

In the twelve verses that follow, we learn how Dante replied to Beatrice's questions by a full confession of his weakness, and how she commended him for his complete admission of his sin, and gave him hopes of forgiveness after he shall have heard from her what his conduct ought to have been.

> Dopo la tratta d' un sospiro amaro,
>   A pena ebbi la voce che rispose,
>   E le labbra a fatica la formaro.
> Piangendo dissi :—" Le presenti cose
>   Col falso lor piacer volser miei passi,   35
>   Tosto che il vostro viso si nascose."—*

After the heaving of a bitter sigh, I scarcely had the voice to make an answer, and my lips only with effort framed it (into words). Weeping, I said : " Things that were present with their false pleasures diverted my steps (from the right path) so soon as thy countenance hid itself from me."

By the false pleasures Dante means the honours,

---

* Scartazzini, in a long note, criticizes those commentators who seek to put an allegorical interpretation on Beatrice's words in verses 22-30. He does not admit that Dante, who was twenty-five years old when Beatrice died, had, before that time, been so given up to the study of the Holy Scriptures or of Theology, and abandoned it afterwards. Is not the *Divina Commedia* itself a convincing proof that he continued that study ? The word *tosto* must not be taken literally. The " *donna gentile* " with whom Dante fell in love, and in consequence became unfaithful to the memory of Beatrice, first appeared to him, he relates in the *Vita Nuova*, § XXXV (Norton's Translation), " on that day on which the year was complete since this lady (Beatrice) was made one of the denizens of life eternal." In § XXXVI of *Vita Nuova* he says : " I saw a gentle lady, young and very beautiful, who was looking at me from a window with a face full of compassion, so that all pity seemed assembled in her."

dignities, glories, liberal arts and poetry, which, with their ensnaring flatteries, absorb the thoughts in the present, and obstruct the contemplation of what is invisible in the future.

Beatrice, seeing Dante's confusion and evident contrition, somewhat relents, and tells him why his confession had benefited him.

> Ed ella :—"Se tacessi o se negassi
>   Ciò che confessi, non fora men nota
>   La colpa tua: da tal giudice sássi.
> Ma quando scoppia dalla propria gota   40
>   L' accusa del peccato, in nostra corte
>   Rivolge sè contra il taglio la ruota.

And she : " Hadst thou suppressed or denied what thou confessest, thy fault would not be the less manifest, by such a Judge is it known. But when the accusation of sin bursts forth from the sinner's own mouth, then, in our tribunal (before the Judgment Seat of God), the grindstone revolves against the edge.

The grindstone is usually turned *(sotto il taglio)* with the edge of the Sword of Justice so as to sharpen it. Beatrice means that, after the confession of the penitent, it would be made to revolve in the opposite direction *(contra il taglio)*, so as to blunt the edge. Divine mercy disarms Divine justice.

Division II. In this Second Division of the Canto, Beatrice proves to Dante that he had no valid excuse to offer for straying from the right path.

Tuttavia, perchè me' vergogna porte
   Del tuo errore, e perchè altra volta
   Udendo le Sirene sie più forte,   45
Pon giù il seme del piangere, ed ascolta ;
   Sì udirai come in contraria parte
   Mover doveati mia carne sepolta.

But still, that thou mayest the better carry shame
for thy transgression, and that thou mayest be more
strong another time if thou shouldst hear the Sirens
(*i.e.* when the temptations of pleasure allure thee), lay
aside the seed of weeping and listen ; so wilt thou
hear how my buried body ought to have led thee in a
course directly opposite (*i.e.* to the course Dante pursued after her death).

Scartazzini explains that by the seed of weeping is
meant the *grave carco* (v. 19), di *confusione e paura
insieme miste* (v. 13). Beatrice wanted Dante's full
attention to the words she was about to address to
him. One who is oppressed by confusion and fear is
not in the best condition of mind to follow attentively
the grave discourse of another.

Benvenuto says that by the Sirens are to be understood the liberal arts and sciences, and poetry. He
adds that St. Jerome called finely written words the
Devil's bait, and said that he was once himself
ensnared by them, at which time the Holy Scriptures
seemed to be rough and uncultivated writing ; but
that when he abandoned the liberal arts and sciences,
and turned his thoughts wholly to religion, the words
of the Scriptures seemed the food of the Angels.

Beatrice now argues that love for her was to be
preferred to love for others, by reason of her excellence.

Mai non t' appresentò natura o arte
   Piacer, quanto le belle membra in ch' io   50
   Rinchiusa fui, e sono in terra sparte :
E se il sommo piacer sì ti fallìo
   Per la mia morte, qual cosa mortale
   Dovea poi trarre te nel suo disìo ?

Never did nature or art set before thee such delight as the fair members wherein I was enclosed, and they are now crumbled into dust. And if the chiefest pleasure thus failed thee through my death, what (other) mortal thing ought afterwards to have drawn thee into loving it?

Benvenuto says that, as Beatrice seemed to Dante more beautiful than any other woman, so in an allegorical sense the science of Theology is the most beautiful of all sciences ; and *le belle membra*, from this point of view, would mean all the Theological writings dispersed throughout the world. In the same way, *qual cosa mortale* may signify "what mortal science."

Beatrice continues her reproaches, telling Dante that having been once deceived, he ought never to have been led astray a second time.

Ben ti dovevi, per lo primo stràle   55
   Delle cose fallaci, levar suso
   Diretro a me, che non era più tale.

It was certainly thy duty, (after being wounded) by the first shaft of delusive things, to have soared aloft after me, who (having ceased to be mortal) was no longer capable (of being led away by fallacies).

Non ti dovea gravar le penne in giuso,
   Ad aspettar più colpi, o pargoletta,*
   O altra vanità con sì breve uso.   60

---

* *o pargoletta:* Dante uses *parvoletti* for bambini in *Par.* XXVII, 128. One of his canzoni begins " Io mi son pargoletta

Neither (the attractions of) a young girl, or other vain things (such as dignities, or sciences), of which the enjoyment is so brief, should have weighed thy wings downwards.

> Nuovo augelletto due o tre* aspetta ;
>> Ma dinanzi dagli occhi dei pennuti†
>> Rete si spiega indarno o si saetta."—

The young bird awaits two or three (blows), but before the eyes of the full fledged is the net in vain spread, or the arrow shot."

Dante is unable to utter a word in self-defence.

> Quale i fanciulli vergognando muti,
>> Con gli occhi a terra, stannosi ascoltando,   65
>> E sè riconoscendo, e ripentuti,
> Tal mi stava io. Ed ella disse :—" Quando
>> Per udir sei dolente, alza la barba,
>> E prenderai più doglia riguardando."—

---

bella e nuova." Scartazzini says that the general consensus of opinions agrees that Beatrice here alludes to a girl.

Benvenuto and others rather think that it is Gentucca of Lucca who is meant. But Beatrice is reproving Dante for *past* loves, not for what are in the *future*. Dante had not, at the time of his supposed mystical journey, even seen Gentucca. Scartazzini says that one need not go deeply into all the opinions that are held as to *pargoletta :* but from the context two things seem pretty clear to him. 1st, that Beatrice is not speaking of abstractions, but of real persons ; 2ndly, that she is not speaking of any one special person, but of young women generally.

* *due o tre :* Benvenuto reads *otte.* *Otta* is an ancient form of *ora,* and he explains it " *aspetta due otte,* scilicet, percussiones antequam fugiat vel evadat." Compare *Inf.* XXI, 112-114 :—

> " Jer, più oltre cinqu' ore che quest' otta
>> Mille dugento con sessantasei
>> Anni compiè che quì la via fu rotta."

† Compare Prov. I, 17 (Vulgate) " Frustra autem jacitur rete ante oculos pennatorum."

Even as children silent in shame stand listening with their eyes upon the ground, both avowing their fault and repentant, so was I standing. And she said : " Since thou art distressed from hearing, raise up thy beard, and thou wilt feel more grief from looking (at me)."

Beatrice commands Dante to raise his beard, instead of his face, by way of reminding him that he is a full-grown man, and cannot plead the extenuating circumstances of youth, knowing moreover that to look her in the face will disconcert him still more.

Dante obeys, but relates that his chin had got such a strong downward bend towards his chest, that he scarcely could do so.

> Con men di resistenza si dibarba 70
> Robusto cerro, o vero al nostral* vento,
> O vero a quel della terra di Iarba,†
> Ch' io non levai al suo comando il mento ;
> E quando per la barba il viso chiese,
> Ben conobbi il velen dell' argomento. 75

With less resistance is a stout oak uprooted, either by a northern gale or by one from the land of Jarbas (*i.e.* from the south-east), than I raised my chin at her command ; and when by ' beard ' she asked for my face, I fully understood the venom of the argument.

Division III. Here commences the third division of the Canto, in which Dante relates how, after his

---

* *nostral vento* means the *Tramontana* or north wind, and coming from Europe was called by the Italians *Nostrale.*

† Iarbas or Hiarbas was King of Gætulia in Libya, and from him Dido bought the land for building Carthage.

penitence and confession, he was washed in Lethe, and conducted to the Four Nymphs who represent the Four Cardinal Virtues.   But we are first told how the Angels, by ceasing from casting clouds of flowers round the car, gave him an. opportunity of seeing Beatrice.

> E come la mia faccia 'si distese,
>> Posarsi quelle prime creature
>> Da loro aspersion l' occhio comprese :
> E le mie luci, ancor poco sicure,
>> Vider Beatrice vôlta in su la fiera,   80
>> Ch' è sola una persona in duo nature.

And as my countenance turned itself upwards, my sight took in that those primal creatures (*i.e.* the Angels) had desisted from their scattering (of flowers); and my eyes, as yet little confident, beheld Beatrice turned round towards the animal (the Gryphon), that is One Person only (Jesus Christ) in twofold nature (God and Man).

Scartazzini says that Beatrice, after concluding her argument, turns her eyes round to the Gryphon, and does not seem to pay further attention to her faithless lover.

Dante, however, rivets his eyes on her, and sees how superhuman is her beauty.

> Sotto suo velo, ed oltre la riviera
>> Vincer* pareami più sè stessa antica,
>> Vincer, che l' altre qui, quand' ella c' era.

---

* Scartazzini says that the reading with *vincer* in both lines makes the sense difficult, but the reading has the authority of all the older Codices. Witte has an excellent alternative reading, but unfortunately lacking good authority :—

  " Sotto suo velo, ed oltre la riviera

(Even) under her veil, and (as far off as) the other
side of the stream, she seemed to me to surpass her
ancient self, to surpass it more than (she surpassed)
all others when she was here (on earth).

> Di pentér sì mi punse ivi l' ortica, 85
>   Che di tutt' altre cose, qual mi torse
>   Più nel suo amor, più mi si fe' nimica.

The sting (*lit.* nettle) of repentance so pricked my
heart (*lit.* me) there (on the far side of the stream),
that of all other things, whatever had most turned
me to its love (in the past) now became the object
most hated by me.

The sight of Beatrice's celestial beauty was to
Dante the decisive moment ; it completed, by resusci-
tating his love, what fear, confusion, and shame had
been preparing in his mind.

Lubin remarks that, now that he feels so much
penitence for his past life, he will soon pass through
Lethe.

Dante falls prostrate on the ground.

> Tanta riconoscenza il cuor mi morse,
>   Ch' io caddi vinto.* E quale allora fêmmi,
>   Sálsi colei che la cagion mi porse. 90

Such keen remorse was gnawing my heart, that I

> Vincer pareami più sè stessa antica,
>   Che vincea l' altre qui, quand' ella c' era."

Dr. Moore remarks, as to disputed readings in Dante, that it
is usually safer to prefer the one which presents the greatest
difficulty, for the copyists, who were not always highly educated
men, were very apt, on coming across a hard passage, to put in
words of their own to make the sense easy.

* Scartazzini draws attention to Dante falling down in a
swoon, and says it is a symbol of dying to sin to rise again to
grace. It is the second time that Dante has so fallen. The

sank down overcome, and what I then became, she (Beatrice) knows, who furnished me the cause.

When Dante recovers consciousness, he finds himself in the waters of Lethe.

> Poi, quando il cuor di fuor virtù rendemmi,
>   La donna ch' io avea trovata sola,
>   Sopra me vidi, e dicea :—" Tiemmi, tiemmi."—
> Tratto m' avea nel fiume infino a gola,
>   E tirandosi me dietro, sen giva   95
>   Sovr' esso* l' acqua lieve come spola.

Then, when the heart restored to me my outward sense, I saw right above me the lady (Matelda) whom I had found wandering alone (*Purg.* XXVIII, 40), and she was saying, " Hold me, hold me." She had drawn me into the stream up to my throat, and dragging me after her, was speeding over the water as lightly as a shuttle.

Instead of *spola*, Benvenuto reads *scola*, which he says is a kind of long light vessel, suitable for naval

---

first occasion is told in *Inf.* V, 140-142, when, after witnessing the anguish of Francesca da Rimini, he says of himself

> " Sì che di pietade
> Io venni men così com' io morisse ;
> E caddi come corpo morto cade."

He is, perhaps, not only struck with compassion, but also with compunction at the sight of the penalty for a sin of which he is himself not altogether innocent. Here in this Canto, Beatrice reproves him for these same faults, and her censure has the same effect on him as had the sufferings and tears of Francesca.

* *Sovr' esso :* Blanc says (*Vocab. Dant.*) that *esso* in this compound word is an indeclinable pronoun, and when placed between the preposition and the noun has no other function than that of making the phrase more precise, so that here *sovr' esso* would have the signification, *proprio sopra*, right over, right above.

warfare and for war. Buti and nearly all the old commentators read *spola*.

Dante, while in the water, hears the soft cadences of a chant.*

> Quando fui presso alla beata riva,
> > *Asperges me* sì dolcemente udissi,
> > Ch' io nol so rimembrar, non ch' io lo scriva.

When I was near the blessed shore, there fell upon my ear (the words) *Asperges me*, so sweetly chanted, that (now that I am returned to the world) I cannot recall it to mind, much less write it.

The sweet notes of Casella's song are still sounding within him, " *la dolcezza ancor dentro mi suona,*" but the song of the Angels is too much for the human mind to retain.

He is now made to swallow the water of Lethe.

> La bella donna nelle braccia aprissi,   100
> > Abbracciommi la testa, e mi sommerse,
> > Ove convenne ch' io l' acqua inghiotissi ;
> Indi mi tolse, e bagnato m' offerse
> > Dentro alla danza delle quattro belle,
> > E ciascuna del braccio mi coperse.   105

The beautiful Lady opened her arms, embraced my head, and immersed me (as far as my mouth) where I had perforce to swallow the water ; then she drew me forth, and presented me dripping into the midst of the dance of the four beauteous ones, and each covered me with her arm.

---

* The words are from Psalm LI, 7, "Purge me with hyssop, &c." in the Vulgate, Psalm L, 9, "Asperges me hyssopo, et mundabor ; lavabis me, et super nivem dealbabor." The words *Asperges me* are used in the Roman Church, when the priest sprinkles the penitent with holy water after confession, and before absolution.

The four cardinal virtues, in the form of four maidens, were dancing by the left wheel of the chariot. The above passage may be taken to mean that, when a man by sacerdotal confession and absolution has been removed from the act and guilt of sin, he is passed on into the company of the cardinal virtues, in order that he may behold the happiness of practising the virtues, and may be the better prepared for the three higher virtues, the handmaidens of sacred Theology. And when each of the four maidens covered Dante with her arms, it was, as it were, a promise that that particular virtue would, from that moment, protect him from the sin to which that virtue is opposed ; namely,

> Justice against Injustice.
> Prudence against Folly.
> Fortitude against Frailty.
> Temperance against Intemperance.

The four Damsels now address Dante.

> —"Noi sem qui ninfe, e nel ciel semo stelle ;*
>   Pria che Beatrice discendesse al mondo,
>   Fummo ordinate a lei per suo ancelle.

---

* Scartazzini says, that it is evident from these words, that the four maidens make Dante to understand that they are " *le quattro chiare stelle*," which guided Dante's steps, as he tells us in *Purg.* VIII, 91, and whose rays illumined the face of Cato (*Purg.* I, 23). Beside this we gather that the four cardinal virtues are both in Heaven and on Earth, but do not wear the same forms in both places ; for on earth they are nymphs, of learned counsel ; in Heaven they are stars, radiant beings, whose light is neither for themselves, nor for the Heaven where they dwell, but for the Earth. Scartazzini thinks the summarized meaning of the passage is, that the cardinal virtues shine in Heaven as lights to illumine the world, and at the same time are the counsellors of mankind.

Merrenti agli occhi suoi ; ma nel giocondo
  Lume ch' è dentro aguzzeranno i tuoi   110
  Le tre di là, che miran più profondo."—

" Here we are nymphs, and in Heaven we are stars ;
before that Beatrice descended to the Earth, we were
appointed to be her handmaidens. We will lead thee
before her eyes, but for the pleasant light that is within
(them), the three on the other side (of the chariot) will
sharpen thy sight for they look more profoundly."

Before Beatrice, who is Sacred Theology, descended
into the world, which she only did after the Incarna-
tion of Jesus Christ, the four cardinal virtues were appointed as her satellites, preparing men's minds, by
disposing them to virtuous and holy lives, in order
that the seeds of Theology might the more readily
bear fruit in them.

Scartazzini says : " There can be no doubt whatever
that there is an allegory in these lines. But Beatrice,
as we have noticed before, does not symbolize Theology in the abstract, but rather ecclesiastical authority, personified by the Supreme Pontiff, the Pope.
The business of that authority is, like that of Beatrice
in the *Divina Commedia*, to direct man to Heaven, or
to the blessedness of Life Eternal. Now the cardinal
virtues are those which formerly, in the Gentile world,
prepared the way for Christianity, of which Ecclesiastical authority is the head. They had then been appointed handmaidens to ecclesiastical authority of old,
before the foundation of the Church.

The cardinal virtues prepare man, and render him
fit to recognize the demonstrations of Truth, driving
away from his mind the passions which obfuscate his
intellect. To arrive afterwards at a full knowledge of

celestial and divine truths, the Theological virtues are
requisite, which refine the mind, and fit it to contemplate divine things, because God opens His secrets, as
Landino says, to whoever has sincere faith, firm hope,
and burning Love."

———

Division IV. In this Fourth and Concluding Division of the Canto, Dante describes how he attained a
more complete cognizance of Beatrice ; and he first
relates how the four handmaidens led him forward and
invited him to look at her.

> Così cantando cominciaro ; e poi
>> Al petto del grifon seco menârmi,
>> Ove Beatrice vôlta stava a noi.

Singing thus (*Noi sem qui Ninfe*) they commenced ;
and then they led me with them to the breast (*i. e.* in
front) of the Gryphon, where Beatrice stood turned
towards us.

Beatrice was standing upon the left hand edge of
the chariot, still covered by her veil (see XXX, 61-69),
and we have just read, in v. 80 of this Canto, that she
had turned round to look at the Gryphon. If therefore Dante was right in front of it, Beatrice was turned
to him also.

The Nymphs continue.

> Disser :—" Fa che le viste non risparmi ;   115
>> Posto t' avém dinanzi agli smeraldi,*
>> Onde Amor già ti trasse le sue armi."—

———

* Lami (*Annotazioni*) says that Beatrice's eyes were of a
greenish hue, like the colour of the sea.

The Ottimo comments thus on this passage :—" Dante very
happily introduces this precious stone, considering its proper-

" See that thou spare not thy gaze," said they; "we have placed thee in front of those emeralds, out of which, in days gone by, Love drew forth his darts to attack thee."

By emeralds Dante means either to express the brightness or the colour of Beatrice's eyes.

Dante at once obeys.

> Mille disiri più che fiamma caldi
> Strinsermi gli occhi agli occhi rilucenti,
> Che pur sovra il grifone stavano saldi.   120

A thousand longings, more burning than fire, (made me) fasten my eyes upon the radiant eyes (of Beatrice), that still rested steadfastly upon the Gryphon.

Francesco da Buti says that Theology, or rather

---

ties, and considering that griffins watch over emeralds. The emerald is the prince of all green stones ; no gem nor herb has greater greenness ; it reflects an image like a mirror ; increases wealth ; is useful in litigation and to orators ; is good for convulsions and epilepsy ; preserves and strengthens the sight ; restrains lust ; restores memory ; is powerful against phantoms and demons ; calms tempests ; staunches blood ; and is useful to soothsayers."

Longfellow remarks that the beauty of green eyes, " Ojuelos verdes," is extolled by Spanish poets ; and is not left unsung by poets of other countries. Compare Shakespeare (*Romeo and Juliet*, act iii, sc. v) :—

> "Oh, he's a lovely gentleman !
> Romeo's a dishclout to him : an eagle, madam,
> Hath not so green, so quick, so fair an eye
> As Paris hath."

In one of the old French Mysteries (*Hist. Theat. Franç.* l, 176), Joseph describes the child Jesus as having

> " Les yeux vers, la chaire blanche et tendre,
> Les cheveulx blonds."

Ecclesiastical Authority, both in its opinions, and in its purposes, ever stands fast on the Divine Word made Man.

Dante now describes what he saw reflected in Beatrice's eyes.

> Come in lo specchio il sol, non altrimenti
>> La doppia fiera dentro vi raggiava,
>> Or con uni, or con altri reggimenti.

As the sun in a mirror, not otherwise, was that animal of two-fold nature beaming therein (*i.e.* was being reflected in Beatrice's eyes), now with one kind of attribute, now with another.

At one moment displaying His human nature, at another His Divine: at one moment bearing a literal, at another an allegorical sense. Sometimes as the Lamb, and sometimes as the Lion. Many commentators think that Dante wished to show that Theology ought to consider Christ at one time as God, and at another as Man, so as not to confound His two natures.

Dante invokes his readers to realize his wonder.

> Pensa, lettor, s' io mi maravigliava,
>> Quando vedea la cosa in sè star queta   125
>> E nell' idolo suo si trasmutava.

Think, reader, if I marvelled, when I saw the thing stand motionless itself, and yet in its image (reflected in the eyes of Beatrice), undergoing transformations (from one attribute to another).

The other three maidens now come forward.

> Mentre che, piena di stupore e lieta,
>> L' anima mia gustava di quel cibo,
>> Che, saziando di sè, di sè asseta ;

Sè dimostrando del più alto tribo 130
   Negli atti, l' altre tre si fêro avanti,
   Danzando al loro angelico caribo.*

While my soul, full of awe and delight, was feasting
on that (heavenly) food, which, while satiating, creates
a longing, the other three (the Theological Virtues)
stepped forward in front (of Beatrice), showing themselves to be of the higher race in their deportment,
dancing in their heavenly saraband.

Benvenuto says that Dante's insatiable longing was
well to be understood, for the delight of seeing the
nine muses is as nothing compared with that of
beholding the nine dames, who were doing honour to
the triumphal car.

· The nine consisted of the four Cardinal and three
Theological virtues, Matelda, and Beatrice.

The Three unite their voices in a song of intercession
on behalf of Dante, beseeching Beatrice to reward his

---

* *Danzando al loro angelico caribo*: Scartazzini says that
this is one of those passages which still remain obscure, and
have not yet found an Œdipus to interpret them. Some read
cantando instead of *danzando*. The reading depends on the
word *caribo*, which is obscure in its meaning and origin. It
would seem that the word was generally understood in the
time of Dante, as the oldest commentators never took the
trouble to explain it, until Benvenuto, whose idea seems to be a
mixture of dancing and song, interpreted it *"canzone da ballo."*
Francesco da Buti reads *garibo*, which he derives from *garbo*,
" cioè, al loro angelico modo." Scartazzini says that the silence
of the oldest expositors proves that, in their time, the word
was not unknown. It is hardly possible that they would pass
it over from not themselves understanding it.

There are numberless other explanations and readings, but
the one I have given here seems to be that most generally
adopted.

return to fidelity, after his humble repentance and purification, in consideration of the long distance he has travelled, and the many hardships he has undergone, in order to get a sight of her eyes, which she is still keeping fixed upon the Gryphon.

—" Volgi, Beatrice, volgi gli occhi santi,"—
  Era la sua canzone,*—" al tuo fedele†
  Che, per vederti, ha mossi passi tanti.‡   135
    Per grazia fa noi grazia che disvele
    A lui la bocca tua, sì che discerna
    La seconda bellezza che tu cele."—

" Turn, Beatrice, turn thy holy eyes," was their song, " to thy faithful one, who, to get sight of thee has taken so many steps. Of thy grace grant us the favour

---

* *Era la* sua *canzone* instead of *era la* lor *canzone*, as many others read. The former reading is that adopted by most of the old commentators. Scartazzini says that Dante often used *suo* and *sua* for *loro*, and that the practice prevailed largely among the older writers.

† *al tuo fedele:* The Three call Dante Beatrice's faithful one, for as a Christian poet he had battled for the faith, as no other poet had done. Beatrice herself, in *Inf.* II, 61, calls him her friend, though he was still lost in the paths of error.

" L' amico mio e non della ventura,
    Nella diserta piaggia è impedito
    Sì nel cammin, che vôlto è per paura."

‡ *ha mossi passi tanti:* Benvenuto points out that this is the fact both historically and allegorically, for when Dante turned to the task of ascending to the glory wherein Beatrice was; that is, to undertake this glorious poem, feeling that he had learned enough of philosophy and poetry, he travelled to Paris, poor, and as an exile; and there, with the greatest zeal and perseverance, studied and mastered theology. He then passed through Hell, next through the gradual ascent of the mountain of Purgatory, and now, at last, after *tanti passi*, he has found his long-lost Beatrice in the Paradise of Delights.

DIGRESSION ON DANTE'S PENITENCE UPON THE
LEFT BANK OF LETHE.

Scartazzini says the problem before us is : " What are the sins which are reproved and censured in Dante, when he had passed beyond the boundaries of that second kingdom where the human spirit is purged? What are the sins to which he confesses, for which he feels shame, and repents of, in that region which the spirits can only enter when they have completed their purgation? And secondly, Why does this penitence of Dante not take place in Purgatory, the place appointed for the purgation of souls, rather than in the Terrestrial Paradise, wherein none are wont to enter until after their sins are covered? A double problem, which, as far as we can see, none have as yet even attempted to solve.

The relations between Dante and Beatrice on earth were of far too slight a nature for her seriously to have intended to reproach Dante with infidelity to her as a woman, except, perhaps, as indicating a censure, under an allegorical veil, for some aberrations of Dante after her death, and we know from Dante himself in the *Vita Nuova*, that they did actually occur ; but what was the extent of the relations between them on earth? A look, full of a timid, pure, child-like love, a graceful salutation, and nothing else ! Dante was bound to Beatrice by no promise to keep for her alone a love which seems never to have been proffered, and, perhaps, never would have been accepted. The wife of Simone de' Bardi would have had no right to reprove Dante for having fallen in love with another maiden. Therefore we may conclude that, in the scene that takes place in the thirty-first Canto between Dante and Beatrice, this infidelity to the real Beatrice is only of secondary importance, and that the reproofs made to him and his confession of sin and error refer principally to his infidelity to the symbolic and allegorical Beatrice. In Canto XXX, 121, she says :—

K K K

'Alcun tempo il sostenni col mio volto;
   Mostrando gli occhi giovinetti a lui,
   Meco il menava in dritta parte vôlto.'

by which she means that Dante walked in the way of eternal
happiness, under the escort and guidance of revealed doctrine,
as taught by the *ideal* Papal authority which Beatrice symbolizes.   In Canto XXX, 124-132, she goes on to accuse him
of having withdrawn himself, shortly after her death, from
the guidance of revelation in order to trust to guides, who do
not lead Man to real happiness, nor can they perform what they
promise.

*Dante's sin, then, is Aberration from the Faith, Doubt of its
Truth, and Unbelief.*

This would explain Beatrice saying :—

'Tanto giù cadde che tutti argomenti
   Alla salute sua eran già corti,
   Fuor che mostrargli le perdute genti.'

But these words would be inexplicable if Dante had nothing
more to reproach himself with than the crime of having loved
another woman after the death of Beatrice."

Scartazzini comes also to the conclusion, that the censure
passed upon Dante in the Terrestrial Paradise is for sins concerning faith, from another discovery that he has made.   Virgil,
Dante's master and guide, says in *Purg.* VII, 7-8 :—

"Io son Virgilio ; e per null' altro rio
   Lo ciel perdei, che per non aver fè."

That is why Virgil is able to walk in complete security
through the regions of eternal and temporal torment, therefore is it granted to him to conduct his disciple as far as the
Terrestrial Paradise, as far as the left bank of Lethe.   But
not one step beyond that.   In like manner it is not permitted
to Dante to reach the right bank of Lethe, as we saw in the last
lines of Canto XXX :—

"senza alcuno scotto
   Di pentimento che lagrime spanda."

The sin, then, which prevents Dante from crossing Lethe must
be the same as that *rio* which excludes Virgil not only from
Heaven, but also from the Terrestrial Paradise.   Therefore a
sin concerning his faith.

In Canto XXXIII, 82, Dante asks Beatrice how it is that her words surpass his power of understanding them. She tells him that it is for the express purpose of making him fully comprehend that the school (*scuola*) he has followed is as far removed from the divine way as is the Earth from the Sphere of Heaven called the *Primo Mobile.*

Therefore Scartazzini claims to have established that the sin for which Dante has to do penance on the left bank of Lethe is one concerning the faith, infidelity towards her who represents those who ought to guide Man in accordance with the doctrines of revelation. It cannot be a sin of Heresy, for Dante shows by his works that he never was an unbeliever. Therefore the school followed by him was a philosophical school ; what seduced and allured him were philosophical speculations, and his sin was one of doubt, and of vacillation in his Faith.

CANTO XXXII.

———

TERRESTRIAL PARADISE (*continued*).
THE TREE OF KNOWLEDGE.
ASCENT OF THE GRYPHON.
TRANSFORMATION OF THE CHARIOT.
THE GIANT AND THE HARLOT.

IN the last Canto Dante gave a description of the
beauty of Beatrice. In the present Canto he relates
how the procession of the Church Militant turned
about and retraced its way; how he followed the
chariot with Beatrice and her handmaidens; how an
eagle struck the Chariot, and divers other strange
events.

Benvenuto divides the Canto into four parts.

In the First Division, from v. 1 to v. 33, Dante is
warned not to look too fixedly at Beatrice. The procession returns through the forest, Dante and Statius
following.

In the Second Division, from v. 34 to v. 60, they
stop at the Tree of Knowledge, to which the Gryphon
fastens the Chariot.

In the Third Division, from v. 61 to v. 99, Dante
falls asleep, and, on awaking, finds Beatrice, Matèlda,
and the seven handmaidens alone by the tree.

In the Fourth Division, from v. 100 to v. 160,
Dante describes in figurative language, the more
notable persecutions which the Church Militant had
suffered.

Division I. At the conclusion of the last Canto Dante had at length been accorded the privilege of beholding Beatrice's countenance in its glorified state. He gazes upon it with such ardent rapture that all other objects around him are forgotten.

> Tanto eran gli occhi miei fissi ed attenti
>   A disbramarsi la decenne sete,
>   Che gli altri sensi m' eran tutti spenti.
> Ed essi quinci e quindi avean parete
>   Di non caler, così lo santo riso   5
>   A sè traéli con l' antica rete;*

So fixed and riveted were my eyes in satisfying the ten years' thirst, that all my other senses were extinguished. And upon either hand, both to the right and left, they (*i.e.* my eyes) had a screen of indifference, and thus the saintly smile (of Beatrice) drew them towards it with its ancient net.

Beatrice had died in 1290, ten years before 1300, the year in which the scene is supposed to take place, and, therefore, Dante's ten years' thirst means the longing that he had had to behold her again. And now that his eyes see the beloved object, his other senses are in abeyance. His concentrated gaze is interrupted.

> Quando per forza mi fu vôlto il viso
>   Vêr la sinistra mia da quelle Dee,
>   Perch' io udia da loro un : *Troppo fiso.*

When perforce my face was turned away towards my left hand by those goddesses (the three divine maidens), because I heard from them a (sound of) " Too intently."

---

* By *l' antica rete* he means :—

> "L' antico amor che già m' avea traffitto
>   Prima che io fuor di puerizia fosse."

In verse 116 of the previous Canto, we saw that
Dante had been placed in front of the emerald eyes
of Beatrice, who was still standing upon the mystic
Chariot, and turned towards the Gryphon.   Dante
was, therefore, standing in front of the Chariot, and
had on *his right* hand the four nymphs dressed in
purple (XXIX, 130), *i.e.* the cardinal virtues, and on
his left the three others (XXIX, 121), *i.e.* the theological virtues.   The latter are, therefore, the goddesses
who speak to him the words : " *Troppo fiso.*"   They
invite him to look at other things that are passing
around him, and notably they would seem to be drawing his attention to the procession of the Church
Militant now about to retrace its steps.   Benvenuto
thinks that they wish to modify the admonition of
the other four damsels, who (in XXXI, 115) told him
Fa che le viste non risparmi.

Dante now explains how impossible it was for him
to see anything at all, so soon as he withdrew his
gaze from Beatrice's eyes, which had completely
dazzled him.

> E la disposizion ch' a veder ée   10
>   Negli occhi pur testè dal sol percossi,
>   Senza la vista alquanto esser mi fee.*

And that condition of the sight which exists in eyes
that have only recently been struck by (the rays of)
the sun bereft me, for some moments, of my sight.

---

* *Fee* : = *mi fece, mi fe.*   Scartazzini says that the second "*e*"
was not added for any poetical license, but because it was the
old rule for the third person singular of the perfect tense.   It
was used as much in prose as in poetry.

 " Con sola la parola gli rendee la salute."
                                                        Dial. S. Greg., I, 4.

Ma poi che al poco il viso riformossi,
   (Io dico al poco, per rispetto al molto
   Sensibile, onde a forza mi rimossi),   15
Vidi in sul braccio destro esser rivolto
   Lo glorioso esercito, e tornarsi
   Col sole e con le sette fiamme al volto.

But when my vision gradually readapted itself to the less—I say the less, out of respect to the greater splendour (*i.e.* the intense radiance of Beatrice), from which perforce I had turned away—I saw that the glorious host had wheeled on its right flank, and was returning with the sun, and the seven flames (of the candlesticks) in its face.

The right wheel of the Chariot (that of the New Testament) was the first to move. Up to this time the procession had been marching towards the West, meeting Dante, who had been walking towards the East, as we gather from Cantos XXVII and XXVIII. The Chariot now wheels about, and they all proceed together towards the East.

Scartazzini here quotes from Benvenuto and Buti to show that *tornarsi* does not mean *volgersi*, but *tornare indietro*, return back again. Antonelli says that if we reflect upon the facts narrated during this day, from the ascent of the stairway up to this point, we shall be led to the conclusion that it was now about ten o'clock in the morning. Therefore, the majestic procession, in wheeling upon its right flank, described a semicircle from west to east, by the north, and thus the personages composing it were struck full in the face by the rays of the sun as they wended their way up the stream along its right bank. Jacopo della Lana remarks on what follows and says that, as when hosts are about to change their camp, all await the standards, and do not march in a straight, but in a circular line, and in such wise that the shields shall always be on the outside, so this mystic host set itself in motion behind its first standards, and the Chariot did not move until the whole of the procession had passed Dante.

> Come sotto gli scudi per salvarsi
>> Volgesi schiera, e sè gira col segno,*   20
>> Prima che possa tutta in sè mutarsi :
> Quella milizia del celeste regno,
>> Che precedeva, tutta trapassonne
>> Pria che piegasse il carro il primo legno.†

Like a battalion wheels round under (the protection of) its shields for safety, and moves round with the standard, before the whole body can change its front: (so) that soldiery of the celestial kingdom, which were

---

* Compare Tasso (*Ger. lib.* XI, st. 33) :—
> " La gente Franca impetuosa e ratta
> Allor quanto più puote affretta i passi :
> E parte scudo a scudo insieme adatta,
> E di quegli un coperchio al capo fassi."

Scartazzini says the simile is quite exact in all its parts. A long column must wheel many times before the whole of it has changed its front. First the van with the standard ; then the main body by degrees, and last of all the rear-guard. In like manner here, first the candlesticks go in front, then the band of the saints, and last of all the Chariot.

† *il primo legno:* There are two interpretations of this line : *first*, that the pole bent the Chariot round to the right ; *second*, that *carro* governs the construction, and must be understood that the chariot, as if animated, turned its own pole. Scartazzini says that the first of these interpretations, as the more simple and natural, deserves the preference.

in the van, had all of them passed us, before the pole had turned the Chariot.

When the line of the elders had passed by, the Chariot also began to turn round to follow them.

> Indi alle ruote si tornâr le donne,*   25
> > E il grifon mosse il benedetto carco,
> > Sì che però nulla penna crollonne.

Then did the ladies return to the wheels (*i.e.* the four to the left wheel, and the three to the right), and the Gryphon set his holy burden in motion, but in such wise (*i.e.* so easily) that not one of his feathers was disturbed.

The operations of Divine Power are set in motion by the sole exercise of the Divine Will. No other external means or instruments are necessary for Christ to guide His Church, than His Word alone, and His Holy Spirit.

Dante himself, with Matelda and Statius, close the procession. It may be noticed that, from the time that Statius enters the Terrestrial Paradise, he never utters a word, but becomes perfectly passive.

> La bella donna che mi trasse al varco,
> > E Stazio† ed io seguitavam la ruota
> > Che fe' l' orbita sua con minore arco.   30

---

* *le donne:* The four damsels had left their appointed post for the purpose of conducting Dante towards Beatrice's eyes (XXXI, 109) ; while the other three had come forward, *danzando al loro angelico caribo*, to entreat Beatrice to display her features (XXXI, 132).

† *Stazio :* Scartazzini says that there is no means of conjecturing what part Statius is now made to serve in the great vision. As a soul purified from every sin, he might have ascended direct up to Heaven, without waiting to behold the mysteries which are shown to Dante in order that he may relate

The fair lady (Matelda), who drew me through the ford, and Statius and I were following that wheel which made its orbit with the lesser arc.

As the procession wheeled on its right hand, the left wheel had to make the longest turn, and the right wheel, consequently, a much shorter one.

Dante now finds himself on the side of the three theological virtues between the Chariot and the bank of Lethe. And he adds that the holy strains of angels singing kept time with their footsteps.

> Sì passeggiando l' alta selva, vôta,
> Colpa di quella ch' al serpente crese,*
> Temprava i passi un' angelica nota.

Thus passing through the lofty forest, empty (of inhabitants) from the fault of her (Eve) who put her trust in the serpent, an angelic strain (of music) regulated the paces (of the glorious host).†

Division II. Here begins the Second Division of the Canto, and in it we read how the mystic procession, followed by Dante and Statius, comes to a stop

---

them to the living (XXXIII, 52 *et seq.*).   Dante certainly must have had some reasons for mentioning Statius up to the end of the *Purgatorio* (XXXIII, 134), but Scartazzini confesses that he cannot guess what the reasons were.

* *Crese :* for credè.   In the middle ages *cresi, crese, cresero,* were freely used both in prose and in verse.

† Dante here repeats the censure which he first passed on Eve in XXIX, 23-30.   In the *De Monarchia,* III, 16, Dante says that by the Terrestrial Paradise is figured the happiness of this life. By saying that the forest is empty of inhabitants, through the

at a tree denuded of its foliage. This is the Tree of Knowledge, and to it the Gryphon fastens the Chariot.

> Forse in tre voli tanto spazio prese
> Disfrenata saetta, quanto erámo   35
> Rimossi, quando Beatrice scese.*

Perchance an arrow loosened from the string had in three flights traversed as great a space as we had moved onward, when Beatrice alighted (from the Chariot).

She alights when the company has reached the Tree, which, as we shall see, is the symbol of obedience, and she goes and sits down on its roots under the boughs. The act of alighting is essentially one of homage to Obedience. But more than that, the Tree is also symbolic of the empire, and thus Beatrice's descent from the Chariot will signify the deference and submission of the ecclesiastical to the civil authority, in accordance with St. Paul's injunction (*Rom.* xiii, 1), " Let every

---

fault of Eve, Dante means to express that by reason of sin no one occupies himself in the practice of virtue, as in the words of the Psalmist (*Ps.* LIII, 3), " There is none that doeth good, no, not one." Dante implies, in the literal sense, that, owing to the fault of our first mother, the Terrestrial Paradise is uninhabited, man having been excluded therefrom on account of sin ; and, in the allegorical sense, that, from the faults of bad government, there is no one in the world who practises virtue, and follows out his own real happiness in this life.

* Scartazzini says : " What is the allegorical meaning of this descent of Beatrice from the mystical Chariot, the symbol of the Church ?" It is, he thinks, a sign of humility, and he quotes *Gen.* XXIV, 64-65, showing how Rebekah alighted off her camel, and covered herself with her veil, when she saw Isaac approaching, and had ascertained who he was.

soul be subject unto the higher powers." And these
two interpretations of the Tree being symbolic both of
obedience and of the empire are not antagonistic to
each other, because deference paid to imperial authority
is precisely homage rendered to obedience.

> Io sentii mormorare a tutti : *Adamo!*
> Poi cerchiaro una pianta,* dispogliata
> Di fiori e d' altra fronda in ciascun ramo.

---

* *una pianta:* Scartazzini says that, to explain and examine
accurately all the divergent opinions as to the allegorical meaning
of *una pianta,* even a long dissertation would not suffice. First
and foremost he says that there is no doubt but that *la pianta*
in its literal sense is the Tree of Knowledge of Good and Evil,
planted by God in the Garden of Eden or Terrestrial Paradise.
In describing the tree the Poet had also under his eye that tree
(mentioned in *Daniel* IV, 20-22), that was great and strong,
whose height reached unto the heaven, and which King Nebu-
chadnezzar saw in "the visions of his head in his bed" (*Dan.*
IV, 10). In many passages in Holy Scripture the tree is introduced as an emblem of power and royal majesty. As a tree
stretches up above all other plants, so the supreme power is
elevated above its subjects, and just as a tree gives shade so the
supreme power protects its subjects. Many commentators think
that the tree of the Dantesque vision is a symbol of obedience,
but that is only part of the full sense. Two figures stand out pro-
minently in the great vision, namely, the Tree and the Chariot.
The Chariot is the emblem of the Church. The Terrestrial Paradise is a figure of the happiness of this life. But in this life we
can have no happiness without well-being (*ben essere*). And to
secure well-being in this world temporal monarchy is necessary,
as Dante maintains in the first Book of his *De Monarchia,* ch. 5.
If Empire be necessary to the well-being of the world, and if the
Terrestrial Paradise be a figure of the world in a state of well-
being where man is happy (*Purg.* XXX, 75), it follows of necessity that Dante, true to his system, was bound to introduce the
symbol of the Empire into his vision with the others. The only
symbol of the Empire admissible is the Mystic Tree. Besides

I heard all murmur (in a tone of censure), "Adam!" then they encircled a Tree that was despoiled of blossoms and leaves on each of its boughs.

The whole company murmur against Adam, through whose disobedience sin entered into the world, and by sin death (*Rom.* v, 12). This murmuring involves censure on any one, even a pope, who is guilty of disobedience. Brunone Bianchi says that we have here a tacit comparison between the sin of Adam, who, having been placed in the Terrestrial Paradise, touched the tree forbidden by God, the Supreme Emperor, on the one hand; and on the other, we have the pope, who, placed in Rome, and under the protection of the imperial throne, withdraws himself from obedience to the emperor, whose authority derives from God, and lays his hands upon the secular jurisdiction belonging to the emperor, and that in direct opposition to the express commands of Christ.

La coma sua, che tanto si dilata*   40

---

this, it is not at all rare to find a tree, amongst the poets, used as a symbol of the Empire, or of a reigning house. Hence Dante could with reason take the Tree as the symbol either of the monarchy or the Roman empire. And in truth all that Dante says of the Tree fits in very well with the empire.

* This Tree would seem to be similar in form to the one described on the sixth cornice (*Purg.* XXII, 130-135). Dante there explains the shape, saying of it :—

"*cred' io perchè persona su non vada.*"

In *Purg.* XXXIII, 58, Beatrice says that whosoever robs or injures the Tree sins against God ; and then, after mentioning the punishment of Adam, who ate of its fruit, she adds (v. 64):—

" Dorme lo ingegno tuo, se non istima
        Per singular cagione essere eccelsa
        Lei tanto, e sì travolta nella cima."

Più, quanto più è su, fora dagl' Indi*
Ne' boschi lor, per altezza,† ammirata.

Its crowning boughs, which widen out the more as
they are higher up, would have been wondered at for
height even by Indians in their woods.

Scartazzini says that this passage (40-42) is intended
above all things to symbolize the inviolability of the
Empire, which, according to the Will of God, must
not be touched.   In *De Monarchia* III, ch. 10, Dante
says that it is not even lawful for the Emperor himself
" *scindere imperium.*"

Dante, having shown how all the company censured
the disobedience of Adam, now shows how they com-
mend the obedience of Christ, Who restored the Tree
which Adam had despoiled.

—" Beato se', grifon, che non discindi‡
    Col becco d' esto legno dolce al gusto,
    Poscia che mal si torce il ventre quindi."—   45

The words *travolta nella cima* describe how that the tree was
inverted on its summit to render it more difficult of access.
Comà is a Latinism for chioma.

  * *dagli Indi :* Compare Virg. *Georg.* II, 122 :—
    ". . . . . gerit India lucos,
      Extremi sinus orbis, ubi aera vincere summum
      Arboris haud ullæ jactu potuere sagittæ."

  † *Per altezza :* Scartazzini says there is a complete parallelism
between the two trees as described by Daniel (IV, 7-19), and this
tree described by Dante.   With Daniel the tree is an emblem
of the Babylonian Empire, with Dante, of the Roman Empire.

  ‡ The Gryphon (*i. e.* Jesus Christ) is praised because he does
not rend the Tree, meaning the Empire, to which our Lord willed
that due homage should be rendered.   He gave the command:
"Render, therefore, unto Cæsar the things which are Cæsar's,
and unto God the things that are God's."—*St. Matt.* XXII, 21.

> Così d' intorno all' arbore robusto
> Gridaron gli altri ; e l' animal binato :
> —" Sì si conserva il seme d' ogni giusto."—

" Blessed art thou, Gryphon, who dost not rend with thy beak this Tree, whose fruit is sweet to the taste (as Eve found it), since by that taste (*quindi*) the belly (of mankind) was contorted with anguish (*i. e.* Man tasted thereof to his own hurt.) " Thus cried the others (*i. e.* the members of the Church Militant) round the mighty Tree ; and the animal of twofold nature (the Gryphon, answered): " Thus is preserved the seed of all the just."

Scartazzini thinks that these words, put into the mouth of the Gryphon, are a paraphrase of those spoken by Christ to St. John the Baptist : " For thus it becometh us to fulfil all righteousness," (in the Vulgate *justice*)."—*St. Matt.* III, 15.

The Gryphon now draws the Chariot up and binds it to the tree ; in consequence of which the Tree throws out fresh blossoms.

> E volto al temo ch' egli avea tirato,
> Trasselo al piè della vedova frasca ;   50
> E quel di lei a lei lasciò legato.

And (the Gryphon), turning to the pole which he had dragged, drew it to the foot of the widowed stem (*i. e.* bare tree), and left bound to it that which was (made) of it (*i. e.* the wooden pole.)

According to Dante He recognized and confirmed the authority of the Empire, first in submitting Himself to the Census ordained in the reign of Cæsar Augustus, thereby registering Himself as a subject of the Empire. At His condemnation He said to Pilate : " Thou couldest have no power at all against me, except it were given thee from above," thereby recognizing his power as legitimate.—*St. John* XIX, 11.

Scartazzini thinks that by the pole is meant the
sacred seat of the Church, and that as the Gryphon
drags the Chariot by the pole, so Christ guides His
Church by means of the Sacred Seat.   The tree then
is, literally : The Tree of Knowledge of Good and
Evil ; allegorically : The Empire.

The Cross of Christ derived from the Tree of
Knowledge is the origin of the Papal Seat.   If the
Cross is made from a branch of the Tree of Knowledge, and the Papal Seat originates in the Cross, it
can well be said that the Papal Seat was formed from
a branch of that Tree.   Christ joins the Papal Seat,
Roman in its origin, to the Roman Empire ; and that
not only in externals, as shown by both Papacy and
Empire having their central abode at Rome ; but also
inwardly, in that, according to Dante, both Pope and
Emperor ought to go hand in hand in guiding the
human race to its two-fold object and end.

Now Dante describes the marvellous change that
came over the Tree after the Gryphon had bound to it
the pole of the Chariot.

> Come le nostre piante, quando casca
>   Giù la gran luce mischiata con quella
>   Che raggia dietro alla celeste lasca,*
> Turgide† fansi, e poi si rinnovella   55

---

* *lasca,* which properly means a roach or mullet, here signifies the Constellation of the Fish.   Aries follows after Pisces,
and when the sun is in Aries we are in spring.

† *turgide fansi:* swell with sap.   Compare Virg. *Eclog.* VII,
48 :—
> " Jam læto turgent in palmite gemmæ."
and *Georg.* I, 315 :—
> " Frumenta in viridi stipula lactentia turgent."

Di suo color* ciascuna, pria che il sole
Giunga li suoi corsier sott' altra stella ;
Men che di rose, e più che di vïole
Colore aprendo, s' innovò la pianta,
Che prima avea le ramora† sì sole. 60

As our plants (*i.e.* those in our world) when (in Spring) the great light (the Sun) falls downwards, mingled with that (of Aries) which beams behind the Celestial Fish (*lit.* roach), begin to swell, and then each is renewed in its own colour, before that the Sun harnesses his steeds beneath another star (the constellation of Taurus); in like manner did the Tree, which before had had its boughs so desolate, renew itself, disclosing a hue less (vivid) than that of roses, but more than that of violets.‡

---

* *di suo color.* Compare Petrarch, *Rim. P. I. son.* 9 :—

"Quando 'l pianeta che distingue l' ore
Ad albergar col Tauro si ritorna,
Cade virtù dall' infiammate corna,
Che veste il mondo di novel colore."

† *ramora*, an ancient form of the plural *rami*; so *campora* for *campi*. See Nannucci, *Teoria dei Nomi*, page 360.

‡ Ruskin (*Mod. Painters*, III, 226) says : "Some three arrow-flights farther up into the wood we come to a tall tree, which is at first barren, but, after some little time, visibly opens into flowers, of a colour 'less than that of roses, but more than that of violets.' It certainly would not be possible, in words, to come nearer to the *definition* of the exact hue which Dante meant—that of the apple blossom. Had he employed any simple colour phrase, as a 'pale pink,' or 'violet pink,' or any other such combined expression, he still could not have completely got at the delicacy of the hue ; he might, perhaps, have indicated its kind, but not its tenderness ; but by taking the rose-leaf as the type of the delicate red, and then enfeebling this with the violet grey, he gets, as closely as lan-

Scartazzini remarks that here again we have one of those passages, which have not yet found their Œdipus to interpret them. Speaking generally, he has no doubt that the allegorical sense of this passage is, that the virtue infused by the mystic Chariot into this Tree, that is, by the Church into the Empire, was so great, that the Tree was seen in a short time to renovate itself entirely, and to clothe itself with foliage and fruits ; implying thereby that the Empire, when converted to Christianity, was endowed with new life. As soon as the Church was joined to the Empire, the latter began at once, at least potentially, to prosper.

Division III. Here begins *the Third Division of the Canto*, in which Dante relates how he falls asleep, and on awaking finds Beatrice, Matelda, and the seven damsels alone by the Tree, and learns that the glorious Procession of the Church Militant, and the Gryphon, have ascended to Heaven.

Dante first tells how the whole of the celestial beings present before him chanted a hymn so sweet, that overwhelmed with emotion he fell asleep.

> Io non lo intesi, e qui non si canta
> L' inno che quella gente allor cantaro,
> Nè la nota soffersi tutta quanta.

----

guage can carry him, to the complete rendering of the vision, though it is evidently felt by him to be in its perfect beauty ineffable ; and rightly so felt, for of all lovely things which grace the spring-time in our fair temperate zone, I am not sure but this blossoming of the apple-tree is the fairest."

I did not understand it, nor here (on earth) is sung the hymn which that company then sang, nor could I bear (to hear) the whole melody throughout.

> S' io potessi ritrar come assonnaro
>> Gli occhi spietati, udendo di Siringa,* 65
>> Gli occhi a cui più vegghiar costò sì caro ;
> Come pintor che con esemplo pinga
>> Disegnerei com' io m' addormentai ;
>> Ma qual vuol sia che l' assonnar ben finga.

If I could portray how the unrelenting eyes (of Argus) sank into slumber, on hearing (tell) of Syrinx, the eyes to which more watching cost so dear; like an artist who paints from a model, I would delineate the way that I fell asleep ; but whosoever wishes (to do so), let him be one who can well depict slumber.

Dante implies that he is not, himself, able to do it, and he only will describe what he saw when he awoke.

---

* Juno, having cause to be jealous of Io, had placed her under the guardianship of Argus, whose hundred eyes watched without intermission. Jupiter, having ordered Mercury to carry off the young nymph, Mercury slew Argus, after lulling him to sleep by telling him the story of Syrinx, the nymph of Arcadia, who was changed into a reed. See Ovid, *Met.* I (Dryden's translation).

> " While Hermes piped, and sung, and told his tale,
> The keeper's winking eyes began to fail,
> And drowsy slumber on the eyes to creep ;
> Till all the watchman was at length asleep.
> Then soon the god his voice and song supprest,
> And with his powerful rod confirmed his rest ;
> Without delay his crooked falchion drew,
> And at one fatal stroke the keeper slew."

Però trascorro a quando mi svegliai,   70
   E dico ch' un splendor mi squarciò* il velo
   Del sonno, ed un chiamar : *Surgi, che fai ?*

Therefore I pass on to when I awoke, and I say
that a dazzling light tore aside the veil of my sleep,
and (also) a crying out, "Arise, what doest thou ? "

The dazzling light is the now distant glory of the
Gryphon, the Elders and the Angels reascending to
Heaven.† It would seem to be Matelda who spoke
the words, and Dante finds her standing over him
after his sleep, like as we read in Canto XXXI, 91-96,
that she had hovered over him after his swoon.

Dante then goes on to compare himself to the
disciples at the Transfiguration.

Quale a veder dei fioretti del melo,‡
   Che del suo pomo gli Angeli fa ghiotti,
   E perpetue nozze fa nel cielo,   75
Pietro e Giovanni e Jacopo condotti
   E vinti ritornaro alla parola,
   Dalla qual furon maggior' sonni rotti,

---

* *mi squarciò il velo del sonno.* Compare *Inf.* XXXIII, 26 :—
    " quand' io feci il mal sonno
   Che del futuro mi squarciò il velame."

† The description of the dazzling light has a close analogy to
that of the Transfiguration. The three disciples fell asleep
(St. Luke, IX, 32) : "But Peter and they that were with him
were heavy with sleep, and when they were awake they saw
his glory, and the two men that stood with him." And in
the description by St. Matthew, XVII, 7, we find the resemblance to "Surgi, che fai ? " "And Jesus came and touched
them, and said : Arise, and be not afraid."

‡ *melo.* Compare *Song of Solomon*, II, 3 : "As the apple-
tree among the trees of the wood, so is my beloved among
the sons." This passage is interpreted as referring to Christ,
and Dante here calls the Transfiguration the blossoming of
that tree.

> E videro scemata loro scuola,
>> Così di Moisè come d' Elia,   80
>> Ed al maestro suo cangiata stola :
> Tal torna' io, e vidi quella pia   ·
>> Sovra me starsi, che conducitrice
>> Fu de' miei passi lungo il fiume pria.

As, to behold the blossoms of that apple-tree which makes the Angels eager for its fruit, and keeps perpetual bridals in Heaven (*i.e.* the glory of Christ, of which the Transfiguration was but a glimpse), Peter and John and James were led (apart), and (having been) overcome (by sleep) recovered at the word (of Christ) by which more profound slumbers have been broken (*i.e.* those of the dead) and they (the three disciples) beheld their company diminished by (the loss of) both Moses, as also of Elias, and (found) that the raiment of their Master changed : so I revived, and beheld that saintly one (Matelda) standing over me, she who before had been the conductress of my steps along the (bank of the) stream.

He now misses Beatrice.

> E tutto in dubbio dissi :—" Ov' è Beatrice ? "—   85
>> Ond' ella—" Vedi lei sotto la fronda
>> Nuova sedere in su la sua radice.*
> Vedi la compagnia che la circonda ;
>> Gli altri dopo il grifon sen vanno suso,
>> Con più dolce canzone e più profonda."—   90

And all in doubt I said : "Where is Beatrice ?" And

---

* Scartazzini says that Beatrice is sitting beneath the foliage and upon the roots of the mystic tree. We have seen that the tree is a symbol of the Empire. Therefore, its roots, speaking allegorically, can only signify the spot on which the Empire itself was situated, and from which it stretched forth its branches, and that spot is Rome.

she : " Behold her under the new foliage, sitting
upon its roots.   Behold the company that surrounds
her : the others are ascending with the Gryphon, with
sweeter song and of deeper import."

Tommaseo thinks that the Angels and the seven
Virtues were round Beatrice, but Scartazzini points
out that as the Angels were mentioned before, and not
now, it is reasonable to suppose that they were included in the glorious host that was following the
Gryphon up to Heaven.

Dante now relates how he concentrated his gaze on
Beatrice.

> E se più fu lo suo parlar diffuso
>   Non so, però che già negli occhi m' era
>   Quella ch' ad altro intender m' avea chiuso.
> Sola sedeasi in su la terra vera,
>   Come guardia lasciata lì del plaustro,   95
>   Che legar vidi alla biforme fiera.

And whether her speech was further poured forth, I
know not, because already she (Beatrice) was before
my eyes, who had distracted my attention from hearing more.   She was sitting alone upon the bare earth,
left there as guardian of the Chariot, which I had seen
bound to the Tree by the animal of twofold nature
(the Gryphon).

Most of the commentators take *la terra vera* to
mean the soil of the Terrestrial Paradise, that pure
soil, uncontaminated by original sin.   Scartazzini
argues that Beatrice was sitting on the roots of the
Tree, which (v. 86) was supposed to signify, that spiritual authority has its seat in Rome, the root of the
Empire.   Here we find two things said of Beatrice.
She is sitting alone, and sitting on *la terra vera.*

Vera must be taken in the sense of *nuda.* Beatrice sits alone ; she has no other court than the seven Virtues. She sits on *la terra vera ;* she has no other throne than the bare earth, thereby imitating Him, who had not where to lay His head. Beatrice symbolizes the spiritual authority, the ideal Papacy of Dante's aspirations. The Bishops of the Primitive Church sat alone in the Imperial City, without any retinue of cardinals, courtiers, or servants. They were poor ; the papal throne had not as yet been set up ; the temporal wealth of the Church had not yet been heaped up ; they assembled their flocks in the Catacombs ; therefore they sat upon the bare earth. In describing Beatrice as alone, and sitting on the bare earth, Dante portrays the humility and poverty of the primitive Vicars of Christ, and satirizes the splendour and worldly pomp of the later Popes, besides those of his own time. Therefore Beatrice may be considered to figure either the primitive successors of St. Peter, or ideal Pope, imagined by Dante.

Dante now describes Beatrice's retinue of handmaidens.

> In cerchio le facevan di sè claustro
> Le sette ninfe, con que' lumi in mano
> Che son sicuri d' Aquilone e d' Austro.

The seven nymphs were making of themselves an enclosure that encircled her, with those lamps in their hands which are secure from Aquilo and Auster (*i.e.* cannot be extinguished either by the north or south wind).

The Virtues formed the sole escort and ornament of the first successors of St. Peter, and the ideal Vicar of Christ should be surrounded by them alone.

It may be inferred that when the Gryphon and the Elders had departed, the seven lamps of gold, which had before that time been preceding the procession, were taken in charge by the nymphs representing the Virtues. Allegorically it may mean that subsequently to the descent of the Holy Ghost upon the disciples of Christ on the Day of Pentecost, the Virtues were no longer to be separated from the Sevenfold Spirit of God.

Division IV. In the Fourth and concluding Division of the Canto, Dante gives a description, in figurative language, of the more notable of the tribulations through which the Church Militant had to pass.

—" Qui sarai tu poco tempo silvano,   100
         E sarai meco, senza fine, cive
         Di quella Roma onde Cristo è Romano.

" Thou shalt be but for a short time a forester here, and shalt be with me for evermore a citizen of that Rome where Christ is a Roman.

Beatrice means that his sojourn in the Terrestrial Paradise will be but short, and that when, after his return to earth, his life ends, he shall be with her an inhabitant of the Kingdom of Heaven, where Christ, as man, is a citizen, and where God reigns as Emperor.

" She now exhorts him to watch the Chariot attentively, and that for the good of the world, he should, after his return there, write what he has seen.

> Però, in pro del mondo che mal vive,
>   Al carro tieni or gli occhi ; e quel che vedi,
>   Ritornato di là, fa che tu scrive."—*   105

Therefore, for the good of the world, which lives
ill, keep thine eyes fixed upon the Chariot, and that
which thou seest, when thou art returned (to the earth)
yonder, take heed that thou write."

The world was living ill both socially and morally,
because neither of the two leaders assigned to it by
Heaven, the Pope and the Emperor, was performing
his proper functions.

Dante relates how he at once obeyed Beatrice's
injunction.

> Così Beatrice ; ed io, che tutto a' piedi †
>   De' suoi comandamenti era devoto,
>   La mente e gli occhi, ov' ella volle, diedi.‡

Thus (said) Beatrice ; and I, who at the feet of her
commandments was all devoted, directed my mind
and my eyes where she willed, (*i.e.* I fixed my eyes
and turned my thoughts upon the Chariot).

Dante now begins to describe the persecutions of the
Church ; the first that he mentions are those of the
early Roman Emperors : Nero, Domitian, Diocletian
and others. These persecutions are figured by an
Eagle swooping down on the Chariot with such great
force as to make it totter.

---

* *fa che tu scrive.* Compare *Rev.* I, 11 : "What thou seest,
write in a book, and send it unto the seven churches which are in
Asia."

† *a' piedi de' suoi comandamenti* is like *le ginocchia della
mente*, in Petrarch ; and *alle mani della sua grazia*, in Boccaccio.

‡ *diedi la mente e gli occhi:* I turned, *rivolsi ;* compare
Purg. III, 14 :—
  "E diedi il viso mio incontro al poggio."

Non scese mai con sì veloce moto
    Fuoco di spessa nube, quando piove   110
    Da quel confine che più va remoto,*
Com' io vidi calar l' uccel di Giove
    Per l' arbor giù, rompendo della scorza,
    Non che dei fiori e delle foglie nuove ;
E ferì il carro di tutta sua forza,   115
    Ond' ei piegò, come nave in fortuna,
    Vinta dall' onda, or da poggia or da orza.

Never descended with such swift motion fire (*i.e.*
lightning) from a thick cloud, when it is raining from
that confine (*i.e.* of Heaven, the sphere of fire) which
moves the most remote (from the earth), as I beheld
the bird of Jove swoop down through the Tree,
rending off the bark, not less the flowers and the
new foliage ; and he smote the Chariot with all his
might, at which it reeled like a ship in a tempest,
driven by the waves, now to starboard now to
port.

Scartazzini says that the eagle not only smites the
mystic Chariot, but likewise seriously damages the mystic Tree. The persecutions of the emperors against the
Christians not only injured the young church, but the
empire itself, depriving it, in part, of that new life
which it had acquired by its union with the Church ;
depriving it, moreover, of many of the most loyal and
faithful because the most virtuous and holy minded
of its subjects. The next tribulation of the Church is
that which it sustained from false prophets and heret-

---

‡ *quel confine che più va remoto.* Scartazzini thinks that in
this passage Dante most probably follows the teaching of
Aristotle, who, in his second book of the Meteors, teaches that
lightning is generated by fire being confined in the clouds, when
the latter rise to the level of the sphere of fire.

ical teachers, and these are symbolized here by a fox,
hungry and lean, who leaps into the body of the
Chariot.

>   Poscia vidi avventarsi nella cuna
>   Del trionfal veiculo una volpe,
>   Che d' ogni pasto buon parea digiuna.   120
>   Ma, riprendendo lei di laide colpe,
>   La donna mia la volse in tanta futa,*
>   Quanto sofferson l' ossa senza polpe.

Next I saw leap into the body of the triumphal
Chariot a fox, that appeared (from excessive leanness)
to be fasting from all wholesome food. But, upbraiding
it for its hideous crimes, my Lady (Beatrice) put it to
as swift a flight, as its fleshless bones would bear.

Scartazzini observes that the fox leaped into the
Chariot from without, and therefore signifies a heresy
that did not take its origin within the body of the
church, but from the outside. He says that Dante, in
this part of his vision, seems to follow a chronological
order, and that if in verse 124 there is an allusion to
the gifts of Constantine to the Church, it is evident
that he here refers to a heresy which took place
before that time. It can neither be the heresy of
Arius, of Mahomet, of Anastasius II, nor of Nova-
tian. He is convinced that the heresy here alluded
to is that of the Gnostics. Gnosticism did not spring
up within the Church, but had its origin in Oriental
philosophy. The fox is put to flight by Beatrice ; and
Gnosticism was victoriously combated by the Fathers
of the church.

---

* *futa*: the same as *fuga*, was formerly in common use. A
mountain on the road between Bologna and Florence is said to
have been called *Montagna della Futa* on account of *la fuga*
the rout and flight of the Ghibellines at that place.

Dante now goes on to describe the Third Tribulation of the Church, which is the rich endowment of it by the Roman Emperors.

> Poscia, per indi ond' era prima venuta,
>> L' aquila vidi scender giù nell' arca   125
>> Del carro, e lasciar lei di sè pennuta.*
> E qual esce di cuor che si rammarca,
>> Tal voce uscì del cielo, e cotal disse :
>> — " Oh navicella mia, com' mal se' carca ! "—

Next, from the same direction whence it came before (*i.e.* through the tree), I saw the eagle descend into the body of the Chariot, and leave it covered with its plumes (*lit.* feathered from itself). And like as issues from a heart that is mourning, so there issued such a voice from Heaven, and thus spoke : " O my little bark, how evil thou art freighted!"

Scartazzini says that all the commentators agree that Dante is here making allusion to the riches and luxuries bestowed on the Apostolic Seat by the Roman Emperors, and more especially to the " Donatio Constantini." He adds that whereas the Church had come victorious out of all its previous tribulations and trials, this last was far more insidious and fatal, and the Church was put to the same temptation which Satan attempted with Jesus Christ, when he showed Him all the kingdoms of the Earth, and the glory of them. With our Lord he failed, but with the Church he was

---

* *lasciar lei di sè pennuta.* This is generally understood to mean that the Emperor Constantine impoverished himself to bestow rich endowments on the Church when he moved the seat of Empire to Constantinople. Compare *Inf.* XIX, 115 :—

> "Ahi, Constantin, di quanto mal fu matre,
>> Non la tua conversion, ma quella dote,
>> Che da te prese il primo ricco patre ! "

successful. Gold, power and earthly glory, became
the god adored by the so-called ministers and servants
of the Living God.

We shall now see how the mystic Chariot gradually
deteriorates. A dragon rises from the earth between
the wheels, strikes the Chariot with his tail, and carries
off the floor of it.

> Poi parve a me che la terra s' aprisse   130
>   Tr' ambo le ruote, e vidi uscirne un drago,
>   Che per lo carro su la coda fisse :
> E, come vespa che ritragge l' ago,
>   A sè traendo la coda maligna,
>   Trasse del fondo, e gissen vago vago.   135

Then methought that the earth opened itself between the two wheels, and I saw issue from it a dragon,
who thrust his tail upward through the Chariot: and
like a wasp that draws back his sting, (the dragon)
drawing back to himself his envenomed tail, dragged
(part) of the bottom forth, and went his way in
malignant eagerness (to work further evil).

Some commentators interpret *vago* as rejoicing,
exulting, but Scartazzini does not agree with them,
and thinks Dante nearly always uses the word to
mean eager (see *Purg.* XXVIII, 1, and many other
passages). The dragon was far from going away satisfied, but like the wolf (*Inf.* I, 99) who *dopo il pasto ha
più fame che pria,* it departed as departs the devil, who
having worked one evil, is eager to work another
worse one.

Now what is this dragon? The figure is most
probably taken from *Rev.* XII, 3-4, " And behold a
great red dragon having seven heads and ten horns,
and seven crowns upon his heads. And his tail drew

the third part of the stars of Heaven, and did cast them
to the earth." In the dragon of the Apocalypse,
Scartazzini says that modern Biblical exegesis sees
figured the Roman Empire, antichristian, the enemy
and persecutor of the church. Its seven heads are the
seven hills of Rome ; the ten horns are the Roman
Emperors from Augustus down to Nero : the tail that
drags away the third part of the stars of Heaven
figures the oppression and desolation of the church.
The dragon is " that old serpent, the Devil and Satan,"
as in the Apocalypse. The dragon issues from the
earth, whereas the Gryphon, or Christ, descended from
Heaven ; and consequently the dragon is the infernal
antithesis to the celestial Gryphon. Up to the time of
the appearance of the dragon, the body of the Chariot
had escaped injury ; but from this point it begins
to degenerate. The dragon in attacking it with his
envenomed tail, typifies the Devil, who instilled
corruption into the Church, and despoiled it of all its
virtues. And the dragon coming forth between the
two wheels of the Chariot is thought to imply that the
demon of cupidity of worldly possessions arose in the
hearts of the clergy, the two wheels typifying the two
orders, the secular and the monastic clergy.

In the next six lines, Dante relates how the
plumage of the eagle covered every part of the Chariot
in an instant of time.

> Quel che rimase, come di gramigna
>> Vivace terra, della piuma offerta,
>> Forse con intenzion sana e benigna,
> Si ricoperse ; e funne ricoperta
>> E l' una e l' altra ruota e il têmo, in tanto   140
>> Che più tiene un sospir la bocca aperta.

What remained (of the Chariot), even as fertile earth with grass, reclothed itself with the plumage offered perchance with pure and benign intention ; and both of the wheels, as also the pole, were covered with it as quickly as a sigh doth longest keep the lips apart.

This evidently alludes to the rich endowments of the Church. Up to this point the mystic Chariot has had the symbolical meaning of the Church universal, inasmuch as it owns the Pope for its head, but thenceforward it seems to have signified the Papal throne. It is now transformed into a monster of terrible appearance.

> Trasformato così il dificio santo
>   Mise fuor teste per le parti sue,
>   Tre sovra il têmo, ed una in ciascun canto.
> Le prime eran cornute come bue ;   145
>   Ma le quattro un sol corno avean per fronte.
>   Simile mostro visto ancor non fue.

Thus transfigured, the holy edifice (*i.e.* the Chariot) put forth heads from its (different) parts, three above the pole, and one at each corner. The first were horned like oxen (*i.e.* each of the three heads had two horns); but the four (at the corners) had (each) a single horn upon the forehead. A monster such as this was never seen before.

Scartazzini thinks that the monster with the seven heads and ten horns in this passage is a symbol of the degeneracy of the Church, and more especially of the corruption of the Papal throne. This monster is the triumphal Chariot, that is, the Church as it ought to be. In the same way the seven heads may be taken as the antitypes of the seven candlesticks with the seven bands of light, and the ten horns as antitypes of the ten paces (*Purg.* XXIX, 81), which Scartazzini believes to imply perfection or excellence, as the number ten symbolizes perfection. Some think the seven heads are the antitypes of the seven damsels who had surrounded the Chariot. Jacopo della Lana is of opinion that the seven heads imply the seven capital sins which entered into the Church as soon as it became possessed of worldly riches.

Pride,
Anger,   } which offend against God and against
Avarice,   } one's neighbour, are two horned sins.

Envy,
Luxury,   } which only offend one's neighbour, are
Sloth,   } one horned sins.
Gluttony,

Most of the principal commentators give this interpretation.

Dante, having now passed rapidly over the vicissitudes of the Church from the earliest epoch of its existence, proceeds to notice its condition in his own times. He carries on the allegory by relating how he beheld upon the Chariot, now transformed into a monster, a bold shameless woman, and beside her a giant, who appeared to guard her and at times they exchanged caresses. But when she turned her eyes upon Dante, the giant scourged her, loosed the Chariot from the Tree to which the Gryphon had bound it, and dragged it and the woman so far into the forest, that they were lost to Dante's sight.

> Sicura, quasi rocca in alto monte,
> Seder sovr' esso una puttana sciolta
> M' apparve, con le ciglia intorno pronte.   150

Firm, as a castle-keep on a high mountain,

methought there sat upon it (*i.e.* the Chariot transformed into a monster) a dishevelled harlot rolling
her eyes with ready glances.

> E, come perchè non gli fosse tolta,
>> Vidi di costa a lei dritto un gigante,
>> E baciavansi insieme alcuna volta.

And, as if in order that she should not be taken
from him, I beheld upright beside her a giant, and ever
and anon they kissed one another.

> Ma, perchè l' occhio cupido e vagante
>> A me rivolse, quel feroce drudo   155
>> La flagellò dal capo insin le piante.

But, because she turned on me her wanton and
roving eye, that savage paramour scourged her from
her head unto her feet.*

> Poi, di sospetto pieno e d' ira crudo,
>> Disciolse il mostro, e trassel per la selva
>> Tanto, che sol di lei mi fece scudo
> Alla puttana ed alla nuova belva.   160

Then, full of jealousy and cruel rage, he unloosed
the monster (from the Tree to which the Gryphon had
bound the Chariot before its transformation), and
dragged it off through the forest, so far, that he made
of that alone a shield unto the harlot and the newly-
formed beast (*i.e.* he made the forest an impediment
to my being able to see them any longer).

Dante has here been giving, in allegorical language,
a sketch of the events that happened in his own time,
which Scartazzini considers to be perfectly clear.
There are two personages : the harlot and the giant.

---

* Tommasèo says that the woman with the wanton glance
reminds one of la *lupa* . . . *di tutte brame, Inf.* I, 49 ; and her
roving eye of *la bestia senza pace, Inf.* I, 58.

The harlot, styled *fuja* in XXXIII, 44, is that harlot of *Rev.* XVII, 1-2, "that sitteth upon many waters: with whom the kings of the earth have committed fornication," and is also "that great city (*Rev.* XVII, 18), which reigneth over the kings of the earth ; " evidently meaning Rome. In the allegory of this Canto there is a symmetrical arrangement, which makes each personage and component part have its antitype or antithesis. Now Dante has taken Beatrice as the ideal type and symbol of the spiritual and papal authority, and therefore the harlot must be the antitype of Beatrice, and thus signify the papal authority degenerate, corrupt, and transformed into the contrary of what it ought to be, and therefore deserving of all censure. Such were in Dante's eyes the Popes of his time, and notably so Boniface VIII, who, in *Par.* XXVII, 22, is called by St. Peter "*quegli ch' usurpa in terra il luogo mio.*" The harlot is therefore the Papal Curia degenerate and corrupt, and is the symbol of the two Popes contemporary with Dante, Boniface VIII and Clement V.

Nearly all the commentators are agreed that the giant, who appears to be an imitator of the kings of the earth, that have committed fornication with the great Whore, symbolizes the Royal House of France, and especially Philippe le Bel, whose contests with Boniface VIII are well known.

Scartazzini sums up the interpretation of the allegory as follows :—

The Monster is the antitype of the Triumphal Chariot.

The Seven Heads form the antitype of the Ten Paces (see *Purg.* XXIX, 81, note).

The Harlot is the antitype of Beatrice.

The Monster being loosed from the Tree, and dragged through the Forest, is the antitype of the Chariot being led to the Tree and bound to it.

The Giant, as Paramour of the Church, is the antitype of the Gryphon, who, as the symbol of Christ, is the Bridegroom.

In the Gospel History, Pontius Pilate is taken as an antitype of Christ. But in *Purg.* XX, 91, Dante calls Philippe le Bel "*il nuovo Pilato.*"

This argument speaks in favour of the common interpretation, and Scartazzini does not for one moment hesitate to accept it, and he explains the episode of the giant dragging the transformed Chariot through the forest out of sight, to be an imaginary prophecy of Dante relating to the translation of the Apostolic Seat from Rome to Avignon in 1305, Dante supposing himself to be looking five years in advance of 1300, when the vision is supposed to have occurred.

Pietro di Dante comments on the passage thus: " Et hoc est quod dicit, scilicet, quomodo traxit eam secum per silvam, idest quod fecit ut Curia romana tracta est ultra montes in suo territorio de Roma."

"And this is what he says, namely, how he dragged her through the forest, that is, what he did in getting the Curia Romana dragged over the mountains (the Alps) into his own dominions, away from Rome."

END OF CANTO XXXII.

CANTO XXXIII.

As in the last Canto Dante described at very great length the persecutions of the Church Militant, he now relates how Beatrice and her attendant ladies mourned over the indignities that the Church was suffering from the Kings of France.

Benvenuto divides the Canto into four parts.

In the First Division, from v. 1 to v. 33, Dante relates the plaintive dirge over the Church, sung by the seven nymphs.

In the Second Division, from v. 34 to v. 63, Beatrice foretells, for his consolation, the swift retribution that is coming, in the person of one who will set the Church free from its persecutors.

In the Third Division, from v. 64 to v. 102, Beatrice enjoins Dante not to be careless about the Vision he had witnessed, and remonstrates with him on his ignorance as to the things he has seen connected with the Tree.

In the Fourth Division, from v. 103 to v. 145, Dante relates how he is led by Matelda to drink of the water of Eunoe, after which he is made fit to ascend to Heaven.

Division I. The sweet nymphs break forth into a plaintive strain of psalmody, of which the responsive

verses are sung alternately by the three Evangelical
and by the four Cardinal Virtues. Beatrice listens
with deep emotion.

> *Deus, venerunt gentes,* alternando,
>> Or tre or quattro, dolce salmodia
>> Le donne incominciaro, e lagrimando ;
> E Beatrice sospirosa e pia
>> Quelle ascoltava sì fatta, che poco   5
>> Più alla croce si cambiò Maria.

" *Deus, venerunt gentes,*" (this) sweet psalmody the
ladies commenced singing, in alternate choirs, now
of three, now of four, weeping the while ; and Beatrice listened to them with sighs of compassion,
(and) with such an aspect (of woe), that Mary at
the cross was but little more changed (in appearance).

Dante, in the above passage, uses the words of the
Psalmist lamenting over the desolation of Jerusalem
by the Assyrians, and applies them to the tribulations
of the Church which he described under an allegory
in the last Canto. Beatrice had been standing on the
Chariot of the Church, when the Gryphon, Jesus Christ,
bound it to the Tree, *i.e.* the Empire. The scene has
now entirely changed. The place of Beatrice, the
representative of the *ideal* ecclesiastical authority, has
been usurped by the shameless harlot that typifies
corrupted ecclesiastical authority, and, as such, is the
antitype to Beatrice. The brutal giant has dragged
his wanton paramour out of sight, that is to say,
Philippe de Bel has transferred the Papal Seat to
Avignon. The *ideal* authority can only rule in Rome,
and therefore Beatrice, its representative, is pictured
here as standing by in desolation and woe.

Having described Beatrice's appearance, Dante tells
how she at length broke silence.

> Ma poi che l' altre vergini dier loco
>   A lei di dir, levata dritta in piè,
>   Rispose, colorata come fuoco :
> —*Modicum, et non videbitis me.*   10
>   *Et iterum*, sorelle mie dilette,
>   *Modicum, et vos videbitis me.*—

But after that the other maidens had given place
for her to speak, she, rising up upon her feet, answered
with a countenance as red as fire : " 'A little while, and
ye shall not see me.   And again a little while,' my
beloved sisters, 'and ye shall see me.' "

These words of our Lord (St. John XVI, 16) are
spoken by Beatrice, partly as a prophecy, partly as an
aspiration for the speedy restoration of the Papal Seat
to Rome.   Her face is burning with indignation at
the wrongs suffered by the Church of which she is the
guardian.

The company now moves on.   The seven nymphs
walk in front ; then Beatrice, while Matelda, Dante
and Statius, bring up the rear.

> Poi le si mise innanzi tutte e sette,
>   E dopo sè, solo accennando, mosse
>   Me e la Donna, e il Savio che ristette.   15

She then placed all the seven in front of her, and,
by a mere sign, motioned me and the Lady (Matelda)
and the Sage who (still) remained to walk after her.

In this new procession, diminished in numbers, the
same kind of order is observed as in the greater procession that had proceeded to the tree.   The candlesticks
are born aloft in the front by the seven damsels, next
walks Beatrice, and then Matelda and the two poets.

Beatrice now invites Dante to step nearer, and walk with her.

> Così sen giva, e non credo che fosse
> Lo decimo suo passo in terra posto,
> Quando con gli occhi gli occhi mi percosse ;
> E con tranquillo aspetto :—" Vien più tosto,"—
> Mi disse,—" tanto che s' io parlo teco,   20
> Ad ascoltarmi tu sie ben disposto."—

Thus she (Beatrice) moved on, and I do not believe that she had planted her tenth step on the ground (*i.e.* had walked as much as ten paces), when with her eyes she encountered my eyes ; and with a tranquil aspect : " Come on more quickly," she said to me, " so much that if I speak with thee, thou mayest be well placed for listening to me."

Scartazzini says that he does not agree with Tommaseo, in thinking that Dante speaks of these ten paces merely from love of mathematical exactness, but believes that, in this number, Dante has again concealed some allegory, which we do not know how to unravel. These ten paces of Beatrice remind us of the ten paces' distance, by which the candlesticks were separated from the mystic procession, of which they were the standards.

Dante obeys the commands of Beatrice, and draws nearer to her. She encourages him to take heart and converse with her.

> Sì com' io fui, com' io doveva, seco,
> Dissemi :—" Frate, perchè non ti attenti
> A domandarmi omai venendo meco ?"—

So soon as I was, as in duty bound, by her side, she said to me : " Brother, why dost thou not venture to question me now that thou art walking with me ?"

Benvenuto says that she implies that she knows

Dante wishes to ask her whether so many offences, committed against God in the person of His Vicar on earth, will be allowed to remain long unpunished.

Dante feels encouraged to ask her what is in his heart, but does so with much timidity.

> Come a color che troppo reverenti,*   25
>   Dinanzi a' suoi maggior' parlando sono,
>   Che non traggon la voce viva ai denti,
> Avvenne a me, che senza intero suono†
>   Incominciai :—" Madonna, mia bisogna
>   Voi conoscete, e ciò che ad essa è buono."—   30

As happens to those who are so over reverent when speaking to their superiors, that they fail to drag any living utterance to their teeth, so it befell me, for I began to speak without any perfect sound : " My Lady, thou knowest my necessity, and that which is good for it."

He means that Beatrice knows how much information it is good for him to have.‡

---

* *Reverenti dinanzi a' suoi maggior, &c.* Compare the answer of Telemachus to Mentor, when exhorted to pay a visit to Nestor, *Odyss.* III, 27, Lord Carnarvon's Translation :—

> " Nay, Mentor, how may I before him come,
>   Or greet him—I who have no skill in speech ?
>   It ill beseemeth youth to question eld."

† *senza intero suono:* Compare Ariosto, *Orland. Fur.,* XLII, 98 :—

> " Spesso la voce dal desio cacciata
>   Viene a Rinaldo sin presso alla bocca
>   Per domandarlo ; e quivi, raffrenata
>   Da cortese modestia, fuor non scocca."

‡ It has been well said that Dante must be commented by Dante. We have in *Convito* IV, cap. 8, Dante's definition of reverence, which we will take in his own words : " Lo più bello ramo che dalla radice razionale consurga si è la *discrezione* . . .

Beatrice commands Dante to put aside all timidity.

> Ed ella a me :—" Da tema e da vergogna*
>   Voglio che tu omai ti disviluppe,
>   Sì che non parli più com' uom che sogna.†

And she to me : " It is my will that henceforward thou disentangle thyself of all timidity and shame, so that thou mayest no longer speak like one who dreams (*i.e.* like one who stammers out his words as if he were asleep).

Fear and shame together entangle the feelings and thoughts as well as the speech.

Division II. In the Second Division, Beatrice foretells the swift retribution that is about to befall the

---

Uno dei più belli e dolci frutti di questo ramo è la *reverenza* che debbe al maggiore il minore . . . *Reverenza* non è altro che confessione di debita suggezione per manifesto segno."

  * *Da tema . . . ti disviluppe.* Compare *Inf.* III, 14, where Virgil says to Dante :—

> " Qui si convien lasciare ogni sospetto,
>   Ogni viltà convien che qui sia morta."

And *Par.* XV, 67 :—

> " La voce tua sicura, balda e lieta
>   Suoni la volontà, suoni il disio,
>   A che la mia risposta è già decreta."

And *Par* XVII, 7 :—

> " ' Manda fuor la vampa
>   Del tuo desio,' mi disse, ' sì ch' ell' esca
>   Segnata bene della eterna stampa.' "

  † *com' uom che sogna:* Compare Petrarch, *Rime*, P. I, Son. 41 :

> " Se parole fai,
>   Sono imperfette, e quasi d' uom che sogna."

And Tasso, *Ger. Lib.* XIII, 30 :—

> " Gli ragiona in guisa d' uom che sogna."

persecutors of the Church from the hand of one who will set her free. She says that the eagle will, in its turn, have an heir, for a messenger of God will, before long, slay the harlot and her paramour, the giant.

> Sappi che il vaso che il serpente ruppe,
> Fu, e non è ;* ma chi n' ha colpa, creda   35
> Che vendetta di Dio non teme suppe.

Know that the vessel, which the serpent (*i.e.* the dragon) broke (with his tail, XXXII, 130-135), was and is not ; but let him who is guilty be assured that the vengeance of God is not to be scared away with sops.

Let not him, Philippe le Bel, who has occasioned the destruction of the Church, the vessel which the serpent broke, hope to appease the anger of the Deity by any outward acts of religious, or rather superstitious, ceremony ; such as that, in Dante's time, performed by a murderer in Florence, who imagined

---

* *Fu, e non è* : Scartazzini says that these words, compared with "*Modicum et videbitis me*," &c., prove, *first*, that the Papal seat, corrupted by wealth, and alienated from the knowledge of God, is no longer as holy, as perfect as it was in its early days, or so efficacious in the sanctification of Christians ; *second*, that before long would be literally fulfilled, what was shown in allegory, of the carrying off of the Chariot. But all this degradation of the Church was but for a little while. *Et iterum modicum et videbitis me.* Hence we must understand *fu, e non è* in two senses : *first*, Il vaso *fu e non è* santo quanto Dio lo fece, *i. e.* the Church no longer has that holiness which it had when God first created it ; *second*, Il vaso *fu e non è* congiunto alla pianta dove Dio lo pose, *i. e.* the Church no longer remains connected to that tree to which God attached it, namely, the seat of the Roman Empire. I use the word "Church" here in the sense that Scartazzini takes it to have gradually acquired towards the end of the last Canto, namely, no longer the Church Universal, but the Papal Seat.

himself secure from vengeance, if he ate a sop of
bread in wine upon the grave of the murdered within
nine days. Corso Donati, Benvenuto tells us, acted
on this belief, and Falso Boccaccio says that, when
Charles Sansterre defeated and captured the youthful
Conradin, son of the Emperor Conrad IV, with young
Frederick of Austria, and the two Lancias, and had
them beheaded at Naples, it was reported that Charles
and his barons caused sops to be prepared, and they
ate them over the dead bodies, saying that thenceforward there could be no vengeance carried out
against them. Scartazzini states that, out of sixty-
four commentators whom he has quoted, forty-nine
are agreed in referring this passage to the popular
superstition of the times, and some mention it as
actually occurring in their days.

Emilio Giudici (*Storia della lett. ital.*, Vol. I, 215)
observes that the present passage is one of the most
sublime touches of the Dantesque pencil, a mode of
speech mysterious to us, which, while it bears in our
eyes the obscurity of the answer of an oracle, must
have been perfectly clear and intelligible to Dante's
contemporaries, but to the Anjous must have contained a bitter sarcasm, deriding their superstitions
and threatening vengeance for their crimes. Scartazzini says that we have here one of the many buried
treasures, with which the whole poem would glitter,
were it to be illustrated by a commentary that was
rigidly historical.

Beatrice now shows how vain is such fancied security on the part of Philippe le Bel, for the outrage on ˙
the Church will be speedily avenged by a special
emissary of God.

Non sarà tutto tempo senza reda*
   L' aquila che lasciò le penne al carro,
   Per che divenne mostro e poscia preda ;
Ch' io veggio certamente, e però il narro,   40
   A darne tempo, già stelle propinque,
   Sicure d' ogni intoppo e d' ogni sbarro ;
Nel quale un cinquecento diece e cinque,
   Messo di Dio, anciderà la fuja
   Con quel gigante che con lei delinque. .   45

Not for ever shall remain without an heir the eagle that left his plumes in the Chariot, from which cause it became (transformed into) a monster, and afterwards the prey (of the giant) ; for I can assuredly discern, and therefore I announce it, that already there are at hand (certain combinations of) stars, secure from any impediment or hindrance (*i. e.*, no power can avert such a conjunction of planets), that will give us a time in which a five hundred, and ten and five, sent from God, shall slay the abandoned woman, together with the giant, the accomplice of her guilt.

Scartazzini remarks that the above passage is one of the most obscure and disputed in the whole of the *Divina Commedia*. In the first place, Dante has again imitated the mystic style of the *Revelations* (XIII, 18), " Here is wisdom. Let him that hath understanding

---

* *L'aquila senza reda* is the vacant imperial throne. The vision is supposed to have taken place in 1300, in which year the imperial throne was not really vacant, but only so in Dante's eyes. In the *Convito* he speaks of Frederick II as the last Emperor and King of the Romans. Dante evidently hoped that, in a short time, an Emperor after his ideal would be elected. Scartazzini thinks that the Purgatorio was written subsequently to the death of Henry of Luxembourg, in 1313, and that, therefore, he cannot be the monarch on whom Dante founded his hopes.

count the number of the beast : for it is the number of a man ; and his number is Six hundred three score and six." Scartazzini says that this last is not a difficult enigma, as St. John was a Jew, and, written in Hebrew letters, the number 666 exactly makes

NERON CÆSAR.

To decipher the number given by Dante, one ought to know whether he was thinking of the symbolic value of the Latin letters, or only thinking of the letters themselves, D.X.V., which transposed, give the word D.V.X., *i. e.* a leader or captain. Whichever way one takes it, the passage evidently implies the hope that a personage would shortly appear, who would reform the Church, and re-establish the imperial authority. It is also clear from the context that Dante is pointing to some well-known contemporary personage, on whom he could found his hopes. Scartazzini feels assured, moreover, that if this passage is compared with the prophecy of the Veltro (*Inf.* I, 100-102), it will be distinctly proved by evidence that the D.X.V. and the Veltro are one and the same person. Again, the context proves that the person foretold by Dante can only be a captain, or secular leader, and not by any means a Pope or a churchman.

Let us look at history. On the 16th December, 1318, Cangrande della Scala, Lord of Verona, was elected by the congregation of Ghibelline Chiefs, as Captain of the League against the power of the Guelfs. It was then he actually received the standard of the Eagle, as the Leader in Italy of all the followers of the Empire. And (according to Scartazzini), it was just at the end of 1318 and at the beginning of

1319, that Dante was putting the last finishing touches
to the Cantica of the *Purgatorio*.   Hence Scartazzini
feels quite clear that it was Cangrande della Scala
who is the D.V.X. foretold by Dante.   Giuseppe
Picci (*I luoghi più oscuri e controversi della Divina
Commedia,* page 158 *et seq.*), observes : " If we write
down the name and qualification of Cangrande as
" Kan Grande de Scala Signore de Verona," and
compute numerically the initials and propositions, we
have the following result :—

$$
\begin{array}{rcl}
K & = & 10 \\
G & = & 7 \\
d & = & 4 \\
e & = & 5 \\
S & = & 90 \\
S & = & 90 \\
d & = & 4 \\
e & = & 5 \\
V & = & 300 \\
\hline
  &   & 515
\end{array}
$$

All things therefore concur in making it intelligible
and probable that the D.X.V. is Cangrande della
Scala—an opinion adopted by the majority of ancient
commentators.

Beatrice now explains that, if her description appears
obscure, it will soon be made clear by facts.

> E forse che la mia narrazion, buja
> > Qual Temi e Sfinge, men ti persuade,
> > Perch' a lor modo lo intelletto attuja ;*

---

* *attuja :* This word only occurs in this one passage of
Dante.   The older commentators never noticed it.   Benvenuto
translates " obscures the intellect," but he reads " *ottura,*"
which spoils the rhyme.   I think it best to take *attuiare* as
signifying *offuscare,* which is the sense given to the word by
the Accademia della Crusca.

> Ma tosto fien li fatti le Naiáde,
> Che solveranno questo enigma forte,   50
> Senza danno di pecore o di biade.

And peradventure my utterance, obscure as (the oracle of) Themis* (to Deucalion), or (the riddles of) the Sphinx (to the Thebans), may persuade thee less, because it clouds the intellect after their fashion (of speaking ambiguously) ; but before long will the facts (that will occur) be the Laïades† [not Naiades but Laïades, *i. e.* Œdipus the son of Laïus], which will solve this difficult enigma without the destruction of flocks or of harvests (like as was wrought by the Sphinx in the neighbourhood of Thebes).

---

* Themis was celebrated for her ambiguous oracles. Homer personifies in her the order of things sanctioned by law and custom.

† It will be observed that, whereas in the text the word *Naiáde* occurs, I have translated it as if it were *Laïade*. It is a very curious episode in the *Divina Commedia*, and I take this opportunity of thanking my friend Dr. Moore, who forewarned me of the passage. The idea of Naiades, or Laïades, was evidently suggested to Dante by these lines from Ovid, *Met.* VII, 759-761 :—

> " Carmina Laïades non intellecta priorum
> Solverat ingeniis, et precipitata jacebat
> Immemor ambagum vates obscura suorum."

In Dante's time a clerical error in all the MSS. of Ovid had substituted Naiàde for Laiàde. Heinsius was the first to discover the error. It seems quite clear that Dante had Œdipus Laïades and the Sphinx in his mind, for the line " Senza danno di pecore o di biade," evidently comes from the lines in Ovid immediately following those quoted above :—

> " Protinus Aoniis immittitur altera Thebis
> Pestis, et exitio multi pecorumque suoque
> Rurigenæ pavere feram."

" Forthwith a second plague is sent to Thebes in Bœotia,

Beatrice now exhorts Dante to relate what he had observed when he returns to the world, and especially not to omit to mention the condition in which he saw the Tree in the Terrestrial Paradise.

> Tu nota ; e, sì come da me son porte,
>   Così queste parole segna ai vivi
>   Del viver ch' è un correre alla morte ;
> Ed ággi a mente, quando tu le scrivi,   55
>   Di non celar qual hai vista la pianta,
>   Ch' è or due volte dirubata quivi.

Mark thou ; and, even as these words are uttered by me, so do thou teach them to those, who are living that life which is a hastening unto death ; and bear in mind, when thou writest them, not to conceal in what plight thou hast seen the Tree, which has already, in this place (the Terrestrial Paradise) been twice pillaged.

All the ancient commentators agree that the first time the Tree was despoiled by Adam ; and the second time by the giant.

Scartazzini says that the passage in **XXXII**, 39, as to the tree being denuded of flowers and other foliage on every branch, and the murmuring of the name of Adam by the glorious company, leave the first beyond any possible dispute. Besides which, in v. 61 of this Canto, Beatrice mentions what a long penalty had befallen Adam for having "bitten at" the Tree. None of the attacks either by the eagle,

---

and many rustics supplied food to the monster, by the destruction of their flocks, and of their own persons ;" while the line :—

> " precipitata jacebat
> Immemor ambagum vates obscura suorum."

Meaning that the prophetess of obscure utterances forgot her riddles, and hurled herself down from a high cliff, can only refer to the Sphinx, and not to the Naiades.

the wolf, or the dragon, robbed the Tree, they only injured either it, or the Chariot. But the giant, by detaching the Chariot, and carrying it away from the Tree, of the wood of which it was formed, did rob the Tree. Therefore Scartazzini thinks that the interpretations of the old commentators are the best. Adam despoiled the Tree the first time, the giant the second time.

Beatrice now draws a general conclusion by affirming, that not only Adam, but every other violator of the Tree, incurs the wrath of God.

> Qualunque ruba quella, o quella schianta,
>> Con bestemmia di fatto offende a Dio,
>> Che solo all' uso suo la creò santa. 60

Whosoever plunders that, or rends that (the Tree), offends with blasphemy of deed against God, Who created it holy for His use alone.

> Per morder quella, in pena ed in disio*
>> Cinquemil' anni e più,† l' anima prima
>> Bramò Colui che il morso in sè punio.

---

* *La pena* refers to the years that Adam lived on earth ; *il disio* to the time he passed in Limbo, where the souls have only this torment, that they abide for ever longing and without hope. (See *Inf.* IV, 41-42.)

† *cinquemil' anni e più*: In *Paradiso*, XXVI, 118, Dante makes Adam to say that he passed 4302 years in Limbo, and 930 years on earth ; for Adam's age see *Gen.* V, 5. According to Eusebius, Jesus Christ was born 5200 years after the creation of the world. The other chronologists differ greatly as to this date, but Dante has evidently followed that given by Eusebius. If Christ was born in the year 5200 from the Creation, and died in the thirty-third year of his age, the date of His descent into Limbo would be 5232, which is the exact date given by Dante. See *Par.* XXVI, 118 :—

N N N

For biting that (*i. e.* for having eaten of its fruit), the first-born soul (Adam) in pain and in desire, for five thousand years and upwards, had to long for the coming of Him who punished on His own Self the sin of that bite.

———

Division III.   The Third Division of the Canto is taken up by a conversation, which Beatrice begins by remonstrating with Dante on his ignorance, as to the things he has seen connected with the Tree.

> Dorme lo ingegno tuo, se non istima
> > Per singular cagione essere eccelsa   65
> > Lei tanto, e sì travolta nella cima.

Thy intelligence must be asleep, if it does not comprehend that it is for a special reason that it (the Tree) is so lofty and so spreading at the top.

Graziani (*Interpret. dell' allegoria della Divina Commedia*, p. 348) says : "The prodigious height of the Tree gives an exact image of the vast size of the Empire, and the inversion of it at the top, that is, tapering downwards in the contrary way to what pine and fir trees do, is perhaps stated for many reasons, but we will confine ourselves to Dante's description of another and similar Tree (*Purg.* XXII, 135), alike too in its

———

> " Quindi, onde mosse tua Donna Virgilio,
> > Quattromila trecento e due volumi
> > Di Sol desiderai questo concilio."

If to the figures 4302 we add the 930 years that Adam lived on earth, we obtain 5232, which is the date of our Lord's death, according to the calculations of Eusebius.

significance : ' *Cred' io perchè persona su non vada,*'
and symbolizing, in the passage now before us, God's
intention that the Empire should be inviolate."

> E, se stati non fossero acqua d' Elsa *
> > Li pensier' vani intorno alla tua mente,
> > E il piacer loro un Piramo alla gelsa,
> Per tante circostanze solamente   70
> > La giustizia di Dio nello interdetto,
> > Conosceresti all' arbor moralmente.†

And if thy vain thoughts had not been as the (petrifying) waters of the Elsa round thy mind, and if thy
delight in them as Pyramus to the mulberry (*i.e.*
stained with the blood of Pyramus), by so many circumstances alone thou wouldst have recognized the
justice of God, in the moral signification of the prohibition of the Tree.

---

* *acqua d' Elsa :* The Elsa is a river in Tuscany, rising in
the mountains near Colle, and flowing northward into the Arno
between Florence and Pisa. Its waters have the power of
incrusting or petrifying anything left in them.

† *moralmente :* In *Convito* II, cap. I, Dante says that the
Scriptures can be understood, and must be expounded chiefly, in
four meanings or senses.

The first is called the *literal sense.*

The second the *allegorical sense ;* and this is the sense which
conceals itself under the mantle of these fables, and is a truth
concealed under a beautiful falsehood.

The third is called the *moral sense ;* and it is the one which
readers of Holy Scripture must intently and continually apply
to it, for their own profit and for that of their pupils.

The fourth is called the *anagogical sense ;* that is, above
sense ; and this is when one expounds a passage in Scripture
in a spiritual sense, which passage, although it be historical in
its literal sense, or in its narration of events that happened on
earth, by the things signified signifies things of eternal glory.

Scartazzini says that Beatrice means that if Dante had not lost himself in vain thoughts, and become as hard as stone, after all that had been shown to him in so many figures and allegories, he would assuredly have understood the moral signification of the justice of God in the precept given by Him to our first parents, almost as if it had borne the identical meaning of what was His Will as to the inviolability of the empire.

Beatrice, in reproving Dante for the vain thoughts that obfuscate his mind, is evidently speaking of his past life, and that his purification can only be complete and perfect after that he shall have tasted of the waters of Eunoe, which will render him, as we read in the concluding words of the *Purgatorio,* "renewed as are young trees with new foliage, pure, and disposed to mount up to the stars." He had been absolved and made free from sin, he had drunk forgetfulness of it in the waters of Lethe, but the consequences of his sin, an obfuscation of his mind, still remained. Scartazzini says that the waters of Lethe take away sin, while those of Eunoe waft away the darkness that, after sin, overclouds the soul.

Beatrice now tells Dante that she wishes him, at all events, to take back to the world what she has just said, and, as she sees his mind is too hardened and impenetrable for her words to be clearly engraved in it, she desires that he should carry away a rough outline of the general sense of what she has said.

> Ma, perch' io veggio te nello intelletto
> Fatto di pietra ed, impietrato, tinto,
> Sì che t' abbaglia il lume del mio detto,   75

Voglio anco, e se non scritto, almen dipinto,
  Che il te ne porti dentro a te, per quello
  Che si reca il bordoñ di palma cinto."—*

But because I see thee with thine intellect (hardened) into stone, and dyed with the colour of stone, so much so, that the light of my discourse dazes thee, it is furthermore my wish, that thou shouldest bear it away with thee (*i.e.* within thee), if not written down, at least sketched in outline, for the same reason that the pilgrim carries with him his staff wreathed with palm leaves.

A conversation now ensues between Dante and Beatrice somewhat to this effect. He assures her that her words are profoundly impressed in his mind. He then asks her why her discourse soars so far above the height of his intelligence. She tells him that it is in order that he may understand how little the school followed by him is of a character, that can rise to the level of her lofty conceptions. " But," says Dante, " I do not remember that I ever was estranged from thee." " Naturally," replies Beatrice, " because only this day hast thou drunk oblivion in the waters of Lethe."

Ed io :—" Sì come cera da suggello,
  Che la figura impressa non trasmuta,   80
  Segnato è or da voi lo mio cervello.

---

* *bordon di palma cinto:* Pilgrims were in the habit of carrying their staff wreathed with palm leaves, the cockle shell in their hats, and sandals, to show that they had been in the Holy Land. See the Old Ballad of "The Friar of Orders Grey":—

  "And how should I your truelove know
    From many another one?
  O by his cockle shell and staff,
    And by his sandal shoon."

> Ma perchè tanto sovra mia veduta
>   Vostra parola disïata vola,
>   Che più la perdé quanto più s' aiuta ?"—

And I : ". As is wax (impressed) by a seal, which changes not the figure stamped upon it, so is my brain (*i.e.* my memory) now imprinted by you. But why is it that your longed-for discourse ranges so far above my sight (*i.e.* my comprehension), that the more it (my intellect) looks for aid, the more it loses it (*i.e.* the more my faculties strive to grasp the sense of your discourse, the less they succeed in doing so)."

> —" Perchè conoschi (disse) quella scuola   85
>   Ch' hai seguitata, e veggi sua dottrina
>   Come può seguitar la mia parola ;
>   E veggi vostra via dalla divina
>   Distar cotanto, quanto si discorda
>   Da terra il ciel che più alto festina."—   90

" In order that thou mayest know," said she, " that school (of philosophy) which thou hast followed, and that thou mayest see how (little) its teaching is able to accord with my discourse (*i.e.* how incapable it is of elevating itself so far as to comprehend the mysteries of revelation) ; and that thou mayest see that the way of you (philosophers) is as widely removed from the way of God, as is distant from the earth the heaven that speeds round highest of all."

She means the Primum Mobile, the farthest off and the highest of the moveable heavens, beyond which was supposed to be the Empyrean, which was still.

The conception of this passage is taken from *Isaiah* LV, 8-9, " For my thoughts are not your thoughts, neither are your ways my ways, saith the Lord. For as the heavens are higher than the earth, so are my

ways higher than your ways, and my thoughts than
your thoughts."

Dante tries to deny what Benvenuto says he had
however already confessed to, namely, that he had
ever deserted Beatrice, and turned his footsteps into a
false way.

> Ond' io risposi lei :—" Non mi ricorda
>   Ch' io straniassi me giammai da voi,
>   Nè honne coscïenza che rimorda."—

Whereupon I answered her : " I cannot recollect
that I ever estranged myself from you, nor have I any
conscience that reproves me (for having deserted
you)."

Beatrice reminds him with a smile that his want of
recollection of his faults is no proof of his innocence,
for the water of Lethe which he had drunk would take
away all memory of his past sins.

> —" E, se tu ricordar non te ne puoi
>   (Sorridendo rispose), or ti rammenta   95
>   Come bevesti di Letè ancòi ;
> E se dal fummo fuoco s' argomenta,
>   Cotesta oblïvion chiaro conchiude
>   Colpa nella tua voglia altrove attenta.

" And if thou art not able to remember anything
about it," she replied with a smile, "recollect how that
only to-day (*ancoi*=ancora oggi) thou hast drunk of
Lethe ; and if from the smoke a fire may be inferred,
this forgetfulness (of thine) clearly proves blame
(against thee), in thy will being turned elsewhere (than
to me).

In the above words Beatrice has replied to Dante's
excuse in verse 93 : *Nè honne coscïenza che rimorda.*
She now promises that from thenceforward she will

confirm him in good hope, only speak to him in clear words, and no longer in enigmatical language.

> Veramente oramai saranno nude   100
>   Le mie parole, quando converrassi
>   Quelle scovrire alla tua vista rude."—

But in good sooth, from this time forward, my words shall be as much denuded (of figurative language) as is befitting, for the purpose of uncovering them (my words) to thy crude vision."

By drinking of Lethe, Dante has lost all memory of sin committed, but his mind is still obfuscated. The water of Eunoe will clear up and illuminate his intellect.

———

Division IV. We now enter upon the Fourth and concluding Division of this last Canto of the *Purgatorio.* In it Dante relates how he is led by Matelda to drink of the water of Eunoe, thereby acquiring the blessing of perfect virtue.

He begins by relating that it was mid-day.

> E più corrusco, e con più lenti passi,
>   Teneva il sole il cerchio di merigge,*
>   Che qua e là, come gli aspetti, fassi,   105

---

* Dr. Moore has a note on this passage, in which he alludes to two others, namely, *Par.* XXII, 151, and *Par.* XXVII, 85, which some commentators have strained to prove to be allusions to time, still subsequent to Easter Wednesday. " I do not consider, therefore, that the discussion of these passages falls within the scope of our present subject. At the same time I admit (as I have already said) that Dante intends to give us generally to understand that, though himself beyond the limits and conditions of time, still the time passing meanwhile on this earth was such that, when he returned to it after his ecstatic

Quando s' affisser, sì come s' affigge
  Chi va dinanzi a gente per iscorta,
  Se trova novitate in sue vestigge,
Le sette donne al fin d' un ombra smorta,
  Qual sotto foglie verdi e rami nigri   110
  Sovra suoi freddi rivi l' Alpe porta.*

And (now) the sun, more resplendent, and with a
more retarded course (*lit.* paces) was holding the
meridian circle (*i.e.* was at noon), which (noon) takes
place here (in our hemisphere) and yonder (in the
other hemisphere) according to the aspects (of the
heavenly bodies), when, just like one who goes before
a company by way of escort, if he encounters anything new upon his way, comes to a halt, so did the
seven ladies come to a stand-still at the edge of a pale
shadow, of the same kind as the Alps bear upon the
icy banks (of their torrents) beneath their dark green
foliage and gloomy branches.

The above allusion to the time of day is the last
that occurs in the Divina Commedia, and is intended
to refer to noon on Easter Wednesday, 13 April, 1300.
Dr. Moore (Time References, p. 127) says that it is
hardly necessary to add that Dante gives us no such
marks of time in the *Paradiso*, since there he has
passed from time to eternity (*Par.* XXXI, 38). Also

---

vision of Paradise, it would be found to be the evening of
Thursday, April 14th."—*Time References*, pp. 126-27.

* *l' Alpe:* The word is used here as a general term for a high
mountain. Benvenuto remarks that, though Dante had doubtless witnessed nature, as here described, in many places on
the Alps, he had especially done so on the Apennines near
Florence, in the upper Val d' Arno, where, between Fiesole and
Arezzo, there is a most fertile territory, through which Hannibal
marched.

there they have " no need of the sun, neither of the moon to shine in it, for there is no night there."

Dante now sees two rivers, which are Lethe and Eunoe, issuing from one source, and, remembering the rivers of Eden recorded in *Genesis*, thinks he sees Euphrates and Tigris.

> Dinanzi ad esse Eufrates e Tigri
> Veder mi parve uscir d' una fontana,
> E quasi amici dipartirsi pigri.

Methought I saw the Euphrates and the Tigris issue forth from one spring in front of them (the seven ladies) and like friends (about to part) linger lazily in their separation.

In *Inf.* II, 76, Dante had told Beatrice that, through her alone, the human race surpassed all within that heaven which has the smallest circles, meaning the sphere of the Moon, which most immediately contains the earth. He now calls her the light of the human race.

> —" O luce, o gloria della gente umana,   115
> Che acqua è questa che qui si dispiega
> Da un principio, e sè da sè lontana ?"—

" O Light, O glory of the human race, what water is this which gushes forth from one source, and then separates itself far apart from itself ?"

One part, Lethe, flows from East to West, and the other part Eunoe, from West to East. Scartazzini says this would be quite exaggerated language, if Dante only intended to speak of the daughter of Folco Portinari. But Beatrice is, in this Canto, an eminently symbolic and allegorical personage. *La luce della gente umana* is the word of God, Divine Revelation. " Thy Word is a light unto my feet and a lantern unto my path " (*Ps.* CXIX, 105). As she symbolizes the authority that is in possession of Divine Revelation, and who, according to the doctrines of that Revelation, ought to guide the human race to the highest felicity, Beatrice is really the light of the human race, she who walks before, with the light of Revelation, with the lamp of the word of God in her hand, and gives light unto whoever follows it. Jesus Christ said : " I am the Light of the World " (*St. John*, VIII, 12). So that the person called here *luce della gente umana* must be either Jesus Christ Himself, or His vicarious representative on earth. Now the Vicar of Jesus Christ on earth, according to the teaching of the Church to which Dante belonged, was the Pope. Therefore, in this passage, as in others, it is made clear that the Beatrice of the *Divina Commedia* symbolizes supreme ecclesiastical authority, that is, the Pope, who represents on earth Him Who is the Light of the World.

Beatrice tells Dante to ask Matelda, who now for the first time is spoken of by name, to answer his question. Fraticelli thinks Matelda is the symbol of devotion to the Holy Catholic Church.*

> Per cotal prego detto mi fu :—" Prega
> Matelda che il ti dica."—E qui rispose,
> Come fa chi da colpa si dislega, 120
> La bella donna :—" Questo, ed altre cose
> Dette gli son per me ; e son sicura
> Che l' acqua di Letè non gliel nascose."—

And to such a prayer (of mine) answer was made to me (by Beatrice) thus : " Ask Matelda to tell it

---

* Scartazzini thinks that, in her allegorical sense, Matelda is the symbol of ecclesiastical ministry.

thee." And hereupon the beautiful Lady answered
like one who defends himself from a fault (imputed to
him) : " This, as well as other matters, have been told
him by me ; and I am certain that the water of Lethe
has not hidden them from him."

Matelda had not only given him the information
he desired (*Purg.* XXVIII, 88-144) about the Terrestrial Paradise, but likewise about the wind of that
elevated region, and the various conditions of it, and
finally had given him *un corollario ancor per grazia.*
She felt quite assured that the waters of Lethe had
not effaced from Dante's memory the information she
had supplied him about the wind and the water,
because the only thing that they are capable of
effacing is the recollection of past sins ; and as we
read in Canto XXX, 142, Lethe cannot be passed
until the sins in question have been repented of and
atoned for. All the information she had given him
would remain in his memory.

Beatrice now tells Matelda that Dante's mind and
memory have undergone a great strain, considering
the whole of the great vision which he has seen, the
weight of Beatrice's own reproofs to him, and finally
the great enigma of the DXV, and that these things
are a greater care on his mind, which may well account
for his forgetting what he saw and heard when he first
entered into the Terrestrial Paradise. She accordingly directs Matelda to lead him to Eunoe.

> E Beatrice :—" Forse maggior cura,
>   Che spesse volte la memoria priva,   125
>   Fatta ha la mente sua negli occhi oscura.
> Ma vedi Eunoè che là deriva :
>   Menalo ad esso, e, come tu sei usa,
>   La tramortita sua virtù ravviva."—

And Beatrice: " Perchance thoughts of much greater importance (*lit.* greater care), which oftentimes take away memory, have darkened the eyes of his mind so. But behold there Eunoe, which takes its source yonder: lead him unto it, and, as thou art wont, revive again in him his languishing powers."

Scartazzini, who has written so fully about Matelda, thinks that the words *come tu sei usa* allude to former friendship in life between Dante and Matelda, whom he takes to be some Florentine lady, a friend of Beatrice, and Dante's confidante about his love for her, and who is probably mentioned, though not by name, in the *Vita Nuova.* He thinks that, in her life-time, she must often have restored Dante's *virtù tramortita.*

Matelda hastens to perform Beatrice's behest, with every loving proof of good will.

> Com' anima gentil che non fa scusa,   130
>   Ma, fa sua voglia della voglia altrui,
>   Tosto ch' ell' è per segno fuor dischiusa ;
> Così, poi che da essa preso fui,
>   La bella donna mossesi, ed a Stazio
>   Donnescamente disse :—" Vien con lui."—   135

Like unto a gentle soul that makes no excuse, but makes its own of the will of another (*i.e.* conforms its will to another's wishes), so soon as that (other one's will) has been manifested (only) by a sign ; thus, after that I had been taken hold of by her, the beautiful Lady moved on, and said courteously to Statius: " Come thou with him."

This is the last time that Statius is mentioned. All through the great vision, and the passage through the Terrestrial Paradise, he has borne but a passive and secondary part, and even here Matelda shows a marked difference between Dante, whom she takes by the hand, and Statius, whom she bids follow after. Scartazzini thinks that Statius is only an allegorical personage in this Canto, without much reality. Most of the old commentators take it for granted that he too drank of the water of Eunoe, and was bathed in it, but Dante does not mention the fact.

Dante now brings the Cantica of the *Purgatorio* to a conclusion, relating how he was taken to Eunoe, and how he returned from it regenerate, and fitted to ascend to Paradise.

> S' io avessi, lettor, più lungo spazio
> Da scrivere, io pur canterei in parte
> Lo dolce ber che mai non m' avria sazio ;
> Ma perchè piene son tutte le carte
> Ordite a questa Cantica seconda, 140
> Non mi lascia più ir lo fren dell' arte.

If, Reader, I possessed a greater space for writing, I would, in part at least, relate in song that sweet draught which never would have satiated me ; but, inasmuch as all the sheets that have been prepared for this second Canticle are now full, the curb of art allows of my going no further (*i.e.,* I may no longer give the rein to art).

Scartazzini says of *piene* and *ordite*, that the thirty-three cantos destined for this second Canticle have now been completed. In the division of his poem, Dante scrupulously observes the laws of symmetry. Each of the three Canticles has thirty-three cantos, inasmuch as the first Canto of the *Inferno* must be regarded as the Introduction or Preface to the whole poem. And in fact, in the *Inferno*, the Invocation to

the Muses is not in the first Canto, as it is in the
Purgatorio and *Paradiso,* but in the second.

> Io ritornai dalla santissim' onda
> Rifatto sì, come piante novelle
> Rinnovellate di novella fronda,
> Puro, e disposto a salire alie stelle.*   145

From this most holy water I returned (to where
Beatrice was awaiting me) renewed as are young
trees with new foliage, pure, and disposed to mount
up to the stars.

Each of the three Cantiche ends with the word
" *stelle.*" " Perhaps," says Scartazzini, " Dante does so
to indicate to his readers what is the ultimate end of his
Poem, and to what point ought to be directed the eye
of every one who does not ignore its lofty origin and
its exalted purpose and aim. With the word " *stelle,*"
as the concluding word of his Poem, Dante practically
points his finger upwards, and exclaims : 'To Heaven !
To Heaven ! To Heaven !'"

---

* *stelle :* Dante, after drinking the water of Eunoe, is so
renewed and refreshed that he feels himself fit to ascend to the
stars.   Compare *St. John* IV, 14 : "the water that I shall give
him shall be in him a well of water springing up into everlasting
life."   Compare also Virg. *Æn.* XII, 788 (Conington's Translation) :—
> " Again the haughty chiefs advance,
> Their strength repaired, their arms restored."

Come piante : Scartazzini says this is not unlike an ode of Pindar's (*Nem.* VIII) : " Virtue increases in wise and just men ; like
as the tree, by vivifying dews, grows up towards the humid air."

Rinnovellate : Compare *Eph.* IV, 23 : "And be ye renewed
in the spirit of your minds." And *Hebrews* VI, 6 : "to renew
themselves unto repentance."

END OF THE PURGATORIO.

INDEX.

Benevenuti de Rambaldis de Imola

---o---

COMENTUM

SUPER

DANTIS ALDIGHERIJ

COMŒDIAM

NUNC PRIMUM INTEGRE IN LUCEM EDITUM

Sumptibus GUILIELMI WARREN VERNON

Curante JACOBO PHILIPPO LACAITA.

Florentiæ, typis G. Barbèra, 1887, 5 *vols. large 8vo.,* 75 *lire*
(£3). (*D. Nutt,* 270, *Strand, London, W.C.*)

*** A limited number of copies on large paper were issued, at
150 lire (£6). Only eight of these remain for sale.

===

"As a matter of interest in the history of the Society should
be mentioned the publication of the first edition of Benvenuto da
Imola's 'Comment on the Divine Comedy.'"—*Sixth Annual
Report of the [American] Dante Society,* May 17, 1887.

"All students of Dante are familiar with the name of Lord Vernon, and with all that he has done for the honour of the poet and
for the illustration of his work. He has used wealth with lavish
munificence in printing splendid and valuable editions of the text,
which not the most enterprising publisher would venture to undertake as a matter of business. And he has added to this a number
of unedited ancient commentaries, which will all have one day to
be critically examined, and has opened a path which Italian literary
societies are following. He had intended to do more, he had

purposed to print the copious and important Latin Commentary
of Benvenuto da Imola, a design which was interrupted by his
death. Meanwhile the Dante Society of the American Cambridge, under the impulse of Mr. Charles Elliot Norton, resolved
to edit and publish the commentary ; but they gave up their
plan when they found, through Sir James Lacaita, that Lord
Vernon's son, Augustus Lord Vernon, was bent on carrying out
his father's wish. The preparation of the text of Benvenuto was
begun, under the superintendence of Sir James Lacaita, when
Lord Vernon (Augustus) died in 1883. But the family enthusiasm
in a noble work was still alive. The work was taken up by Lord
Vernon's brother, the Hon. William Warren Vernon, and finished
at his expense. Readers of Dante have to thank him for accom
plishing his father's design, and for giving them at length the
opportunity of seeing in its integrity a work the value and interest
of which are in their way unique. The book is handsomely
printed in five large volumes at the Barbéra Press, with intro-
ductory notices by Sir James Lacaita ; . . . . . . [whose] notices
are a model of what such things ought to be, succinct and clear."
—*The Guardian*, July 27, 1887.

" It is not inopportune that the publication of the important old
Latin Commentary of Benvenuto da Imola upon the great poem of
Dante should occur in the present year of Jubilee in England, for
it will be remembered that the action of the Divine Comedy is
supposed to have taken place in the year of the famous Roman
Jubilee of 1300. Benvenuto was writing his commentary in 1375,
as is indicated in one of the historical and biographical extracts
quoted by Muratori in his *Antiquitates Italiæ*, and it must contain the substance of the lectures delivered by him at Bologna
during a period of ten years. Its subsequent history is interesting. Other early commentators made large use of Benvenuto's
work in MS., especially Landino and Talice da Ricaldone, whose
own Latin Commentary, completed in 1474, has recently been
edited at the expense of the King of Italy. Castelvetro proposed
to print Benvenuto da Imola in the sixteenth century, but was
unable to execute his design in consequence of his own banishment from Italy. In 1855 the stupid blunder was made of
printing at Imola a so-called translation in Italian from the

quaint and racy Latin of Benvenuto, a proceeding which did no credit to the faithless and ignorant translator, or to the birth-place of the old citizen of the town whom it was intended to honour. Lord Vernon, the grandfather of the present Baron, desired to add an edition of the Commentary of Benvenuto to his many other valuable and liberal contributions to the study of Dante. It was announced in 1846 by Colomb de Batines, in his *Bibliografia Dantesca*, that the editorship of the intended work had been confided to the well-known Italian critic and scholar, Nannucci, and that he had selected for his text a manu-script in the Laurentian Library, collating it also with the well-known Estense MS. at Modena, from which Muratori's extracts were obtained. The further progress of Lord Vernon's project was unfortunately stopped by his death in 1866."—*The Saturday Review*, June 25, 1887.

"Fortune was not propitious to Benvenuto Rambaldi, of Imola, for, if his name did not actually fall, as happened to so many of his contemporaries, into absolute oblivion, the details of his life remained almost entirely unknown to posterity, his writings were either ignored, or very little known, and his greatest work was either issued in fragments, or so clumsily remanipulated as to lose its true character. To refresh the fame of Benvenuto, and to satisfy, at the same time, a long-felt want among Italian students, provision has been made by an English gentleman, in whose family the study of Dante is a tradition, and he has confided the publication of the entire commentary of the Imolese to the care of Senator James Philip Lacaita ; and thus the work of Benvenuto, reintegrated from the excisions of Muratori, and liberated from the interpolations of Tamburini, at last takes again its fitting place among the commentaries of the sacred poem, and presents itself as an assistance, and an instrument of great value for the interpret-ing of the Commedia, at a moment in which Italy is setting up at Rome a chair of Dantesque literature . . . . That of Benvenuto belongs to the second series of Dantesque com-mentaries, to the series of official lectures that began with those at Florence, given by Boccaccio in 1373, and which finished in the fourteenth century with those at Pisa by Buti about 1390. It (Benvenuto's) was delivered in Latin, for that probably appeared to the Imolese to be the only language worthy of science, and it may boast of superiority over the exposition of the Italian novelist in its completeness, extending as it does over the whole Commedia, and over that of the Pisan lecturer in its greater value of more varied, and richer classical culture. . . . . But however solicitous Benvenuto has been in adapting his commentary to the minds of the many, his work will for ever remain scholastic : scholastic, in its mediæval sense we mean, full of varied erudition, nor are wanting mythological dissertation and doctrinal digression. At the same time what is noteworthy in this fourteenth century commentator of our greatest poet is the unity of method that is constantly preserved ; whence his work does not bear the slightest trace of weariness in any place, nor does it present those disproportions that are to be seen in the different parts of other Dantesque commentaries : nor is this beautiful uniformity obtained by the sacrifice of anything that is necessary, as one may perceive in the commentary of Jacopo della Lana, but (it is obtained) by the matured preparation of a plan from which the author never turns aside his thought."—*Rivista Critica della Letteratura Italiana.* January, 1888.

"The Latin Commentary of Benvenuto Rambaldi da Imola is to be found in a considerable number of manuscripts, of which the one held in the highest repute is the *Estensis* (1408), at Modena. In the Eighteeth Century Muratori made it appreciated by the lovers of historical studies, through the fragments which he gave in his *Antiquitates italicæ.* The Avvocato Tamburini published a translation of it in 1855, which he in vain attempted to pass off as complete and faithful. The illustrious and generous English Dantophilist, George Lord Vernon, had resolved once more to take on himself the expense of its publication, the editing of which was to be entrusted to Professor Nannucci. The death of Lord Vernon interrupted the execution of this project, but his son, William Warren Vernon, has magnificently honoured the engagement which his noble father had contracted with the lovers of Dante. It is, in fact, some little while since that the edition of the complete commentary has come out at the expense of the Honble. William Warren Vernon, and under the direction of the learned Sir James Philip Lacaita. The Vernon family has not deserved less well of Dantesque science than those of the Trivulzio or the Caetani. of which the Italian nobility can well be proud.

Benvenuto da Imola (Rambaldi, from the name of his family) is also known by the *Liber Augustalis*, an abridgement of the history of the Emperors, by his intercourse with Petrarch, who names him in his letters, and also by inedited writings on Valerius Maximus and the *Pharsalia*. In his commentary he speaks of his birthplace, Imola, where his father, Magnus Compagnus, gave a course of lectures; he speaks too of his residence at Bologna, with the language and customs of which he is well acquainted, says he, *quia fui ibi per decennium*, by which one may understand that he was no longer there when he wrote his ! ook dedicated to the Marchese Nicholas II of Este (1388), fc whom also he made the *Liber Augustalis*. He celebrates his masters Petrarch and Boccaccio, both already dead.

His political judgments bear the impress of great independance : he gives a severe estimate both of Popes and Emperors, as also of the epoch in which he writes, compared with which he finds that of Dante almost a time of tranquillity. He naturally makes use of Boccaccio, but without naming him, unless it be to report some anecdote which he has had from him ; as, for instance, that of Dante's reputed residence at Monte Cassino. He borrows from him his dissertations on the different kinds of tragedy, comedy, and satire, and on the idea that Dante seems to have had of composing his poem in latin ; and he reproduces Petrarch's opinion on this subject, that the experiment might quite well have been a success. He borrows again from Boccaccio the anecdote of the first seven cantos lost and then found ; and from (Jacopo della) Lana some details; as for example the combat between the Christians and the pagans at Arles, where the bodies of the former were said to have been distinguishable by a scroll that had fallen from heaven. All the same he maintains entire freedom as to interpretation.

But it is from the historical side that the commentary of Benvenuto da Imola is of incomparable value : it is, from this

point of view, the source from which all the other commentators have come to draw. Benvenuto is, among the scholiasts of Dante, specially the historian (*l'historien par excellence*) as Pietro Dante is the scholiast. Separated as he was, by a considerable interval of time, from the author of the *Divina Commedia*, and living besides far from Florence, he has only been able to have recourse to written and not to local traditions : the historian that he oftenest consults is Villani. To make up for this, he is intimately acquainted with the history of Bologna and the Romagna in general. If he accepts the popular legend of the journey of Saladin to France, or of the outrage committed against the Princess of Antioch by Frederick II, on the other hand he repudiates the fabulous histories about the foundation of the Italian cities to which national pride had given credence."
—"*Les Anciens Commentateurs de la Divine Comédie*" by Professeur Maxime Formont, in *L'Instruction Publique*, 1ᵉʳ Septembre, 1888.

DRYDEN PRESS : J. DAVY & SONS, 137, Long Acre, London

www.ingramcontent.com/pod-product-compliance
Lightning Source LLC
Chambersburg PA
CBHW052343110726
47901CB00005B/1340